Advance Praise from Cynthia Ozick for Tova Reich's *My Holocaust*

I have now read, with an accelerating sense of astonishment, every stupefying word of Tova Reich's *My Holocaust*, and have been mentally rehearsing how best to express my conviction that this is a novel before which one ought to fall on one's knees. Put it that Philip Roth's merited status as our most acerbic contemporary American satirist melts away in the blaze of Tova Reich's burning brand. In *My Holocaust* (aha, the title alone!), she is ten times wickeder than Roth, a hundred times wilder, and his sharpest jabs seem in comparison no more than the irritable umbrella-pokes of a meek little old lady in a lace cap, faintheartedly peering into her reticule to pluck out a complaint. In Tova Reich's unafraid boldness, in her heroic recklessness, there is something to offend everyone and everything, every preening and every piety. Nothing and no one 'scapes whipping—not even the institutions and persons one might most wish, for fear of public opprobrium, to spare.

Here is a novel that cuts, cuts, cuts: it is satire, caricature, comedy, farce; it makes you laugh and wince, often simultaneously; it judges and condemns; but it also clears away cant and pomposity and fakery. And much more than merely cant and pomposity and fakery: it accuses the prevailing tone of American society, a cultishness cultivated from the top down—the cult of rivalrous victimization, celebrated among the humanities in all American universities, from women's studies to black studies to postcolonial studies, from literature departments to history departments to Middle Eastern departments, all those braggart elitist realms where grievance and suffering are crowned with laurel.

Tova Reich's verbal blade is amazingly, ingeniously, startlingly, all-consumingly, all-encompassingly, deservedly, and brilliantly savage. All the same, she doesn't lecture or scold; her language is not that of a moralizing jeremiad. It is (seemingly) as detached as any of the natural disasters our planet has lately endured: with the force of a tsunami, a flood, an earthquake, it rolls over what human hands and minds have made of civilization. She is Dean Swift's Jewish sister; but poor deprived Swift had only human nature to deal with. Reich has what Swift, that unlucky goy, lacked, and (even with all his mammoth pessimism) could not have imagined: Reich has the Holocaust—or, better yet, the Holocausts, since, as she elucidates, everyone covets his or her own supremely desirable Holocaust. Her deadpan riffs and ironies, those long cresting waves of shocking wit, wash over egotism, greed, envy, falsehood, corruption, exposing their bones and stones without mercy. And still we laugh. There is no cranny of American crank culture (or couture) that is invulnerable to Reich's skewer. Her several fantastically imagined rosters of all the possible copycat Holocausts that our competitive American spirit has devised are outdone only by reality.

Tova Reich's *My Holocaust* is a ferocious work of serious satiric genius. I believe it to be one of the most penetrating social and political novels of the early twenty-first century next to which the last century's *Animal Farm* is a mere bleat. Its publication is certain to raise a howling hullabaloo; but if there was ever a hullabaloo worth raising, this is the one. Yet this extraordinary writer's intent is the very opposite of destructive. She shows us how the temple of Holocaust memory has been defiled. She means to cleanse the temple.

My Holocaust

ALSO BY TOVA REICH

The Jewish War
Master of the Return
Mara

My Holocaust

✳ A Novel ✳

Tova Reich

HarperCollins*Publishers*

Part I of this book first appeared, in somewhat different form, in the *Atlantic Monthly.*

HarperCollins books may be purchased for educational, business, or sales promotional use. For information, please write: Special Markets Department, HarperCollins Publishers, 10 East 53rd Street, New York, NY 10022.

Library of Congress Cataloging-in-Publication Data is available upon request.

ISBN-10: 0-06-117345-2
ISBN: 978-0-06-117345-5

07 08 09 10 11   ID/RRD   10 9 8 7 6 5 4 3 2

To the memory of
Esther Stone

You shall not make for yourself an idol nor any image of what is in the heaven above and in the earth below and in the water under the earth. You shall not bow down to them nor serve them. Because I the Lord your God am a jealous God, visiting the sin of the fathers upon the children unto the third and fourth generation of those who despise me.

EXODUS 20:4–6

* PART ONE *

The Holocaust Princess

I T WAS NOT THE FIRST TIME that the father-and-son team Maurice and Norman Messer, respectively chairman of the board and president of Holocaust Connections, Inc., were traveling home from Poland, but it was definitely the saddest. In all their business dealings for clients they had always come through with flying colors, which was how they had built their enviable reputation and their legendary success. But this time, in a most painful personal matter involving an exceedingly close member of their own immediate family, indeed, the very future of their line, they had failed completely. Nechama, only child of an only son, had absolutely refused to see her father or her grandfather, either one-on-one or in any constellation. She had, in any case, as they were categorically informed, taken a vow of silence. This was communicated to the two men by a matronly nun in sunglasses who came to meet them outside the gate of the Carmelite convent—the new convent, that is, some five hundred meters from the perimeter of the Auschwitz death camp, to which the nuns had moved after all that ridiculous fuss. "Sister Consolatia requests that you respect her right to choose," the nun told them with finality, in English, though Maurice of course knew Polish. From the signature phrasing, the Messers, father and son, could not deceive themselves that this was anything other than a direct quotation from their apostate offspring, now reborn as Sister Consolatia of the Cross, their lost Nechama.

Nevertheless, despite their unquestionably genuine and heartbreaking disappointment, they made themselves comfortable, as usual, in their ample seats in the first-class compartment of the LOT airplane. They always flew Polish, as a matter of policy, to maintain healthy relations with the government with which they had most of their dealings, and they always flew first class, because to do otherwise would be unseemly for men like themselves, steeped as they were in such nearly mythic tragic history, a history that set them apart from ordinary people and therefore necessitated that they be seated apart. And from a business point of view, from the purely practical side, it would look bad to go economy, it would look as if their enterprise were falling on hard times. Everything in their line of work, naturally, hung on image. "Look," as Norman formulated it, with the usual pauses and swallows that heralded the delivery of one of his aphorisms, "we already did cattle cars. From now on, it's first class all the way." Clients expected a premium operation from the Messers, and Holocaust Connections, Inc., billed them accordingly. This trip, for example, was covered by an anti-fur organization that was eager to firm up its honorary Holocaust status, and Norman had managed, even in the midst of his private anguish, to do a little work for them, still in its early stages admittedly, involving the creative use of the mountains of shorn hair of the gassed victims in the Auschwitz museum—a ghoulish idea on the face of it, which he was now massaging and dignifying in order to establish the relevant ethical connection that would ennoble the agenda of the fur account and give it that moral stamp of the Holocaust.

By now, of course, the father and son partners knew all the flight attendants on the airline, specializing in the women. Maurice persisted in referring to them politically incorrectly

as "hoistesses," a teasing liberty for which he took the precaution of propitiating them, just in case, with small offerings
from the luxury hotels of Warsaw and Krakow—miniature
shampoos or scented soaps from the bathrooms, chocolate
hearts wrapped in gold foil plucked off the pillows atop the
turned-down bedsheets. He squeezed and harassed their vivid
blondness and springy buxomness hello and good-bye and
thank you, muttering, "Don't worry, girls, don't worry, I'm
safe." "And he gets away with it too," as Norman painstakingly
and unnecessarily explained to his wife, Arlene, "because he's
this cute little tubby old bald Jewish guy with pudgy hands and
a funny accent, and the dumb chicks from Czestochowa, they
think he's harmless—big mistake, ladies!—so it turns into a
stereotypical Polish joke."

They boarded the plane ahead of the common passengers,
wearing to the very last minute their trademark trench coats—
the sexy semiotics, as they interpreted it, of international mystery and intrigue. Then one of the attendants, Magda or Wanda
or someone, without even inquiring, her brain imprinted with
their preferences as if the storage of such information were her
reason for existence, glided forward with a welcoming smile
such as had long vanished from their wives' repertoires, bearing before her living and breathing breasts a tray with their
usual—for Maurice, his glass of Bordeaux ("I'm a red wine
male," as he liked to confide urbanely at official functions), for
Norman, rum with Coca-Cola, two containers of chocolate
milk, and a dozen bags of honey-roasted peanuts.

For a long time they sat side by side in silence, each with his
own thoughts, perfectly at ease with the other, apart yet joined,
Norman tearing open with his teeth pack after pack of the
peanuts, pouring them out into the ladle of his palm, jiggling

them around like dice, and then, with his head tilted slightly back, dumping them into his mouth with a sharp flat smack. He went on doing this automatically, mechanically. It was okay to dispatch the nuts this way when he traveled with his father. The old man didn't mind, most likely didn't even notice, like other survivor parents maybe just registered gratefully that at least his son was eating, and for Norman it was a stolen pleasure because this was not a snacking style in which he could ever have indulged had he been with his wife or daughter. That robotic, cranelike up-and-down motion of his arm drove the two of them crazy, they could feel its vibration even if they weren't looking directly at him. Maybe that's why Nechama went into the convent, Norman speculated—because of his annoying habits.

As for Arlene, well, he was just not going to spoil everything by thinking about his upcoming meeting with her while he was masticating. He simply refused even to start thinking about how he was going to manage her on the Nechama problem when he got home, how he would confirm that, yes, unfortunately, it looked, at least for the time being, as if this nun thing was a done deal, there was nothing they could do about it for the moment except, of course, to use Arlene's idiom, to go on being supportive, to love their daughter unconditionally, it goes without saying, to always be there for her, but, at the same time, we need to allow time to grieve—figuratively grieve, that is, not actually go into mourning by sitting shiva for seven days like those ultra-Orthodox fanatics when one of their kids converts—and then, of course, we need closure, we need to move on with our own lives, to let go of all this bad stuff, put it behind us, give the healing process a chance to work, blah blah. "Look at it this way," he could say to Arlene, "the bad news is, it's a fact—she's a nun, so that makes her a Christian, I guess, a goy, a shiksa, even worse, a Catholic, we just have to face it. And also it's a problem, I suppose, that she had to go and pick that Carmelite convent right by Auschwitz, of all places, for her nun phase, where three-quarters of our family were incinerated. Know what I mean? On the other hand"—and here he would slow down and suck in air for greater effect—"the good news is, she's safe, she has a guaranteed roof over her head and what to eat every day, guys can't bother her anymore, and, from a parent's point of view, we will now always know exactly where she is at all times."

Hey, he loved the girl as much as Arlene did, Norman thought resentfully. Why was he always the one on the defensive? Did he really need this added grief? Nechama was his daughter too, for God's sake. This whole mess was no less of an embarrassment for him than it was for Arlene. Jesus, this could even impact their business, their lifestyle—you hear that, Mrs. Messer, hello? How was it going to look? he demanded of the wife in his head: Holocaust Heiress Dumps Jews. It was an emergency damage-control situation requiring a rapid response. He had to figure out some way to market this negative to their advantage, to turn it around—something like, you know, the ongoing trauma of the Holocaust, the continuing threat to our survival, the Holocaust is not yet over, et cetera et cetera.

No problem; he was prepared to deal with it. But there was one thing he wanted to know, just one thing—why was it the case that he was always the one who had to be, as Arlene would put it, supportive, like some kind of jockstrap? Why couldn't she be supportive of him once in a while? Had it penetrated her ozone layer yet that everywhere her poor schlump of a husband went he was a big man, he was greeted like a hero? Was she cognizant of that fact? In Warsaw, the women adored him, especially since he had lost all that weight; but the fact is, over there they had always loved him, they loved him in any shape or form, they loved him for himself. They came up to his hotel room carrying bouquets of flowers and bottles of champagne, with beautifully made-up faces and beautifully sprayed hair, in shiny high-heeled shoes and gorgeous real-leather minidresses with exposed industrial-strength steel zippers running from neck to hem—not that he carped the diem, needless to say. In the States they worshiped him, idolized him for his aura of suffering, like a saint, like a holy man out of Dostoyevsky, they revered him for never letting up on this miserable Holocaust business, for immersing himself in it every minute, for schlepping the Shoah around on his back day and night, for sacrificing his happiness to keep the flame going—not for his own health, obviously, but for the moral and ethical health of humankind. The anguish in his eyes, the melancholy in the set of his mouth, the manifest depression in how he blow-dried his hair, the sorrowful awareness of man's-inhumanity-to-man in the way he belted his trench coat—it turned them on, yes, it turned them on.

So big deal, his wife didn't appreciate him. So what else was new? She was happiest when he was away from home, that was obvious, she was delighted that his job required so much traveling. Fine, he could live with all that, too, so long as somebody appreciated him, so long as someone somewhere was glad to see him once in a while and showed him a little respect. But it was another thing entirely to blame him for the whole fiasco. C'mon, was he the one who put the kid in the nunnery? Please! And why was he going home now, of his own free will, to listen to all that garbage? He must be out of his mind, meshuga. It was

masochism, pure and simple, a sick craving for punishment—
he should call a shrink, seek counseling, as the mental health-
niks say. Did he have any doubts whatsoever about what Arlene
was going to dump on him, with her squeegee social worker's
brain and her prepackaged psychological explanations? Oh, it
was an old song, he had heard it a thousand times already. She
would start in again with the whole bloody litany—how it was
all his fault, everything that had happened was his fault. Right
from the start. First of all, what kind of sick idea was it to
insist on naming a baby Nechama? A poor, innocent baby, to
give her a name like Comfort, as in "Comfort ye, comfort ye,
oh my people," like some sort of replacement Jew, like some
sort of postcatastrophe consolation prize, as if they were all
depending on her to make things right again after the disaster.
Such a heavy load, such an impossible burden to saddle a kid
with—no wonder the poor girl took herself out of this world.
Did he think names don't matter? There was a whole literature
on the subject, on the effect of names on development and
identity and self-image. What kind of father would do such a
thing to his own flesh and blood? It was criminal, unforgivable.
Why couldn't she have been given a normal name, some sort
of hopeful, pursuit-of-happiness American name that people
could at least pronounce, like Stacy, or Tracy?

And then this whole second-generation business that he had
gotten himself involved with, dragging Nechama along like
some sort of archetypal sacrificial lamb, like Jephtah's daughter, like Iphigenia. As a matter of fact, Norman knew very well
that most mental health types just loved the second-generation
concept, they ate it up, but Arlene—surprise, surprise—didn't
believe in it at all. Why? It was completely predictable: because
it served Norman's agenda, that's why, because it legitimized

and explained his obsession, and gave it status. There was nothing in it for Arlene. As far as Arlene was concerned, second generation was a made-up category, an indulgence for a bunch of
whiners and self-pitiers with a terminal case of arrested development. The so-called survivors, they were the first generation;
they were the ones who had been there, they had experienced
it all firsthand, and after them came their children, this bogus
second generation, these Holocaust hangers-on, Norman and
company, throwing a tantrum for a piece of Shoah action. So all
of those tough, shrewd, paranoid refugees who came out of the
war—you don't even want to begin to think about how they
made it through—suddenly they get turned into sacred, saintly
survivors with unutterable knowledge, and then the second
generation, born and reared in Brooklyn or somewhere, far,
far from the gas chambers and crematoria, gets crowned as
honorary survivors. Suddenly these lightweight descendants
are endowed with gravitas, with importance, with all the seriousness and rewards that come from sucking up to suffering.
What could be neater? All the benefits of Auschwitz without
having to actually live through that nastiness—Holocaust lite.

And what did they do to deserve this honor, this second
generation? What exactly are their suffering bona fides? Well,
they had it rough, poor babies—they were victims too, you
can't take it away from them, as they reassured one another at
regularly scheduled 2-G Anonymous support group meetings
in synagogue basements. They were damaged by the damaged,
suffered the psychic wounds of being raised by mistrustful,
traumatized, overprotective parents with impossible expecta-
tions. They bore the weight of having to transmit the torch of
memory, that kitschy memorial candle, from past to future.

They endured a devastating blow to their self-esteem in consequence of the knowledge that their lives were a paltry sideshow compared to their parents' epic stories. It was sick, sick, pathetic—"Holocaust envy," a new term for professionals, coming your way soon in the next updated, revised edition of the DSM-IV bible of mental disorders. And to think he would expose his own child to such a pathological situation—to think he'd go ahead now and render this acute condition chronic by prolonging the agony, by trying to pass the whole load on to Nechama like a life sentence, like indentured servitude, like guilt unto the tenth generation. Is it an accident, then, that she abandoned the Jews for the ultimate martyr religion, complete with vicarious suffering as its main value and a tortured skinny guy on a cross as its main icon? Is it an accident that she found her way back to the gates of Auschwitz? Had it never dawned on him where this morbid Holocaust fixation would lead?

✳

"Maybe we should've come mit one of those deprogramming fellas," Maurice was now saying. "Maybe we should've climbed the wall from the convent like that crazy rabbi—what's his name?—when it used to be in the other building where they used to keep the gas in the war. Maybe we should've kidnapped her from the *schwesters*."

Norman shook his head. "Bad idea, Pop." He swallowed portentously before elaborating. "It would have been disastrous for Polish-Jewish relations, a nightmare for Catholic-Jewish relations, not to mention curtains for business relations."

"Nu, anyway, you have to be a younger man for that kind of monkey business, climbing walls—you know what I mean? And you're not so young anymore, Normie, ha ha, and I'm not in such good shape—like your mama says, svelte. I'm not so svelte like I used to be when I was a leader from the partisans and fought against the Nazis in the woods."

Norman had to catch his breath and squeeze the bridge of his nose to stem the keen rush of longing for his daughter that swept over him at that moment, as Maurice recited that familiar refrain in exactly those words about having been a partisan leader who fought the Nazis in the woods. It was a private joke between Norman and Nechama. They would mouth those exact words of Maurice's every time he uttered them, flawlessly imitating his grimaces and gestures and accent, mouth them behind the old man's back at gatherings with friends and family or even at the public speeches that he regularly gave in synagogues or community centers or schools about his career as a resistance fighter, which he always began with the sentence, "I'm here to debunk the myt' that the Jews went like sheep to the shlaughter." Norman and Nechama would mouth this sentence, too, in fits of choking, mute hilarity. It was a harmless father-daughter ritual that had started when she was about eighteen or nineteen years old, after Maurice had given his standard talk, at Nechama's invitation, in the Jewish student's center at her college, opening, as usual, with that sentence about the sheep-to-the-slaughter myth, and ending, as usual, by snapping smartly to attention when they played the Partisan's Hymn, "Never Say This Is the Final Road for You."

In a moment alone with Nechama during the reception following Maurice's talk, the two of them facing each other with their clear plastic wineglasses filled with sparkling cider, as if playing a couple just introduced at a social gathering, Norman casually mentioned—in another context entirely, he forgot what—that of course nobody really knew exactly what Mau-

rice Messer had done during the Holocaust except that he had
hidden in the woods all day and stolen chickens at night. No
shame in that, of course, under the circumstances. "You just
gotta face it, kiddo," Norman went on, in the grip of something
beyond his control, "he never shot in the woods—he shat in the
woods!"

"You mean Grandpa wasn't really a partisan leader who
fought the Nazis?" The child seemed genuinely shocked.

Norman raised an eyebrow. His daughter was not being
ironic. Maybe he had gone too far this time, maybe she really
was an innocent, maybe she was just too fragile for this kind
of realpolitik. Incredibly, it looked as if she truly had not fathomed until that moment that her grandfather's story was just
an innocuous piece of self-promoting fiction. For a devastating
pause, Norman felt as if he might have violated his child in some
irreparable, unforgivable way, but when, after a long silence to
absorb the new information, she mischievously blurted out,
"Okay, Dad, I won't be the one to tell the Holocaust deniers
that it's all made up," he breathed again with relief, impressed
by how quickly she had caught on, how alert she was to where
her interests lay and her loyalties belonged, how sophisticated
she was in accepting human weakness as another amusing fact
of life.

"Look," Norman intoned, "it's not as if he didn't really suffer. You think it's easy being considered a victim all the time,
having people feel sorry for you—especially for such a macho
type like Grandpa? You're a big girl now, Nechama, you can
understand these things. The Shoah was an extremely emascu-
lating event, as your mother might put it; strangers could come
along and really screw you. For men like your Grandpa, this was
very hard to take—so that afterward it became psychologically

critical for him to find ways to prove that he hadn't been castrated, that, to put it bluntly, he still had balls—and he turned
himself into a resistance fighter. It's as simple as that. Anyway,
who's going to be hurt by an old man's little screenplay starring
himself as the big hero?" He slowed down emphatically now to
make way for the bottom line. "The Holocaust market is not
about to collapse due to one old man's pathetic inflations, trust
me. Those loonies who say the whole thing never happened
should not take comfort."

Should not take comfort, he had said—not take *nechama*.
Anyway, it was from that time on, as he recalled it, that they
began their tradition of delicious mockery, all in affectionate
fun, whenever Maurice warmed up and delivered his partisan
spiel. It had evolved into their own personal father-daughter
thing. And it was the memory of this innocent conspiratorial
bonding with his child that took possession of him now and
overcame him.

"Nu, Normie," Maurice was saying, "yes or no? Why you
not talking? You remember that hoo-hah mit the *schwesters* at
the convent mit that crazy rabbi, like your mama calls him?"

Maurice liked to quote his wife whenever possible, to
whom he gallantly conceded superior mastery of English idiom
and pronunciation, and whom he regarded as a nearly oracular
source of common sense. For example, whenever the subject
came up of that rabbi who had created an international incident with his protest against the presence of a Catholic convent at Auschwitz, where more than a million Jews had been
gassed—the very same convent in which, in a more acceptable
location ordained by the pope himself, their granddaughter
Nechama was now a nun praying for the salvation of the souls
of the Jewish dead—Blanche would open her eyes wide and

exclaim, "But, darling, he's crazy!" In consequence, Maurice never failed, when referring to that event at the old Carmelite convent, to include the epithet "that crazy rabbi"—as if the rabbi's mental state were a certifiable clinical diagnosis, since Blanche, with her peerless common sense, had declared it to be so. Common sense, in Maurice's opinion, was an exceedingly desirable quality in a woman, and there was a time when he had advised Norman to put it at the top of his list in choosing a mate. To which Blanche would always remark coyly, "When they tell you a girl has common sense, that's code language for not so ay-yay-yay, if you know what I mean—in other words, not so pretty." "Common sense together mit pretty," Maurice would then chime in with alacrity, "just like mine Blanchie."

They discussed everything, he and Blanche, even the subjects they did not discuss. They discussed but did not discuss, for instance, their shared sense of the limitations of their Norman's capabilities—it was not an understanding that they cared to seal in words. But around the time they sold their ladies' undergarments company, Messers' Foundations, from which they had made a more than comfortable living, the Holocaust had become fashionable, more fashionable even than padded brassieres and lycra girdles. At first, the two of them booked up their retirement by becoming leaders in the survivor community and popular lecturers on the oral-testimony circuit. The Holocaust was hot, no question about it. Blanche then urged Maurice to start the new consulting business, Holocaust Connections, Inc., and to take Norman in as an equal partner—"Make Your Cause a Holocaust," as their smart-aleck Norman packaged it, he was just too much. It would be first and second generation working and playing together, an ideal setup, a perfect outlet for their Norman, the original futzer and putzer, as they lovingly called him, whose jobs until then, they both agreed, had been totally beneath him, totally unsatisfactory and unchallenging. Now Norman could hang around all day long, talking creatively with clients on the telephone, holding forth with all his brilliant opinions, cracking his wicked jokes, writing an article now and then for a Jewish newspaper, traveling and schmoozing in diplomatic channels and the corridors of power with all the other politicians and insiders and players—the best possible use of his considerable gifts and talents. Unspoken was their shared sense that Norman needed their help, that fundamentally he was a weak person, that he could never manage on his own. Never mind that he had gone to Princeton University—Princeton Shminceton!—where he had even taken part in a sit-in in the president's office for three days and nights, though his mother had not hesitated to march right into the middle of that nonstop orgy to personally hand him his allergy medicine. Never mind that he had a law degree from Rutgers, where they trained poor schlemiels to become a bunch of creepers and crawlers. Never mind that he was an adult, to all appearances a grown man, with a social-worker wife and a beautiful but moody daughter. If the war broke out tomorrow, they knew in their hearts that their Norman would never make it. Without saying it out loud, they recognized that, unlike themselves, Norman would not have survived.

Survival—that was the bottom line. You couldn't argue with it. It was the fact on the ground that separated the living from the dead. That was the lesson they had struggled to drum into their Norman: first you survive, then you worry about such niceties as morality and feelings. When someone tells you he's going to kill you, you pay attention, you take him seriously, you believe him. You wake up earlier the next morning and you kill him. If you survive, you win. If you don't survive, you lose. If you lose, you're nothing. What is rule number one for survival? Never trust anyone, suspect everyone, take it as a given that the other guy is out to destroy you and eat him alive before he gets the chance. Why had they survived? Luck, it was luck, they always said. But they didn't believe it for a minute. It was the accepted thing to say, so as not to insult the memory of the ones who hadn't survived, the ones who, let's face it, had failed, the ones who were now piles of gray ash and crushed bone that people stepped on. The real truth, they knew, was that they had survived because they were stronger, better—fitter. Survival was success, but even among the successful, there were categories and degrees. Look at your survivors today, for example, the ones who had staggered out of the camps like the living dead. There were your classic greenhorns, eternal immigrants, afraid to offend by harping on the Holocaust—why make a federal case of it?—a bunch of nobodies until they had their consciousness raised by the survivor elite, by Blanche and Maurice's circle, the ones who survived with style, the fearless ones. "Me? I'm never afraid!" Maurice always said; it was his motto. Now, thanks to them, the Holocaust was a household word. They built monuments and museums. They were millionaires, big shots, movers and shakers. They ran the country. Survival of the fittest. Blanche had once read in a magazine that cancer cells were the fittest form of life because they ate everything else up, they spread, they reproduced, they succeeded, they survived, they won. Maybe this wasn't such a wonderful example; maybe this didn't reflect so nicely on her and Maurice and the rest—to be compared to cancer. Cancer was bad, but in this world if you survive, you win, and if you win, you're good.

They were a formidable team, Blanche and Maurice Messer, a fierce couple, and proud of it. For their fortieth wedding anniversary, Norman and Arlene had given them a plaque engraved with the words "Don't Mess with the Messers," which they hung in "Holocaust Central," their den off the living room, right above the composition that Nechama had written when she was eight years old, in third grade. The topic was "My Hero"; Nechama had chosen Maurice. "Grandpa had a gun in World War II. He killed bad Germans with the gun. He was a Germ killer. He saved the Jewish people. He loved the gun. He kissed the gun goodnight every night. He slept with the gun. After the war they gave Grandpa a ride on a tank. He was holding the gun. Then they took the gun away. Grandpa was sad. He cried because he missed his gun. So he married Grandma." The teacher gave her only a "Fair" for this effort, but Blanche said, "What does she know? It's not by accident that she's a teacher," and she hung the composition, expensively framed, on the wall. "I'm the gun," she asserted defiantly. Maurice also didn't much care for this composition. "What for is she telling the *ganze velt* this partisan story? It's private, just for family." "What are you worrying about, Maurie?" Blanche demanded. "Every survivor is a partisan. Survival is resistance." "Don't be so paranoid, Pop," Norman put in. "It's safe to come out of the closet now." Then, swallowing deliberately and pausing pregnantly, he added, "Ziggy and Manny and Feivel and Yankel, and everyone else who was with you in the woods in those days, they're all dead by now, may they rest in peace—and quiet."

Again, it was a question of survival, this time the survival of the Jewish people in an age of assimilation and intermarriage and the mixed-blessing decline of anti-Semitism in America—another Holocaust, frankly, even more dangerous in its way because it was insidious, invisible, underground. There was nothing that Blanche and Maurice would not do to ensure Jewish survival, no effort or sacrifice was too great, and, as they knew very well, there was nothing like the Holocaust to bag a straying Jew—it was the best seller, it was top-of-the-line, it got the customer every time. Why did God give us the Holocaust? For one reason only: to drive home the lesson that once a Jew, always a Jew. You could try to blend in and fade out, you could try to mix and match, but it was all useless, hopeless. There was no place to hide, no way to run. Hitler with his Nuremberg Laws of racial and blood purity, almost as if he'd cut some kind of deal with the anti-intermarriage rabbis, would find you wherever you were and flush you out like a cockroach. Thank you, Mr. Hitler!

And what could be more effective in sending this message loud and clear than a partisan leader and his wife—herself a survivor of three concentration camps, maybe four, depending on how you counted—telling their story over and over again until they were blue in the face, pounding in nonstop, day and night, the lessons of the Holocaust. Whatever it took to beat in the message, even if it meant pushing themselves into the limelight in crude ways that ran thoroughly counter to their nature, even if it meant giving the misleading impression that they were exploiting the dead, they would do it, not for personal fame and glory, God forbid, but for the cause, because this was their mission, this was why they had been chosen, it was for this purpose that they had survived. They were the first generation, the eyewitnesses. Norman was the connecting link. Nechama was continuity.

Yes, continuity. She was their designated Kaddish, their living memorial candle, the third generation. And now she was a Christian. This was tragic—tragic! How could it have happened? Who could ever have foreseen such an outcome? It was beyond human imagining. They had thrown everything they had into that girl, she had always been the ideal apprentice and protégée. She was, as Maurice used to say in his speeches, the spitting image of his mother, Shprintza Chaya Messer the guerrilla fighter, murdered by the Nazis during the roundup in Wieliczka while screaming at the top of her lungs, "Fight, *Yidalech*, fight!"

To this day, people still talked about Nechama's bat mitzvah speech—how she had turned to address the ghost of the Vilna girl with whom she had insisted on being twinned with the words, "Rosa, my sister, you were cruelly cut down by the Nazis during the Holocaust. You never had a bat mitzvah. Today I give back to you what was so wrongfully taken away—because today I am you." Arlene, with her naive American O-say-can-you-see attitudes, had called this gruesome, morbid, a form of child abuse, and had threatened to walk out of the sanctuary, but everyone else felt spiritually uplifted and morally renewed by Nechama's words, and wept contentedly. And who could forget the Holocaust assemblies that Nechama had organized in high school, at which either Maurice or Blanche gave testimony, and once even Norman, as the ambassador of the second generation, addressed the teenagers with their yellow paper stars for Jews pinned to their Nine-Inch Nails T-shirts, pink triangles for homosexuals, black triangles for Gypsies, and especially who could forget Nechama's original dance composition, presented each year, entitled "Requiem for the Absent," with the flowing, twisting scarves and the arms reaching poignantly toward the heavens? She had always been so proud of her family, those Holocaust relics who would have mortified your average adolescent, and had even invited her grandparents and her father to accompany her to Poland for the March of the Living, with thousands of other Jewish girls and boys from all over the world, but she was in a class apart, she was a Holocaust princess. And she wasn't ashamed of the VIP treatment that she then received because of her family's position in the Holocaust hierarchy, and she wasn't embarrassed to walk at a slower pace alongside the old folks for the three-kilometer march from Auschwitz to the actual killing center in Birkenau, with its remains of the gas chambers and crematoria, and ash and powdered bone underfoot; she had turned to them and said, they would never forget it—"I see them, I hear them, I feel them, the dead are walking beside us." And then there was her essay on her college application in which she had written, "The one thing about me that you may or may not have learned so far from this application is that I am, in the most positive and constructive sense, a Holocaust nut. What this means is that I am totally obsessed by the Holocaust, the murder of six million of my people, and am determined to do everything in my power to make sure that these dead shall not have died in vain." "Beautiful, beautiful," Maurice declared, "like the Shtar Shpangled Banner!" She was rejected by Princeton, even though she was legacy, because deep down they were, as Maurice put it, "a bunch of anti-Semitten and shtinkers." So she went to Brown.

With such Holocaust credentials, who would ever have predicted that she would turn her back on her people and become, of all things, a nun? Convent and continuity—these were two concepts that definitely did not go together, they did not mix well, they were not a natural couple. The idea of a nun was foreign to Jewish thinking; among Jews every girl got married one way or another, every girl had children, and if one didn't—well, that just never happened, who ever heard of such a thing? Ever since she was a little girl she had talked so movingly about how she would have at least twelve children to help make up for the millions who had been murdered—heads bashed against stone walls, hurled alive into flaming pits, shot and gassed. She was going to be a baby machine for Jewish continuity. She was a pretty girl, everyone remarked—a little full maybe, "zaftig," as Maurice said; "baby fat," said Blanche. Her favorite food, according to family lore, was marzipan, and even that preference was regarded as a sign of her superiority; it was so European, so Old World—what ordinary American Mars Bar kid knows from marzipan? The boys who were attracted to her were usually considerably older, usually foreigners. One of the family's favorite stories was about how she had stayed out very late one night, and when she finally came home, at five in the morning, her excuse to her parents was that this Salvadoran guy named Salvador had asked her out, and she didn't want to hurt his feelings, so she had to explain to him that she could never date a non-Jew because of the Holocaust—it was nothing personal, but it was her duty to replace the six million. And then, of course, she had to tell him the whole history of the Holocaust so that he'd understand where she was coming from—starting with Hitler's rise to power in 1933, and so forth until the end of World War II in 1945, which took a long time, which was why she was so late, she hoped they weren't mad. "So what did Salvador say?" Norman asked, obviously not mad at all, obviously swelling with pride. "Oh, he said, 'I only asked you out for a cup of coffee. I didn't ask you to marry me.' But that's not the point."

And she never did date a non-Jew, so far as they knew. In any case, soon after she entered college, her romantic life became a mystery to them, off-limits as a subject. She did, it is true, bring home a number of gentile boys, but this was "purely platonic," as she put it—"We're just friends." She knew them in connection with her activities to end the persecution of Christians throughout the world. "There's a Christian Holocaust going on as we speak," she declared at dinner in the presence of one of these guests, "and as a Jew who could have been turned into a lampshade, I cannot in good conscience remain a silent bystander." She brought home a Chinese graduate student who described how he had been beaten and tortured because of his membership in an underground church. She brought home a Sudanese lab technician whose family members had been burned or sold into slavery for practicing their faith. As they narrated their stories at the table, she listened raptly, her eyes moist, her mouth slightly open, even though she had surely heard them before. "Any guy who wants her will have to show torture marks," Arlene said. "What for is she fooling mit the goyim?" Maurice complained to Norman. "Where you think Hitler got all his big ideas from about the Jews, tell me that? And the pope, you should excuse me, his holiness, what was he doing during the war playing pinochle?" "They're trying to hijack the Holocaust," Norman wailed. "Christians are not—I repeat, not!—acceptable Holocaust material. This is where we draw the line." They tried to wean her from this new fixation by offering her a partnership in their business—complete control of the Women's Holocaust portfolio: abortion, sexual harassment, female genital mutilation, rape, the whole gamut—but she wasn't buying. "The Christians are the new Jews," she said. "Christians have a right to a Holocaust too. Since when do Jews have a monopoly? That's the problem with Jews. They think they own it all, they never share." So they broke down after all and offered to take on the Christian Holocaust as part of their business, however alien and distasteful it was to them—to have her create and head up, in fact, a new department devoted entirely to this area. "Forget it," she said. "You guys are too compromised and politicized for me. You'd sell out the victims for the first embassy dinner invitation."

*

The last time any member of the family had seen her was a few days after she called to tell them that she would be entering the Carmelite convent near Auschwitz as a postulant, and since it was a contemplative, enclosed, "hermit" order, she would not be available much afterward for visitors. She insisted that though she would soon become a novice and then eventually take vows, she would always consider herself to be a Jewish nun. They should keep that in mind. They were not losing her. They should not despair. It was decided that Arlene would go alone to see her. She accepted the mission despite her frequently voiced resolve never to step foot in that "huge cemetery called Poland—it's no place for a live Jew; this back-to-the-shtetl heritage nostalgia trip is obscene; these grand tours of the death camps are grotesque." The day after Nechama called, Arlene flew to Warsaw.

When Nechama converted to Catholicism, she had told them that this was a necessary step toward the fulfillment of her "vocation," but they should know and understand that, like the first Christians, she remained also a Jew. "What you mean?" Maurice had demanded. "Are you mit us or against us, are you a goy or a Jew? You can't have it bot' ways. You can't have your kishke and eat it also! Better you should for a little while just make believe like you're a Catholic—then finished, *fartig*—it will be just the same like you did it." Norman wanted to know if this was some kind of Jews-for-Jesus deal, but no, she said, it was in the best tradition of the early Church fathers. Norman then made the hopeful point to the family that nowadays maybe you could be both a Christian and a Jew, just as you could, as everyone knew, be both a Buddhist and a Jew—a Jew-Bude, it was called, something pareve, nothing to get excited about, neither milk nor meat.

Even so, her conversion was a devastating blow, though not entirely unexpected, given her increasing immersion in the Christian Holocaust. After college she had worked full-time for the cause at its Washington headquarters, and then she had set out on what she called her "pilgrimage," her "crusade," to bear witness to the persecution firsthand at the actual sites throughout the world, and to offer comfort and strength to the oppressed. She had been kicked out of Pakistan for agitation and promoting disorder. In Ethiopia she had been arrested, and it had required major string-pulling to spring her, which, fortunately, they were able to discreetly pull off thanks to her family's position in the world and their fancy connections in high places—"a little schmear here, a little kvetch there," as Maurice recounted with satisfaction. As it became clearer and clearer to them that she was heading toward conversion, Norman tried to make the case to her that she was far more useful to the Christian Holocaust as a Jew, that her Jewishness was an extremely effective media hook, it piqued people's curiosity—what was a nice Jewish girl like her doing in a place like this? It made her far more interesting and, let's face it, bizarre, especially as she was so Jewishly identified, with her family so prominent in Holocaust circles, bringing even greater atten-

tion and visibility to the cause. "Besides," Norman added deliberately, "you don't have to be Christian to love the Christian
Holocaust. When I do the Whale Holocaust, do I become a
whale? Think about it, Nechama'le. Think again, baby."

From contacts in Poland, they knew almost immediately
when Nechama had arrived there. She began a slow circuit
of the main extermination camps, stopping for a few days
at each one to fast and pray—starting with Treblinka, then
Chelmno, Sobibor, Majdanek, Belzec, until she came, finally,
to Auschwitz-Birkenau. She called home to say that she had
lit a memorial candle in front of the Carmelite convent for a
"blessed Jewish nun," Saint Edith Stein—"Sister Teresa Benedicta of the Cross," as she called her—who was martyred in the
gas chambers there. "Oy vey," Maurice had said. "She's talking
about that convert Edit' Shtein? I'm not feeling so good!" In
another telephone conversation she made the comment that
traditional Judaism provides no real outlet for a woman's spirituality. "I mean, suppose a Jewish woman wants to dedicate her
whole heart and soul and all of her strength to loving God and
to prayer. Where is there a Jewish convent for that? Does Judaism even acknowledge the existence of a woman's spirituality
in any context other than home and family?" She took a room
in Oswiecim to be near the nuns. "They're such holy, holy
women, it's humbling and uplifting, both at once. How could
anyone ever accuse them of trying to Christianize Auschwitz?
It's just ridiculous. Everything they do, they do out of love."

Nechama arranged to have Arlene meet her at the large
cross near the now abandoned old convent, the building in
which, during the Holocaust, the canisters of Zyklon B gas
with which the Jews were asphyxiated had been stored, just at
the edge of the death camp. She was already there, praying on

her knees, when Arlene's car drove up. Arlene asked the driver to wait for her; she had no intention whatsoever of visiting the camp. After she finished with Nechama, she would go directly back to Krakow, she would be in Warsaw by evening, she would be on a plane flying out of this cursed country the next morning. As she approached the cross with her daughter kneeling before it, she could see two nuns in full habit posted in the distance. Nechama herself was wearing an unfamiliar type of rough garment—probably some sort of nun's training outfit, Arlene thought.

Nechama heard Arlene approaching, and with her back still turned she signaled with her thumb and index finger rounded into a circlet—a gesture she had picked up during a teen trip to Israel—for her mother to wait a few seconds more as she finished her devotions. Then, after placing her lips directly on the wood of the cross and kissing it passionately, she rose to her feet. "Mommy," she cried, and she ran to embrace her mother. Arlene shocked herself by breaking out in racking sobs that swept over her like a flash storm. Her mascara streaked down her cheeks.

"I'm sorry, I'm sorry," she kept on repeating.

"What are you sorry about? Go on, cry. Crying is good for you—it cleanses the spirit. There's nothing to be ashamed of."

"I'm sorry for letting them screw you up," Arlene sputtered into the coarse cloth of Nechama's shirt. She had not planned to begin this way, but she could not stop herself now. "I'm sorry for not fighting harder to keep them from poisoning you with their Holocaust craziness. I should have fought them like a lioness protecting her cub. They crippled you, crippled you, they destroyed any chance you might have had to lead a normal life—and I did nothing to prevent it."

"Mom?" Nechama pushed Arlene to arm's length. "Two things, Mom. Number one, I'm not screwed up, and number two, the Holocaust, believe it or not, is the best thing that ever happened to me. It has made me what I am today. I'm proud of what I am. I'm doing vital, redemptive work. By dedicating myself to the dead I bring healing to the world. Do you understand? I don't want you to pathologize me—okay, Mom? I'm not a sicko."

Wiping her eyes with a tissue that she clutched in her fist, Arlene now took the time to look closely at her daughter. Nechama's face, framed by a kerchief that concealed all of her thick, curly hair, her best feature, was exposed and clear—no makeup, and no sign either of the acne that had troubled her well into her twenties. So convents are good for the complexion, Arlene concluded bitterly. Instead of contact lenses she was wearing glasses with a translucent pale pink plastic frame. The expression in her eyes was serene and benevolent—too placid, Arlene thought, she looked drugged, brainwashed, dead to life. There was a faint mustache over her upper lip; in her new life of poverty, chastity, and obedience, there was no place any longer for the facial bleaching in which Arlene had instructed her as part of the beauty regimen of every dark-haired woman. Around her neck hung a daunting cross made from some base metal. The womanly fullness of her barren hips bore down earthward against her skirts, pulled down inevitably by gravity whether they fulfilled their biological function or not, Arlene could see that. She had put on a little weight—not that it mattered anymore. At least she was getting enough to eat.

Nechama quickly sensed her mother's appraising eye, and for a moment she was seized by a familiar irritation that she recognized from the past, from those times when her mother would rate her appearance down to the last fraction of an ounce, and would register mute disappointment. By an act of the will, Nechama shook off this feeling, which she considered unworthy and a vanity.

"You look nice," Arlene finally said. She avoided Nechama's eyes, gazing up instead at the twenty-six-foot wooden cross looming behind them. "So this is the famous cross that the Jews and the Poles are beating up on each other about."

"Yes—isn't it ridiculous?" Nechama said. "I guess I'll just never understand what Jews have against a cross."

The Crusades. The Inquisition. Pogroms. Blood libels. The Holocaust. If she can't figure out what we have against the cross, Arlene thought, especially when it is planted right in this spot, where over a million Jews were gassed and burned, then she has strayed a long, long way from home, she has gone very far indeed, she is lost to us.

"I mean," Nechama went on, "what everyone needs to realize now, if we're ever going to get beyond this, is that each Jew who was murdered in the Holocaust is another Christ crucified on the cross. When I pray to Him, I pray to each one of them. I pray every day to each of the six million Christs."

Suffering and salvation. Martyrdom and redemption. This was not a language that Arlene recognized. The cross cast its long dark shadow over them and onto the blood-soaked ground beyond. The afternoon was passing. Arlene adjusted the strap of the stylish black leather bag on her shoulder and glanced toward the waiting car. More than anything else in the world now, she wanted to get away from here, from this madness that breeds more madness, from this alien sacred imagery that justifies unspeakable atrocities. She wanted ordinariness, dailiness, routine—plans, schedules, menus, lists, programs, things, material goods. "Do you need anything, Nechama?" Arlene asked. "I mean, before I go—like underwear, vitamins, toiletries? Tell me what you need, and I'll see that you get it."

"Oh, I don't need anything anymore—I'm finished with needing things," Nechama said, breaking her mother's heart. "We live very simply here. Other people have needs. They send us long lists of what they need, and we pray for them. That's what we do. I can pray for you, too, Mommy. Tell me what you need."

What did she need? She needed to think and see clearly. She needed to remember everything she had forgotten—or she would soon lose faith that she had ever existed at all. "I need to have you back with me," Arlene said quietly, in the voice she would use when she would lie down in bed beside her daughter at night, to ease the child into sleep.

Nechama smiled rapturously. "We'll pray for you," she said, and her gaze moved from her mother and the cross above them to encompass her whole world, the two nuns motionless in the distance, and the more than a million dead inside the camp who never rested.

* PART TWO *

Camp Auschwitz

1

In ROOM FOUR, BLOCK FOUR of the Auschwitz death camp museum, as they were brought to a halt in front of the display case of a canister of Zyklon B poison gas with an arrangement of white pellets spilling out like a bridal train, Monty Pincus suddenly slapped his forehead audibly, remembering that he had better telephone his wife Honey in Arlington, Virginia. Moving a perfunctory step or two away from the group, he pulled his mobile phone from the inside pocket of his disheveled iridescent fly-blue suit jacket, stretched by a single button across his prospering paunch, and with his eyes absentmindedly tracing the outline of the inspiring architectural hoist of a Slavic brassiere through the snug fuzzy pink sweater of the guide, Krystyna Jesudowicz, as she went on with her spiel about how between 1942 and 1943 alone almost twenty thousand tons of this pesticide were shipped by the Degesch division of the German monster company I. G. Farben to this site alone in order to efficiently carry out what was classified as a sanitary operation to exterminate Jews and other vermin et cetera et cetera, and casually ignoring the venomous rays of annoyance she focused so personally on him as he raised his voice to the Jewish decibel level required for long distance, he yelled into the phone, "Honey? Honey, I know you're there! Pick up the phone, Honey! Is something wrong with your brain? Goddamn it, pick up the phone!" He didn't care how long he'd have to wait on the line before she got up off her fat behind to answer the telephone, or how many times she would force him to redial. This was crucial business touching on the well-being and survival of the United States Holocaust Memorial Museum. He would charge it to the federal government.

With his left hand, the one that wasn't flattening the phone like a muff against his ear, Monty scratched his smudge of a beard and then, through his trouser pocket, he discreetly, as he liked to believe, adjusted the lay of his manhood, shouting the whole time, "Honey, for Christ's sake, pick up the goddamn phone!"—practically drowning out Krystyna and her decadent Eastern European accent as she carried on with how in the so-called shower rooms, which were actually gas chambers in disguise, this Zyklon B was released from special outlets to asphyxiate the naked prisoners packed inside, children, women, and men, fifteen hundred to two thousand human beings at a time, for which about five to seven kilograms of the chemical were needed, and so forth, piling on the full authority of the numbers. "Is he always so rude?" demanded Bunny Bacon in a voice meant to be heard specifically by the miscreant, glaring at Monty through her oversize eyeglasses with their red frames, enunciating precisely in her strict kindergarten-teacher's syllables. Norman Messer, at his post beside her, having been stationed there by his father to help ease her through all of this traumatic material to which she was being exposed for the first time, and also, as Maurice said, to "massage her nice so she'll get mama to give out good," cleared his throat twice and explained laboriously, "Well, with such a prima donna like our Monty here, it's a matter of personal policy for him to talk only when someone else is also talking—to maintain his image that he already knows it all."

Monty listened cheerfully to all of this with his one available ear, calmly unperturbed and unchastened, taking it all in with a complacent sense of how natural and right it was for him to be the topic of conversation. By way of a token excuse, though, because he knew that Maurice would eat him alive if he alienated this money Bunny, he shrugged the shoulder that was unencumbered by the telephone and held out his arms palms upward in a "What can I do? This is an emergency" gesture, presenting her, at the same time, with his lopsided, crinkly-eyed, guaranteed irresistible grin. He could sense from her exaggerated signs of aversion and her confrontational hostility toward him that he was beginning to win her over, that he would soon have her panting at his feet with her tongue hanging out, ripe and ready to do whatever he wanted, exactly as he had been ordered by Maurice—or, as he was now known, the Honorable Maurice Messer, who in his new position as the presidentially appointed chairman of the board of the Holocaust Museum was hoping to extract a major donation from Bunny's mother, Mrs. Gloria Bacon Lieb. Monty would have much preferred to have been assigned to the mother. The daughter, with her limp brown bangs and her boyish haircut peaking in a kind of cowlick at the top of her disproportionately small, pointed head, was thick-ankled, pear-shaped, "a little broad from the beam," as Maurice phrased it rather tactfully, he thought, while the elegantly groomed and sumptuously costumed mother was a babe, the sleek poster girl for money and maintenance, spa and salon, accommodatingly blond, with a willing and attentive look meant for men. But Maurice had decreed, "Gloria, she's mine. First I squeeze a big one out from her in the name from Husband Number One, the late Mel Bacon, from discount wholesale manufacturing in Third World countries fame, may he rest in peace. Next I work on her for the goods from

Husband Number Two, mine fellow partisan and resistance fighter, Leon Lieb, originally from nursing homes until he got investigated by a bunch of anti-Semitten no-goodniks, and after that, like the rest from us wandering Jews since time immemorial, starting all over again from scratch—this time in slum and tenement real estate. Your job is to schmear the daughter, the old maid. Hit the jackpot, Pinky, and God willing, pretty soon I twist the arm from the council from the museum and I make you director." Only from Maurice who could make him director did Monty tolerate this despised diminutive of his last name, this Pinky infestation, which had tormented him through adolescence, unmanning him, pounding into him the doctrine that, physically, in all his parts, he was the runt, and also intellectually, number ninety-nine in a class of one hundred of his yeshiva high school, legendary for advance distribution to students of the answers to all state and national exams on the principle, which Monty had absorbed in his molecules, that from the religious perspective, officials, authorities, governments, and the like were mere temporal impediments and irritants meant to be outwitted.

Maurice now stroked the luscious fabric of Gloria Bacon Lieb's jacket sleeve, shaking his head at Monty's bad telephone manners—such a wise guy, that Monty!—while gazing adoringly and forgivingly at him. He truly had a passion for Monty, wishing in his heart at times that his Norman could have been even half so bold and confident and inventive, though naturally he would never have uttered such a thought out loud even to his own wife Blanche. Not to imply that Norman was a nothing, of course, and especially now with Maurice "very romantically involved mit the museum," as he liked to say, he, Norman, was the de facto big chief of their business, Holocaust Connections, Inc., ran the whole shop himself, "hook, crook, and shtinker," while Maurice was the silent partner—"well, maybe not so silent," as his Blanchie would lovingly remind him. Still, Monty—Monty was truly "hoo-hah, he was something, a shuper shtar!" "Mine Monty," Maurice elaborated to Gloria, "absolutely brilliant, a creative genius par excellence! You see that can over there?" He indicated the Zyklon B in the display. "Nu, so the Auschwitz museum here out from the goodness of its heart breaks down and loans to us a couple of cans for our place in Washington from the thousands left behind here like garbage by the Nazi criminals and murderers, they should rot in hell. But what happens next? When we try to get it through customs into the good old U.S.A.—such problems, you shouldn't know from it, such aggravation! EPA, ShmeePA, they're all making us crazy. Where are we going to store it? That's all what these geniuses wanted to know. What precautions are we taking it shouldn't explode? Maybe it will be the end from the world, maybe it will give gas to the whole Congress as if we would ever notice the difference anyway, maybe—who knows what else maybe? Environmental! You know why the word *environmental* has mental in it? Now you know why! But mine Monty here—he solves everything. Mine crazy Monty! Chutzpah mit charisma—that's mine Monty in a nut's shell. This boy never met a rule he wouldn't break, never met a risk he wouldn't take, a little reckless maybe, sometimes we have to hold him back mit wild horses, but the trut' is, Gloria darling—an incredible talent, a true visionary. Believe me, when it comes to making the Holocaust a household word—Nobel Prize material!"

Gloria stepped forward and pressed her cool palm over the place where Maurice's heart was hammering passionately, drawing her molded bosom in its expensively tailored suit up to him, her face so close to his he could inhale her gourmet mouthwash. "Now listen up, Mr. Chairman," she whispered, "if you know what's good for you, you had better tell me right this minute how your little genius boychik did it." She must really have wanted to know. "Ah, Gloria darling," Maurice said, sandwiching that creamy hand of hers between his two pudgy ones with those anomalously manicured fingernails, and rubbing it up and down rhythmically, "the answer to that question will cost you a minimum five million from Mel's foundation. But seriously speaking, darling, even if you gave to me ten million, I wouldn't tell to you, because of mine love for you, Gloria, not to mention mine respect for your mind—for your own good, darling, in case the G-men torture you mit dripping prune juice on top of your beautiful hairdo or mit shticking pins and needles under your gorgeous manicure God forbid to get out from you the information. Better for your own health you shouldn't know what kind of finaglings and problems we had to go through in the name of creating our sacred institution!"

Krystyna was now enumerating that gruesome litany regarding the disposal of the corpses following twenty minutes or so of torture in the gas—the extracting of the gold teeth, the probing of the orifices for concealed treasure, the cutting off of the women's hair—ad nauseam, literally and figuratively, though there were a lot of perverts and sadists out there who always got a big charge from it all, Norman knew. Ah Krystyna, our Lady of Brzezinka—she gives good Shoah! He observed her as she pumped on relentlessly, totally on automatic like an old hooker, staring blankly into the contaminated space of this barrack where who knows what suffering had once been endured, her fingers raking unconsciously through her champagne-colored hair, teasing it out even fuller. What with everyone but himself ignoring her—Monty still hollering into his telephone, his father conducting museum business with Gloria, and now Bunny foaming at the mouth over something or other—well, if by some miracle Krystyna wasn't already an anti-Semite like every other single Pole he had ever met, Norman reflected, and especially with her close personal contact with particularly obnoxious Jewish types in her job as the museum's acquisitions agent in Warsaw and occasional VIP tour guide for fund-raising junkets such as this one, which enabled her to get to know the species intimately and, from her point of view, no doubt gave her open-and-shut grounds and justification to despise them even more, she would definitely turn into a flaming Jew-hater now. "Maurice, look," Gloria was saying, jutting her chin toward Bunny, "Barbara is very upset about something. Stand up straight, Barbara," she added reflexively.

"What's the matter, Bunny honey?" Maurice appealed with sincere concern, turning in alarm from the mother to the daughter. Bunny furiously jabbed a finger toward Monty, who was still braying into the telephone. "I really really find it offensive the way he swears and takes the Lord's name in vain," she responded. With the same accusatory pointer she pushed up the bridge of her eyeglasses, but she had hooked even Monty's attention for a second. "I consider such language very very inappropriate in this place of holy Christian and Jewish martyrs," she elaborated. Uh-oh, Monty thought, I'm in big trouble; this chick has really fallen for me hard.

"Mrs. Lieb?" Maurice looked admiringly from Bunny to Gloria. "I must compliment you on bringing up such a sensitive daughter. Such antennas she has, such rabbit's ears, you should excuse me, and she is still only a Holocaust virgin! Need

I say more? Amazing!" Then walking a few paces up to Monty, he hissed into his free ear, "Get off the goddamn telephone, you schmuck, before I kill you. You gonna cost me a couple of million, imbecile!"

Monty contemplated Maurice disdainfully. "Okay, Honey," he rasped at last into the phone so that only Maurice could hear him, resigned under the circumstances to leaving his message on the machine, "you win this time. But I'm telling you right now, Honey, you'd just better not fuck me over if that reporter from the *Post* shows up at the house—you hear me, Honey?—the one I told you about, the guy who's doing a profile on me in connection with the museum? I'm warning you! You'd better not give him any information at all. Don't let him in. Don't show him anything—no scrapbooks, no pictures, no nothing. Don't take him around—you hear?—no upstairs, no downstairs, no attic, no cellar, no garage. The operative phrase is 'No comment'—get it, Honey? If you screw me, you're finished—and that's a promise. I'll take everything, every last goddamn thing, including the kids. I'll call a press conference, I'll tell the media what a nutcase you are, I'll get the museum lawyer pro bono in court on my side and I'll wipe you out, Honey, if you mess with me—you have my word on that!" He was out of control. "Moron!" Maurice ejaculated. "Such a message you leave on a tape? For evidence for later? Idiot!"

"Shut up, Mr. Honorable Asshole Partisan!" Monty shot back, and, stuffing the phone in disgust into his pocket, he pivoted sharply, heading straight toward the next room, Room Five, with the others following instinctively behind like a tribe of ducklings—despite everything, Maurice once again recognized in awe, despite the fact that he let such vile words out of his dirty, filthy *pisk* and was so fresh and ungrateful and even

cruel, despite the fact that he was blowing all his chances of
ever being named the director of their moral-beacon museum
much less surviving the vetting process and media scrutiny
with all his scandals and cowboy shenanigans and fooling
around, despite the fact that he, Maurice, so many times felt
like wringing out the boy's neck good and hard like a chicken,
he could not deny the truth staring him now as always right
in the face—that his Monty was a true leader, just look how
everyone else spontaneously and docilely followed him like
sheep, a born trailblazer, he was a natural, a latter-day hero of
our Holocaust.

*

As they all filed behind Monty into Room Five, however, Maurice could feel the rage rising once again like a hot bolus in
his throat. Madame Jadwiga Switon, the top potato of this
State Museum in Auschwitz-Birkenau, had personally sworn
to him on everything that's holy—ha!—that they would have
the entire place to themselves. He had patiently struggled to
drill into her thick Polack head how important these donors
could be to him, how essential it was that they feel they are getting the exclusive, red-carpet, five-star treatment, and she had
promised—yes, promised!—that during their tour the premises would be closed to the general public. "You have my word
of honor, Pan Messer," she had assured him. So how did you
explain, then, the presence in this chamber of horrors of those
three creatures in the corner over there who could loosely be
classified as human? Maybe they looked like statues, maybe
they resembled some kind of conceptual sculpture installation
iconography in the museum-speak Maurice was beginning to
absorb, the way they sat there perfectly still, frozen like the dead,
but Maurice wasn't tricked. He knew this place inside out, he

knew they were aliens here, they didn't belong, whether they were animate or whether they were so-called art, and when he marched right up to them to tell them in no uncertain terms where to go, he could see that they were alive all right, their chests were rising and falling evenly, their eyeballs were rolling gently behind their drawn lids, a low underwaterish buzz was coming regularly from somewhere deep down inside them.

"Excuse me, mister," Maurice said, giving a deliberate cough and addressing the one sitting erect in a wheelchair in the middle who seemed like the boss—the fat one with that merry cushion of a gut, the long gray beard like dry straw, the shaved head with that ridiculous little ponytail in the back like a misplaced *pupik*, dolled up in a long white embroidered blouse like some sort of swami salami. Slipping his hand into the back pocket of the trousers of his made-to-order suit, Maurice extracted an ornate silver case, clicked it open, took out his chairman's card embossed in gold with the seal of the museum, and waved it in front of the impassive face. But, to his shock and embarrassment before potential donors, the reflexive deference that his position invariably evoked in normal people, which he had come to expect, did not materialize, not from this kook in the wheelchair who didn't even bother to open his eyes, and not from the other two freaks sitting on the floor there with their legs curled under them like a contortionist Indians, or, you should excuse me, Native Americans at a powwow—the pregnant girl in all those gypsy *schmattehs*, rows and rows of beads, and small round steel-rimmed glasses, and, on the other side of the cripple, a tall—you could tell he was a giant even though he was all folded up—clean-cut fellow who was definitely a goy, maybe even a goy with a trust fund who gets a kick out of giving the finger to his ancestors by pledging

to Jewish causes—who knows?—the last of the WASPs; the
other two, the guru and the hippie, they were Jews, no question
about it, most probably penniless worthless Jews, you couldn't
fool Maurice in a million years, he could smell it. "What do we
have here?" Maurice demanded, turning to Krystyna, his paid
employee, for an explanation. "The three stooges? The *ganze*
holy *mishpoche*, the virgin mother mit her two husbands, including the holy ghost?" "It's called meditation, Pop," Norman vol-
unteered wearily, depositing this information with a sigh from
the depths of his sullen sophistication. His father waved him
away impatiently, though Norman had wanted to say more, but
the words just could not be dredged up fast enough. "Don't
give me no meditation!" Maurice barked. "Get the bums out
from here. They're trespassing on mine Holocaust!"

"Um, Maurice?" Bunny Bacon now stepped forward pur-
posefully to make a point. "Don't you think there's enough
Holocaust to go around for everyone? I mean, I really really
like this diversity." Her eyes like fishes behind the bowls of her
glasses shifted from the weird threesome, still unavailable in
their trance, then back to Maurice. "And, you know," she went
on, flashing her encouraging pedagogic smile, "I really really
appreciate it that Auschwitz is wheelchair-accessible. You know
what I mean? Was it always that way—I mean, even at the time
of the Holocaust?"

Then, feeling reinforced about having voiced her position
on this matter, Bunny turned her attention to the main exhibit
in the room, which extended behind a glass partition along one
entire wall about the length of her kindergarten classroom in
New York City where the miniature rainbow-colored cubbies
were lined up. "What's that?" she asked Norman, her personal
docent. "Some kind of installation art?" By way of an answer,

Norman signaled with a look in the direction of Krystyna, who was duly delivering what the American taxpayer was paying her for. "Two tons of human hair," Krystyna was reciting for the thousandth time, "from the seven tons found by Soviet troops when they liberated Auschwitz in 1945, shorn from the heads of the gassed female corpses, baled and labeled for shipment to Germany for use in the war industry—for cloth, carpets, insulation, et cetera et cetera."

"A hair mountain? Oh my God, this is *so* gross!" Bunny exclaimed. And finding some amusement in hearing herself sound like one of her five-year-olds staring down into a plate of snot-green brussels sprouts in the lunchroom of the exclusive private school where she taught, she went on for good effect: "A humongous hairball! Yuck!" She turned to face Monty. "I really really hope you don't make your visitors do hair at your Washington museum!"

Monty was opening his mouth to reply when Maurice leapt, with a spryness impressive for his age, in front of him and seized both of Bunny's nail-gnawed hands, kissing them lavishly. "What a soul! I'm telling you"—and he beamed at Gloria—"your daughter is sensitive like the proverbial open sore. We survivors said this very same thing, ditto ditto—no hair! It's a part from the human body! This could be hair from the head of mine mama, mine *bubbe,* mine *tante,* mine *schwester!* We Jews, we bury in the ground the body parts and we say a Kaddish, we respect the dead, not like these Polish anti-Semitten here who get a thrill you shouldn't know about from showing the physical remains from dead Jews." Then, smiling proudly at Bunny, he added, "I can assure you, Miss Bunny honey, that not even one single hair from the head from even one single murdered Jewish lady is on display at our museum in Washington to defile our temple to the Holocaust. This was a battle that I led personally and that we survivors fought on principle and won. And"—here he gave a pause like a fanfare before proceeding—"because of your beautiful and sensitive soul that you let me have a tiny peek today, I want to say that it gives me great pleasure here and now in this factory of death we call Auschwitz to hereby award you mit the official title of Honorary Survivor mit all the rights and privileges thereof and thereto."

Monty kept his mouth shut in solidarity with Maurice as the old man went on like this, spinning his revisionist history of the hair war in which he now fully believed. Monty stood transfixed, overflowing with respect for the shameless guile and gall of the old rogue—they were as alike, Maurice used to say, like two foxes in a foxhole, and Monty recognized this as the ultimate compliment—remembering how ruthlessly Maurice had fought some of the other survivors, Lipman Krakowski and Henny Soskis, for instance, in the battle over the hair, swearing on all that is holy that he would destroy them, how imperiously Maurice had insisted that they display the real thing due to the proven ghoulish popularity and drawing power of this exhibit at the Auschwitz museum, how doggedly he had even arranged to have a couple of hundred pounds of the stuff schlepped home from Poland in laundry sacks that were now buried in storage somewhere out in the malls of Maryland, how in the end he had been forced to retreat and give in only because he had gotten that call directly from the White House—Henny had a granddaughter who was an intern there with face time—advising him that he'd better back off on the hair business if he ever wanted to be renamed to the museum council much less be reappointed chair.

"You don't know how right you are, Maurice," Gloria was saying. "Barbara is extremely sensitive. Thank you so much for noticing." She was thinking about all those years of analysis, starting when Bunny was three years old, right down to the present day—exactly forty years of psychiatric treatment so far; maybe they should throw an anniversary party. Even from Poland, Bunny faithfully kept her appointments by daily scheduled telephone calls; minus her shrink, she would turn into an absolute wreck like that hair over there, she would let herself go, fall apart, it was as critical as that. With such a high-strung and neurotic daughter, phobic and panicked about everything from mice to men, requiring couturier designer care, could anyone in all fairness fault Gloria for protecting her assets, sticking only to millionaires? It was a practical necessity, a survival thing. All that dieting because the Nazi was within, the endless shopping like a life sentence with no possibility of parole, the brain damage that comes from a lifelong career of pleasing men—she did it all out of maternal love. She was sensitive too, she too was a survivor. Why didn't anyone give *her* an award?

"Maurice?" Gloria now asserted herself. "Don't you think you should at least talk to someone in this Auschwitz museum about the condition of this hair? I mean, look at it! It's a mess. Who knows what's crawling around in there—mice, lice— who knows what? It's all matted—ugly! They could at least try to do something with it—don't you think?—something creative, to make it a little more presentable and attractive? And for goodness sake, in this day and age, why does it all have to be so gray?"

"It is gray because of a chemical reaction in the gas chamber," Krystyna spoke up, as if a button had been pushed, "the effect of contact with the Zyklon B—diatomite saturated in hydrogen cyanide."

"Wrong," came a mellow voice from the other side of the room. "It is gray because it awaits karmic retribution."

"Hey!" Maurice pounced. "You some kind of a denier, Mac?"

"I am an affirmer—of the universal energy of transcendence," replied the wacko in the wheelchair.

"As far as I am concerned, fella," Maurice said, moving in on him menacingly, "you mit your sidekick squatters here are trespassers, pure and simple, and I for one am not going to take it shitting down, so to speak. I'm calling the authorities here right this minute to kick you out but good. This place is not your place, Mr. Whatever-Your-Name-Is."

"Pop?" Norman whispered as fast as he could into his father's ear, trying to resist the temptation under the pressure of circumstances of overexplaining, embarrassed to the bone yet again by the old man's siege mentality, his paranoia, his propensity to make a scene, his provincialism. "Pop, don't you recognize this guy from TV? It's Mickey Fisher, the Zen master—he's a very big *roshi,* like a chief rabbi. He's on cable every Sunday morning—Arlene always watches. I'm going to get his autograph. She'll be thrilled. Maybe she'll even be nice to me for a day. She does the meditation exercises with him when he's on the tube. I actually heard from La Switon's own mouth that he's here with about a hundred groupies on some kind of interfaith retreat. I think they've got rooms right here in the museum. So technically, Pop, I can tell you as an attorney, you don't have a leg to stand on. They're not trespassing."

Maurice took a step or two back, as if to reposition himself on the battlefield of survival, to consider the new facts on the ground, which now encompassed even his own daughter-in-law. "Very nice," he said to the guru after some reflection, "very nice. Mine son explained me, now I understand everything. So Pisher, tell me—you came here mit a t'eme?"

"Oh, yes! I came here with minds and bodies reborn countless times across space and time, from every land, embracing every color and faith and gender, and yes, also with my personal team, Jake Gilguli," Fisher motioned to the WASP to his left, "my chief of staff, and," indicating the pregnant hippie on his other side, "Marano—one name, like Madonna—my personal assistant."

Maurice's face went crimson. "I didn't say *team*," he sputtered, "I said"—and here he twisted his mouth grotesquely, stuck out about a third of his tongue while biting down excruciatingly on it with his teeth, and with an enormous spritz of saliva he extracted that almost impossible sound that came so easily to every lisping dumbbell—"*theme!*"

"Ah, theme! Yes, yes, we also have a theme. Our theme—our teaching, as we prefer to call it—is 'From Horror to Healing.' But meditating and chanting now in this space of the unconsoled, I am visualizing enlarging it to "From Hair to Horror to Healing."

"Why not 'From Hair to Eternity'?" Monty cracked.

"Maybe it should be 'From Hair to Maternity,' " Norman put in, not to be outdone by this rival for his father's love and approval and munificence, as he rather crudely zoomed in on that belly nesting like a great egg in the lotus of Fisher's personal assistant, this so-called Marano. He could take this liberty, he felt confident, because she obviously did not matter much in the scheme of things, she was expendable, the kind of woman who got knocked up—Norman could sense that.

The *roshi* went on, separating himself from the illusion of their mockery. "We are seeking awareness by focusing our chakra centers on the breath coming out of our bodies in the letter H, as in the mantras Hair, Horror, Healing, Hiroshima—Holocaust! As in, Ha, Ha, Ha—laughter! We are birthing the bliss of the dead by visualizing their repose away from this space in which their suffering and lamentation are on display, and every eye gazing upon them is an affront."

"Maurice?" Gloria now spoke up, commanding an audience. "You know, we may consider this guy a little cuckoo and everything he says sounds like mumbo jumbo, but in my humble opinion he does have a point—about this display business? Because what exactly *is* on display here when you come to think about it—and also in your great big museum on the Mall in downtown Washington, D.C., where all those millions of tourists from all over the world come filing through to gape and stare? Us! We're on display, we're exhibit A, let's face it, we Jews, you and me—Jews being gassed, Jews being shot, Jews being hanged, Jews being electrocuted, Jews being beaten, Jews being raped, Jews being tortured. Don't you find it all a little bit vulgar and coarse and in bad taste? Do you really think when all is said and done that this is a good thing for the Jews? Do you really consider this a project worth supporting?"

"Gloria, Gloria," Maurice began, "why you mixing in your pretty little head mit all this mystical shmystical?" But Monty cut him off at once, progressive and canny enough to recognize the importance of at least giving the appearance of taking a woman—and especially a woman loaded in every sense of the word who is flirting with an idea—seriously. "That's actually very perceptive of you, Gloria," Monty said, screwing a finger in his ear and then absentmindedly rolling the yield between thumb and forefinger and examining it. "You've touched directly on a problem that we scholars have been wrestling with from the beginning. In the end, though, we've concluded based on all of our research and analysis that the benefits of presenting the Holocaust to the world and displaying ourselves as victims—of normalizing the abnormal, as it were—far outweigh the disadvantages in terms of the social, historical, and ethical lessons that can be learned about the human potential for evil—and also for good. We Jews have a moral obligation to offer our suffering and humiliation to the world as a cautionary tale, and for the lessons governing future personal and political behavior that can be drawn from it. We must think of the Holocaust, in effect, as the Gift of the Jews."

"Really?" Norman geared up. "And I always thought it was the Gift of the Germans." Norman's face puckered in disgust. The Holocaust as the Gift of the Jews—what a repulsive idea! Another sound bite for the simpleminded, another kernel of instant kitsch from Monty Pincus, King Kitsch himself.

"Your name is Gloria?" the guru now intoned, combing with his fingers through his bushy gray beard, plowing ahead, indifferent to the ego-warped dialectics of the two men, capturing the woman with his piercing, intimate gaze. "Forgive me, but I can sense from your manifestations that you are not a Gloria. You are a Jiriki. From now on, I shall call you Jiriki because of your struggle to find enlightenment on your own power. You have a very special soul, a holy holy soul, Jiriki, I can visualize the karma streams coming from it, I can sense your personal struggle to actualize our vision of the oneness of all living things past, present, and future, whether it be the oneness of all the dead souls here at Auschwitz—Jews, Poles, Gypsies, Soviet prisoners of war, and so on, all equal in victimhood, all one and the same—or whether it be the oneness and interdependence of all the living souls of every faith and color and gender who have come here seeking healing and enlightenment. But it is holy holy souls like yours above all, Jiriki, that we are searching for at our *zendo* in East Hampton, on Long Island. You know, you really ought to come and visit us there when you get back to the States. You would be our most welcome and honored guest, I promise you. Of course, at the moment, we're in a temporary trailer, but if you came to see us there, I would be delighted to personally show you the architect's drawings for our new complex, the Center for High Energy Metaphysics, that we're planning to build, and it would be my great pleasure, I assure you, to escort you on a private tour of the oceanfront property we're hoping to buy. In the meantime, though—why don't you come and meditate with us at Execution Wall, linking Block Ten, where sterilization experiments were performed on Jewish women, with Block Eleven, where the Polish Catholic martyr Saint Maximilian Kolbe was tortured? It's a very interesting interfaith must-see attraction in case you haven't done it yet, Jiriki—the black wall where prisoners were taken out and shot? You can lay a wreath there. Marano will make one for you from the grass and flowers blooming in the organically enriched soil here at the camp. Please do join us, Jiriki. We will be sitting there in meditation until sunset."

Gloria was flattered, and torn. On one side was a man appealing to her mind; on the other, a man beckoning to her spirit. And, in the middle, Maurice Messer, the familiar type of man comfortable in his conviction that she possessed neither but whom she was an expert at handling—and he was laying claim. "Well, well, well! Look what we have here! A Buddha *schnorrer*! Very nice, very nice! So what else is news? You think

I don't know what you're up to, mister? I've been in the fund-raising business since before you could even say yoga, or yogi bear, or yogurt—or Harry Krishma, or Harry Karry, or whatever. It takes one to know one, fella—let me tell you. Gloria darling, listen to me—this guru shmuru knows from nothing! What does he mean—one and the same? Over one million gassed Jews in Auschwitz processed and mass-murdered like a factory is the same thing like seventy-five thousand Poles, most of them political prisoners, given the dignity of being shot one by one at a wall if they weren't lucky enough to starve to death first? How can you compare? Believe me, Gloria darling, there's no contest. We Jews win this one hands down! And this so-called Execution Wall, this black wall, this wall of death, or whatever name they want to give to it—I'm telling you, Gloria darling, this wall is not your wall, this wall is special for the Poles and the pope. I got a bigger and better wall for you, and I'm not talking here from the Great Wall from China. The wall I'm talking is your wall, a Jewish wall—the Founders' Wall in our museum, the million-dollar donors' wall—your personal wall, Gloria darling, where you can have a personalized plaque of your own, that's the wall where you belong! Of course you can't go to this *goyische* wall mit this *gonif*—this swami shake-down artist, this yogi used-car salesman! Number one, I made a promise to Leon to take good care from you—so how could I ever explain to him that I let you run around a death camp mit a bunch of meshuga meditators? Number two, you will spoil your beautiful Armani suit from sitting outside on the hard stone floor meditating mit these kooks, not to mention maybe getting piles, God forbid, from the cold and wet."

"Of course we shall provide Jiriki with a *zafu* to sit on, compliments of the Center for High Energy Metaphysics."

"And number three, we have on our schedule next a private tour from the gas chamber, which is a very special treat that doesn't happen every day to any old *schmendrik*. Come on, gang," Maurice called out to the others with the tense and desperate jollity of a social director on a cruise ship, "we're going to the gas chamber! The limo is waiting by the door."

And urged on anxiously by Maurice and Krystyna, they were hustled out of the room as Mickey Fisher-roshi and Chief of Staff Jake Gilguli observed them with calm detachment, serenely letting go of the sensation of their reality, unlike Personal Assistant Marano, who lifted her eyes as Norman rushed by and smiled mysteriously. "See ya later, Normie," Marano sang out in an exotic accent that was totally untraceable to any land or to any language he had ever known.

*

"Did you hear that?" Norman kept repeating during their one-minute drive in the Mercedes on the camp streets from Block Four to the gas chamber just beyond the barbed wire that surrounded the barracks. "How the hell did she know my name? Do I know that aging hippie from somewhere? Do you recognize her, Pop?"

"You're famous, Norman, that's what it is, you're a celebrity," Monty said, profoundly bored by the long-running performance of Norman stuck in another one of his ruts. "You're a public figure from your second generation work—what do you expect? You're instantly recognizable. You just don't have the luxury of anonymity like the rest of us poor schnooks here. That's the price you have to pay for fame—sorry. Come to think of it, though, I'm pretty sure I called you by your name in there when we were looking at the hair, like when I said, 'Shut up, Norman you putz,' or 'Shut up, Norman you asshole,' or something like that—so that probably explains it, okay? All right? Do you think you can finally shut up already?"

But it continued to bother him, he could not stop mulling over it even long enough to lash back at Monty for this mean-spirited sarcasm, this totally undeserved attack. She had called him Normie, not Norman. What could that mean? Did she recognize him from his past, his childhood, boyhood, youth—school, some party somewhere? Had they smoked pot together once long ago in his glorious weed days? Was this Auschwitz trip going to turn into some kind of trip trip? He was so absorbed in trying to figure out the connection—the way it fluttered there so elusively bedeviled him like a filmy web he just could not grasp—that he had absolutely no memory at all of stepping out of the limousine with the others in front of the gas chamber of Crematorium I, or of pausing with the group as Krystyna informed the ladies that the gallows they may have noticed set up opposite the entrance here were used only once, in 1947, to execute the camp's first commandant, Rudolf Höss, the mastermind who had introduced the Zyklon B in 1941 as a method of killing Jews—for a grand total by the war's end, according to Höss's own written estimate, of one million one hundred and thirty thousand Jews gassed at Auschwitz alone.

Was he boasting or something? Norman wondered, as his focus on pinning down this Marano creature was thoughtlessly interrupted by his father puffing up and holding forth—"You know, ladies," Maurice was expatiating, "this reminds me from when I was a leader from the partisans and fought against the Nazis in the woods." Norman rolled his eyes. "Pop? C'mon, Pop, there's no time for this now. We have to get to the gas chamber." "You should excuse me, Mr. Smart-Alex, Esquire," Maurice responded defensively to his son. "Maybe I didn't go to fancy-schmancy Princeton University like you did. Maybe I just got mine degree from the University from the Holocaust. But let me tell you something, sonny boy—nowadays, that's a very hot school. Everybody and his uncle wants to get in!" Then, turning triumphantly to Gloria and Bunny, for whom his reference to his wartime exploits had been intended, Maurice started again. "Like I was saying before I was so rudely interrupted by mine own flesh and blood here"—and he launched directly into that tale that Norman had anticipated and dreaded, all the more so now since his father had become such a public figure, chairman of the premier Holocaust shop in the world, the consequences of exposure of these lies would have been not only personally catastrophic but also potentially ruinous to faith in the integrity of Holocaust history, deniers everywhere who insisted that the entire Holocaust was a hoax would be given a field day thanks to the old man's pitiful bragging, for the life of him Norman could not understand what suicidal urge impelled his father to persist in risking everything by telling these pathetic stories. On this particular occasion, Norman realized with dispirited resignation, Maurice had no doubt been prompted, like Pavlov's dog, by the stimulus of the gallows at the entrance to the gas chamber. It was a preposterous but vintage story, Norman knew from personal mortifying experience as he girded himself to be inflicted with it yet again, packaged and formulaic from overtelling, fantasy wantonly mutated into fact—how, when his father "was a leader from the partisans and fought against the Nazis in the woods," he had led his band of resistance fighters on a night raid into a hovel in Galicia, dragged the vodka-stupefied peasant off his straw mattress, tied a rope around his fat neck, and hanged him from a rafter on the ceiling with a warning sign pinned to his filthy nightshirt, "This is what happens to anyone who hands a Jew over to the Nazis."

"Oh my God!" Bunny exclaimed. "You mean, you *lynched* the poor guy—without even a trial? Haven't you ever heard of the concept of due process, of innocent until proven guilty?"

Maurice sighed. Every so often he encountered a specimen like this; his Blanchie called them the PCniks, the even-Hitler-has-rights delegation. Their daughter-in-law Arlene was a card-carrying member of this union—soft-in-the-head sheltered coddled American liberal do-gooder types with absolutely no clue about what was possible on this planet in the department of chaos and horror. Arlene, however, could be dismissed; she did not possess Bunny's bank account. Bunny, on the other hand, had to be stroked. "Bunny honey," Maurice pleaded, "the point from the story is to debunk the myt' that we Jews went like sheep to the shlaughter. That's all what I wanted you ladies to understand."

"I guess what my father is trying to say here is that the story needs to be taken as a paradigmatic or archetypal conceit rather than literally or at face value," Norman enlarged, attempting through abstraction to give the impression that he was making everything clear once and for all.

Maurice did not at all appreciate being accused of conceit, nor did he appreciate hearing another human being, even his own son, decoding what he was *trying* to say, as if he were some kind of mental defective who could not speak for himself. But before he could mess things up even further with these two naive women by opening his mouth to amplify, and before Norman could go on with his interpretation of the story, which essentially confirmed that the old man was fantasizing, which was the most charitable explication of the text that even these gals might fathom, Monty stepped forward to defend his patron and to straighten things out—with the extra dividend of adding yet another chit to the pile that he would soon call in without mercy. "Of course there was a trial, Bunny. What kind of person do you think Maurice is? He just told you the short version of the story, a little jazzed up maybe to give it some drama, but I can assure you based on the scholarly analysis and survivor testimony on this particular case that twelve peasant volunteers were duly and lawfully summoned so that this fellow could be tried by a jury of his peers. You don't have to worry; all of his rights were protected. Maurice was just giving you the *Reader's Digest* condensed version because we're in a rush, you know, we still have to do this gas chamber and crematorium in Auschwitz I, and tomorrow there's still Auschwitz II-Birkenau, which is the real quote-unquote heart of darkness, not a fun place at all, believe me. Touring is hard work, I'm sure you've noticed. We're all tired. You probably want to get back to Krakow to do a little shopping for souvenirs, and maybe to freshen up at the hotel before dinner, so I really do think we ought to get moving. As the writer said, This way for the gas, ladies and gentlemen," Monty wound up, tossing out that mordant grabber title with his customary casual show of erudition, though he had never, of course, read the Borowski story, as he had also never read a word by the author of *Heart of Darkness.* Ducking his head winsomely, Monty directed their gaze toward the door of the gas chamber, sweeping his arm flamboyantly like the ringmaster of the circus introducing the next freak and stunt act of the Greatest Show on Earth.

They proceeded along the level path to the reconstructed Crematorium I, including model gas chamber, furnace room, and re-created chimney, with the earth banked up to the roof on either side giving off a constricting feeling of irreversible descent. Squeezing the maximum out of their short walk, Krystyna used it to give them a concise briefing about the space they would enter first, which between 1941 and 1943 had variously served as a mortuary, an execution site, and also as a gas chamber until the vortex of the liquidation was moved to the larger and more efficient killing center at Birkenau three kilometers away, and this facility was converted into a bomb shelter for Nazi staff. It was a lucky thing too that she had had the foresight to administer their information dose in advance, because they would not have heard a single word she was saying had she waited until they got inside. The screams of maybe two dozen teenagers were crashing off the stuccoed walls with its black patches and the brick showing through. Not one of the juvenile delinquents in that gas chamber displayed any inter-est whatsoever in the contingent of adults that had just made its entrance. Maurice was furious. Once again they were not alone; he would murder Madame Jadwiga Switon for this later, you could depend on it. Most of the kids were in a primitive clot, howling rock songs and gyrating in what appeared to be a drugged state; a few were grabbing their throats, grimacing like gargoyles, and emitting mock agonized gagging noises inspired by the surroundings; in the corner a boy and girl were groping each other down the slippery slope to the next stage; another girl was absorbed in scratching a graffiti haiku into the wall; two kids were methodically cracking sunflower seeds with their teeth and spitting the shells out at a bull's-eye they had marked off; a gang of hooligans were rolling on top of each other, lust-ily pummeling and pounding; a grown-up, ostensibly mature, ruggedly handsome man with a shaved head and a gold hoop in one ear, their chaperon no doubt, was sitting on the floor with his arms encircling his drawn-up knees, leaning against the wall, smoking placidly; and in the center of the room, two boys in eyeglasses who must have been twins, smaller than the others, the designated class scapegoats and objects of ridicule, most probably, were running around in circles yelling over and over at the tops of their lungs in their puberty-stricken voices, "*Ayn mah lir'ot poh! Ayn mah lir'ot poh!*"

Even though Norman understood Hebrew, the three women and also his own father wounded him deeply by turning automatically to Monty for the translation. Monty was a rabbi, they knew, having received his ordination, as Norman could have told them, in 1968, after undergoing a grand total of two months of training on a chicken farm in New Jersey in the ritual slaughtering and koshering of poultry to avoid being drafted in the Vietnam War. As it happened, he also had a doctorate, from the Reverend Jerry Falwell's Liberty University in Lynchburg, Virginia, with its flexible, user-friendly programs and forgiving correspondence courses, for which, as Honey in a fit of vindictiveness had once informed Norman, she had ghostwritten his dissertation on Simon Wiesenthal, the Nazi hunter and Nobel Prize loser. These two advanced degrees inspired Maurice on numerous occasions to introduce him proudly as "Rabbi Dr. Monty Pincus, mine outstanding academic director and spiritual mentor." His status as an expert was something that Monty cultivated and prized, and was touchy about, so he was quietly relieved that his reputation would not be assaulted this time by the spectacle of Norman jumping in to correct him, since the short simple sentence of the two demented kids running around in circles over there was manageable even with his botched Hebrew. He shook his head sagely, as befitted the somberness of the occasion, like Virgil leading Dante and company in this case through the circles of the Inferno, another unread work he could adorn himself with like an accessory. "Believe it or not," Monty struggled to be heard over the crazed kids, "they're saying that there's nothing worth seeing here." He glared at the lunatic twins as if he were about to spit. "Mengele material!" he muttered.

Maurice marched right up to the adult sitting there smoking tranquilly against the wall presumably in charge, and planted himself in front of him with his hands on his hips. "What's going on here?" he yelled. "You the teacher? This is a sacrilege!" Without getting up, the teacher took his time stubbing out his cigarette on the concrete floor of the long, narrow gas chamber and then stuffed the flattened butt into the pocket of his army camouflage pants. He folded his ear over like a crepe to mime his interest in hearing Maurice more clearly. "Eh?" he asked, looking up at the old man. "A sacrilege, I said, a sacrilege!" Maurice shouted. The teacher leapt up nimbly, stuck two fingers in his mouth, and let out a shrill whistle that jolted Maurice like a thunderclap, but it also had the effect of quieting the kids down to an almost tolerable degree for a blessed respite. The begoggled twin dervishes in the center of the room, however, carried on as maniacally as ever, until the teacher megaphoned his hands and barked out like a drill sergeant, "Eldad! Medad! Shut up!"—when they froze in their tracks as if bewitched.

The teacher then extended his hand so genially that Maurice took it before he could think of checking himself. "Shalom, shalom. Eh, I am Shimshon ben-Yishai from Kibbutz Beit Hamita," he said in a testosterone-timbred voice with that ponderous Israeli accent as, with his mighty grip, he took Maurice's measure. "Eh, and this is our youth and the hope of our future"—his conspicuously blue-veined muscled arm took in the adolescents in their frenzy—"fulfilling the final unit of the eleventh grade Shoah curriculum." He gave Maurice a sweet, wry grin. "Eh, so what were you trying to say to me a minute ago?" he inquired.

"I was saying," Maurice replied, oddly subdued by this disorientingly physical phenomenon of a Jew, "that how these youngsters are behaving here in this place where so many from our people were shlaughtered is—inappropriate!"

"Eh, inappropriate? How—inappropriate?"

"Look, Shimshon," Monty stepped in, riding again to the rescue of Maurice's dignity, "this is the Honorable Maurice Messer you're talking to—Maurice, give him one of your cards!—chairman of the governing council of the United States Holocaust Memorial Museum, the premier institution in the capital city of the most powerful nation on earth dedicated to the memory of the eleven million victims—six million Jews and five million others—some of whom perished in this very room in which your kids are going bonkers. So stop being cute. You know perfectly well what he means by inappropriate behavior."

"Eh, no—not really. Inappropriate for teenagers?"

"Look here, Shimshon," Monty made a second attempt, even risking appearing pathetically absurd for Maurice's sake by drawing his own woefully out-of-shape, shorter-than-average Diaspora body pugnaciously up to the hunk. "The mission of our museum is not only remembrance, it is also education. You're an educator. In fact, by your own admission, you teach a course on the Holocaust—right? So the way I see it, you're just being a pain in the butt. Otherwise, how can you justify dragging a bunch of teeny-boppers all the way to Auschwitz?"

"Eh, well, since you ask me so nicely, I will tell you. I am fulfilling the mandate from the Israel Ministry of Education for a course in Shoah history culminating in an on-site heritage tour. Personally, I do not believe we need such a course. But I teach it because it is my job, because it is required for high school graduation, because pah-pah-pah. Maybe you need the Holocaust in the Diaspora, in America, but as far as I am concerned, we Israelis have no trouble maintaining our Jewish identity without it, thank you very much. To be absolutely honest, all of this emphasis on the Shoah is, eh, if you will excuse me, overkill. What you see here today in the inappropriate behavior, as you call it, of my kids is, I am very sorry to say, a terminal case of Shoah backlash." He would soon get them out of this graveyard, Shimshon was thinking as he spoke. He would take them back to the hostel to cool down. And then tonight they would all go to that convenient little shopping center that that thoughtful and enterprising Polish developer had had the brilliant idea of building within a stone's throw of this death camp theme park—to bring a measure of normalcy to this miserable tourist town with mass murder as its main and sole attraction. They would eat cheeseburgers and fries at the fast-food restaurant, and after that they would sweat all of this sick stuff out of their systems at Disco Auschwitz, dancing until daybreak in defiance of mortality.

"I'll tell you what I think is inappropriate," Bunny piped up now, summoning every fiber of her inner resolve to take on this uncontrollable male. "I really really think smoking is inappropriate in this sacred place." She jutted out her lower lip and blew her bangs apart like a curtain. "In my opinion," she added, "Auschwitz should remain a smoke-free zone."

The twins, Eldad and Medad, were running in mad circles again, screaming, "*Yallah! Yallah! Kadimah!* Let's go! Let's get out of here!" Shimshon unhurriedly lit another cigarette, getting double service from the flame by absentmindedly igniting the corner of Maurice's card and letting it burn closer and closer to his fingertips until it curled up into a cinder and dropped to the gas-chamber floor. Rounding up his mad flock at the same time, he turned casually to Monty as he went about his job and inquired almost as an afterthought, "Eh, these 'others' you mentioned—five million others? Who are they, if I may know?"

"Holocaust-victim wannabes." Norman managed by some miracle to beat Monty out with the answer. "You have no idea how many of them there are out there. Poles, Gypsies—pardon me, Roma and Sinti—Russians, Catholics, et cetera and so forth, you name it. Everyone and his cousin wants to get into the act, everyone wants a piece of the Holocaust pie."

"Eh, but five million? Where did you get that number?"

"Oh, we just made it up," Norman explained blithely. "It was a political necessity—to justify a Jewish museum on the National Mall. It was kind of a victim inclusiveness gesture—you know what I mean?—sort of like sharing the Shoah wealth. The main thing, though," he added confidingly, "was that, after all the political bloodletting, when all the smoke had cleared, so to speak, we were still ahead by a million."

"Great, *yofi, kol hakavod*, congratulations, *mazal tov*," Shimshon boomed. "But, eh, if you don't mind, me and my kids—we would like to resign from your victims' club." And with his sultry cigarette dangling flaccidly from the corner of his lips and his two gorgeously toned Zionist pioneer arms spread wide, he skillfully herded the frenetic teenagers out of the gas chamber, which, as Gloria was now breathlessly remarking, she had recognized immediately. It was an exact replica of that truly creepy gas chamber she had seen that you could actually walk into at the Wiesenthal Center in Los Angeles, the Museum of Tolerance, where she and her late husband, Mel Bacon, had been given a *really* private tour by the executive director. "I guess this one is sort of the original though," Gloria added stupidly, but she couldn't stop herself, she had flipped automatically into her long-playing role of a woman programmed to charm and amuse as they were led by Monty into the adjacent crematorium, where, shaken for a moment out of character by the rawness of the ovens, she cried, "Oh, they're just like altars!"

There were two red brick furnaces in the room, reconstructed out of original parts after the war, with black metal doors through which corpses on gurneys riding on tracks could be shoved. When this facility was in operation, Krystyna told them, there had actually been three ovens, with a capacity to incinerate three hundred and forty bodies over a twenty-four-hour period with accompanying side effects, including smells and sights and sounds potentially so counterproductive to discipline and order in the Auschwitz I work camp so close by that it became yet another efficiency-driven reason to relocate the entire killing operation to Auschwitz II, or Birkenau, or Brzezinka in Polish—Krystyna's hometown, as it happened, she added defiantly. She snapped open the capacious faux-alligator-skin tote bag she was lugging and rummaged around inside, extracting and setting out one by one the supplies for the ritual she knew from experience Maurice would conduct at this point: memorial candles in small glasses; a book of matches she had picked up, this one, as it happened, with a drawing on the cover of naked figures in chains and the legend "Hades, Krakow"; white synthetic lace doilies with bobby pins attached for the ladies to pancake on their heads; cardboard skullcaps like tepees in a school project for the men; a gleaming white plastic hard hat for Maurice to use in lieu of a yarmulke, imprinted with an American eagle seal with a star of David in a halo over its head, and below it the slogan, "A Campaign to Remember, the United States Holocaust Memorial Museum"; two small bouquets of shriveled red carnations and rusted ferns wrapped in soggy newspaper; and scented tissues in a gilded box pinched from the Grand Hotel's ladies' lounge. She lined up the candles on one of the cast-iron corpse-conveyor trolleys. "Pop?" Norman whispered desperately to Maurice. "You're not going to do your *din Torah* number again—are you?" Maurice wasted no time retaliating. "Are you telling me how to run mine business? Maybe you seen it before already, but for the ladies it's news. They will love it. It's a very moving ceremony, for your information. Just watch me. I'll have them crying into their borscht in two minutes flat. And when they cry, Mr. Hotshot Businessman, they buy." Then, while the mother and daughter were adjusting their doilies to avoid disturbing their hairdos and as the men donned their headgear, Maurice sidled over to Krystyna and hissed into her ear, "Such crappy flowers you bring for mine donors? What happened mit all the money what I gave to you? How many times do I have to tell you? The Washington museum is a Tiffany operation! What? Don't tell me! You never heard from Tiffany's in Brzezinka?"

Having manfully voiced his dissatisfaction to the subordinate, Maurice now strode proprietarily up to the open door of one of the ovens, basking in his position and prestige, like a minister making his way to the front of the congregation. Solemnly and ceremoniously, he lowered the hard hat over his pate with both hands, the liner inside preadjusted to his dimensions, crowning himself like Napoleon. Indicating the slogan on the front of the hat with the tapping of a manicured fingernail, Maurice smiled at Gloria and said, "A Campaign to Remember—get it? Mine Monty—such a genius!" Suddenly, he thrust his arms so abruptly upward to the blackened wooden beams of the ceiling of the crematorium that the women gasped and slammed their hands in fright flat over their hearts. "God, Creator of the Universe!" Maurice cried out in a thundering voice, "I, the Honorable Maurice Messer, Chairman from the United States Holocaust Memorial Council, the presidentially appointed governing board from the United States Holocaust Memorial Museum, hereby summon You mit all the powers invested in me to this holy court in the crematorium from the Auschwitz-Birkenau death camp where so many from our sisters and brothers were annihilated. I am subpoenaing You, Lord Almighty, to this awful place where the cries from the dead can still be heard—to stand trial on the charge of abandoning Your children. I accuse You, God, of remaining a silent bystander while Your people, Your holy and pure martyrs, were murdered, shlaughtered, burned, drowned, and shtrangled for the sanctification of Your name at the hands of the German perpetrators and their collaborators, the evil ones, may their name and memory be blotted out! Where were You, God, when mine sainted mama, Shprintza Chaya Messer the guerrilla fighter, was shot down in the streets of Wieliczka screaming, 'Fight, *Yidalech*, fight!'? I demand an answer, Lord! How could You have remained silent?"

Gloria and Bunny were clutching each other, staring at Maurice, stunned, obviously drained and overcome, one of Gloria's arms invoking the One Above, too, by pointing urgently and heartbreakingly to the heavens. He took note. Of course they're moved; he had even successfully moved himself to a degree, it was a kind of autoeroticism. Though he had performed this ritualized trial of God many times before for the benefit of so many other prospective contributors, it touched him now to be reminded yet again through the visible effect of his own words on these blank slates of how real the tragedy he was selling truly was. "Where were You, God," he pushed on now even more ardently, aroused to even greater heights by the undeniable emotional response he was getting, "when mine *tateh*, Kalman Zissel of blessed memory, mine sisters the twins Manya and Fanya, mine brothers Zelig and Berel, together mit their entire families were turned into ash here in this godforsaken—yes, God forsaken!—place, this death factory, this cursed universe called Auschwitz? How could You have forsaken Your children, God? Why did You hide Your face? Why did You remain silent? Why do You remain silent still? Answer me, Lord! Let me hear Your voice—now!"

Here Maurice paused, as if to give the defendant a chance to respond. This was when he noticed that not only Gloria, but now Bunny too, standing beside Krystyna, who was engrossed in filing her fingernails, was jabbing her arm heavenward, while the two men, Monty and Norman, were listening with slightly cocked heads to something clearly over and on top of them, their eyes turned quizzically to the ceiling, drawing Maurice's attention in that direction above the crematorium, from which, no question about it, a distinctive noise was emanating. What had he done? He had not realized the extent of his own powers. What terrible spirits had he called forth to rain down fire and brimstone upon them? It was a good thing he was wearing his hard hat, that was for sure. A dreadful crescendo-like rumbling noise was coming from up there, as if the heavenly hosts had been awakened, as if the dead were rising to demand an accounting, the smoke sucked back down through the chimney, the ash turned to bone, the bone like in the vision of Ezekiel to flesh. "Pop?" Norman announced, drawing his words out even more than usual to dominate the moment. "I think you might have finally gotten Him to answer. Congratulations!"

"This is ridiculous," Monty said. He pushed out the back door of the crematorium into a stone courtyard, proceeded up the grassy slope flanking the walls of the complex like a scout leading a climbing expedition, with the others, even Gloria and Krystyna wobbling on their high heels, clambering up behind him, until they were all standing together on the flat roof. That was where they saw them—running around like the possessed, shrieking like savages in a demonic trance, pounding and drumming furiously with sticks and stones on the air vents of the gas chamber and the crematorium, on the holes for dropping in the Zyklon B crystals, on the chimney for letting out the smoke of the burning dead.

It was Eldad and Medad, prophesying in the camp.

2

A T DINNER THAT EVENING in the upstairs dining room of Krakow's Hawelka restaurant, which Maurice had reserved for their private use, justifiably deploying congressional Holocaust appropriations for that purpose, unstintingly ordering a full array of Polish culinary classics specially prepared by the chef—pigeon stuffed with kasha and mushrooms, white sausage, tongue in Polish sauce, pork roast, cabbage pierogi, salmon *kulebiak*, beet *zurek*, each presentation accompanied by a wine from the restaurant's own cellar—Norman felt himself to be utterly disconnected and apart, dissociated from the reality of his companions, like a visitor from another planet who had been dropped on the ice sculpture at a bar mitzvah smorgasbord, the broiled red faces of alien gorgers and fornicators swirling bizarrely around him. Let them think what they want, he reflected morosely as he clinically observed Gloria leaning against Monty, who was stuffing into his mouth something fleshy and glistening and wet. So I'm uptight—a wallflower, a prig, a puritan at a bacchanal, a bumpkin among the sophisticates, gloomy when everyone else is having a blast—I don't care what they think of me. Oh, a death camp can certainly make a person work up an appetite, like the flagellants in old Russia he had read about who would get so turned on, the priests as a precaution recommended castration. What loathsome lowlifes they were, Norman thought, assessing his dinner companions—revolting!

His father was kicking him under the table, as if he were an old TV set on the blink, to get him to start running again, entertain them, give them their money's worth, sing for his supper. Well, he definitely was not about to knock himself out for the old man tonight, no way, not after their curt but painful conversation before dinner this evening when, in response to his request uttered with such obvious trepidation and embarrassment, instead of showing a single sign of paternal tenderness and sympathy toward his supplicant son, Maurice had cut him down without ceremony, icily informed him that there was absolutely no chance in hell that he would ever get his wish, he could just forget about it, turn off his heart's desire, he would never be named director of the museum, certainly not while Maurice was chairman, and Maurice had no plans whatsoever of retiring in the near or distant future, they would have to drag him off the premises kicking and screaming, or in a body bag even—didn't he deserve a little tribute and reward after what he went through in the war, why should Norman begrudge him?—that for Norman to push to be director under the circumstances was selfish in the extreme, inexcusably piggish, not to mention suicidal for both of them. "Why you being such a *chazzer?*" Maurice had demanded harshly. "Why you not satisfied mit what you have? It's not enough for you to be the big boss from our business, Holocaust Connections, Inc.? What's wrong mit you? You never heard from nepotism?" "So who's going to get the job?" Norman had asked, abashed, defeated by the hopeless finality of it all, dreading to hear the answer, which of course he knew beforehand. "Monty—who then? Unless he fucks a goat in broad daylight on the front lawn from the White House—it's his for the taking, on a silver platter." The best Maurice could do for his own son at this sensitive time, the old man had added, softening a bit at last as he recognized the quivering little boy about to cry behind the grizzle of the grown man, was to use their contacts in the West Wing to get Norman appointed to the council—Monty's girlfriend, for instance, that old grandma, that *alter cocker* who only wanted to feel Monty's Holocaust pain, the Jewish liaison for the president, Zelda Knecht or whatever her name was, she could maybe lobby for it from the inside. Then, after a decent interval—because even putting his name forward for a seat on the council at this critical time was risky, bound to raise eyebrows, sure to incite their enemies to sharpen their teeth—but still, after a respectable interval, once Norman had become a council member, once he had been sworn in, it might be possible to arrange for him to be placed at the head of one of the committees, Second Generation maybe, or Death Camp Preservation, or, with a little luck, maybe even the heart of the heart where Norman's trusty vote would earn double value by solidifying Maurice's majority, the kitchen cabinet, the war room itself—Politics and Perks.

Then, as if the disappointment inflicted upon him by his own father had not been grievous enough, as he was waiting at the elevators to go up to the privacy of his room for the pitiful purpose of calling his wife to tell her what had happened to him and abjectly accept whatever paltry shred of solace she might condescend to dole out from her vestigial sense of spousal obligation, a clerk from reception scurried over and handed him a message that Arlene had indiscreetly, shamelessly dictated to a complete stranger over the telephone. Norman got rid of the peasant with a few zlotys, unfolded the edible sheet of creamy Grand Hotel stationery, and read: "If you don't get in to see Nechama, don't bother coming home." For Christ's sake,

Norman thought, now everyone knows our business! Instead of comfort from a cold wife, what does she cast at him? Consolatia—their lost child, Sister Consolatia of the Cross. Well, maybe this was the opportunity he had been waiting for; maybe he should shock Arlene out of her smugness, take her up on her offer—and not come home. But, of course, whether he came home or not was beside the point, because after all, more than anything else in the world, he too longed to see Nechama, she was his baby too. What kind of a father did Arlene think he was? He didn't need her to remind him—or to offer incentives. Almost three years had gone by since anyone from the family had laid eyes on their Nechama, though once in a while a terse letter came, and sometimes even a staticky phone call. So much had changed since she had vanished, above all Maurice being named chairman of the Holocaust, for which, it should be noted, the fact that he had a Catholic nun granddaughter contributed very positively toward his appointment, and the old man, once so appalled by the idea, had not hesitated to package his personal cultural diversity as a major plus. But ever since they had arrived in Krakow the previous evening, not for a single minute had Norman forgotten that Nechama was alive and breathing in the neighborhood—not at Auschwitz today with the Carmelite convent achingly within a short walking distance, and not at this moment either, here at Hawelka, at this obscene dinner party to which Maurice had even offered to invite her, "for some decent food and a little quality time," he had said. "What's the matter?" he'd added when he noticed Norman's incredulous expression. "I talk mit the president from the United States himself and mit big-shot senators and mit all the members from the diplomatic corpse. You think I can't talk mit some *fershtunkene* old Mother Superior? Believe me, they'll have her delivered to Hawelka wrapped up in a pink bow faster than you can say 'Pope Pius the Twelfth the Nazi Sympat'izer.'"

Norman could just picture it: special delivery to this profane restaurant, wrapped in a pink ribbon like a stripper popping out of a cake—his daughter, the nun. Quality time—what a joke! Where did the old man pick up that phrase anyway? Even if Maurice were right and the convent released her for the night to avert a major crisis in Catholic-Jewish relations, he could just picture her here in this garish room in her nun's getup, squeezed into her grandfather's tight schedule between the Krakovian duck and the big plunge into Gloria's pants in quest of her purse. No thank you, Pop; I'll figure out some other more practicable way to get to her on my own. At dawn tomorrow morning, before they all set out in the chauffeur-driven limousine for their leisurely afternoon tour of the killing center at Birkenau, he would make a pilgrimage alone to the Carmelite convent. He would kneel outside the gate like King Henry in the snow at Canossa, even though it was June now at Auschwitz and the grass was eerily thick, almost blue, thanks to all that human fertilizer. Of course, he would never climb the convent fence like that crazy spiderman rabbi—did they think he was out of his mind?—but he would respectfully and non-violently declare to one and all in the huge crowd that would quickly gather there of high-level clergy, politicians, press, and other assorted celebrities, and also, naturally, ordinary curious bystanders, that he would not move from that spot until they let him see his daughter. "Give me back my Nechama," he would cry. Norman wondered if he should alert the media.

He looked around the table, his internal vision bulging with images of his not-so-bad-looking-after-all face splashed across the front pages of all the newspapers around the globe, future prizewinning photos of his really rather strikingly handsome face when you came to think about it, even when contorted with the noble anguish of a father relentlessly and at enormous personal sacrifice pursuing his righteous cause with which any human parent could empathize. His external vision, on the other hand, was still filmed by estrangement. His father, glumly chewing his goulash, did not look happy, Norman could tell—not that it mattered to him at the moment, but he was condemned, even in his present state of supreme indifference, to be privy to the privies inside the old man's head. Maybe Maurice had finally achieved the exclusivity he had so vainly sought in the death camp tour today by forking over a hefty wad of American taxpayer dollars this evening to this overpriced Polish restaurant, it is true, but the main purpose for which this whole event had been staged still eluded him. Things were not going well at this table. "*Tuches oif dem tisch,*" Maurice would have liked to say, let's get our asses in gear, let's cut to the chase, let's get down to the bottom line, let's talk *tachlis*, let's deal—five million big ones, Mrs. Lieb, not a penny less, hand them over, wham, bam, thank you, ma'am. But no, that was not the way it was done. Foreplay—he was sentenced to kill himself performing fund-raising foreplay. What had there ever been in foreplay for a man? And to make matters worse, he was getting no help from his team. Norman was sitting over there in a mood, on the warpath. Krystyna was stuffing her face like it was the last supper, bending over occasionally to spear a morsel off Bunny's plate, the two of them exploding in great poufs of giggles that sent disgusting sprays of expensive wet food flying out of the gothic circlets of their matching burgundy lipstick. And his Monty here, instead of sticking to someone closer to his own age, instead of working on the daughter as Maurice had ordered, Monty was doing a major job on the mother, flashing for Gloria's titillation his professionally packaged Holocaust melancholy, which never let him down, a proven aphrodisiac, it never failed, ladies of every age and shape were driven to recline and comfort him every time. Maurice just watched in awe as Monty wrapped himself in the erotic robes of borrowed suffering, he listened reverentially to the seductive agonizing of his star pupil. "There are no tears," Monty was riffing, ripping off the most decorated Holocaust gigolo of them all, the Holocaust High Priest. "There are no words, we cannot speak, yet we cannot remain silent; silence is forbidden, talk is impossible, yet talk we must." Maurice could see Gloria weakening, surrendering, submitting. Monty's stump speech was as potent as the scent of musk. No woman, except maybe a frigidaire, could listen to this stuff and not have an irresistible urge to immediately go down on her knees and light a candle. Monty shook his head with lyrical sadness. "As for myself, I was not privileged to be there, I was not worthy," he said—which was, as far as Maurice was concerned, A-plus-plus, a gem, a masterful line, the kid should copyright it. Gloria also appreciated it; she nodded solemnly—she understood. "But dealing with the subject every waking hour," Monty was going on, "and even in my dreams—my nightmares, I should say—living and breathing this material day and night for the last ten years working in the museum, and for the next I-don't-know-how-many years also when I'm director, it's like a life sentence—you know what I'm saying?"

Yes, Gloria knew—one look at her told you that she knew, you didn't have to be an Einstein or even a Weinstein to figure that out. The boy definitely had a way with older women, Maurice had to hand it to him. For example, to take another case, the president's Jewish liaison, Zelda Knecht, not as it happened a still juicy albeit aging broad like Gloria Bacon Lieb, but a bona fide dried-up, decaying senior citizen—it was, Maurice had to admit, to some degree thanks to Monty's very personal interventions with this Zelda, which you wouldn't even want to begin to think about, that he, Maurice, had been installed in his wonderful new job of chairman, the dream job of a lifetime, though of course Maurice's own considerable merit should by no means be discounted, as Blanche never failed to remind him. Nevertheless, Maurice recognized that he owed Monty an enormous debt, and there was no question that as a man of honor he was not only obligated to repay him, but he also wanted to, with his whole heart and soul, he wanted to hand Monty the prize, to make him director of the museum, the two of them together would be an unbeatable team. Monty was the best friend a person could have, and also, it should not for a minute be forgotten, potentially the most dangerous of enemies. Maurice absolutely did not need Monty as an enemy with all the inside dirt and garbage that he had stored away as ammunition, ready to deploy at a moment's notice. Still, Maurice made a mental note to himself to admonish the kid not to talk so publicly about becoming director—*Gottenyu*, why was he counting his chickens already?—even if it puffed him up for a second while oiling the ladies, this "who-knows-how-long as director," as Maurice had just heard Monty casually let drop to Gloria whom he was still moving in on so disgracefully, neglecting his main assignment, the old-maid daughter, which meant, of course, that for the meanwhile, in this emergency at least, Maurice had to cover for him, Maurice was left with the cheese, with Miss Bunny, to whom, because it was absolutely imperative for the success of their endeavor that the targeted donor's ferocious maternal instinct not be slighted, he now turned his attention. What in the world did he have to say to her? Even so, for the sake of ultimately milking the mother, for the sake of his museum for which he was ready to endure anything, Maurice strode valiantly into the breach.

"You know, Bunny"—Maurice made a stab at conversation—"there's definitely something different about you tonight. You look very pretty, if I may say so. You should excuse an old man, but did your face clear up or something?" Bunny squinted at him, speechless. "Ah, now I know what it is!" Maurice exclaimed. "You're not wearing your eyeglasses. That's what it is. It's very becoming, I might add. And you put on a little makeup too—am I right? That should make your mama very happy." When Bunny still failed to run with this small-talk baton that he had relayed to her, Maurice persisted, ready to exhaust himself terminally by stroking her all night long if necessary until he finally figured out what the hell it was that she wanted. "So you're a kindergarten teacher, I hear." Maurice took another shot. "Well, if you want to know mine opinion, Bunny honey, I always say that kindergarten teachers are the unsung heroes from the universe, they have the world's most important job, the molding and shaping from young minds— what could be more important than that? Tell me please, if you don't mind! Believe me, I myself would personally not hesitate for one minute to trade in mine own job as chairman from the United States Holocaust Memorial Museum no matter how hotsy-totsy everybody and his uncle thinks it is, to be a kindergarten teacher and teach—what do you teach, by the way?"

"Self-esteem," Bunny replied sulkily, displaying the contents of her mouth.

"Very nice, very nice. And what else?"

"Small motor skills."

"Small motor? That's very good, very useful. You mean, like the children should learn how to fix a toaster?"

Monty and Gloria now pushed their chairs back and stood up. "I'm going to show Gloria the Kazimierz," Monty announced, twisting his head with a grimace as he loosened his tie.

"Yeah," Gloria slurred as she slumped against him, sliding her hand slowly down the front of his torso in a manner seen only in movies of a certain genre. "Monty promised to show me his Jewish quarter." She was overripe and reckless from the establishment's vaunted red wine.

"Gloria darling," Maurice whimpered in desperation, "you promised to have a drink mit me tonight. A night cup. Remember? We have a date. I want you should know—I'll be waiting for you in mine lounging pajamas and mine slippers, I'll be waiting for you all night long if I have to, in mine suite, Mrs. Lieb. You remember where mine suite is—yes, Gloria darling?" And he glared furiously at Monty, his treacherous protégé, as the couple swept brazenly out, waving to those left behind, like royalty at the open door of their fabulous cabin about to embark for places about which the rabble could not even begin to dream.

＊

Gloria also had a suite of her own, the Palace Suite, a sensible investment of Holocaust discretionary funds, Maurice had calculated, but they made their way instead to Monty's far from frugal expense-account room where, even in the rash and glazed condition they were in, they recognized they were less likely to be disturbed. In no time flat, all of Monty's rumpled and limp clothing molted in a heap on the medallion of the Persian rug. He stretched out on his back in the king-size bed, his furry sponge of a belly overlapping the sheet drawn up to the general vicinity of his former waist, one hand, as he waited for Gloria to emerge from the bathroom, idly performing a housekeeping chore, picking the lint from his navel, the other arm winged on the pillow, propping up his head, which he swiveled slowly toward her when she finally appeared. "Hey, you're a real chick," he observed appreciatively as she stood alongside the bed, draped from breast to drumstick in a plush white towel embroidered in gold with the Grand Hotel monogram, held clutched together at the cleavage with one pampered hand. "Great legs," Monty went on with appealing boyish enthusiasm, and then, thankfully, instead of tagging on, "for a woman your age," which was what Gloria was vaguely expecting and dreading, already ducking figuratively against the impending blow, he added, "You should really have them insured."

Va-va-va-voom, Gloria mused, the little champ thinks he's about to add Marlene Dietrich to his trophy case.

"So," Monty casually rapped out, "I hope you don't mind being on top."

Gloria's eyebrows shot up. Oh, my God, I'm too old to be on top, she was thinking. Under the towel, even with all the extravagant maintenance, things were withering relentlessly, things were drooping and sagging, things, alas, would never be the same, never be as tight, as smooth, as fresh, or as firm as once they had been.

"See, I've been diagnosed with chronic Holocaust fatigue syndrome," Monty explained. "I'm under strict doctor's orders not to exert myself."

Ah, handicapped by the Holocaust. Who could argue with

that? "Sure," Gloria said after some reflection. "No problem, Rabbi." She began to strut around the room. For a minute Monty thought she was going to entertain him with some kind of mature-woman grinding number before dutifully climbing on top, but then she began switching off all the lights with her one free hand, drawing all the draperies gaplessly tight, inspecting the venue meticulously for even a single rogue ray of light that might have sneaked through to illuminate her, the stealth invasion of even one revealing pale moonbeam, releasing the towel shielding her only to grope her way invisibly into the bed, flinging it directly over the telephone on the nightstand, to cover the message bulb, which was glowing urgent red.

Luckily, it was only after she had hastily dressed and tiptoed considerately out of the room in the pitch-dark, only after she had shut the door softly behind her and he had popped his eyes open from the simulated sleep of the mythical sated male, that Monty pressed that button to listen to the message. "Pincus? Crusher Casey here from the *Washington Post*. I got your number from your wife. Look, I'm on deadline on the museum piece, and I wanna run a couple of things by you for your input. Okay, number one, according to a very reliable source, when you were a reporter for the *Jewish Journal*, you were responsible for the deaths of a couple of hundred, maybe even a few thousand, Jewish refugees when you charged ahead to scoop a story about a secret airlift that all the other newspapers knew about too but were sitting on for fear of endangering the escapees. Care to comment? Number two, re that police record of yours on a domestic violence spousal abuse rap, i.e., wife beating, and also for bloodying a hooker—any comment? Three, we've got eyewitness confirmation here that you've been keeping a couple of cans of poison gas from the concentration camps on a shelf in your garage. Comment? Okay, let's see, that's about it for now. So Pincus, give me a call, you've got my number. The ball's in your court. The way I figure it, it's probably in your best interest to tell your side of the story, or whatever the hell, but like I said, I'm on deadline. If I don't hear from you in time, we'll have to run with it as is, with, you know, that great old one-liner, for whatever it's worth, 'The Holocaust Museum's Dr. Monty Pincus was unavailable for comment.' So okay, Pincus, *ciao,* looking forward to hearing from you."

That was enough to deflate any man. Sitting up stark naked with his thin legs hanging over the side of the bed, Monty looked at the clock next to the telephone. It was past midnight in the charnel house of Poland, which meant that it was about six hours earlier in the giddy capital of the free world. He would call that son of a bitch in Washington and if he actually got the living and breathing version on the line, he would hang up immediately. As it happened, he got the machine version. "Mr. Casey? This is Rabbi Dr. Monty Pincus, director of scholarship and academics at the United States Holocaust Memorial Museum, calling you from the Auschwitz death camp. I would like to make three points to you. First, you should be aware that my wife is not a reliable source. She is a sick woman not responsible for any-thing she says or does, of whom you are unconscionably taking advantage. There is a wealth of certified psychiatric documen-tation attesting to this fact. Second, you should be advised that if you move ahead and publish your scurrilous article, it is not only me that you will be hurting, but, far more importantly, the six million Jewish martyrs, including men, women, and over one and one half million innocent children, exterminated by Hitler during the Holocaust, whom you will be murdering for a second time, not to mention the fact that you will also be seriously harming the museum that has been erected in their memory. I therefore advise you to consult your conscience and to consider very carefully whether you are ready to take upon yourself such a heavy weight of responsibility and guilt. Finally, I'm giving you fair warning here and now, you bastard—if you go ahead and print this shit, I'm gonna sue the crap out of you, I'm gonna take you to court and wipe you out, sue you for everything you've got, your last fucking nickel. That's a promise—and let me tell you something, motherfucker, rabbis always keep their fucking promises. It goes with the job description. Any comments?"

He was practically reeling when he smashed down the receiver. There was no point trying to sleep now. In painfully swelling agitation he threw on his gamy and rumpled pants and shirt from the pile in the middle of the floor, not bothering with underwear, and blundered barefoot straight to Krystyna's room on the cheaper side of the hotel. "Didn't I tell you it was him?" Krystyna commented to Bunny, who was sprawled on the bed. "I could smell you from down the hall," she said to Monty as she stood aside to let him through the door. "You smell like her mommy," she added in a whisper, bobbing her head toward Bunny. "Joy, the world's most expensive perfume."

The two women, wearing matching white terry-cloth bathrobes with the gold Grand Hotel insignia pressed onto the breast like a badge, had been watching *Ilsa: She-Wolf of the SS,* dubbed into Serbo-Croatian, which Bunny now clicked to mute. Good old Ilsa of the splendid boobs, the leather boots, the black gloves, the shiny whip, the swastika armband, the Aryan tresses, the death's-head cap—just what he needed at the moment! Still twitching with fury over that phone call, Monty swatted aside the candy wrappers, empty soda bottles, greasy potato chip bags, and other nauseating trash that was strewn across the befouled bed, evidence of a barbaric and costly expense-account raid of the minibar. He churned his weight down into the mattress alongside Bunny, who instantly recoiled, sprang up immediately as if scorched by a hot poker. He narrowed his eyes at her as she squeezed next to Krystyna on the brown velvet club chair, the two of them in their twin assembly-line robes resembling spent porno extras on a break on the set from the drudgery of boring, pointless girl-gropes-girl scenes. There was no chance of a threesome tonight, he figured resentfully as he glared at them sitting there with perfectly serviceable bodies under their robes, especially when you factored in the subfreezing signals that Bunny was giving off almost audibly, even though he really deserved an extra-special treat of some kind after what he had just gone through with that punk reporter, not to mention deserving some kind of special thank-you just in principle, just in a general sense, for all those hours, days, weeks, months, years, of his life that he had at such incalculable personal emotional and spiritual cost sacrificed to the museum, to making the Holocaust number one on the horror hit parade, the paradigm and model against which all past and future atrocities must strive but can never quite succeed to measure up. But if the Holocaust had taught him anything at all, it was that there was no justice in this world, it was foolishly naive, childishly innocent, to expect it. No, there would be no threesome for him tonight no matter how truly he deserved it, no matter even how desperately badly he needed it for the sake of his health—he was under such pressure from all that museum work, so stressed out, so tense, he needed some relief, some release, by all rights the two of them over there on that chair compacted together in their identical snow-white robes like some kind of freaky two-headed ice queen, should just break down, they should just give in, just say to themselves, Oh, what's the big deal, we'll do it for the cause. But no, he was not fated this night to be part of a fun trio. Their pathetic threesome, instead of getting down to business like any normal lusty threesome in this day and age, would just go on staring at the tube as if they'd been hit over the head with a sledgehammer, watching dopily with jaws hanging down while Commandant Ilsa, as part of her job description, soundlessly tortured a naked nubile female prisoner for purely scientific reasons, in compliance with the camp's medical experimentation program to test the limits of pain endurance, and then as she went on, with equal professionalism, to chop off the useless member of a male prisoner who, like the other losers before him, could not hold back long enough to gratify her.

Monty turned from the evening's entertainment and eyed Bunny like a rival he was about to trump. "You don't by any chance find this stuff in any way in violation of your principles by being just a teensy-weensy bit sadomasochistic, or maybe really really offensive to women, not to mention a trivialization of Holocaust memory?" he inquired.

Deliberately avoiding returning his gaze, Bunny shook her head in wordless communion with Krystyna; this guy just doesn't get it, was what she was beaming. "As far as I'm concerned," she proceeded to lecture with grim didacticism, "when it comes to artistic expression, I reject all forms of censorship. In my opinion, artistically speaking, nothing's off-limits, even with respect to the Holocaust—except, of course, denial. Holocaust denial? That's where I draw the line, that's the only no-no. Denial has to be outlawed everywhere, across the board, universally banned as a hate crime. I personally wouldn't dignify a denier by arguing with him even for two seconds. Give a denier a platform, and you give him legitimacy, it's as simple as that. But as long as you don't deny that the Holocaust happened more or less the way it happened, it's out there for everyone's creative expression—kind of like my kids' finger paints, for example, or their Play-Doh. It's raw material for all humanity, so to speak. The Jews don't own the Holocaust."

So now it was denial, the latest heresy. Burn the denier at the stake and turn the pathetic little fruitcake into a major martyr. What a tiresome, self-righteous, stupid bitch! What had he ever done, Monty pondered morosely, to be named the designated receptacle of her pieties, her totalitarianism couched as liberalism, her simpleminded political correctness? So new to the Holocaust game, so fundamentally ignorant on the subject, and already she was spouting her canned opinions. Thank God he had managed in the nick of time to avoid that lurid threesome they were tempting him with, he would have shot his reputation by falling asleep in the middle out of sheer brain-numbing tedium. Still, he was keenly aware that she was the vital link to the big check that Maurice was gunning for, Maurice would strangle him plain and simple if he screwed things up, it was essential to be polite, to carry on as if he took her seriously. "Well, Ilsa's definitely not a denier," Monty conceded, "she doesn't deny herself a single thing." Then, struggling to keep the conversation going, he pushed on, taking up even in this incongruous context his handy persona of the eternal expert. "Did you know that they shot this schlock on the sly over just a couple of days, on the old set of *Hogan's Heroes*—you know, the television series with that crazy Nazi Klink, 'Co-lo-nel Klink,' as Maurice used to say, he just loved that show?"

"Excuse me, but I really really can't even begin to tell

you how offensive it is to hear you making fun of a harmless little senior citizen's mispronunciations," Bunny scolded in her scariest kindergarten teacher's tones. "How would you like it if someone made fun of something about you that you couldn't help? And, by the way, calling this movie 'schlock'? It just so happens that this 'schlock' is part of the academic curriculum of the prestigious UCLA film school."

Maurice harmless? That's a good one. But with the old man so bent on the grand prize of her mother's big bucks, he wasn't even going to begin to get into it. Instead, he went on flashing his expert's license. "You know, it's really too bad you weren't at UCLA when I gave a lecture on the Holocaust in cinema. It's one of my scholarly specialties, as it happens. Of course everyone knows that Ilsa's a bona fide cult classic, based on a real person, as a matter of fact, the Nazi camp guard Irma Grese, who would whip female prisoners until she reached orgasm—this tidbit comes from oral testimony, needless to say, so it has been a little hard for researchers to document. In any case, one thing's for sure—Hitler has made a major contribution to the fantasies of sadists and masochists worldwide, greater even, in my humble opinion, than the Catholic church, the medical profession, and the educational system combined. The S-and-M crowd has a lot to thank him for."

Bunny flicked a look at Krystyna. "Where in the world did you guys ever pick up this jerk?" she asked blandly, as if getting an answer to her question did not really matter to her anyway.

Monty did not quite know how to interpret this unremitting stream of apparent hostility, so accustomed was he to regarding himself as lovable; some kindergarten teacher almost half a century earlier had done an excellent job on him in the self-esteem department. He therefore concluded once again that this nasty display of attitude from Bunny was merely superficial, the flip side of adoration, and he plunged ahead doggedly with another factoid. "Well, since you have such a high opinion of this cinematic masterpiece," he informed, "I'm sure you'll be pleased to learn that the producer is one of our own—Friedman, a Jew, *naturlich*."

"Oh, please," Bunny said, pursing her lips in weary disapproval. "Is it at all possible for just once in your life to look at something minus the Jewish connection? I mean, it's just so dull and provincial. You are aware, I hope, that there are other varieties of experience in this world besides the Jewish one? To take just one example, how important do you think the Jewish question or the Holocaust is to those little guys with the loincloths and feathers in the Amazon rain forest?"

Monty set about with feigned academic earnestness to tackle her openly hostile question—even he could recognize that. "Well, if you don't count the exploiters of the Amazon, a bunch of whom, true to stereotype, are no doubt Jewish, or the fact that some of those natives in penis gourds might very possibly be descendants of the ten lost tribes of Israel exiled by the Assyrians in 722 BCE, which future DNA testing might one day prove conclusively, there are, for your information, also probably at least a dozen or so Nazis still hiding out there in your rain forest, very much connected to the Jewish question and the Holocaust, as a matter of fact. Oh, and by the way, speaking of which, Nazis, I mean—Ilsa? The actress who plays Ilsa? I'll bet you she's Jewish too. She looks Jewish. She looks exactly like a Jewish mother from hell. And she's no spring chicken either. She's definitely over forty, about your age more or less, I'd guess. Check her out—there are unmistakable signs of wear and tear."

"Oh, so he's an ageist, too." By now, Bunny was addressing herself exclusively to Krystyna.

Monty leaned over and grasped her hand, forcing her to acknowledge him. "Believe me, I have nothing against older women," he articulated with precision. "I love older women. Trust me."

Bunny freed herself with a shudder and stood up. "I'm out of here," she said. She gathered up her clothing and stomped off to the bathroom. A minute later, she emerged haphazardly dressed. "Where are you going?" Krystyna asked anxiously.

"This place stinks," Bunny declared, irrevocably on her way out. "I need some air."

As soon as the door slammed shut, Monty stretched out his arm and roughly pulled Krystyna over to him down onto the groaning bed. "Come here, shiksa," he said, and in an impressive feat of carnal dexterity, with one motion tore off her ridiculous robe while almost simultaneously shedding his own overworked rags. But she turned her face pettishly away from him to the stained fleur-de-lis wallpaper. "I think you may have spoiled everything this time," she said, a fetching wenchlike pout in her voice.

Even though she was an underling and beholden, Monty recognized that there was no way he was going to score with her that night until he let her talk herself out. He did not possess the will or the energy at the moment to use brute force, which in principle, he was firmly convinced Polish girls were accustomed to and actually preferred. He was just too tired and preoccupied right then for that kind of heavy investment. For his part, there was no chance at all that he would confide his problems to her, she was too simple and alien. So lying naked on their backs side by side with their noses pointed up to the peeling ceiling under one sheet on the bed paid for through a combination of private Holocaust donations and U.S. government funding, he channeled the bulk of his mental powers to sifting and resifting through the situation with the reporter, reviewing and rehashing also in that framework his private troubles with his wife Honey at home, yet he still managed at the same time, thanks to his long experience faking listening to women, to devote a rationed number of brain cells of an inferior quality to more or less taking her story in, lubricating this show of attention with grunts and snorts now and then at what must have been approximately the right pauses and intervals, judging from the fact that she kept on going, she hadn't yet stopped suddenly to accuse him of not listening as sometimes happened with women in similar circumstances, though not very often, he was such a pro. She was as selfishly and as single-mindedly focused on her story as he was on his own, he suspected, too absorbed in her own saga to pay attention to him; probably in the end she didn't really care one way or another whether he was listening or not as long as she could go on unwinding her tedious soap opera—something about how Bunny was planning to get a job in the museum, in the education department or some other division, her mom would arrange it, and then Bunny would bring her, little Krystyna Jesudowicz from Brzezinka, Poland, to Washington, D.C., in the great and glorious United States of America, to work in the press office or in public relations or as chief of the guides or in collections and acquisitions or whatever, because Bunny was not only fond of her, they had so much in common despite their differences in background, it was really remarkable, but also because Bunny firmly believed that the museum should hire employees of all races and religions and minorities and sexual orientation in order to elevate the Holocaust from just a Jewish hang-up with which the Jews were guilt-tripping the rest of the world to the level of a universal archetype with all-purpose generic lessons and implications for everyone. Bunny would sponsor her, Bunny would get her a green card, Bunny would bless her with citizenship, he could have no idea what an opportunity this was for her, what all this meant to her, and now because he had been so obnoxious to Bunny, so condescending and vulgar and insulting, maybe she would change her mind, maybe it would not happen at all.

Krystyna was rambling on and on, over and over again, with the same obsessive refrain, like a broken record; by now he had tuned out almost completely, she was droning him to sleep, his eyelids were drooping, and it was only when a second voice, not Krystyna's, jolted his flattening sleep line like an electric shock, only then did he snap his eyes open with animal alertness. "I'm looking for Barbara," the voice was saying. "She's not in her room. Do you know where she is?"

Krystyna, with the heedlessness of a creature not fully evolved to a higher stage of self-consciousness, must have at some point while he was dozing off unthinkingly made her way to open the door when she heard a knock. That was where she was now, standing with their once shared cover sheet spilling loosely over the front of her body, the entire undulating length of her rosy back turned to him for his viewing pleasure, while he lay on the bed utterly exposed from head to toe at the very moment when his eyes met Gloria's.

*

From Krystyna's room Gloria went on to keep her date as promised with Maurice in his suite—the Papal Suite, it had been christened. Whenever he was scheduled to go to Krakow he always made sure to have his secretary request it specifically. The brass plate on the door was such a conversation piece, such an icebreaker with visitors, and the paradox and irony of it—himself, an eighty-year-old-give-or-take Jewish survivor with corns and bunions, toiling for the Holocaust from his command post in, of all places, the Papal Suite—in addition to being gratifying, also made him appear laudably ecumenical for the same money. The money, it is true, was nothing to sneeze at, but the benefits you got from this budgetary allocation gave you one hundred percent bang for your buck, like flying first class. But now that he was chairman, because he was getting around on the government's nickel, for which only economy class was authorized and legal, the only way he could wing it, so to speak, was, unfortunately, even in the face of Blanche's superstitious terrors, to claim for himself a sickness that necessitated an in-flight upgrade, chronic aggravation or heartburn or slipped disc or hemorrhoids or whatever, for which, like a schoolboy, he was reduced to submitting to some bureaucrat the corroboration of a doctor's note, which he had no trouble getting, thank God, from his dear friend and fellow partisan fighter, Dr. Adolf Schmaltz, the world-famous proctologist and private hospital chain magnate. Having a suite was, likewise, a big-deal red tape fuss and potential scandal brouhaha for such a high official of a major government institution like himself, but he insisted nevertheless that it was an absolutely justified expenditure to dip into the federal budget pool for this purpose, not for his own comfort or prestige, God forbid, but for the sake of the six million, because he was their ambassador, he needed to look good while representing them in hotels all over the world, entertaining big shots and so on and so forth, it would be unseemly to usher dignitaries into your basic hotel room in which right in front of their faces would be the bed in which they could imagine him emitting bodily fluids and noises that had no place in polite society, not to mention how it looked in front of potential big donors, especially lady donors like Gloria, whom he was now rousing himself from a snatched sleep on the antique silk sofa wet with his drool to let in.

A quick check of his watch told him that it was past two in the morning, but Gloria made no apologies or excuses. Even at this late hour, she was flawlessly coiffed and dressed like a country club matron at ease in her luxury, having obviously showered since dinner that evening, judging by the fresh luster of her hair, and changed into casual dark slacks and a white tailored shirt unbuttoned at the throat, that great betrayer of age, but in her case still under control, her only jewelry discreet but unquestionably costly pearl and diamond earrings nestled securely somewhere near one of her face-lift seams—as his Blanchie used to say, "We should all look so good at age seventy-plus like Gloria Bacon Lieb." Having refused his offer of a drink, even a small ethnic toast of slivovitz or a shot of vodka in honor of their host country, the Republic of Polska, asserting, which was either a good or a bad sign, Maurice was not yet sure, that she liked to have a clear head when she talked money, she sat down on one of the gold-framed Louis number-something chairs and crossed her legs, her spike-heeled, toeless, and backless sandal dangling from her foot like an open mouth as Maurice placed a glass of mineral water on the ornate marble coffee table in front of her. This gave him an opening to call her attention to the centerpiece on that table, a silver fountain in the shape of the museum, on the roof of which was an object that resembled a human eyeball from which a constant stream of water, like tears, flowed, and at its base the words, "Lest We

Forget," inscribed in fancy gold script. "Beautiful—no?" Maurice said, displaying it with pride. "One hundred percent sterling, filled on the inside mit ashes from the dead. One of our premiums—yours for only five million dollars, heh heh." Gloria examined it uncertainly, not touching, keeping her distance as from a contagious animal. "The dripping would drive me crazy," she said finally. "I'd be running all day to the ladies'."

Maurice slid to the edge of the sofa, as close as possible to Gloria without actually climbing into her lap, and flashing the clear polish on his manicured fingernails with glints of pearl pink, he anxiously stroked the back of her barely mottled and for her age amazingly tight-skinned hand, as if to soften her recalcitrant mood, to coax her into compliance. "Gloria, darling," he implored, spraying her with a great burst of saliva, "I want you should go on the wall. You belong on the wall."

There was no need for him to interpret. She knew exactly what he meant. He meant what she had good-humoredly dubbed to her husband Leon, when they had discussed the matter in advance of this trip, the "*gonifs*' wall," the famous wall in the alcove off the museum's Hall of Witness where visitors stood waiting for the elevators like steel freight cars to transport them to the virtual Holocaust; many of her best friends were showcased on that wall, Gloria was aware, the whole congregation of operators and *machers* who had donated a million dollars or more, every little boaster and finagler from Palm Springs to Palm Beach was killing each other to get on that wall—exploit the poor and the wretched, was Gloria's kept-woman's suppressed thought, make deals with dictators and tyrants, then cleanse and beautify yourself in the Holocaust, like a ritual bath for your guilt. "Leon is already on the wall," she responded coldly, refraining nevertheless from wiping Maurice's spit from her face due to her deeply instilled deference to male sensitivities. "Ah, but Gloria darling," Maurice shot back, "that's mit his first wife, mit Rose, may she rest in peace, a lovely lady, I think you knew her. But now, for another lousy million—and what's a million bucks between old friends like us?—he can go on the wall for a record second time, this time mit you. You should work on him, Gloria darling. Soon there will be no more room, the original Founders' Wall will be closed for business, we'll have to put up a backup wall—but for Leon and you, darling, we can maybe still make an exception, we can maybe still squeeze you in." Even if the wall is packed to the gills, Maurice was thinking, he could sell the same space twice—why not? like plots in a cemetery, just pile them on, do the dead know the difference?—on the model of the sainted filmmaker who sold the same original outtakes of his celebrated movie twice, at a cool quarter million a pop, once to the Holocaust Museum in Washington, D.C., and once to the competition in the Holy Land—the son of a gun, such a wise guy, despite himself, Maurice shook his head in admiration.

"Okay, I'll get back to you," Gloria was saying, and, sliding both hands along her thighs to smooth her trousers, she rose to leave. With astonishing swiftness, Maurice got up too and swooped ahead of her to the door, throwing himself against it with the front of his body facing the room, blocking her way, splaying himself across that exit with his arms outstretched, looking as she approached as if he would surge to the heights of rapture at that moment if only someone would do him a favor and crucify him for the cause. "I'm not letting you out from here," Maurice cried, breathing heavily, far more heavily, she recalled bitterly, than his protégé Monty, the Holocaust

Casanova, earlier this evening, in what now oddly felt to her like a related situation. "I'm not letting you out from here until you give to me two things, Gloria darling. Number one, a promise that you'll get Leon to go on the wall again mit you for another million. And number two, five million dollars from Mel's foundation—for a grand total of six million, a very very holy number."

Gloria shook her head somberly. "Mel gave to Yad Vashem and to Wiesenthal. He didn't approve of your museum. He thought it was a big mistake to put up a Jewish institution on the Mall in Washington, D.C., on federal land with federal funding. He was against involving the government with the Holocaust, mixing church with state. He said it was bad for the Jews—and more and more I think maybe he was right."

"Gloria darling, listen to me—for five million bucks, you know what I can give to you? I can give to you the cattle car! You can have the whole cattle car named for Mel and you. Think what an honor! You know, the aut'entic Polish railway car right in the middle from the third floor from the museum just like the one the killers used to ship the Jews to the camps in, it's the biggest thing in our collection. Just picture it, Gloria darling"—and here Maurice risked removing one of his arms from the door to illustrate in the air what he envisioned in his mind's eye—"beautiful, top-of-the-line signage with raised lettering that millions of visitors would read as they walk through it to know what it feels like for a minute to be the victim: 'The Gloria and Melvin Bacon Cattle Car.' I can just see it! What a privilege, what a memorial to Mel! Believe me, this is something special, this is something one-of-a-kind, this is not an offer I would make to just anybody."

Maurice was panting so feverishly, he was straining so hard, that Gloria was afraid he would keel over with a heart attack right there in front of her on the precious Aubusson rug of the Papal Suite. For his part, Maurice was ready, though preferably it should not be a fatal one, he was having so much fun. But if she would just give in, it would be worth it, like those fishes he once saw on television that drop their seed and then drop dead. When you thought about it, it wasn't such a bad way to go.

Gloria stood there in front of him, gazing down at her pedicure. "Why in the world would I ever want a cattle car named for Mel and me?" she said quietly.

"Tell me, tell me what you want, Gloria darling. Whatever you want I'll give to you. Even if it's half mine kingdom." Maurice was almost weeping.

"Okay, Maurice. If you really mean it, since you ask, I'll tell you what I want. Here's the deal. For five million bucks from Mel's foundation? For five million, I want you to bring my Barbara into the museum right away and make her director of education. Then, by the end of one year exactly, after she learns the ropes, I want her named director of the whole museum—the whole kit and caboodle. So that's what I want. Aren't you sorry now that you asked? That's my offer. Take it or leave it."

Maurice's arms dropped to his sides with a thump, his entire body wilting before her eyes. "I can't do it," he muttered, shaking his head, "I just can't do it. Your Bunny is a very nice girl, don't get me wrong, but what does she know from the Holocaust? A kindergarten teacher! I'm not saying this as a criticism from the way you brought her up, God forbid, but what does she even know from Yiddishkeit, from Jewishness? She's all wrong for the job, that's the bottom line. She'll turn the place into a goyische human rights genocide universalist community center, I'm telling you. It would be a tragedy, a terrible betrayal from the six million and from all the survivors. I'm sorry, Gloria darling, it's impossible, I can't do it. Five million is very tempting, believe me, but I can't do it even for five. Ten? Maybe. But definitely not five."

Gloria paused to consider. "Ten?" she brought out at last. Then lowering her voice, as if for privacy, she went on, "For ten you'd have to throw in a little something extra—something for my Michael. His name on the wall, with an inscription of course."

God help me, Maurice was thinking, I should have asked for fifteen. "Twenty, I meant," he blurted out.

Gloria wagged a finger at him. "Now, Maurice Messer, don't you be such a little piggie." She cocked her head, set her hands on her hips, and glared at him as at a naughty boy. "Ten million dollars. That's my final offer. Do we have a deal?"

Maurice regarded her in misery. "She'll have to be investigated, you should know—like a colonoscopy," he said, "to make sure she's clean like a whistle. Are you ready to put her through that? By the FBI, by the CIA, and even more invasion from privacy than that, by mine own personal Roto-Rooter man, mine council lawyer, a very big shtickler for appearances from impropriety, more important than the impropriety itself, like he says, to protect our sacred institution, every piece of toilet paper he collects—to find out if she ever smoked LSD maybe, or maybe hired an illegal nanny from Guatemala."

Gloria stood there before him in silence. No, Maurice thought, no nanny for Bunny, no skeletons in the closet, because there was no life—no husband, no child, no grandchild for her mother, as for the more blessed members of society such as himself.

"All right already," Maurice gave in grudgingly. "What can I do? It's out from mine hands. Okay, so we have a deal. But on one condition—you pay it out in one lump sum, not schlepped out over twenty years like slow torture, kvetching and squeezing like constipation."

"The first five million the day she's made head of education," Gloria said firmly. "The last five on the day she's sworn in as director. At that time, I'll also give you the inscription for Michael. And don't worry, Mr. Chairman," Gloria added, leaning forward to kiss him lightly on his cushiony nose, "it will be our little secret."

"That's all what I get after we were just so lovey-dovey? A kiss on the nose? Mit me you're so platonic? You think mine sex drive is a raisin? What—you have something against older men? I still have mine original prostate, you should know—in working order, for your information."

She smiled coquettishly and delivered another kiss, this one launched from a distance off the pads of two slim fingers as she made her way out the door. "And an extra million from Leon," Maurice grumbled as her perfume wafted by, "don't forget. To go on the wall. For a grand total from eleven million—also a holy number."

3

VERY EARLY THE NEXT MORNING, the limousine pulled up in front of the imposing red brick administration building of the Auschwitz I death camp. Painstakingly reminding the driver for perhaps the fifth time to inform the others that he would meet up with them when they arrived at the Auschwitz II–Birkenau killing center following their exclusive lunch with a top-ranking Polish diplomat at Cyrano de Bergerac, winner of the *Zlota Kawka* prize for best restaurant in all of Galicia, which unfortunately he would have to miss, Norman stepped out, dispatching the car back to Krakow.

It was a beautiful day at Auschwitz, a mild spring breeze carrying the hopeful smell of abundant young grass, a few innocent clouds in an otherwise heartless blue sky. His old man would never contemplate bringing fat cats to this place in winter, Norman reflected condescendingly, their soft, spoiled fingers would have gotten too frozen stiff to write the check; springtime in Auschwitz was just about the limit of spoon-fed, feel-good horror they could handle. Obviously no one, not even a janitor peasant, was around yet this morning, but Norman nevertheless marched straight up to the door of this former brothel for camp guards, this erstwhile processing and delousing center for Jews who had been temporarily reprieved from gassing in order to be worked to death, and pounded insistently with both fists. He didn't even really know what he would have asked had some administrator actually opened the door; most likely he would have just accommodatingly made a fool of himself by falling inside flat on his face, as in some predictable old farce, utterly stunned to be getting some attention. It was simply a procrastinating maneuver, he was fully aware, this busy work of going first through administration, following the official route—to bolster himself with the feeling that he was doing something, anything at all, toward the ultimate goal of penetrating that convent. Meanwhile, though, he still had no idea whatsoever how he was going to go about it, his brain was still swarming with fantasies of feats of personal daring and rescue and public outcry too absurd, too childish, to merit repeating, but he had no realistic strategy at all, no plan of action. He had come to the administration building first partly because he didn't know where else to go; he could not very well have had the limo deposit him right in front of the convent, with the nuns sitting with binoculars spying through the windows, waiting in ambush day and night. And what could the administrators have done for him in any case, even if they had been around? The Carmelites weren't even in that old Zyklon B storehouse inside the camp anymore. They had packed up on the orders of the pope and moved a couple of hundred meters away to the new convent outside the camp's jurisdiction, leaving behind, so that no one should ever forget their existence, that mess of a cross for others to wipe up. Even so, Norman's wrath mushroomed by the minute as he stood there, neglected and ignored, banging on that door. This place belonged to him; he had earned it with family blood and suffering. They had always been around when it was an urgent matter of tattooing and shaving and humiliating and robbing and torturing. So where were they now when he really needed them? He demanded—he deserved—service.

He understood, however, that he could not wait there indefinitely until the staff strolled leisurely in, belching their breakfasts of black bread and blood sausage, to continue their cynical diversion of the profits from the spoils of this mind-boggling Jew-killing project in which every last one of them was directly or indirectly complicit. He wanted at least to be able to truthfully report to Arlene, and have witnesses who could corroborate his story, that he had tried—that he had gotten past the gate of the convent and maybe through the front door, even if he never actually succeeded in seeing Nechama. And what if by some miracle he did get to see her? He was on a very tight schedule, with a commitment in concrete to meet the others by two in Birkenau. So, giving that stubborn door a furious kick, which, he recognized instantly, hurt him more than it would ever hurt them, he hobbled around to the back of the administration building, where, suddenly, rising to his right, he was confronted by the wrought-iron entrance gate to the original camp with that terrific old sick joke immortalized on top, "Arbeit Macht Frei," and its underlying meaning, *Lasciate ogni speranza, voi ch'entrate,* showing through like the sepia cartoon of the creator's true intention and design. Beyond that gate he could see the black wooden kitchen alongside of which the camp orchestra used to be stationed morning and night, setting the beat—*adagio, andante, allegretto, allegro, presto*—the highest cultural expression of the most advanced civilized nation on earth, playing Beethoven and Schubert for the self-improvement and edification not to mention the enjoyment of the slaves as they marched in their wooden clogs through the gate to and from the work that the motto above promised would set them free. Who is the bigot who claims that Huns have no sense of humor?

The Arbeit Macht Frei gate was padlocked, Norman could see, but the orchestra space was filled with dazed creatures who had been overcome by the subtext, who had entered there and abandoned all hope, wandering about lost and aimless like a fresh crop of the dead newly delivered to the Inferno. This was Mickey Fisher's crowd, Norman realized—Buddhists, Hare Krishnas, Christian monks and nuns, Sufis, New Age Jews, Rastafarians, Native Americans, Vietnam veterans, holistic healers, hippies, Rainbow Family and spiritual seekers of all ages. They were locked into the death camp, while he, Norman, clutching the iron stakes of the gate in both translucent white-knuckled fists, was locked out. A young spectacularly freckled woman wearing a long ruffled gauzy orange skirt and nothing else other than a wreath of wildflowers in her tangled red hair approached. "I just want to say that I'm wearing this skirt out of deference to the dead," she felt it necessary to explain, assuming, in her endearing self-absorption, which reminded him so poignantly of Nechama when she was younger, that Norman had recognized at once that she was compromising her principles as an ideological nudist. "Like, I'm into the Body-Image Holocaust? But they said I can't go all the way here at Auschwitz, it would offend too many people? So, like, I just wanted you to know?" Norman nodded; he was cool. He was straining not to let his eyes descend below the speckled tip of her nose, though an earlier glance had impressed him with the rich density of her freckles, which seemed almost like a pointillist mantle thrown modestly over her shoulders, her pale brown nipples merely somewhat larger spots, barely noticeable. Jutting his jaw in the direction of the throng milling about on her side of the gate, floating in that early-morning ether like the damned, he asked, "What's happening?" "Oh, we're like just hanging out—waiting for someone to come and open the gate so that we can go to Birkenau to meditate? Everyone's all spaced out—you know? We've been up all night—because of that shofar? It was so, like, yeah—it just blew our minds."

Amazingly, it was only then, when she mentioned the shofar, that Norman became aware that the high-pitched wail that had been irritating him so acutely from the minute he had arrived at the camp that morning and that had been making him, he now realized, so excruciatingly tense, as if a string stretched too tightly inside his head had been plucked and would not stop vibrating, was not the screeching of a kind of internal alarm that had jammed, but rather an actual ram's horn that was such an integral part of his tribal references—how could he have missed it?—and it was coming piercingly and relentlessly from outside of him. He shook his head in disbelief at his own obtuseness. He had not questioned that sound; he had just accepted it, endured it as the subliminal undertone of Auschwitz, the keening of the massing dead that had penetrated him, a thing that came with the territory. "Who's blowing?" Norman asked the girl, peering over her head into the depths of the camp as if to search out for himself the source of those shofar blasts. "Oh, Jake. Jake Gilguli? You know him? Over at Execution Wall? Like, he's trying to raise the dead? He was killed here once, during the Holocaust—in the gas chamber? But now he's been reincarnated, and he wants to get all the others resurrected too? It's, like, way out of sight, yeah—way way far out."

Norman would have truly wanted to find out more, not only about Gilguli but also about the elusive Marano who had teased and tormented him so cruelly yesterday, but he was growing increasingly uncomfortable conversing here of all places with this half-naked girl. What if some dignitary or member of the press who happened to be on a VIP tour of the death camp today walked by and recognized him from his international, high-profile Holocaust work? How would it look with him standing here chatting so familiarly with this topless—over-the-top!—exhibitionist? It could cause a major scandal, it could be very damaging not only to himself personally and to his family, but also to the museum and, above all, to the Holocaust and the six million. If only that emaciated Hare Krishna fellow over there with the shaved head and the saffron-colored robe would come over, or that turned-on-looking priest in the collar and jeans, so that he could talk to them instead. But no, they showed no signs at all of knowing who he was, they seemed not even to notice him at all. Not that it mattered one way or another. He had no time at the moment to spare for these dropouts or to satisfy his recreational curiosity regarding Gilguli or Marano or any other freak. The morning had been set aside for Nechama; it was his only chance to accomplish something constructive with regard to her case. They were leaving that evening for Warsaw, and tomorrow it was back to the States.

*

Giving the ideological nudist a jaunty little salute and mumbling a neutral, impersonal, impeccably unincriminating good-bye, Norman turned away from this potential big problem that he needed like a hole in the head, luring him from inside the camp like a siren, planted there to entrap him, and walked back around administration and across the parking lot, resolved to waste no more time. He would head straight to the convent now. Once there, he would just play it by ear and hope for the best, it was all he could do. Arlene would just have to take it or leave it, let's see if she could do better. As he emerged from the main entrance of the camp into the street that ran along its perimeter, however, he noticed a small stand draped in a skirt of red and white plastic streamers, the colors of the Polish flag, that he was one hundred percent sure had not been there when he had been driven up in the limo just a short while earlier. Behind the stand, the lanky, olive-complexioned proprietor with dark curly hair, wearing a lavender shirt made from some shimmery synthetic material open to mid-chest to reveal festoons of bright gold chains—Turkish or North African or Iberian Peninsula or thereabouts, Norman figured, guest worker type, in other words—was unpacking his merchandise from two worn black plastic garbage bags patched with duct tape and laying it out on the tabletop. Apart from your usual tourist souvenirs, T-shirts, buttons, bumper stickers, postcards, guide booklets, and so forth, there were also faith-specific paraphernalia and trinkets, such as prayer books, memorial candles, and yarmulkes for the Jews, and for the Christians, crosses, rosaries, and glossy holy pictures that shifted from a depiction of Jesus to Mary depending on how you angled them, and a similar one in that line that slid back and forth hypnotically between the images of the two local Auschwitz saints, Father Maximilian Kolbe, the anti-Semitic pamphleteer, prisoner number 16670, and Sister Teresa Benedicta of the Cross, the Jewish girl Edith Stein, number 44070. This, of course, was all kitsch, junk, which Norman dismissed at once. Not so that dusty, forsaken-looking pile of rags in the corner over there, which caught his eye immediately. An astute shopper with an expertise in the area of Holocaust art (the daring piece *My Mother's Holocaust Quilt VI*, a real collector's item by abstract artist Sherri Shapiro-Pecker, had pride of place in his study—Arlene refused to let it into the living room) and memorabilia, Norman instantly recognized these strips of cloth as genuine ghetto and concentration-camp artifacts, extremely rare and of excellent quality, with a value that, he was certain, this hustler could in no way appreciate. Here was an opportunity to pick up an incredible bargain, perhaps even something that could eventually be incorporated into the museum's permanent exhibition after the usual curator-and-committee red tape runaround, with a discreet and dignified plaque affixed to the display case honoring him as the collector and donor. There was even an original blue-and-white-striped concentration camp uniform including matching cap, in perfect condition, complete with certificate of authenticity, which Norman was sorely tempted to buy, picturing himself showing up at the convent costumed in this—the ghost of crimes past, the nuns would *have* to let him in if only as a small down payment on atonement. But he rejected it as too large an object, too bulky and cumbersome to lug about with the busy schedule ahead of him; he couldn't very well walk around wearing it all day either, turning the place into some kind of ossified theme park, nor could he trust this sleazebag vendor to ship it if he paid in advance, as the guy would no doubt demand.

Although Norman knew that it was imperative that he hurry and get to Nechama and take care of his affairs at the convent in order to meet the others in Birkenau by two, he rationalized his delay as he casually flipped through the cloths in that pile, shrewdly taking pains to conceal his throbbing excitement over this fantastic find, by telling himself that he was performing the necessary and obligatory function of buying gifts for his family to bring home from the trip. He pulled out four armbands—a *kapo* armband for his father, ghetto police for his mother, pink homosexual triangle for Arlene, and the yellow Star of David with the word *Jude* for Nechama, which would have the added bonus of transmitting to Sister Consolatia of the Cross a very subtle message concerning her roots, he decided—and pushed them across the counter. "How much?" he inquired with a show of nonchalance. "Ten thousand dollars," the vendor replied with a suave Mediterranean inflection, in a tone that implied that these goods were meant for a customer of a higher class and a deeper pocket than the one blocking his view at the moment. Norman's eyebrows arced up and his jaw bowed down; this fellow was far more formidable than he had given him credit for, he needed to be alert. They began to haggle, an activity, like spotting a *metziyah* such as these rare artifacts, at which Norman reckoned himself to be singularly adept, closing the deal finally at three thousand dollars, which Norman regarded as a personal triumph. Already he was congratulating himself, already he was itching to tell someone about it, picturing how he would prod Arlene to guess how much he had paid—go on, honey, take a guess.

"Do you take credit cards?" Norman inquired.

Credit cards! The vendor looked around expressively at their bizarre environs, the dilapidated Zasole commercial district of the Polish town of Oswiecim, the anus of the world, well within the contaminated zone of the Auschwitz slave labor and death camp where they happened to be situated at the moment, and then he turned his attention back to Norman as if to an extraterrestrial that had just alit from a spaceship from some distant planet, and answered in one word: "Green." Norman complied by peeling the dollar bills out from the special robbery-proof travel security pouches hidden under his clothing—one thousand strapped to each calf and another thousand secreted frontally inside the waistband of his pants—and paying in full; the amount was just about all the cash he had left to his name at this final leg of the trip. Almost as an afterthought, he asked the peddler if he happened to have a business card for future reference. He was immediately handed the one the fellow had been using throughout their transaction to pick his teeth, soggy and dog-eared. Norman read out loud: "Tommy Messiah, Specialist."

"You Jewish?" Norman asked.

"I am a Jew," Tommy Messiah said. "I don't know anything about ish."

What kind of specialist? Norman was thinking of asking, but dismissed the question as pointless and idle for a nonentity like this who most likely just plucked the word *specialist* from the airwaves, imagining it sounded impressive. Instead, as he was about to set off again for the dreaded showdown at the Carmelite convent, Norman inquired if there might be anything else of historic or antiquarian interest worth looking at. He had been so intensely, so exquisitely focused on consummating the deal involving those precious armbands to the exclusion of everything else around him that it was not until then, not until Tommy Messiah bent down behind his stand and drew out from under it a pile of steel Nazi helmets, one nestled cozily inside the other like teacups, that Norman registered the presence of the pregnant woman sitting in a striped collapsible beach chair off to the side in the shadow of the scraggly trees growing along the camp fence. "Hiya, Normie," she said softly in her unplaceable accent.

Shaken, Norman appealed to Tommy Messiah for support. "You know her?" he entreated.

"Everyone knows Marano," Tommy Messiah answered enigmatically, dumping the helmets on the table with a raucous clatter.

"I don't know her," Norman insisted. "She seems to know me, but I never saw her in my life—until yesterday."

"Oh, c'mon, Normie, don't be such a drag. Of course you know me. Wait, I'll give you a hint." Removing her round, steel-framed glasses and lifting her necklaces of silver, turquoise, and amber beads over her head, she leaned over with difficulty and set them down under her beach chair. She braced her two hands on the plastic armrests, planted her feet firmly apart on the ground, heaving her massively pregnant body in its capacious Indian embroidered and mirrored caftan to a standing position. Without further ado, with the death camp crouched behind her like a stalking beast waiting to pounce, she launched into her routine. "Bo-bo skee wotten-dotten, hey hey hey!" she sang out the cheer with infectious vim, vigor, and vitality, her arms with fingers fluttering like pompoms shooting up into the air, first to one side of her head, then to the other. "Ees-ke wotten, bees-ke dotten, hey hey hey!" Her expansive hips, hands framing them for flirtatious emphasis, swung right, left, right. "Boom-a-lay, Bam-a-lay, wah wah wah!" One swollen, purple-veined leg sprang out in a peppy kick, followed snappily by the other. "Camp Ziona, rah rah rah!" With arms jackknifing up and out in a stirring V for victory, she leaped into the air so precipitously that Norman nearly collapsed in terror.

"Baby pops out at Auschwitz," Tommy Messiah commented blandly. He applauded ironically, "Brava Marano!" But Norman only shook his head in slow, discomfited recognition. "Camp Ziona, of course," he enunciated like a new dawning, "Mara Lieb of the rousing bo-bo-skee-wotten-dotten cheer—how could I not have known? But, of course, you were just a little brat in Tadpoles then while I was already a big-man junior counselor. Still, who would have ever thought we'd one day have a camp reunion, here of all places? All roads lead to Auschwitz, as they say. So—how ya doin', Mara?"

But she turned on him suddenly, poking a finger in imperious censure. "Do not call me Mara," she declared with passion. "Call me Mara-*no*. I am not Mara anymore. Mara is bitterness, Mara is delusion. I have rejected and shed that past life. I am now in a negative transition stage, working on myself toward the next stage, toward my rebirth, toward no longer being Mara but her permutation—toward evolving into Rama." Breathless with agitation, she squatted on the ground, groped around among the weeds and rubbish for her glasses and necklaces, rearmed herself in them, and then, as if deflating in a full-body sigh, sank back down into her beach chair.

Norman cleared his throat. "Well, you're definitely cryptic, I was right about that at least," he pronounced syllable by syllable with an ingratiating grin, anticipating a reward for his witticism. "Okay, so let's see now. You're not Mara and you're not really Marrano—neither a crypto-Jew, according to the accepted usage of the word, and certainly not a swine, which of course is what Marrano means literally, it was a pejorative," he expounded pedantically, showing off perversely. But he was thinking, too, that she was also not from anywhere, she spoke no language without a foreign accent, not even her native tongue. "So what are you, if I may ask?"

She was a Buddhist past-life therapist, she told him after she had caught her breath and calmed down. What she did was help clients to heal and renew themselves by excavating their former lives in order to pinpoint the impact, both positive and negative, in terms of obsessions and compulsions, repetitive patterns and cycles, on the present. "You mean, like Gilguli?" Norman asked. She did not seem at all surprised at this reference, or curious as to how he had so effortlessly drawn the connection. "Jake's the real thing," she said, nodding her head with satisfaction, "a genuine *gilgul*, one of our great reincarnation success stories. He used to be Jack Gallagher, raking in a whole lot of bread as an investment banker in New York. One day, he showed up at our zendo, totally bummed out, an awful mess, on a really bad trip. But with a lot of very hard work on everyone's part, we uncovered his past life as Yankel Galitzianer, gassed and cremated right here at Auschwitz, and now he has returned to search for his ashes so as to put everything to rest and move on. It's been a really heavy journey for him, he's Roshi's prize disciple, a real *phenomen*."

But even though her life's work focused on the past, Marano was stubbornly reluctant to fill Norman in on her own, though she was ready, it is true, even avid, to share updates on some of the people they knew in common. Norman offered her the latest on Camp Ziona's head counselor, Jerry Goldberg, the owner's charismatic son. He had mutated into a world famous zealot known as Yehudi HaGoel, Norman reported, a notorious settlement leader on Israel's West Bank, a polygamist in the Old Testament mold who had been anointed king of the secessionist realm of Judea and Samaria, prompting the remainder of the state of Israel to petition the Arabs to hurl their stones exclusively at Yehudi's fanatic kingdom and leave the rest of them alone—"a *shondeh* and disgrace to our people," Norman concluded, shaking his head in disgust. Marano smiled complacently. "You just really have to dig it, though," she marveled from the depths of her mysterious Eastern wisdom, "the way human beings are so cyclic in their behavior. Look at Jerry Goldberg, for example. Check him out, and what do you see? Still a head counselor after all these years—on the wheel of life, even in the Holy Land, always and forever, the once and future head counselor, he can't escape it, it's his karma." For her part, though, Marano wondered how it had happened that Norman had failed to recognize Mickey Fisher-roshi. "Don't you remember him from Camp Ziona?" she asked with a superior smile of mild reproach. "The lifeguard, Moish Fisher—how could you have missed him? But then again, you didn't recognize me either. You're too into yourself to really see out, that's your problem, Normie, you were probably a carthorse with blinders pulling a junk wagon in one of your past lives; you should come to the zendo, we can work on you. But really— how could you forget Moish Fisher the lifeguard? He was the big man on campus at Ziona! And isn't it really heavy—I mean, talk about cyclic patterns? Just like in those days he would float around the pool with a net on a pole, fishing out the turds that the campers dropped in the water, so too today, in his present incarnation, he cleanses our impurities, he continues the holy holy work of guarding our lives." She wove her fingers over her taut belly, which was visibly undulating like the waves of a rocking sea, and smiled with calm mysterious wisdom. Norman was inspired to ask if what was struggling and kicking inside that animate belly was Fisher's, but he was suddenly struck silent, seized by shyness, unable to enter so private a zone. He recalled how in the Auschwitz museum Fisher had introduced her as "one name, like Madonna," which perhaps was not, as Norman had at first assumed, a reference to the celebrity and superstar, but, rather, a scriptural hint that this conception was meant to be accepted on faith as immaculate, and probing was forbidden. So the question he asked instead was, "Is that how Fisher landed in a wheelchair—because of a swimming accident?"

Marano eyed him peremptorily. "It's too heavy to talk about," she cautioned by way of an answer. "Suffice it to say that Roshi chooses to view his present life from a sitting position."

Norman wanted to find out more—for example, whatever happened to that suspiciously dark-skinned hippie she had run off with, provoking such a scandal in their circles from Riverside Drive to Park Avenue, and also, how in the world had she, an elite Ziona alumna, crossed paths with such a low-caste type like this Tommy Messiah? But Marano drew in her lips, sealing them defiantly, until Norman let drop with tantalizing disingenuousness that he happened to possess some extraordinarily fascinating news about her mother, which she evidently appeared not to know.

"My mother's been dead for over fifteen years," Marano reminded him frostily.

Norman was well aware of that, of course, but in terms of giving off vital signs, surely the fact that a person is dead should not be a hindrance, to Marano, of all people, it should be meaningless, especially in her line of work as a past-life therapist. This, as it happened, was news about her mother's present incarnation. At first Marano stared at him as at some benighted primitive caught up in a dark-age web of voodoo and superstition, but then she remembered her position; he possessed information that she wanted, she was his hostage, and she reconsidered, capitulated. The last she had heard, she told him, her ex-husband was a convert to Islam, fulfilling the commandment of jihad in Afghanistan, earning a small living on the side by giving private tai chi lessons to the children of terrorist sheikhs dwelling sumptuously in their mountain complexes, with a separate cave for each wife. As for Tommy Mashiach, as she referred to him, she knew him from when she was living in

Israel, when she was crashing in an alcove in the Western Wall tunnels, surviving by hawking her poems for a shekel a piece at the Dung Gate. At the time, Tommy had a heavy metal club called the Holy Rock Café where he specialized in trance music and making people happy, in the Muslim Quarter of the Old City, as close as you could get to the Temple Mount, the most sacred piece of real estate on earth, from where the golden age of redemption and nirvana will someday be ushered in—even as a Buddhist she believed this.

"Now what about my mother?" Marano asked, a bit like a woman who had just been violated and was demanding compensation.

"I'm surprised you didn't realize it yesterday when we met you in the hair room at the Auschwitz museum," Norman began with almost unbearable deliberateness, stretching out every syllable, holding her captive. "Your problem is that you're too rigid and dogmatic, too fixated on your latest ism, which makes you, I'm afraid, remarkably clueless. You must have been a mule in one of your past lives, butting your hard head against a stone wall." He glanced at her face vindictively, imagining that she looked properly insulted. Good, he thought, he had gotten her back. Then he went on to inform her that that very attractive older woman who was part of their group—Gloria, the blonde, had Marano despite her meditative state bothered to notice?—this blond chick was, for Marano's information, her mother's successor, none other than Mrs. Leon Lieb, her father's second wife, which made her, if Norman had this figured out correctly, Marano's wicked stepmother. And, what was more, to add to the festivities, that dumpy woman with the short hair and red-framed glasses—Bunny?—she was Gloria's daughter from a previous marriage, which made her—you got

it!—Marano's wicked stepsister. "Isn't this all so heartwarming?" Norman was winding up, like someone far too urbane
for such mawkish family togetherness. "It's like the happy ending of a Victorian novel, when all the characters discover that
they're related to each other through an incredible windfall of
coincidences. But really, how is it possible that you didn't know
who they were? Don't tell me you've never met them. As far
as I recall, your father's been married to Gloria for ten years
at least."

Marano lowered her head. "I'd heard he remarried," she
whispered flatly, as if to strengthen and restore herself. "I
haven't seen him for years, since before my mother's funeral. I
was living with wild dogs in a cave in Ibiza, and they couldn't
find me in time. So that's his new wife. Well, she's thin—at
least he finally got himself someone thin. She doesn't look religious, though. It's hard to believe that my father would ever
have married someone who isn't religious."

"No, she's not religious, that's for sure," Norman drawled
out snidely, "definitely not religious, trust me." Then, taking on
the role of newly anointed counselor and comforter, he very
slowly and ostentatiously went on to dish out his trove wrapped
up as sage reflections. "In a way, I think you can say that your
father has shifted denominations—from Orthodox Judaism to
Holocaust Judaism, which has emerged as the main branch of
Judaism nowadays in any case. He's been very active in our
museum in Washington, a mega donor, right up there on the
wall at the head of the pack, for over a million bucks. He actually competed against my father for the chairmanship of the
museum, he wanted it pretty badly, but then, of course, he had
to withdraw his candidacy because of his legal problems—you
know, the nursing home scandals? Somehow that old story got

out—God alone knows who leaked it. Anyway, don't worry, there are no hard feelings at all between our dads—mine actually just named yours chairman of the first annual ten-thousand-dollars-a-plate partisan and resistance fighters dinner at the Waldorf-Astoria. You'll be happy to hear that your father has made tremendous strides with respect to coming out of the closet about his Holocaust past, opening up and talking about what happened to him during the war."

"What are you saying? My father came to the States in 1939—before the war."

"I know that's what you think. That's what we all thought, as a matter of fact—because your father, like so many other survivors, could not talk about the past, it was not only much too painful but the subject was also taboo. There was a conspiracy of silence. But thanks to the whole exciting and supportive Back to the Holocaust movement, he has become a shining example of recovered memory. If you can cheer on Jack Gallagher as he morphs into Yankel Galitzianer on the path to becoming Jake Gilguli, how can you begrudge your own father the well-earned rewards of his brave saga during the Holocaust, when, for your information, as a resistance fighter, he courageously dressed up in women's clothing to smuggle ammunition into the Warsaw Ghetto in the most perilous and life-threatening of circumstances? Really, Marano, you should be very proud to be the child of such a Holocaust hero, just as I am. My father, as it happens, was also a partisan, who, in his particular case, fought against the Nazis in the woods. Our dads are comrades in arms, so to speak, or whatever—the Holocaust can make pretty strange bedfellows, you know. And don't think there aren't any benefits from all this for you. I'm happy to inform you that you are now fully eligible and qualified to join the Second Generation Club. I'm the president. Give me your address at the zendo, and I'll send you an application. We 2-Gers need to close ranks and stick together for the moral betterment of all mankind. The simple fact is, we're more human than other people because of what our parents went through."

Marano began fishing in a pouch of her caftan for something, which Norman truly wanted to believe was pen and paper to write down her address as he had requested, were it not for the fact that her shoulders were heaving so uncontrollably. He grew acutely concerned that, because of him, she had been dangerously overcome with grief at the awakening of these painful family memories—she, a woman in such a vulnerable physical state—it would be disastrous if she went into labor right here of all vile places on earth, right now when he was on such an exacting schedule, he had to get to Nechama, and then off to Birkenau by two, they were expecting him. Drawing a limp tissue out of his pants pocket and dangling it squeamishly from the pincer of two fingertips, he tried to shove it at her. She pushed his hand away. Lifting her head, she sputtered, "My father dressed up as a woman—that is so far out!" Great spasmodic brays of hilarious laughter were coming out of her, hysterical tears of delight streaming down her cheeks. Norman was inexpressibly relieved that he had succeeded so brilliantly at amusing her, that she was, thanks to him, so obviously entertained, so deliriously happy, when, all of the sudden, in a flash, for which he was totally unprepared, the howls of laughter shifted to howls of lamentation so convulsive and terrible, so splitting and cataclysmic, it was as if she were being torn in two. Instinctively, Norman clapped his hands to the sides of his head to cover his ears.

"My poor, poor, poor mommy," Marano wailed.

Tommy Messiah ambled over from his stand, along with Shimshon ben-Yishai, the kibbutznik teacher, who must have made an appearance, Norman calculated, while he and Marano were catching up on old times. Both cowboys were smoking marijuana, and Tommy Messiah passed his joint to Marano. "Is this what you're looking for?" he asked. "Here, take—you need it." "Are you crazy?" Norman screamed. "This is against the law!" Then, abruptly switching tactics in an attempt to sway them through blunt self-interest, he added, "What about the baby?" Marano took a long toke, relaxing instantly, as if washed gently under a spell. "Oh, don't worry, Normie," she said, her composure astonishingly restored, "Rumi's used to it." "Rumi?" Norman cried, beside himself. "The baby's Rumi? How do you know it's a boy?" "Boy or girl," Marano asserted with conviction, "it's Rumi. I don't *ever* need to know what it is. I'm channeling Rumi."

Norman was furious. They were trying to destroy him with their contraband, their filthy cannabis; pot was illegal in Eastern Europe, plain and simple, open-and-shut. What if a local Oswiecim cop just happened to stroll by right at that moment, whistling his favorite Jew-baiting tune, his paws clasped behind his back swinging a caveman cudgel? They could be arrested on the spot, thrown into some sort of primitive rat-infested Polish dungeon with a stinking hole in the ground for a latrine, they would be disappeared, no one would ever hear from them again. And if by some miracle the Poles discovered what kind of colossal big fish they had caught—Norman Messer himself, president of Holocaust Connections, Inc., only son of the chairman of the United States Holocaust Memorial Museum, et cetera and so forth—all hell would break loose, the shit would hit the fan, a scandal would erupt of major diplomatic and international proportions on the front pages of every newspaper across the globe, it would be a field day for the world's anti-Semitic cartel, not only his own reputation was on the line but the future of the entire museum, of the Holocaust itself, of the six million, of all Jews dead and alive. He glared poisonously at the three of them as they mindlessly, insolently passed the dope back and forth right in front of Auschwitz, of all places. They had not one iota of respect, what did they care? They had nothing left to lose, they were already bandits, outlaws, renegades; even Marano, once a registered card-carrying member of the Jewish aristocracy, was now an outcast, a dropout, a nonentity, she had burned all her bridges behind her. But why drag him into their smelly little losers' circle? They were spitefully plotting to get him into big-time trouble, that was for sure, they were trying to ruin him, but he would not allow it, he would not let it happen. He zoomed in on Shimshon. "What are you doing here?" he lashed out. "Who's minding the kids? Where are the little darlings?"

Shimshon treated himself to another long and satisfying drag on a joint, and then, with a cordial dip of his shaven head, graciously offered it to Tommy Messiah. "Eh, to answer your friendly questions in the order they were asked, as our sages advise, I am here, as you can see for yourself, hanging out on a beautiful day in Auschwitz, the largest Jewish cemetery in the world minus the insignificant convenience of graves, partaking of some weed with my old comrade, Tommy Mashiach. With regard to who is minding my kids—eh, I am happy to report that they have minds of their own, thank you very much. Finally, as to where they are at the moment—they are in the fresh air and wide open spaces of Birkenau park, running freely around among the ashes and bones. They need the exercise, they are all pent up from this unwholesome trip. Eh, we hired a stripper last night to give them some release, but it did not work, I regret to say."

"Is this guy for real?" Norman was practically screeching in consternation, turning to Marano, his only hope, however feeble, of an ally in this impossible situation.

"Normie?" she said, drawing in the last precious bit of essence of grass from the roach of her joint, which she brought smoldering up to her lips pincered at the tip of a pair of rusty tweezers that Tommy Messiah had provided. "Chill—okay? Nobody's going to get busted. We're all cool here. Everything's under control—okay?"

"Okay, okay," Norman said, straining every neuron to map out a plan of action—and then to figure out a backup plan just in case. His heart in his chest was pounding so violently he thought it would burst from its cage. "So, okay, if we're arrested, I'll just tell them that my daughter's a nun at the Carmelite convent here. Then they'll have to let me go. They'll have to hush it up—to avoid a major embarrassment to the Catholic church."

"Your daughter's a nun?" Marano exclaimed. "Normie, that's the coolest thing! Who would have ever thought? Normie Messer, the biggest *schlump, schmegegie,* and *schlemiel* at Camp Ziona, the most uptight, pompous jerk-off on the scene, that insufferable, mean-spirited suck-up who made all the girls gag—and he would be the one to grow up to have a daughter a nun! Way to go, Normie!"

For the first time in a very long time, Norman was again filled with that indescribably satisfying sensation of *nachas,* of pride in one's child, of which he had been so sorely deprived for far too long. He put off dealing for the meantime with the palpable affronts directed against him personally, to which he was of course painfully alive—he would get her back for them later, you could depend on it—choosing instead to bask vicariously in the reflected glory of the compliments to his daughter. He smiled with radiant parental pleasure. "Yes," he confirmed, "Nechama's a nun, Sister Consolatia of the Cross, right here at the Carmelite convent at Auschwitz. I've been trying to get there all morning."

"The Carmelite convent? I know exactly where that is," Marano said. "It's right next door to the interfaith center where I'm staying with Roshi."

"You're staying at the interfaith center?" Norman was truly perplexed. "I thought you were staying in the camp itself. I was wondering how you got out here—since all the others were locked in. I saw them behind the gate myself, they were like prisoners."

Marano shook her head. "That's so ridiculous," she said. "There are a million ways to get out. They probably just got a charge out of pretending to be prisoners—it's a radical turn-on, for sure. Of course Roshi and I aren't staying in the camp itself, the vibes are much too heavy there. We've been doing this horror-healing tour for years. We're way past that scene. The camp is for—campers."

Norman decided then and there to abandon all pretense and claims to dignity, to bare himself in his pressing if temporary and uncharacteristic neediness to this inconsequential person whom, in any case, he would probably never see again in his entire life. "The thing is," he explained, "I have to get into that convent to see Nechama. Arlene—that's my wife—she'll kill me if I don't get in, but I don't have a clue how to go about it."

"Piece of cake, Normie," Marano assured him, "piece of cake! You should have said something before. Tommy's on very intimate terms with the nuns. He does business with them all the time. He'll get you in—and it won't be that expensive either, don't worry. He'll probably even be willing to take a check this time since he knows you're out of cash. I'm pretty sure he feels he can trust you by now. And you know what? I can walk you over most of the way. I've got to split anyhow, I've got to get back to the center. Roshi's probably still sleeping. I have to go wake him up now and help him get ready so that he can get to Birkenau to lead a meditation session." Sighing the tamed, domesticated sigh of a beset, put-upon but withal tolerant and fulfilled personal assistant to an important player voluptuous with power, Marano began the task of extricating herself from that too-low chair, rising with difficulty to her edematous feet in their embroidered Chinese slippers and turning to Tommy Messiah, who had wandered off a short distance for a private consultation with Shimshon. "Tommy," she called out, "can you get Normie into the convent?"

Tommy Messiah cupped his ear with an exaggerated flourish. "The coven?" he echoed.

"The convent, Tommy, the convent!"

He took a few steps closer. "The covenant?" he made another stab, his face screwed in uncertainty.

"Tommy, please, just pay attention for a minute." Marano pronounced exactly: "The con-vent, the Carmelite convent—you know, the nuns? Can you get Normie in?"

"Ah, the fucking convent!" Tommy Messiah gave an angelic smile. "No problem! Five thousand bucks. Make it out to 'Cash.' "

When Norman handed him the check—a museum check,

unfortunately, but it was all he had with him at the moment, it made him very uneasy to use it but this was an emergency, it was his only chance to get in to see Nechama, he would reimburse it the minute he got home—Tommy Messiah stood there scrutinizing it for too long, like a doctor mulling over the X-ray of a fatal diagnosis. Maybe he doesn't read English very well, Norman reassured himself, trying to quell his simmering anxiety. Then, apparently satisfied, Tommy Messiah folded the check carefully and slipped it into one of his glowing new running shoes, which he wore without socks. He had to be at the convent that day anyway, he advised Norman, to deliver an order to the nuns—"a splinter from the true cross," he added with a grin. From his pocket, he produced a small black velvet jewelry box, snapped it open, and, like an illusionist about to perform an amazing trick, showed each of them in turn how it was absolutely empty, there was nothing in there at all. With the same tweezers that he had loaned to Marano to squeeze the last drop from her joint, he picked up a tiny wood sliver from the ground and set it down with a minor flourish, like a priceless gem, on the plush black cushion of the box, displaying it all around again, this time to demonstrate the wondrous phenomenon of the splinter's appearance for their universal gasps and applause. Then he clicked the box shut, slipped it back into his pocket, and, pleased with his performance, executed a sweeping bow.

*

While Norman was struggling to convince himself that whereas Tommy Messiah might quite properly be ready to cheat a bunch of ignorant and unenlightened nuns, he would certainly draw the line at ripping off a fellow Jew, especially such a savvy Jew as Norman Messer who would never let him get away with

it in the end, and especially when it involved sacred relics
pertaining to the Holocaust, the sound of a siren, so distant
and ignorable at first, someone else's headache, grew steadily
louder and more searing. "Oh, my God!" Norman cried, as if
vaulting out of a trance, "it's the cops! This is a disaster! Get
rid of the grass! Get me out of here!" Yet even in the grip of
his panic and distress, Norman was struck by how similar the
sound was to the sirens featured in every single World War II
and Nazi movie he had ever seen—pulsating, ominous, mounting and then subsiding in intensity, a new wave rising as the old
wave faded out, a menacing descent into inescapable doom.
For Norman, it rendered everything that was happening to him
at that moment cinematic, unreal, fictional, slow-motion, and
dreamlike. "Time to split," Tommy Messiah announced.

In the next frame, as if they had carried out this emergency
routine a thousand times before, like the crew of a submarine
fathoms deep in the ocean in dozens of thrillers that he had
also seen, Norman watched with detached interest as each of
them swung into action, performing what looked like assigned,
well-rehearsed roles in a planned maneuver. Marano shoved the
minuscule remnants of the cannabis into a cleft in her loincloth.
She calmly folded her chair, scooped up in her arms all the Nazi
helmets, firmly placed one on her own head, and distributed
three of the others to the three men. "Walla!" she exclaimed at
the completion of these tasks, personalizing *Voilà!* as she did
every other word, and she took her designated place alongside the cart, clutching the two remaining helmets along with
her portable chair. Meanwhile, Tommy Messiah and Shimshon
swept all of the merchandise off the stand into the two patched
garbage bags and tied them securely. Shimshon handed one bag
to Norman, stationing him on the side of the cart opposite

to where Marano was waiting, and with the second bag over his shoulder, he single-handedly, in a truly dazzling feat of strength, hoisted Marano and child, plus helmets and chair, onto the tabletop. Holding Marano securely in place from that side, he indicated to Norman to do the same from his. At this point, Tommy Messiah, already positioned at the head of the stand, began to push, which was when Norman first realized with the pop of a quiet, interior *O,* that the entire shop was on wheels. In this way they ran for their lives—four Jews in Nazi helmets, two carrying a bundle over a shoulder with one hand, trotting on either side of the cart, holding on to it and its passenger with the other, the third bent over straining and pushing energetically with both hands, and the fourth, a stupendously pregnant woman, perched on top with two Nazi helmets upside down nestled in the bowl of her lap and a flattened beach chair like a lid over it all. Panting and sweating, Norman both ran along and watched himself running at one and the same time. Shimshon was bellowing out enthusiastically, "Onward Christian soldiers, marching hup, hup, hup!" to spur on and goad their pursuers, as the Polish police in their vehicle with its throbbing, oscillating siren flashing its heart-clamping red light drew nearer and nearer until the tires screeched to a halt on that provincial street pitted with potholes. Tommy Messiah stopped short, whirled around, and rocketed the erect middle finger of his right hand triumphantly into the air. "One hundred meters, *kurwa twoja mac,* you sons of whores!" he yelled. Then, turning to his comrades, he announced, "We have crossed the line. They can't touch us now."

From that point on it was a companionable stroll on that balmy June day in the gravitational field of the Auschwitz death camp, as they went on taking in the overrich air of this cloaca of the universe on their promenade in the direction of the interfaith center and the Carmelite convent, Lady Marano still being conveyed like a prize melon or a blue-ribbon sow on the way to the fair on the pinnacle of the cart by her three gallant musketeers, Athos, Porthos, and Norman. Tommy Messiah tersely allowed that the invigorating chase episode that had just done them all so much good in the exercise and physical fitness department had no connection whatsoever to the smoke curling upward from their illegal substance, as some might have rashly supposed. Rather, it was one of the byproducts of restraints imposed on the free-market system, which banned within one hundred meters of the death camp complex kiosks, stalls, and other forms of commercial competition that would cut into the profits of the Auschwitz museum's own souvenir, *tchotchke*, and Nazi and Holocaust memento and memorabilia reproduction and knockoff shop. This was information for all of them, but especially for Norman, to absorb and ponder as they walked on in silence. When they reached the new red brick Center of Information, Meetings, Dialogue, Education, and Prayer in Auschwitz, Shimshon effortlessly lifted Marano off the cart, with both hands this time, and set her lightly down on the ground. "I better go see how my kids are doing in Birkenau," he said. "Eh, it was very nice running for dear life from a Polish pogrom again, along with my fellow Jews, thank you very much for the déjà vu. Eh, I think the time has come to get my dreamers ready for the return to Zion." Marano, looking now like a chastened and reformed little girl, sang out in her unique and elusive accent, "See ya, Normie," and turned to take up the personal assistant duties that awaited her in the interfaith center. Norman and Tommy Messiah then set off again, pushing the cart, now loaded with both bags of merchandise, the beach chair, and all the helmets except for the one still on Norman's head, toward the new Carmelite convent, which very soon loomed up in front of them with its overhanging roof and eaves draped like the coif and veil of a nun—a giant, monster, nightmare nun, Norman thought, and she has swallowed up my Nechama.

As they waited at the door of the convent for someone to admit them, Norman took off his Nazi helmet and handed it back to Tommy Messiah. "Keep it," Tommy Messiah said, "it's worthless." Norman, who really did appreciate a freebie, especially one with a value that a philistine and a nobody like Tommy Messiah was in no way qualified to assess, stood there holding the helmet in front of him with both hands, like a proper suitor who had respectfully removed his hat coming to pay a call. The door was opened by a nun in a brown habit, with head lowered and eyes chastely cast down beneath the shade of her veil. Norman's heart leapt—could this one be his Nechama?—but she betrayed no sign of recognition, perhaps under threat to her life, Norman speculated. "I have a delivery for Mother Flagelatta," Tommy Messiah said, "two items." First, from his pocket he drew out the small black velvet box and handed it to the nun. Next, pushing Norman like an oversize package into the darkened building, he added, "And the Holocaust Museum American."

"Sign here, please," Norman heard Tommy Messiah request of the nun. Turning toward the light for a farewell glimpse of the outside world, Norman watched as the hustler extracted from another pocket an Etch-a-Sketch key chain that he held like a small slate in the palm of one hand for the nun to affix her signature, stroking her cheek with the hairy backs of the fingers of his other hand as she labored with the tip of her tongue between her teeth. Get your filthy paws off my daughter, you scumbag, Norman was thinking, fuming within—don't you have any respect at all for a woman who has dedicated her life to prayer and contemplation?

*

He was led into a long, high-ceilinged reception area with a stone-tiled floor, paneled in dark wood and furnished very sparsely with a few rough tables and scattered straight-backed, uncomfortable-looking chairs, on one of which, almost exactly in the center of the room, the nun who was perhaps Nechama but who was restrained from communicating with him, her own father, on pain of dire punishment, indicated he should sit. She did not linger but noiselessly left him almost at once, sitting there alone on that ungenerous chair in the middle of that long room with his legs squeezed tightly together, the Nazi helmet resting in his lap like a codpiece, like the sole article of clothing left for reasons of modesty to a patient who, with heart pounding, awaits the momentous entry of the examining physician. Extending the length of the room along two walls, a little higher than halfway up to the beamed ceiling, was a narrow gallery with a wooden balustrade, along which ran a row of open archways, with corresponding open archways in a row along both lengths of the walls of the ground floor, where he had been ordered to remain seated. Through those openings he could see identical nuns in brown habits moving silently, floating dizzyingly, flickering in the archways like distress signals at sea and then vanishing. Perhaps there were many nuns—he had read somewhere, though, that they rarely kept much more than twenty at any one time in a convent, which, he reminded himself as he *kvelled* and gloated inwardly, rendered all the more impressive Nechama's acceptance by the Auschwitz Carmelites, the Harvard of convents—or perhaps it was just one nun passing swiftly through those mysterious inner chambers, creating the impression that she was many, just one busy little brown bird of a nun with a luminous white breast flitting softly from nest to nest, an optical illusion. Then, emerging from one of the ground-floor archways, bending her head, stooping because of her great height, an Amazon nun was dieseling toward him like a truck driver, which signified to Norman that there had to be at least two nuns. By a process of elimination the second, normal-sized nun desperately letting herself be glimpsed in those openings and then frantically disappearing was surely his Nechama.

The towering nun, no doubt the inspiration for the terrifying abstraction on the prow of the building's roof, was looking not at him as she surged ahead confidently toward his chair in the center of the room, but rather with evident pleasure down at the contents of the small black-velvet jewelry box, which she held open before her as she made her way forward. This giant must be Mother Flagelatta, then, the prioress for whom the box was intended, Norman reasoned as he stood up abruptly, the Nazi helmet striking the stone floor with a sharp clang that reverberated alarmingly throughout that silent cavernous hall. Hovering over him, Mother Flagelatta displayed the contents of the velvet box for his admiration. In the no-frills English of her native Chicago, she delivered a short welcoming homily. "The Holy Father has called Auschwitz the Golgotha of the modern world. The meaning of this is that like our Lord Jesus at Golgotha, all Jews murdered at Auschwitz carried on their shoulders Christ's cross and endured the agonies of crucifixion. It follows then that every Jew crucified at Auschwitz awaits salvation, redemption, and resurrection through our prayers. Thus, every piece of wood in the vicinity of Auschwitz-Golgotha is holy, and may be regarded as a fragment of the true cross upon which a Jew was crucified, especially blessed when brought to us by a fellow Jew. So do not imagine for one minute that we have been taken in or duped or deceived by your Pan Messiah." Her face, framed by the starched white linen of her stiff coif and wimple, Norman noted as he glanced furtively from beneath his brows up at her, was shocking in its coarse redness. He could see directly into the dark, swampy underbrush of her fleshy nose, and her breath that poured down upon him reeked of old cheese and garlic. Over her shoulders she wore the brown scapular of Our Lady of Mount Carmel to shield her from the eternal fires. He was powerless against her.

With two thick fingers, Mother Flagelatta casually flicked off that splinter of wood displayed to such advantage on the black velvet cushion and sent it flying across the room to oblivion, and then buried the box somewhere within the folds of her ample brown habit. She raised her commanding arm in a sweeping gesture to take in the great chamber in which they were standing, and by implication the entire structure. "We built this without the help of a single zloty from the Jews," she declared. "If the Jews had even one drop of decency and gratitude, they would have financed it entirely, as it was they who forced us to move five hundred meters from the camp, it was they who exiled us from our convent where we were best situated to offer our prayers on behalf of the souls of their dead brethren of the Jewish persuasion." She paused to take Norman in for the first time, probing him with her gaze; a few seconds later, having apparently seen her fill, she went on from her intimidating heights. "I regret that it is not possible to show you around, Pan Messer. The sisters are cloistered. We would disturb them in their devotions, and soon it will be time for the noon prayers of the sixth canonical hour. Yet you in particular, as a member of the Jewish persuasion, a tribe with legendary moneymaking facility, and as the ex-father of a young professed who has reached almost the end of her third and last year of temporary vows as she grows toward the fullness of her vocation—you in particular have the responsibility to put an end to this stubbornness that has turned you Jews into little more than ungrateful barking dogs molesting everything in their path. You must lead the way and set an example by making a substantial contribution to our convent, no different than if your daughter were a student at a great university and you were quite properly the recipient of a solicitation. And when you return home you must also organize a telephone campaign to raise funds in our behalf. We are in need of so many things. We have almost nothing at all, only these bare rooms and our two Teresas."

She indicated the two paintings high on the wall at either end of the room, one of a woman robed in a draped, flowing garment, reclining in an ecstatic pose with head thrown back, eyes closed and mouth open rapturously, presenting to be pierced by the spear of the winged male figure erect over her—Teresa of Avila, founder of the Discalced Carmelites, fun-loving mystic with a bias against sullen saints. The other was a portrait of a Jewish girl who, as usual, was having much less fun, Norman noted despondently, too serious, too intense, in brown nun's habit and white wimple, dark shadows from staying up nights studying circling her formidably intelligent eyes, no doubt first in her class in every faculty at the university—Teresa Benedicta, born Edith Stein of Breslau, Germany, a nice Jewish girl gassed at Auschwitz.

What was the deal here? Norman was anxiously struggling

to figure it out. This pituitary wonder who insulted him so unforgivably by referring to his people as dogs and to himself as his own daughter's "ex-father," whatever that meant, this big brother cross-dressing as big sister who knew without benefit of introduction not only exactly who he was but also evidently everything there was to know about him—was this hideous extortionist intimating rather crudely to him that if he wrote a major check right this minute she would let him see Nechama, novitiate and postulancy, cloister and contemplation, be damned? God help him, what was he to do? All he had on him were museum checks. It was bad enough that he had already used one to pay off a blackmailer like Tommy Messiah. But if it ever got out that he had made a mega-donation with a United States Holocaust Museum check to the Carmelite convent at Auschwitz, of all places—to the notorious nuns who had once taken over the camp's Zyklon B storehouse, who prayed every canonical hour for the conversion of the Jewish dead, who when they moved to these new quarters left behind inside the death camp that twenty-six-foot cross like a finger in the eye of the Jews—all hell would break loose, it would be the end of the party, the end of the Holocaust. If only he still had cash on him; cash could always be finessed, laundered, camouflaged from the authorities. But of course she would want far more than he would ever have carried around, even if he had bedecked himself in secret traveling pouches from clavicle to anklebone; she probably would accept no less than fifty thousand at the minimum just for starters. Maybe what he should do is to give her the *kapo* and *Jude* and gay and ghetto-police armbands as a down payment, as a kind of security, as a token of goodwill, and at the same time make a pledge for fifty grand to be sent as soon as he got home by Federal Express in cash that left no fingerprints, on condition that she would allow him to see Nechama now. He was formulating in his mind how to segue into the negotiations—Does FedEx deliver to Auschwitz? he was thinking of asking, but it came out instead, Does Auschwitz deliver to Fed-Cross?—which set her off again, like a firecracker igniting under her seat, like a gunshot at the starting line. "The cross? Your mind is still stuck on the cross? The cross, I would have you know, was blessed by the Holy Father before a million of his faithful compatriots, at a solemn mass in an open field in Krakow, and carried by the nuns to its present spot in Auschwitz, planted in the holy soil in front of our old convent, where it shall remain forever. You can tell your people of the Jewish persuasion that although they may have succeeded in getting the Carmelite sisters out of the camp temporarily, they will never uproot the cross even for one minute—never! Why do you people of the Jewish persuasion insist on acting as if you were the only victims at Auschwitz? Seventy-five thousand Polish Catholics were martyred there too. Let there be equality of worship, I say. You can have a little synagogue, and we shall have our churches. You Jews—why must you always demand special treatment and privileges? Why must you pride yourselves on being the chosen people of suffering?"

Somewhere a bell was tolling twelve, and Norman understood very clearly, as if an antiphonal bell were pealing inside his own head, that this anti-Semite held in her merciless hands not only his own immediate fate, not only whether or not he would get to see Nechama in the small window of time allotted on this June afternoon, but also the fate, twenty-four hours of every day, of his hostage child—her essential survival. This was not a person to antagonize. There was no advantage to him on the face of this earth in engaging in a competitive victims' match with this terrorist and abductor by pointing out to her that seventy-five thousand dead Polish prisoners of war were small potatoes compared to over one million Jews, men, women, and children, gassed and incinerated at Auschwitz alone for no reason other than that they were Jews—we Jews, madam, are still the undisputed winners and champions in this category, I'll have you know. Why were the Poles trying to elbow in so crassly on the rewards of victimhood, such as they were? What was the meaning of all these sordid attempts to Christianize the camp with churches and convents and crosses if not blatant historical revisionism, to disguise the pope's complicity in Hitler's grand scheme, to skew the future perception of Auschwitz by establishing it as a place of Christian martyrdom? But there was nothing for him to gain by hammering all this bile and bitterness through the thick crust of her Polack head, Norman recognized, and what is more, there was everything to lose in terms of safeguarding his Nechama. Instead, he foraged desperately in the dregs of his brain for a sop to offer to this implacable enemy, a deal of some sort. We of the Jewish persuasion are famous for making deals, he would say to her, a compromise with something for everybody—for example, why not replace the twenty-six-foot wooden cross, which was perishable after all and would one day rot, with a circle of permanent time- and weatherproof stone slabs embedded forever in the ground in concrete, each one engraved with a quote, from a Catholic pope, from a Jewish rabbi, from a Muslim imam, from a Buddhist monk, and so on, a regular convention of equal-opportunity, religiously correct, pluralistic diversity staking an eternal claim right in the heart of the death camp. But just as he was about to propose this creative solution of which he was certain that his father, in his lust for a deal, would have signed off on with a huge gala and media extravaganza, and his daughter also would have approved in the spirit of shared ecumenical victimhood, the pure sound of women's voices lifted in song bathed his ears. Mother Flagelatta announced, "It is the hour of Sext, the hour that Jesus was nailed to the cross." A procession of nuns clutching rosaries at their breasts, Nechama from the shtetls surely among them, with heads bowed and pale faces tunneled deep within their brown hoods, appeared at the far end of the room from beneath the portrait of Saint Teresa of Avila, chanting "Gloria Patri" with crystalline sweetness, "Kyrie Christic Kyrie" as they crossed the center of the hall past Norman standing in the shadow of the prioress, "Ave Maria" as they disappeared at the other end under the vigilant eye of Saint Teresa Benedicta of the Cross, that headstrong Jewess, Edith Stein.

He was desperate to know—which of these hollowed-out faces, these wistful, enigmatic voices calling to him, which one was his daughter? It was too cruel to go on tormenting him like this. He was ready to debase himself, to fall on his knees, which in most cases a good Jew would rather die than do, especially before an overgrown Christian of questionable gender dressed in nun's drag, but, as he fervently hoped, at least no one he knew was watching him at this moment, and even if someone were, as a father he was still nevertheless prepared to prostrate himself in supplication at the jumbo-size feet of this torturer for the simple grace of an answer to his question— which of these worshippers is my daughter? But gazing down with contempt upon him, the prioress replied to his thoughts as if he had already uttered them out loud: "Sister Consolatia is a daughter of the Church. *Your* daughter no longer exists." An anguished plea then burst impulsively, wildly, out of him from some uncharted internal wellspring of self-degradation. "I must see her, you have to let me see her," Norman cried deliriously. "I'm being eaten up alive. I've been diagnosed with terminal cancer. It has spread all over my body. I've come from my deathbed for one last glimpse of my child. The doctors say I have just a few weeks left to live." She must have thought he was raving, but—who could say?—maybe he was unwittingly speaking the truth. Cancer was a stealth operator. Maybe he had already been invaded, maybe, unbeknownst to him, sentence had already been passed.

"Cancer is as a grasshopper in the eyes of the true Church," Mother Flagelatta somberly intoned. From the folds of her habit, she extracted a card, which she lowered to him. "This is our Web site. When you get home, you may log on. Go directly to the prayer and blessing reservoir link. Check off 'For Better Health, Physical and Mental,' with a double check for Mental. It is my opinion based on long experience with those of your persuasion that you would also benefit from 'For Overcoming Temptation,' 'For a Conversion,' 'For a Good Confession,' 'For the Grace to Bear My Cross,' and 'For a Happy Death,' which I advise you to check off as well while you're at it, since although the prices vary depending upon the request, there is also a special package deal for three or more prayers and blessings ordered at the same time. Then just type in your credit card information and your expiration date—and send. Within three days' time you will receive confirmation that we have offered the requested prayers for you. It's as easy as that, much less expensive and painful and time-consuming than surgery or chemotherapy or radiation, I might add, and no less effective. You can also send us an e-mail. The address is on the card.

As you can see, Pan Messer, in this day and age, cancer is no excuse, it will get you nowhere."

So they had a computer. This interesting piece of information registered deeply with Norman. It turned out that the Carmelite nuns of Auschwitz were on the technological cutting edge, just like the death camp they had targeted in the heyday of its killing operations. He wondered if they might even have more than one computer, perhaps an entire roomful. And here she had just a short while earlier pleaded poverty, lamented that their convent had nothing, put the squeeze on him for a dole-out, set him up for a major fund-raising sting. Still, what would have been the value now of throwing all of her hypocrisy and conniving right back up into her face? She had his Nechama in the vise of her hands, it was much too risky. Instead, with an exaggerated show of humility, he implored obsequiously: Out of the gracious goodness of her heart and in the spirit of Christian charity of which she was the premier exemplar, would it be at all possible for her to allow him to be in occasional, even monitored and censored, sporadic e-mail contact with his daughter? In response, she gestured up to the balconies where once again identical nuns indistinguishable from one another were sailing from archway to archway in their billowing brown habits with now and then the bright flash of white coif and wimple appearing and disappearing in the openings. "Your daughter?" she said. "All of our sisters are your daughters, and at the same time none of our sisters is your daughter. There is no identity or self in our convent, no individual in the e-mail. The individual and self are erased in all forms of expression. The author of every message is Anonymous." She gripped his elbow forcefully and began to steer him firmly across the room in the direction of the exit—he was practically levitating. "What's your problem, Pan Messer—you can't tell us apart?" she inquired caustically. "Or is it that you can no longer recognize who your own daughter is? But, for that matter, you never really knew who she was—did you? For a person with such limited insight and understanding as yourself, I strongly recommend that you resolve your dilemma in the simplest way—by regarding all of us, myself included, as your daughters, and also that you make your peace with the fact that you no longer have a daughter. This is a paradox and a seeming contradiction, I know, but it is one that a poor soul with inborn handicaps like yourself must learn to live with."

Norman wrestled himself free from her hold, hit solid ground hard, planted himself just inside the door like a dead weight, refusing to budge, poised to go limp like a noodle in nonviolent passive resistance using the method he had honed during his heady student protest days at the university. "I refuse to accept that," he said boldly, liberated at last from her tyranny now that he had gotten such a negative evaluation, been extinguished as both a parent and a human being, not to mention the terminal diagnosis and fatal prognosis that he had inflicted upon himself; there was nothing left to lose. "I need to know right now," he insisted, his composure as well as his resolve now fully restored. "When will I see my Nechama again?"

Mother Flagelatta, in the semiotics of piety, clasped her hands on the ledge of her imposing chest over the image of the Virgin on her scapular. "Most likely never," she replied evenly. "Then again, perhaps one day soon we might deem it useful to release Sister Consolatia from cloister for short periods to serve as the public relations representative of our convent and our cross at Auschwitz—on television and other image-and-opinion-shaping media outlets controlled entirely by persons of the Jewish persuasion. It will be a daunting task, but she has taken a vow to obey and she will do whatever is necessary. As a convert from Judaism who has become a Carmelite nun at Auschwitz, and as the granddaughter of little Mr. Holocaust himself of the famous United States Holocaust Museum, she can be a most effective spokeswoman on our behalf. But of course that will never happen as long as your museum exhibition continues in its present form, especially your libelous anti-Christian film on the origins and sources of anti-Semitism, which has offended us so deeply. Until that film viewed by millions of visitors and impressionable youth is revised and corrected or, better still, burned with all of its clones and copies in a blazing auto-da-fé, I can assure you, Sister Consolatia of the Cross will remain profoundly cloistered, unavailable, and incommunicado, you may consider her case closed, she is dead to you."

The prioress pulled out a sheet of paper from the bottomless cache within her habit. Norman could see the words "Holocaust Museum American" scrawled in red letters on top. Reading directly from this, she listed, frame by frame, her charges against the movie, but what it all boiled down to, as far as Norman could tell, was a nonnegotiable demand to cut out any and all narrative and imagery, overt or implied, that linked Christianity to anti-Semitic persecution or to Nazism or to Hitler himself if he ever wanted to see Nechama again. "Is it absolutely necessary to mention so gratuitously the irrelevant fact that the Führer was baptized a Catholic?" she demanded, her voice spiraling shrilly. "Does the only quote that you use of the Führer's have to be something about finishing the job that the Church had begun? Are you not aware that the Führer's anti-Semitism was racially motivated, the product of the god-

less Enlightenment, a neo-pagan manifestation with no connection whatsoever to Christianity, which has always been a moral
and civilizing force throughout the ages? Is there no gratitude
at all in the hearts of you people of the Jewish persuasion to the
righteous gentiles, almost all of them Christians, who made
such enormous sacrifices in your behalf in the Holocaust? How
could I ever allow Sister Consolatia of the Cross, with her
delicate and refined sensibility, to go out into a world where
such lies and propaganda are promulgated—and by her former
biological family no less!"

What's the big deal? Norman was thinking. Though he had
not one single smidgen of doubt that two millennia of Christian
anti-Semitism and crusades and pogroms and blood libels and
wall-to-wall persecution and oppression had led directly to the
Holocaust, prepared the ground, and ripened the mindset, what
difference did it make one way or another whether or not that
point was rammed home in their stupid little museum movie
when it was already written in blood, enshrined in hundreds
of authoritative history texts, and was common knowledge
throughout the universe? It struck Norman as monumentally
absurd that this old battle-ax hovering above him armed with
the mighty weight of the Church should care so much about an
inconsequential little flick, and especially because, as a museum
insider, he was fully aware of what a sloppy piece of work that
movie was, put together by Monty Pincus in his usual botched,
half-assed, it's-good-enough-for-the-goyim way—that "finishing the job" Hitler quote, for example, plucked from some
obscure, questionable source that could never be verified, those
particular choice words might actually never have been spoken
at all, at least by the "Führer," and then spliced to another quote
from *Mein Kampf* with which it was in no way connected. As a

matter of fact, that film had always troubled Norman, he was reminded now very crisply. He had always felt that something ought to be done about that film because of Monty's cavalier inaccuracies. He had always maintained that the ethical thing would be to compel that slob Monty to publicly own up to his crappy scholarship and take the heat despite the scandal it would bring down on the museum, which would give his father a conniption for sure. But the old man would get over it. It was the right thing to do. If the Holocaust had taught even one lesson at all, Norman now reminded himself vehemently, it was that to remain a silent bystander as the perpetrator assaults the victim is just plain wrong. He could no longer remain a silent bystander as Monty perpetrated his deception against an innocent victim—the trusting public. It was a matter of personal conscience.

Norman gazed up at the chin bristles of Mother Flagelatta. Really, what he ought to do right now was to leak to this odious nun, off the record and not for attribution of course, the real inside poop about the film. He would be her deep throat. He would provide her with the ammunition so that she could follow through and do what was necessary and take Monty out. What did it matter if history was falsified in this film because he gave in to the demands of this fanatic nun, when it had already been so disdainfully tampered with by Monty? How many times had he obsessed to Arlene about his deeply held moral concerns with regard to that movie? She was his witness. Now when he returned home, he would be able to say to her that, at long last, although the job had not yet been completed, something was going to be done. There was hope.

From somewhere behind him, a nun with lowered head under her brown veil appeared without a sound and breathed softly for a moment at his side. His hand brushed lightly against hers as she gave him back his helmet. He longed to pull out his gift of the *Jude* armband and slip it to her like a secret message, like a password, but she flew off far too quickly, his Nechama—because she was Nechama, he believed this with full faith. He lifted his eyes to the mother superior. "I'll take care of her," he said. Then he corrected himself. "I beg your pardon, Sister. It—I meant it—your movie. I'll take care of it. Consider it done."

4

THE LOVELY JUNE WEATHER, one of the first warm and clear days after weeks of bleak spring rain, brought out the pensioners from the nearby towns of Oswiecim and Brzezinka for an afternoon of recreation in the Field of Ashes at the far end of the Birkenau killing center. Stocky men in straw hats chewing the stems of rustic pipes that hung from under the eaves of their mustaches, wearing only black vests over their open-collared shirts with sleeves rolled up, strolled about among the large white wooden crosses and Stars of David that had been stuck by Polish scouts in a touching gesture of shared victimhood into the ashes of Jews who had been burned in open roasting pits fueled by their own fat when the four working crematoria with an official capacity to incinerate one hundred and thirty-two thousand corpses per month could no longer handle the load. In their rubber galoshes, the old men traipsed through the marshy acres of meadow overgrown with weeds, brush, and still unmowed grass rising out of the thick bed of gray ashes, ambling at a leisurely pace over occasional low hillocks of ashes, sloshing playfully through depressions of ash pools filmed with algae. Instead of their usual picturesque gnarled walking sticks, they wielded in their rough peasant hands their rusted old metal detectors, poking them down into the ash piles in front of them as they rambled about, though it is true that for a long time now it had been very seldom indeed for these newfangled devices that their children had sent to them as clever gifts from the Radio Shacks of Chicago to emit any signal at all. There was a time, though, when it was still possible to find gold or precious jewels or rare coins that the Sonderkommando teams of prisoners had overlooked while inspecting the orifices of the gassed Jewish bodies prior to shoving them into the ovens, but that was in the old days, long ago. Since then, the place had been effectively ransacked, pillaged, stripped bare by hooligans, and nothing remained for the respectable citizens except an occasional worthless twisted fork or a hollow pair of spectacles or a hinge from a prosthetic limb or a metal photo frame sometimes even with a faded picture still inside of a chubby naked baby stretched out contentedly on a warm quilt. Still, it was a very pleasant and peaceful way to pass a spring afternoon sauntering about in the Field of Ashes park, and their old women too seemed to be enjoying themselves as they wandered with a basket over their arms among the long grass in their flowered housecoats and colorful babushkas and their oversize men's black rubber boots, gathering the mushrooms that were in season to be fried with onions that night and ladled onto their plates with kasha and slabs of ham on the side. Everywhere you turned there were signs of industry and activity—hayricks set up to dry the grass that grew so abundantly out of the ashes, workers shoveling ashes into wheelbarrows to be spread as fertilizer and on the winter-ravaged roads. Birkenau, with its ash pits, had justifiably come to be valued and appreciated as the main natural resource of the area. Nearby, sailboats skimmed peacefully under the blue sky on the Vistula River, into whose waters tubs of ashes had also been dumped, upon whose banks men now sat dreamily holding their rods, lazily anticipating the tug of their supper of ash-fattened jewfish.

Shimshon's teenagers were also making the most of that
perfect June afternoon, exploring the Field of Ashes as if under
an enchantment, meandering in small clusters of twos or threes
among the wooden crosses and Stars of David with their Israel
scout knapsacks on their backs in which they were stowing the
ash-coated pieces of white human bone that they were collecting—bone chips of varying sizes mostly, but also an occasional
recognizable section of jawbone, or a part of a collarbone, a bit
of femur, and once, an almost-complete skull, which inspired
great brays of boasting and thumbs-up signals and flurries of
triumphant fists pumping the air and chest-pounding from the
lucky finders. As he turned off the back road running behind
the camp, with the smell of wet ashes rising from the ground
like the residue of an apocalyptic campfire infusing every pore
in his nostrils, Shimshon spotted his kids immediately. He
scooted through an opening in the formerly electrified fence,
made his way past the marker with the hermaphroditic sym-
bol of a Star of David affixed to a cross indicating the ruins
of the peasant cottage that in 1942 had served as a primitive
gas chamber in which Saint Edith Stein and other Jews were
exterminated, coming to rest finally at what was for him the
most amusing spot in all of Birkenau—the white sign on a post
stuck straight into the ashes, a depiction of a smoldering cigarette with a thin wisp of smoke rising from it crossed out by a
no-no diagonal red line inside an arresting red warning circle.
Leaning against this sustaining piece of comic relief, Shimshon
lit up and surveyed the scene.

In the distance, he could make out on that extraordinarily clear day what had always been for him the emblematic
moonscape of Birkenau—the forest of tall red brick chimneys
brooding like the eerie tombstones of a devastated primitive

civilization, all that remained of the wooden barracks of the men's camp. Closer to the no-smoking sign against which he was propping himself up, on the western boundary of the camp, he could see the stately red brick Sauna, which had served as a processing center for incoming transports of prisoners, including a women's shower room unforgettably packed in the mega-hit *Schindler's List* with luscious young nude Jewesses who miraculously actually got a real shower—a bevy of beauties unquestionably worth rescuing. From there his eyes moved to the spot where the ruins of Crematorium IV, always his favorite by virtue of having been blown up by Jewish inmates in October of 1944, and Crematorium V had been located, expecting to see nothing at all since, like Crematoria II and III, all of them had been blasted to rubble and collapse by the Nazis in the final days of the war to eradicate the evidence. This time, though, as he gazed casually in that direction, he was confronted, as in a mirage or a dream or a hallucination, by the full presence of Crematorium IV rising in front of his eyes in a place where it should no longer have been, complete with the gas-chamber wing and the two tall redbrick chimneys of the furnaces. Again and again it happens like this, Shimshon reflected; their death factories designed according to the most advanced technological standards to delete every trace of the killing project festering just below the surface, heaving up the evidence, ashes here, bones there, and now Crematorium IV come back to haunt them again. That's not supposed to be there, Shimshon told himself. It was only then, as that bizarre reality swirled into focus and made itself manifest in all of its perceptible urgency, that he came to his senses, remembering everything that he had to do; he could not afford to waste another minute.

Stubbing his cigarette out in the Coke bottle cap he carried around and used selectively as an environment-friendly portable ashtray, which came in handy now in preventing the mingling of ashes, and stuffing the entire mess into the pocket of his army camouflage pants, he set out decisively across the field toward the irrefutably solid edifice of the resurrected Crematorium IV. The ground upon which he trod seemed to give way as he advanced, his feet in their Old Testament sandals sinking disconcertingly into the muck of the ash bed. Now as always when he crossed this woeful place, he had the unnerving sensation that he was walking on something alive and palpitating, a great cushiony maternal breast and womb that would endure eternal abuse with martyred Jewish resignation. He was thinking about this weird phenomenon as he moved forward, and thinking about seeing Leyla, and thinking also that he must rally his troops to carry out Operation Ben-Zeruya, for which they had trained so carefully and so hard, in just a little more than an hour from now, when he idly pulled a tall weed out from the ground he was traversing. It came up with alarming ease, as if from the scum of a viscous swamp, trailing a long forked root thickly breaded with ashes, looking as he held it up before him like a homunculus, a witch's mandrake, a humanoid monster. Discarding this mutant with a shudder, he surged ahead now even more briskly, strewing as he went along upon the old peasant men and women searching for treasure and fungi muttered curses in five languages—*chara, zift, dreck*, shit, *gownó*—stimulating one or two of the less dull-witted among them to swivel around stunned, but he was already gone before they could retaliate for what had been dropped on them. To each of his bone-collecting kids he offered encouragement and motivation as he passed—a comradely slap on the back, a playful punch in the gut, an affectionate mussing of the hair,

a hug, an embrace, as well as a word or two to remind them
to prepare their minds and hearts for the difficult task that lay
before them. When he came to Eldad and Medad, their glasses
steamy from the intensity of their concentration on the bone
hunt, their cheeks roseate and their breathing congested from
allergy to the entire heaving organic cosmos underneath them,
he paused for a brief conference. "Eh, Operation Ben-Zeruya
will commence in one hour exactly," Shimshon advised, glancing at his indestructible Israeli elite air force pilot's watch. "It is
now T minus sixty. You are my lieutenants. You must order the
troops to start loosening and digging out the pah-pah-pahs. Act
like you're playing a game. If any of these old farts here try to
stop you, pretend you don't understand what they're talking
about, cross your eyes and stick out your tongue and blow out
your snot and drool and go spastic like you're insane. I have
some business to take care of, but at T minus ten I shall return
to give the signal for the final countdown."

     Touching his crotch, breast, and head in quick succession
with both hands, Shimshon then spread his arms and swiftly
repeated this sequence with one hand on the same points of
the bodies of each of the twins, intoning as he did so, "Remember—Jewish balls, Jewish heart, Jewish brain," like a revered
lord enacting a mystical rite by passing on a portion of his powers to his knights before their entry into battle. The ceremony
completed, he pivoted sharply without another word and set
off at once, jogging at a hearty clip to Crematorium IV, skirting
the resurrected gas chamber/furnace room that had shocked
him from the distance of the ash field, heading directly into the
annex behind it that had not been visible from that perspective—an exact replica of the SS commandant's headquarters
with special creative attention devoted to the authenticity

of the room and all of its paraphernalia in which the Jewish women were raped, which, unfortunately, had to be reproduced at considerable expense since the real building in which this took place, though still standing intact right at the edge of the camp and perfectly usable, was unavailable due to the fact that it had been converted into a church.

From this facsimile of the Kommandantur, Shimshon made his way into an uncannily faithful re-creation of the dark interior of the horse-stable prisoners' barracks complete with three tiers of wide-planked bunks, the lowest set right on the dirt floor and the highest directly under the rough wooden rafters. On this lovely June afternoon, each of these tiers, but the middle one especially because it was squarely within the camera's range, was packed with more than thirty female extras recruited in the Polish countryside from as far away as Rzeszow and Kolbuszowa, their large black Jewish-issue eyes made up to express the extreme limits of gauntness and soulfulness, turned with depleted curiosity upon the three actresses in tattered and soiled striped prisoner uniforms shooting a scene by the furnace in the center of the room.

Shimshon stood some distance away and watched as his friend, the Palestinian beauty Leyla Salmani, played Yael, the SS commandant's favorite Jewess, the one who, in the sensational climactic scenes of the movie, would get the decadently handsome Nazi warrior and rapist slobbering drunk, drive a nail through his skull with a rock, and then triumphantly dash out to lead the revolt that would blow up the multimillion-dollar Hollywood reproduction of Crematorium IV. In the episode they were filming on that day, however, Yael, to establish her leadership credentials, was struggling to break up a fight between two starving fellow inmates who were clawing savagely at each other over possession of a dried-out crust of bread, pulling instinctively at one another's shaved head as if the hair were still growing from it. Over and over again, because the director's personal unique vision of this original idea was never quite satisfied, Leyla had to reenact this scene, repeating the words, "Sisters, it's okay to be angry, but let us manage our anger to direct it against the enemy," until they came out like chopped meat worming through the holes of a grinder. This director, who was also the screenwriter, a soft-hearted Jewish boy from Los Angeles named R. C. Hammer, wearing a backward baseball cap over his receding hairline, had been particularly thrilled and gratified to cast an Arab woman in the role of Yael, and especially one of such distinguished lineage, the Oxford-educated daughter of the moderate Palestinian hero Abu Salman of Hebron, who had been crippled by a bomb planted by the Jewish underground led by the fanatical settlement firebrand Yehudi HaGoel. This amazing trivia morsel, this fusing of opposites, of classic enemies, Jew and Arab united in the service of high art, would be a super marketing feature when the film was released, a truly inspirational selling point in the trailer with the appropriate background music, there was no question about it. When Leyla had learned that she had gotten the lead part of Yael in *The Triumph of the Traumatized,* she sat Shimshon down on the ancient mosaic-tiled floor of her apartment on Omari Street in the Muslim Quarter of the Old City of Jerusalem with its ravishing view of the golden Dome of the Rock through the tall windows, and they shaved off each other's hair. Thick black glossy waist-length tresses tumbled equally from both of their heads in massive hanks, piling up around them like the softest, the most voluptuous, the most tempting and treacherous of nests.

Finally, R. C. Hammer came out with his definitive "Cut!" Immediately, Leyla snapped out of character and began walking toward Shimshon, inserting into her earlobe the matching gold hoop to his, which together made a pair. He anticipated her approach in a squatting position so that she could promptly climb upon his back. He carried her off the set, out of the prisoners' barracks and commandant's headquarters annex, behind the replica of Crematorium IV, into one of the birch groves that gave Birkenau its name, where incoming transports of prisoners would undress—men, women, and children, old and young, grandparents and parents stripped naked in front of their children and grandchildren amid the meager screening of the mottled slender trees in those final moments before filing in assembly lines into the waiting gas chambers. Roaming in and out in the sun-dappled shade of the birches, avoiding the ash pit that had been dug to accommodate the overflow corpses during the operationally challenging Hungarian transports of 1944, Shimshon wordlessly slipped a hand under Leyla's prison trousers and caressed the shapely leg that was draped over his shoulders, while she absentmindedly played a tune with her fingers on his shaven head, staring down at the pulsing veins, marveling at the strange desire welling gradually up in her, like a newfound power, to squeeze the life out of this man of whom she was after all rather fond, a feeling that was in some ways similar to the not altogether unpleasant constriction in her loins that she would experience while standing on a ledge at a great height that seemed to call out to her to jump, to throw herself away, pulling her over, drawing her inevitably downward, when she really had as far as she knew no wish at all to end her life just then. Her heart pumping violently, she went on drumming on Shimshon's exposed head and pondered the source of this unforeseen feeling. The next moment, though, unexpectedly overcome by a wild panic that this giant Jew might at any second drop her into the ash pit from his not inconsequential height of well over six feet, might even deliberately hurl her over, the acknowledged enemy, with all the force of his superior strength, she began to beat rhythmically on his shoulders, in thinly concealed desperation, with her two little fists, insisting that he let her down at once. "You must trust," Shimshon admonished, cuffing her ankles firmly in place. "Let me down, let me down, you Zionist Nazi!" she cried, emitting high-pitched gulps that resembled laughter to demonstrate that she was only joking in calling him by that name as she went on hammering, now on the unprotected crown of his head. Shimshon crouched on the ground to allow her to dismount. "You should have had faith that I would take care of you," he commented mournfully. Leyla stiffened. "Take care of your own," she responded. "We can take care of ourselves." Shimshon took her two hands and held them. "Leyla, Leyla," he said. "It was so good between us for a little while there among the birches—what happened?" He rummaged deep inside the pocket of his army pants. "Here," he went on soothingly, handing her a small white envelope, "I brought you a little present—premium grade, direct from Tommy Mashiach. It will improve your mood. Eh, take two before bedtime—but only if I'm the guy who's with you."

She emptied the little pink pills, some stamped with a Star of David, others hatched with the letter *x,* into the small embroidered Bedouin pouch attached to a thin string of yarn around her neck and resting under her costume low between her breasts. Then, returning the envelope to him, she said, "Here, you can use this to write me a letter from jail when you're arrested with your kids." Shimshon gave her a sly smile. "Eh, arrested for what?" he asked, though he knew very well to what she was alluding—Operation Ben-Zeruya, about which she happened to possess privileged information, and had already expressed her passionate disapproval. Then, he added, "Eh, who knows? Maybe you will be sitting in jail with me. Wouldn't that be cozy?"—which was meant as a pointed reminder, to put her on notice that he also had her by the balls, so to speak, literally by the *kadurim*, by virtue of the pills, the Ecstasy that was between them.

Still, even with all of her heartless belligerence, he was madly drawn to her. She was irresistible, a goddess, the most bewitchingly mysterious and unknowable woman he had ever known. In the early days even a glimpse of her from a distance would so overcome him he felt he would collapse; once, even, he had been obliged to turn away to throw up, as if in a fever. They battled over every centimeter, all of his friends warned she would destroy him. Most recently she had threatened to organize her own competing scout pilgrimage to Auschwitz-Birkenau, of veteran West Bank stone-throwing *shabab* youth, to add the crescent of Islam to the stars and crosses in the ash field in commemoration of the Palestinian Holocaust. She could not understand why he objected even to the Stars of David stuck into the mortal remains of the dead Jews; it was just too precious, too manipulative and calculating of him, she insisted, the way he rejected all concessions so that none would have to be extended in return. She insisted that the idea of having his kids collect bones for burial in Israel was morbid and sentimental child exploitation, that the rabbis, though in most instances insufferable thugs, were absolutely justified in this case in refusing to permit interment in hallowed ground even if their reasons were plainly racist, to prevent possible pollution by non-Jewish remains. Go ahead, she declared, stick your bags of bones into the mud of your kibbutz and cover them up with your manure and chant your mumbo jumbo and dance your "Am Yisrael Chai" hora over them if that deludes you into believing that you're still alive, that you've escaped annihilation once and for all. Yet even without a single hair on her head, even in her shapeless inmate's uniform, Leyla was luminous, she was magnificent, it was exquisitely painful to let her go, excruciatingly difficult to part from her even now when she was being so cold, so cruel, so impossible, just the thought that he must now leave her aroused in his soul an aching longing, every molecule in him was already missing her fearfully in advance, it was like giving up light, intensity, the rush of feeling alive. But his kids were drawing him away, he could not fail them, it was his duty to transform this trip from passive ghetto mourning to hopeful Zionist defiance, so he turned to Leyla and said, "Eh, if I stay with you one minute longer, I will lose all my strength and become like any other man," and with no other farewell, he turned and hurried away.

When he arrived at the ash field with only ten minutes remaining until blastoff, they were standing at their assigned posts, just as he had ordered, regarding him with the unforgiving judgmental scrutiny of children, testing to see how he would react now to the unanticipated obstacle that had arisen in the form of the vehicles, two gleaming limousines and a jeep parked at the edge of the field, and their passengers—that little nudnik of a museum chairman he had met the day before in Auschwitz in the gas chamber of Crematorium I, a trim all-American camera-ready type he did not recognize, and an Auschwitz-Birkenau official decked out in the uniform of a park ranger with a coiled wire trailing down behind one ear like a bionic creature plugged into central control. The two dignitaries were strutting around the expanse of the ash field like lords surveying their rightful domain, followed a few paces behind by the proprietary bailiff explaining the improvements and amenities, all of them ignoring for the moment as beneath their notice the underage interlopers stationed at the crosses and the stars, and the peasant poachers. The kids had their eyes mercilessly upon Shimshon. Would he abort the mission? Would he remain true to them, or would he go over to the enemy?

As he approached the trio in order to better assess the situation and what adjustments in their tactics might be required, he could hear the old man lapping his tongue like a *shtadlan*, groveling like a caricature of a court Jew; everything that had always disgusted Shimshon about the pathology of the Diaspora was confirmed for him once again. "Congressman," Maurice Messer was holding forth to the camera-ready specimen, "I want you should know I left before the dessert today a lunch in a five star restaurant from Krakow mit a top-notch ten-star Polish diplomat who was mine personal guest. Why? Because it was more important to me to be mit you here by the ashes—mit you, Representative Jedediah Jaspers, chairman from the House Appropriations Committee, so that I can show to you mit mine own eyes why our museum must always get the maximum plus in government funding from your appropriations committee, not one penny less. Every time you sit down mit your gavel to *hock* your committee to order, you must remember these ashes, J. J., you must never forget what I am showing to you here today. What are the ashes from the six million worth in dollars and cents? That's the question you must ask to yourself, and that's the question you must answer mit your heart and mit your conscience and mit the whole complete allocation from the annual federal budget. I'm talking to you now not like one human being to another, not even like one American-success-story Jew to another American-success-story Mormon, but more important, I am appealing to you today here on these sacred ashes—chairman to chairman."

Maurice looked up sharply, suddenly distracted from his performance, recognizing Shimshon. "Uh-oh," he said, tugging the congressman's jacket sleeve, as if to pull him out of the path of an oncoming locomotive, "watch out, J. J., this fella's a major *uch* and a *vey*, a big troublemaker, no respect whatsoever."

The guard in his uniform boldly stepped up to Shimshon, standing too close, like a boot-camp commander. "Can I help, sir?" he demanded with a spray of sausage-scented saliva. "Eh, thank you, as a matter of fact, yes," Shimshon answered, gazing down at him benignly. "Eh, I was wondering if the distinguished chairman of the Holocaust Museum is the one who hired that Nazi car over there?" He pointed to the Mercedes limo idling at the perimeter of the field. "Because, eh, if you will excuse me, there is no ethical difference in my opinion between driving in a Nazi car and using the data from Nazi medical experiments. Eh, personally, even if I were stranded in Death Valley and Steven Spielberg's Shoah Foundation Nazi car from *Raiders of the Lost Ark* happened to stop to pick me up, I would refuse to get in, I would not accept the ride."

"Take advice, Mac," the guard warned confidentially, with a kind of menacing solicitude in masterful film-and-television-acquired albeit Slavic-stamped English, "do not attempt comical business—which applies to minors too, I must add." He illustrated by glancing in the direction of the kids scattered through the field. "Is it clear as mud? Good. So it covers ground. Do not believe one minute even you will exit premises with loot. We have you below surveillance—do you comprehend? Every bone and ash flake hooligans stuff into rucksacks, I beg to remind, is legal property of Auschwitz State Museum and citizens of Poland." He raised his wrist to his lips, and in staccato Polish he communicated harshly and rapidly into a tiny radio embedded near his watch.

But the congressman was forging ahead, oblivious to these developments. "My friend," he said in his sonorous tones, laying his right hand on Maurice's shoulder but gazing well over his head, at a constituency of ashes, "nobody loves the Jewish people, dead or alive, more than I do. And I say this without any self-interest, since only a minuscule percentage of the voters in the great state of Utah are Jews, and at present, I am planning to spend more time with my family and have no intention of running for president. But I say to you here and now on these sacred ashes, the Jewish people will never have a better friend in the United States Congress than Jed Jaspers—and that's a promise. As a Saint in the lineage of Ephraim, one of the ten lost tribes of Zion, deep in my heart I feel a special kinship to you and to your Holocaust and to your great state of Israel." With the same hand with which he had singled out Maurice for his beneficence he now struck his left breast in an ardent pledge of allegiance.

"I never doubted it for one minute, J. J.," Maurice responded. "And speaking in the name from the Jewish people, I can tell you that when it comes to you Mormons and to all of your wives and to your Tabernacle Choir, the feeling is one hundred percent mutual."

"Yes, we members of the Church of Jesus Christ of Latter-day Saints feel a special bond with our Jewish brethren. We have both suffered persecution and attempts at extermination, and we have both been blessed by the Lord with a special gift for survival and finance. And that is why our elders have decided to tap our great genealogical index—the largest and most complete genealogical database in the world, I might add—to baptize by proxy our deceased Jewish brothers and sisters whom we love so much, in order to bestow upon their dead souls in the afterlife eternal salvation, as well as all of the privileges and blessings of our great faith. I am happy to report to you that, to date, among the late Jews who have been privileged to receive posthumous conversion into the Church of Jesus Christ of Latter-day Saints we are proud to count Brother Israel Ba'al Shem Tov, founder of Hasidism, Brother David Ben-Gurion, first prime minister of the state of Israel, Brother Sigmund Freud, father of psychoanalysis, and every single victim of the Holocaust whose name is in our genealogical records— and you can bet your life that there are plenty of names on our charts, we're targeting all six million or however many you've got—including that beautiful and spirited little gal that everyone has such a great big crush on, Sister Annie Frank, who, I might add, no longer belongs to you alone but to all of us, to all of mankind, to the entire universe."

"How can we ever express our gratitude to you for your generosity?" Maurice said. "I'm telling you, Congressman, if we could reciprocate by making an after-death circumcision for Reb Brigham Young, we would not hesitate for one minute—mit a top-of-the-line catering affair! To live as a Jew, to die as a Jew, and then to wake up in the next life as a Mormon LSD, mit out even having to go to the trouble of applying for admission—what could be better, especially mit your multiple-wives package deal? But you know something, J. J., I just have to tell you, so you shouldn't be blindsided or God forbid caught off guard—sometimes mit the Jews, it just so happens that the baptism doesn't take."

"Oh, it will take all right—as long as I'm chairman of appropriations holding the purse strings for federal funding of the Holocaust, it will take. What person in his right mind would ever turn down such a generous gift as free membership in our glorious Church, when it is offered with such sincere and unselfish goodwill? Why shouldn't you Jews appreciate the great benefits of belonging to the Church of Jesus Christ of Latter-day Saints when I myself am not one bit ashamed to consider myself an honorary member of the Jewish faith—and to bear its mark upon my body?" Maurice's eyes popped wide open, alarmed for an instant that Jaspers was about to drop his pants then and there by way of demonstration of his Jewish membership. Instead, the congressman pulled a gold Star of David out from under his shirt and held it up under Maurice's nose for inspection. "You see what it says there, my friend?" he pressed on. "Zion—as in Zion National Park, in the great state of Utah—inside a Jewish star, like these terrific Stars of David here, set down among these terrific crosses on this sacred sea of ashes to honor the union of the Jewish and Christian faiths and their equal and shared suffering. I'm telling you, my friend, I love it. It touches my heart real deep. God bless you and God bless America. These crosses and stars send a great big chill right down my spine."

"Yes," Maurice said, "the crosses mit the stars. A very nice decorative touch, like mine wife Blanche would say, a bit of white in the gray, it cheers things up—a very thoughtful gesture on the part from the Polish scouts."

"The Polish scouts put them in," Shimshon cried, "and the Jewish scouts will take them out!" Inserting two fingers between his lips, he let out a piercing whistle. "Operation Ben-Zeruya has begun!" he shouted. "Let's go, *chevra*—comrades, *kadimah*!"

At this signal, the kids at their assigned stations pulled the loosened posts out of the ash-glutinous earth and began running across the dolorous field bearing the white wooden crosses and the stars on their backs just as the three police cars and the paddy wagon drew up with sirens blaring. When Shimshon realized that the officers spilling out of the cars charging toward them were armed with pistols and truncheons, he yelled, "They're prepared to murder Jews again in Auschwitz!" and he ordered his troops to drop their burdens at once and to surrender. Eldad and Medad smashed the crosses they were carrying against one another like swords, shattering them to pieces, provoking a zealous avenger of a guard to throw each boy over a shoulder like a bundle of rags for the heretic's pyre, sending their glasses sinking into a dark pool in the ash marsh, hustling them to the paddy wagon flailing and screaming in hopeless Hebrew, "Help, I can't see! I can't see—help!"

"*Chevra*, do not lose heart!" Shimshon cried out. "We have prevailed! Symbolically, we are victorious!"

The old peasant pensioners scuttled forward, abandoning their metal detectors and mushroom baskets, to pick up the remaining crosses and replant them in the ashes with extravagant kisses and mumbled prayers and tears rolling down their leathery cheeks. The stars they left where they had fallen. Maurice Messer turned to the congressman. "This fella is a fringe character," he said, pointing contemptuously at Shimshon being herded into a police car along with his children's crusade. "I hope the Poles teach him mit his juvenile delinquents a good lesson once and for all. You don't have to worry about him. He has nothing to do mit us. He does not represent our Holocaust."

*

The fact is, Maurice Messer was stretching the truth a bit when he told Congressman Jedediah Jaspers that he had left the five-star Krakow restaurant without having had his dessert, though in his defense it ought to be noted that he permitted himself this harmless fib in his devotion to the cause, to impress upon the appropriations chairman the gravity, the urgency, the sacrificial nature of his responsibility with respect to full funding for the museum. Not to begrudge him, but just for the record, the real story is that he had had a very nice crème brûlée with raspberries along with what he called a *kichel*, though Gloria had described it as a chocolate hazelnut madeleine, to accompany his coffee, followed by an excellent brandy compliments of the house, after which he had corralled them all into the limousine for the ride to Birkenau, dropping them off at the imposing watchtower entrance now functioning as an administration center—the arched gateway through which, by war's end, trains pulling cattle cars packed with human freight rode efficiently through straight to the gas chamber terminus—and then giving the order to the chauffeur to drive him on to the ash field to catch up with the congressman. As Krystyna detained her charges at the gateway in order to prep them with the stats—the killing center's size when in operation, four hundred and twenty-three acres with three hundred buildings housing two hundred and fifty thousand prisoners at its height, gassing an average of thirty-four thousand people a month between March of 1942 and November of 1944 for a grand total of one million one hundred thousand exterminated, ninety-five percent of them Jews—Gloria noticed off to the right on the perimeter of the camp, in front of what looked like a church with a huge cross on top looming over the two-hundred-and-twenty-volt-capacity electrified barbed-wire fence, a small souvenir kiosk that caught her eye thanks to its cheerful red-and-white plastic fringe bunting rustling lightly in the warm breeze. Declaring that she absolutely could not return home the next day without all of the gifts that she still needed to buy for her maids, her cook, her hairdresser, her personal trainer, her dog walker, her chauffeur, Bunny's shrink, her doorman, and so on and so forth, she led the way to this roadside attraction with the others following submissively behind, resigned to the whims of this consort of millionaires.

That is how they found themselves in front of the SS commandant's headquarters in which the Jewish women had been raped, now transformed into the parish church of Brzezinka with, in addition to the imposing crucifix on its roof, another one in front, and Polish women dressed in black crossing themselves as they made their way unmolested to and from confession—at Tommy Messiah's stand, when he got that call on his mobile phone from Shimshon in the Oswiecim county jail. Though Tommy Messiah was speaking in rapid-fire Hebrew, both Norman and Monty could make out the gist of what had happened—basically, what it came down to was that there had been an arrest of some sort over some kind of cross-related protest action—and then something further about the need for posting bond, or bail, or whatever, at which point Monty lost interest, thank God, and went off to fool around with Krystyna, while Norman's ears truly perked up especially sharply when he caught a reference to a check for five thousand dollars that

Tommy Messiah ebulliently declared he would sign over to the Polish authorities immediately since, as luck would have it, this was exactly the amount they were holding out for. Of course they would take this check, *ayn ba'ayah*, no problem, it was an official United States government check, from the Holocaust Museum of Washington, D.C., for Christ's sake, made out by the son of the chairman no less, a kind of scalper's fee, you might call it, or a consultant's commission, for helping the poor *schlimazel* gain admission to the Carmelite convent, believe it or not, which any schmuck could get into simply by knocking on the door—this check was one-hundred-percent certified, as good as gold from Fort Knox, don't worry, *hakol beseder*, everything is okey-dokey, I'll be there in less than an hour. Norman was nearly choking with anxiety and agitation, trying desperately to figure out how to intervene and prevent this catastrophe as Tommy Messiah clicked off his phone, stuck it into the back pocket of his jeans, and announced, "Closing time, friends, special bargain prices, every item on the table— three for a dollar," and began moving things along at a nice clip with the charade of placing his goods out of reach, rendering them thereby irresistibly appealing, ostentatiously stuffing them piece by piece into his worn garbage bags, swatting away like an annoying gnat the frantic entreaties with which Norman was seeking to get his attention, albeit as inconspicuously as possible to avoid arousing the suspicions of Monty and all of his other latent enemies lurking in readiness.

As Tommy Messiah rushed off, rolling his cart to his brokendown van parked in the Birkenau lot in front of the Gate of Death alongside a sparkling yellow Volkswagen tour bus from Munich, and as Krystyna, hauling Gloria's purchases in two used and wrinkled "Auschwitz Gift Shop" shopping bags courtesy of

Tommy Messiah, led the group through the arched entryway
under the watchtower into the killing center, Norman was
thinking despairingly that he would just run ahead straight to
the massive stone and granite monument at the end of the rail
spur, between the ruins of Crematoria II and III, light a memorial candle, and beseech God to save him from imminent scandal and disgrace. Maybe he would even scribble a little note
and insert it between the stones, the way petitioners did at
the Western Wall in Jerusalem—"Dear God," he would write,
"For the sake of Your Holocaust, don't let me get fucked over
again. Love, Norman." This was not idolatry, he told himself, it
was an emergency stopgap measure, it was crisis intervention.
To add to his problems, he was still lugging around that Nazi
helmet, which he could not figure out what to do with. He had
thought of simply abandoning it on the roadside, or in the taxi
as he rode from the convent to meet the group at Birkenau,
but then reconsidered—it might really have some value, what
did a peddler like Tommy Messiah know? Maybe, though, he
would leave it after all, like an offering, near the stone slabs at
the international memorial here in Birkenau with the inscrip-
tions in all those languages—at the German slab perhaps. He
could fill it with flowers that other visitors had left, they would
never miss them, with a note inside, "From a repentant Storm
Trooper, we Germans are a new people," or, more realistically,
"Remember Dresden! Remember the German Holocaust!"
or, better still, "The Holocaust Is a Hoax, Neo-Nazis Unite!"
No, that was too incendiary. And what if they traced it back to
him? Then the federal government Holocaust Museum check
he had made out to a small-time crook and hustler for personal, non-business-related access to the notorious Auschwitz-
defiling Carmelite convent that had ended up in the hands of

Polish police to bail out a gang of Zionist hoodlums who had uprooted the crosses and vandalized Polish national property would look like peanuts by comparison. And of course, for the sake of authenticity, for verisimilitude, he would need to write whichever note he decided to leave inside the Nazi helmet in German. That was a problem. His German, he had to admit, if only to himself, was essentially little more than his kitchen Yiddish tarted up, spiked with a sharper edge.

Krystyna, for her part, as she entered Birkenau at the head of her charges, was, as always when she arrived at this place, bitterly reminded of the stories her mother used to tell her of how the invading German forces had marched Soviet prisoners of war into their town of Brzezinka to raze and demolish their homes in order to carry off the used bricks to build the barracks of the women's camp, which were still standing to the left of the tracks alongside which they were walking. Of course, after the war, to rebuild their homes, some of the citizens, her mother had told her, had understandably taken part in the dismantling of the wooden barracks to the right of the tracks, leaving only the haunting desolation of the brick chimneys within those stone rubble outlines of the rectangular foundations. But, as every child to whom the cautionary universal tale of the three little pigs had ever been whispered in the darkness of bedtime could attest, a wooden house could never make up for the loss of the solidity and the security of brick, and, in any case, the main point, as far as Krystyna was concerned, was the utter absence of any sympathy at all for the suffering and the besmirching of their good name that the Polish locals had endured as a result of the Nazi occupation and the proximity of the camps. Why didn't anyone ever consider their feelings? What kind of obscene blasphemy was it to insinuate that the Poles were worse even than the German barbarians, that the Poles hurled themselves upon their Jewish neighbors with pitchforks and scythes and flaming torches to do the Germans' dirty work, that the Poles were common collaborationists like your maniacal Croat killer, your debauched Ukrainian peasant? Jesus Christ, the Poles were victims too—martyrs, Christians. Why was all the attention focused only on the Jews? That's all anyone ever heard—Jews, Jews, Jews. In places like China with over a billion population, they must be stunned when they discover one fine morning that there are after all so few Jews in the world, given all the noise and trouble these Jews stir up and the landfills of verbiage they generate. Even the inscription on the granite slabs of the memorial here in Birkenau, which had once so equitably and inclusively acknowledged everyone who had suffered and perished without singling out any particular group for the victim's prize, even that innocent inscription had to be revised to give center stage to the Jews. Krystyna shuddered as she pictured the merciless squeeze that must have been applied to bring about this change. She dealt with these Jews all the time, she knew what ruthlessness they were capable of. They were the world-class memorialists, they made their memories their religion, they worshipped their memories like an idol, they made their memories everyone else's memories, they had the corner on the memory market.

She would have liked to talk to Bunny about this. Bunny was open to suffering diversity, Bunny was not a genocide xenophobe, Bunny was not a Holocaust hog, but Bunny had been ignoring her rather coldly since last night, avoiding looking into her eyes, hovering like a traumatized child with her thumb stuck in her mouth close to the designer skirts of her champion shopper mother, whose bags she, Krystyna, was now schlepping like some kind of coolie, like a Slavic serf as they walked along the tracks deeper into the vastness of the camp. There was no one on whom she could rely, no one she could trust, no one who would not in the end abandon or betray her. Monty over there had detached himself pointedly from the group and was behaving, as usual, as if there were nothing he could possibly learn from her of all people, giving off signals that all of the information she was spoon-feeding them with was special sugarcoated watered-down tourist packets utterly beneath him. He was kicking the pebbles across the rails with his signature macho cockiness and his jaunty strut, though she could tell of course that something was bothering him, she knew him too intimately, as much as it mattered to him that the whole world regard him as immune to worrying, she knew he was beset. Up ahead she could see Norman surging in the direction of the monument like some sort of wreck gasping on its last cylinder, evidently panic-stricken by his latest crisis, whatever that was, totally useless as usual. And as for her boss, the Honorable Maurice, king of the Holocaust, any minute now, if he hadn't finally keeled over with a hemorrhage from perpetual overexcitement, he would be charging back from turning the screws on that dumb cowboy congressman from some state in the American Wild West, expecting her to have already delivered his audience to the monument at the end of the tracks so that he could do his routine of the Kaddish and the candles and the canned speech with the corrupt tears.

Krystyna made up her mind to give them the quick tour—they had all, herself not least among them, had it up to the kazoo with this lousy Holocaust. She would point out to them the major sites along the way, the blocks of barracks, some still standing, most in ruins, the rows of vertical columns like a chorus of witnesses with bowed heads between which the electrified barbed wire had been strung, the guard towers lining the tracks, the unloading ramp, the remains of Crematoria II and III, et cetera et cetera—and that's as far as they would go. They would skip the rubble of the other two crematoria and the ash field. She would bring them directly up to the monument, she decided, discreetly sweep away whatever memento might have been left this time by some visiting joker, a tampon in a condom, for example, a standard favorite, and park them there to await the advent of Maurice.

They continued walking along the railway spur, drawing closer to the end of the line, arriving at the unloading ramp where, as she explained to them, selections had taken place, conducted personally, most memorably, by Mengele M.D. himself—the prisoners dragged out of the cattle cars marched straight to the gas chambers, with a few of the more able-bodied and unencumbered spared for the interim, singled out to die more slowly from slave labor and starvation and despair and disease. As they came closer to the unloading ramp, however, there seemed to suddenly materialize, like a supernatural vision in a clearing mist, a large circle of human beings frozen in a sitting posture on the muddy ground around the railway track, with that bushy-bearded guru robed from head to foot in celestial white presiding from the elevation of his wheelchair, like a benevolent godfather officiating at the last supper.

He strummed a few chords on the guitar resting in his lap to rivet their attention as Krystyna and her charges approached. "Welcome, oh welcome, my sweetest friends and welcome to you, holy holy Jiriki," he chanted in a minor key with a husky catch in his voice, while plucking the strings of his guitar, serenading Gloria almost exclusively. "You are so so special, Jiriki, we believe in you so much. How we have waited for you, holy holy Jiriki, how we have longed only for you. Come rest from your spiritual journey here on the healing soil of Birkenau filled with such great knowing and such holiness. Come cry with us, come laugh with us, come meditate with us. The holy holy souls of the dead and of those of us living in our present lives will open up and make room for you in our circle. Sit down beside our good friend Marano carrying her Rumi. It is the sitting place in our circle of samsara that has been held for you since the beginning of time." All of this he sang to the accompaniment of his guitar in a kind of improvised lamentation melody that combined the chanting of Tibetan monks with the cantillation of the synagogue.

Gloria clapped her hands. "Oh, let's," she cried. "It would be so much fun! And I'm so tired anyway from all that shopping—I'm just dying. I've got to rest, my feet are killing me, I've got to slip off my heels, I've got to sit down, so I might as well meditate while I'm at it—even though I have no idea how," she added with a giggle.

"Oh, it's just an old Chanel anyway," she went on distractedly, brushing her skirt as if it were a rag not worth paying any attention to as the redhead whom Norman had met that morning behind the Auschwitz gate, now covered chastely by a long batik poncho, came softly forward on bare feet and slipped a cushion under her. Gloria sat down on the ground next to Marano, greeting her with a cordial smile, like a well-bred dinner party guest taking her assigned place at the table. "I think Rumi is a very nice name for a baby, honey," she said sociably. "Is it short for something, like Abrumi—which is short for Abraham? Because I had a cousin named Abraham, Abraham Mitnik, but we called him Abrumi. He was a dentist." The oth-

ers in their group, seeing Gloria settling in for a stretch of time
to be arbitrarily dictated by herself alone, bowed to their fates
and found places for themselves in the circle as well.

Mickey Fisher-roshi played a rippling chord on his guitar to
scatter the distractions. "You know, my beautiful friends," he
began again, continuing with his chant like an ancient storytell-
ing minstrel around a fire, "I want to tell you something very
very deep. We are in a concentration camp. A concentration
camp blesses you with concentration, so my holy holy friends,
concentrate your chakra centers to take this in, this is the deepest thing. There is so much hunger in this world—hunger for
dharma, hunger for enlightenment, hunger for satori, hunger
for self-realization, hunger for transformation, hunger for nirvana, hunger for oneness. Sometimes I am hungry. So I eat a
schnitzel—a tofu schnitzel. I eat ten tofu schnitzels, and my
hunger is satisfied, I am all schnitzeled out. But, my beautiful friends, and this is one of the deepest levels, there are also
spiritual schnitzels, and however many spiritual schnitzels I
eat, I can never be satisfied. Spiritually I always remain hungry,
spiritually I am always seeking. Now listen to this, my sweetest
friends. Say you are hungry now, even though eating is forbidden in Birkenau by the rules of the camp. Say, though, that you
really could use a coffee break, with a doughnut maybe, or a
bagel with cream cheese, or a bialy and butter, or a pineapple-
walnut muffin, perhaps, even though if eating were allowed
here we would of course permit ourselves only a thin soup
made from potato peels, which we would drink from a tin
bowl without a spoon, and maybe also a chunk of moldy bread.
What is the biggest problem in the world? My friends, we do
not know how to nourish ourselves. That is the problem. It is
so so deep! Listen to this, my beautiful friends. We must nour-

ish ourselves now by reading out the names of the dead souls whose lives were interrupted and who cannot rest. As we read these names, some of us may be moved to add names from our own private Holocausts and some of us may be moved to speak, to cry out from the deepest depths of our hearts. Do not be afraid, my beautiful friends, the main thing is not to be afraid at all. There is holy holy healing energy here in Birkenau. Open your souls to Auschwitz and let yourselves be nourished. My friends, let us now remember the dead souls. Read!"

Jake Gilguli lifted his shofar to his lips and blew a long doleful wail as everyone in the circle resumed their meditative practice while a Japanese Zen Buddhist nun rose from her *zafu* and made her way noiselessly through a ring of memorial candles to the large carved cinnabar bowl resting on a rosewood stand set between the rails like an offering in the center of the circle. She took one of the lists of names out of the bowl and began to read: Horowitz, Anna; Horowitz, Eva; Horowitz, Henrik; Horowitz, Hinda; Horowitz, Joseph; Horowitz, Laszlo; Horowitz, Milka; Horowitz, Reiza; Horowitz, Shlomo; Horowitz, Tibi. She continued the naming of the members of the Horowitz tribe for many minutes. Were they related at the start, she wondered, as they were at the end? When she reached Horowitz, Zygmunt, she had completed the names on her list. Bending down to return it to the bowl, she added in a high trembling voice, "And Sadako Sasaki and all of the other children radiated and vaporized in Hiroshima and Nagasaki in the Japanese Holocaust."

A black man in an impeccably tailored three-piece suit and an orange dashiki-cloth tie, with a close-fitting white crocheted openwork skullcap pulled over his head, stood up in the circle. "Brother Mickey," he began in confident resonant revivalist tones accustomed to the podium, "I, Pushkin Jones, am moved by the words of the good sister to bear witness for the sake of our forefathers and foremothers by naming the nameless of the Jones clan, the lawful property of the slave master Jefferson Jones, who were among the more than sixty million—*sixty million, I stress!*—victims of the African-American Holocaust." Closing his eyes, he sang in a deep bass riffing on the blues: Jones, Negro girl, age eight. Jones, Negro boy, branded. Jones, Negro female, age twelve, lactating. Jones, mulatto boy, age three months. Jones, Negro male, age twenty-two, scarred back. Jones, Negro female, possessed by the devil. Jones, Negro male, age thirty-eight, no teeth. Jones, Negro female, runaway."

From the other side of the circle, Reb Tikkun from the Shtetls, the former Sheldon B. Noodleman from the Office of Management and Budget, dressed like a Polish peasant except for the fringed garment over his white shirt and black vest, and the beard and curled sidelocks dangling like coiled ribbons from under his cap, took up his klezmer fiddle to jam with Pushkin Jones, and then began to sing counterpoint to him, in a melody like a Yiddish dirge. "We also must name *our* nameless. Prisoners numbers 74883 to 74885—three Jewish females from Oppeln. Number 172853—baby boy born in the Birkenau women's camp. Numbers 74889 to 74901—group transport of thirteen Jewish females. Numbers 172860 to 173049—one hundred and ninety Jewish men from Westerbork, Holland. Numbers 74902 to 74970—sixty-nine Jewish women on the same transport from Holland. No numbers—the six hundred and eighty nine others on the transport from Holland, including one hundred and twenty-two children, killed in the gas chambers."

The two gladiators, Pushkin Jones and Reb Tikkun from the Shtetls, were sufficiently armed and ready to carry on with this musical duel until the camp closed and they were chased out by the guards, but they were silenced by a chain of actions that began with Fisher-roshi jabbing his elbow into Jake Gilguli's side, who, in turn, was catapulted out of his profound meditative state, fumbled to retrieve his shofar, took it up to his lips, and let out a startling blast. After allowing some time for the purity of the meditation practice to be restored in the ensuing silence, Fisher-roshi began to strum his guitar again and weave his mantras into the mind streams. "My sweetest friends, remember these words— peace and oneness. Peace to all the souls of the victims, living and dead, nameless and named. Oneness to all of our Holocausts, oneness in honoring our Holocaust diversity. So deep, so deep! We will never know, my beautiful friends, we will never know what mysteries lie in the depths of the human heart. For the sake of peace and one-ness, for the sake of enlightenment and healing, my holy holy friend Jake Gilguli will now share the testimony of his karmic transformation."

Jake Gilguli stood up, taking some time to unfold to his full six feet four inches in his brown robe for this special occasion, presenting himself before them in all the blond perfection of a superhero in mufti. As Jack Gallagher, he told them in the confident tones of the hereditary senior corporate executive, he had been trained from the earliest years of his privileged childhood to become a warrior on Wall Street, mowing down and slaying all of his competitors. But all along he was trou-bled by strange phobias and nightmares. He was terrified, for example, of high black leather boots and of trains. Trains were the dominant motif in his dreams—being pushed into and out

of trains to the accompaniment of the screams and lashes of
uniformed officers, standing on crowded platforms wedged
among weeping women and children and men weighed down
with bundles, huddling inside dark boxcars unable to breathe,
with no possibility of escape. At the same time, he was inex-
plicably attracted to movies about the Holocaust and to Jews,
especially to Jewish women of more zaftig proportions, with
dark mustaches over their lips, and a black mole in the crevice
of the nostril, and prizewinning puckered thighs—the kind of
stereotypical Jewess who, for a Jack Gallagher, must remain
a secret vice, with whom he could never be seen in public. It
was one such woman, a drill sergeant from the Israeli army
named Bathsheba, who led him to the discovery of his past life
as Yankel Galitzianer when she showed him an ad in a Hebrew
newspaper, a language he could not read or understand, for
the New Jersey burial society of the shtetl of Przemysl, seeking other survivors. Immediately he recited the names and
described the physical characteristics of his two comrades,
Jacek Lustiger and Henryk Pfefferkorn, who had escaped into
the forest three days before the roundups in Przemysl, while he,
Yankel Galitzianer, had been herded into a cattle car by black-
booted guards, and he rode for a week on the rails without
water or food until he came here to Birkenau, where he was
sent to the left at this very unloading ramp during the selections by Dr. Mengele himself, and marched with the others
into the gas chamber of Crematorium III—from which all that
remains is that pile of imploded rubble over there. The Przemysl burial society ad was like a lightbulb being switched on
in his brain; it was—enlightenment. Everything came back to
him at that moment, his entire childhood, his mother's Sabbath
candlesticks, his father's melodies amazingly authentic, like the

tunes in *Fiddler on the Roof*. As for the mundane details of what happened to him after his spiritual awakening, he did not really want to go into that, it was much too hurtful—how the surviving members of the Przemysl burial society refused to recognize him as one of their own, as the reincarnation of Yankel Galitzianer, and to give him a plot; how the rabbis from every Jewish denomination repeatedly rejected him as a candidate for conversion; how even his own Gallagher family had sought to have him declared legally incompetent and committed to a mental institution and divested of his fortune, though thanks to his excellent attorneys, they were foiled in this nefarious scheme resoundingly and expensively—boy, were they sorry that they ever started up with him! Suffice it to say, however, that his life was renewed when he met his great Zen master, Mickey Fisher-roshi, who illuminated his karma, who saved him from annihilation a second time and rebirthed him as Jake Gilguli, an awakening for which he would be eternally grateful and indebted, in this and in all his future lives.

Fisher-roshi nodded his head sagely and indicated to Gilguli to come forward and kneel down before him on the railroad track behind which the wheelchair was braked. He took up his guitar again and resumed his chant. "My sweetest friends, and my holy holy soul mate Jake Gilguli, this is so heartbreaking and so deep! Today, amidst the horror of Birkenau and the healing, here in this space of endless crying where the ashes of your former life as Yankel Galitzianer lie scattered, I bestow on you a new name to mark the beginning of your one-thousand-day journey as a lay monk toward dharma transmission, toward more supreme enlightenment and perfection, and to acknowledge at one and the same time the oneness of duality, the oneness of your Zen karma with your *Yiddishe neshama,* your Jewish

soul. Your new name as a monk is Koan—like Cohen, resonat-
ing richly of the word for a priest of Israel, *kohain*. From today
and henceforth you will be known as Jake Koan Gilguli—Buddhist monk, Jewish priest. I also present to you on this day of
your ordination as a lay monk the first of your koans, the first
of the enigmatic questions that through *zazen* and fidelity to
your master will lead you as you set forth in fulfillment of your
vows beyond the boundaries of reason to ultimate awakening.
Your koan of the week is: Who is a Jew?"

*

"Who is a Jew?" Maurice Messer repeated far too loudly as he
stood over Krystyna, panting heavily, having found them at last
after running around the camp searching for them everywhere.
"What kind of a *fercockte* question is that to ask a mixed-up kid
like this Gilguli-Shmilguli over here who doesn't even know
who he is one day to the next? The real question is, Who is a *good*
Jew? And the answer, ladies and gentlemen, is, It depends on
the size of the donation." Then he turned to his paid employee.
"What's going on here?" he demanded. "I thought I told you to
have them waiting for me by the plint'." Krystyna glanced at
him dismissively. "Madam Fifi over there decided she wanted to
meditate with the hippies," she answered smugly, swiveling her
jaw perfunctorily to indicate the other side of the circle, where
Gloria was happily installed on her cushion with Marano to her
left and Bunny at her right. Maurice shook his head in resignation. "So where are the boys?" he asked brusquely. She pointed
first to Norman, who was sitting outside the circle with his
legs stretched straight out in front of him like a toddler in a
sandbox, sullenly filling his helmet with mud and dirt, scoop-
ing it up, packing it in, and then flipping it over and dumping it into little rounded molds in the shape of Nazi brains,

five such mounds at least lined up already like a barricade on either side of him. Next she pointed farther down the circle to where Monty was contorted in an inane imitation of the lotus position next to the redheaded ideological nudist in her poncho, attempting to enter into conversation with her like an old creep who has wandered into a coed dorm party. Maurice glanced at his son, then headed toward Monty for an unscheduled meeting regarding museum affairs.

To Monty's astonishment, at the opposite end of the circle, not far from where the guru was enthroned, Bunny was venturing to speak up. "Hi," she began, sliding her red-framed glasses up her nose with her index finger as her mother smiled and bobbed her blond head encouragingly. "My name is Barbara 'Bunny' Bacon and I just wanted to say how really really happy I am to be visiting with you here today in your circle of diverse Holocaust worshippers and especially how deeply moved I was listening to the recovered-memory testimony of Jake Koan Gilguli. I also want to tell you how much I really really appreciate your interfaith intergender inter-sexual-orientation inter-age, well, just about inter everything, ceremony. I'm a little nervous now but I've got to get used to public speaking because I just got this really terrific news that I'm about to switch jobs. I'm about to become a Holocaust professional, and I'm really really excited. I just want to say that I've been learning a lot about the Holocaust, and I've concluded that what it all comes down to, like all the other problems in the world, is child abuse. I used to be a kindergarten teacher before becoming a Holocaust professional, so I know all about child abuse. My main source for studying the Holocaust is this incredible little book that I carry around with me at all times—you'll never find me anywhere without it, it's like my bible, my lucky charm. I read a passage from this book every night before bedtime like a prayer. Some day, I hope, portions from this classic will be included in the official Passover seder service. And, just to do my little bit, I want you to know that when I start my new job as a Holocaust professional at the United States Holocaust Memorial Museum, I intend to make communal readings of passages from this book a daily mandatory requirement for my entire staff. So if you don't mind, I'd like to read a short selection from this master-piece because as far as I'm concerned, it explains it all. Okay, so here goes: 'Yes, it's a sickness called hunger. Frozen fingers don't hurt. Sometime in the night they chewed their fingers down to the bone—but they're dead now.' Isn't that just amaz-ing? Doesn't that just say it all—and in a child's voice, too? In case you're interested—and I really really believe that you and all women and men of goodwill have a moral obligation to be interested!—the book is a true-life memoir called *Fragments* by a Swiss Jew named Binjamin Wilkormirski. I can't begin to tell you how highly I recommend it, it's a definite must-read; there'll be a quiz tomorrow—okay, just kidding. Oh, and I just wanted to say one more thing—thank you so so much for listening."

Monty's eyes darted toward Maurice. "Since when did she get a job in the museum?" he demanded. "You mean you went ahead and hired her—without even consulting me?"

"Relax, Pinky." Maurice placed a restraining hand on Mon-ty's shoulder. "I had to do it—you're a shmart boy, how come you don't understand? Don't worry so much! I'm gonna shtick her in the bowels from the education department. She'll shit there the whole day and futz around mit the Holocaust work-shops and lesson plans for high school teachers from Podunk to Peoria, and answer the letters from the kids who write in to

say that the Holocaust really really sucked. It has nothing to do
mit you." Eager to change the subject, Maurice looked around
the circle to locate the person who was moved to speak at that
moment, a young man with a soaring white eagle feather in
his long dark hair. "I don't know why," Maurice whispered to
Monty, "but that kid who's talking over there, the one mit the
schmatteh wrapped around his head like he has a terrible headache? He looks to me very familiar."

"My father is a Holocaust survivor," the young man was
saying with intense earnestness, "and my mother is the Hopi
peaceful little people. I, the sum of their parts, am a spiritual
crusader for the Native American Holocaust. I regard myself
as a nomad and a traveler. Everywhere I go I make a pilgrimage to the natural wonder of the place, bearing crystal earth
pods in my pocket, and take on a new name to honor the gods
who dwell there. When I came to Poland I descended into the
depths of the Wieliczka salt mines into a rock salt chapel where
I knelt down and made an offering upon a salt altar by the light
of a salt chandelier. The offering that I made was a photograph
of my father's family before the war, including the brother
and two sisters who passed out of the pollution and contami-
nation of this Third World through the gas chambers here in
Auschwitz-Birkenau. In front of this offering of the family portrait I placed another offering—a kachina doll, three small ears
of blue corn, and a handful of red beans. In this way I honor the
Native American Holocaust and vow to work for redress and
reparation and restitution. Then, in my Hopi way, I took on my
new name—Salt Mines. As long as I sojourn in Poland I shall
be known as Salt Mines, Eliot Salt Mines Schmaltz—the spirits
will allow me to answer to no other name."

"Oy vey," Maurice groaned, struggling to keep his voice

down, "I'm glad his papa is not here to see this—the boy is completely cuckoo from the mushrooms." He tapped his temple with one manicured finger, and turned sorrowfully to Monty. "Pinky, don't you recognize who this is? Eliot Schmaltz, the son from mine proctologist, Adolf Schmaltz, mit the oxblood shoe-polish toupee? You know Adolf—he's up on the wall in the museum, from his chain of private hospitals thanks to all the insurance policies that nobody can understand. Of course you know him, the one who gives to me the doctor's notes every fiscal year so I can fly in the first class on the government's expense account? Oy vey! This is his son from his second marriage, when he divorced his first wife Yetta mit the warts from Bialystok, mine Blanchie's girlfriend from the same hometown, and married that glamour puss, Vonda Schmaltz, mit the legs, from the Taj Mahal Casino in Atlantic City. I think you met Vonda Schmaltz one night—you sat next to her at the Babi Yar testimonial dinner, five thousand dollars a plate, you were very deep in conversation or whatever mit her, I noticed. Mine Blanchie says she has a nose job and I can tell you personally from mine years in the foundation business that everything on top is not only manhandled, it is also man-made, heh heh— maybe that's why the boy traded her in for Mother Nature."

As Maurice went on riffing in this way, discharging waves of discordant vibrations all around the circle, penetrating concentration, snapping detachment, provoking a chorus of shushing, a fusillade of indignant glares, Monty recalled something he had never told his boss, not because he had been pledged to secrecy, which he may or may not have been, he didn't remember, but simply because it had never seemed that important or useful to him. The day after sitting next to Vonda Schmaltz at the Babi Yar dinner, he had been summoned into her husband's

office and dispatched that very evening with his vaunted rabbinical charismatic and spiritual powers and a fat check in his
pocket on a private plane to Flagstaff, Arizona, and from there
in a waiting limousine to the desert reservation on a top-secret
mission to deprogram the son. In the end, the kid had granted
him an audience of a few minutes only, arriving to the meeting surrounded by painted and feathered extras with arms
folded across their bare chests and tomahawks in their leather
loincloths to guard him from kidnappers. This distracting
entourage, plus the brevity of their meeting, plus the fact that
Monty had taken along on the junket a fresh-faced Holocaust
groupie and had better things to do, probably explained why
he hadn't recognized the boy now. In their brief meeting, however, Monty had managed to extract from Eliot a promise that
he would do the death camp tour in Poland for comparative
Holocaust shopping. Monty had duly reported this back to old
man Schmaltz, asserting that such an exercise would doubtless
confirm the superiority of Jewish suffering to all others—what
was the trail of tears, after all, compared to the forced marches
of death camps and gas chambers and crematoria?—and bring
the boy back into the fold. As he pocketed a nice bonus for this
success, it had permeated even Monty's self-congratulatory
miasma that Schmaltz was heartbroken, desolate, he would do
anything to save his son, crawl and grovel, humiliate himself in
any way. What Monty was now witnessing here at Birkenau, he
figured, was Eliot Salt Mines Schmaltz in the act of fulfilling his
promise to his father.

Maurice was now raising his voice even louder, ignoring the
implicit and overt censure all around, hurling his words across
the ring directly at the *roshi* himself. "I'm telling you, Mickey
Mouse baba," Maurice announced, "this is a tragedy. This boy is

Eliot, the son from mine oldest and dearest friend, Dr. Adolf Schmaltz, M.D., the distinguished physician, entrepreneur, and philant'ropist, mine boyhood pal, mine *lantzman* from mine hometown of Wieliczka, mine comrade in arms who served under me as mine aide-de-camp when I was a leader from the partisans and fought against the Nazis in the woods. Just look at what happened, it can break your heart to pieces. Instead of going back to Wieliczka, his papa's shtetl, for a heritage tour from the ruins from the Jewish community and the cemetery and so forth and so on, the boy goes to the Wieliczka salt mines to make a pagan offering in the Blessed Kinga chapel mit all those *getchkehs* and idols and icons. I'm telling you, it's a calamity. We are losing the best and the brightest from our second and our third generations to the New Agers and the nutcases and the nuns."

"That's Adolf's and Vonda's boy, Eliot the Indian?" Gloria exclaimed. "Such an interesting and well-spoken young man, with such a pretty feather! I'll be seeing your mother in two weeks at our ladies book club meeting, Salt Mines," she addressed him directly. "Your mom's the discussion leader. She'll be so happy and excited to hear that I ran into you at Auschwitz. I'll give her your regards. We're reading the *Critique of Pure Reason*—by Immanuel Kant?"

From within his fortress of Nazi mud pies, Norman raised the stakes by taking spiteful aim at Gloria. "And that's your husband Leon's girl, Mara the hippie and dropout," he announced portentously, extending his arm with the helmet hanging from it, like a weapon spearing a decapitated head, pointing it toward Marano in deep meditation at Gloria's left. "Such an interesting old girl our Mara is—don't you think?—maybe a little too interesting? And what a pretty belly she has, so well cooked—maybe a little too well cooked, huh? Maybe a little too pregnant? Hey, aren't we having a fun second-generation reunion today here amongst the scenic wonders of Camp Auschwitz?"

"Oy vey," Maurice cried. "That's Leon's girl Mara, the one who gave him so much aggravation and heartburn that he was too upset to pay attention to his nursing homes and got into such big-time trouble mit the government you wouldn't want to know from it? What did mine dearest friend, the outstanding financier and benefactor Leon Lieb, ever do to deserve such a punishment? Those were mine very own words what I said to the president from the United States himself when I wrote to him a letter asking for a pardon for mine dear friend Leon. I explained him mit all mine credentials as chairman from the United States Holocaust Memorial Museum speaking on behalf from the six million that Leon was one from the great heroes from the Holocaust, a partisan fighter par excellence, he put on a dress mit a brassiere mit *schmattehs* stuffed inside the size D cups, and lipstick and a *teiche'le* around his head, to smuggle rifles in his bloomers into the Warsaw Ghetto. He was not ashamed to make a fool from himself in ladies' garments for the sake of showing to the whole world that the Jewish people will never—no, never!—go like sheep to the shlaughter. That's what I wrote to the president. The pardon came special delivery the next day. But what does it matter, what good is it all for Leon, when he has a daughter like this—a daughter who had every advantage money can buy, and then she turns around and gives to her papa the finger? Look at her, she's dressed like a bag lady in the gutter mooching around in a garbage dump by a subway station in the south Bronx!"

But when Maurice noticed the radiant look on Gloria's face

he was silenced. "Oh my God," Gloria exulted, "oh my God, I'm going to be a grandma, I'm so excited, I've always wanted to be a grandma." Patting and stroking Marano's belly reverently, she chattered on about how she hoped Buddhists weren't hung up by that primitive Jewish superstition that bans buying anything before the baby is born, alerting the evil eye, like counting chickens before they hatch, because there were so many things they needed, there was so much fun shopping to do, a complete layette—adorable little embroidered smocks and teeny-weeny bonnets, irresistible bibs and itsy-bitsy booties and cuddly blankets. She would host a baby shower in the coming weeks in their Fifth Avenue duplex, that was the solution. Leon would be thrilled to see how well his Mara has turned out after all, he had invested so much worrying into that girl, almost as much as into his real estate, and now at last he would collect the returns. But they were definitely going to have to do something about that name. Rumi was just too odd and peculiar. They needed something the other kids could never find a way to make fun of in Yale preschool, like Peter or Richard or William, something reliable like that, something that would keep the boy safe from despair. Because she was certain it was going to be a boy, though instantly she rejected the idea of linking him in her thoughts with Michael. That was something she would never do, something she would not permit herself. It had happened so long ago, nothing in this life could ever be done now to alter or remedy it.

Gloria gazed tenderly at Marano, struck by the resemblance to Leon in the droop of the cheeks that defined the contours of the face and the swarthiness of the complexion, it was a wonder she hadn't noticed it earlier. And especially now, with Marano lost behind those glasses in meditation reciting a mantra under her breath, Gloria was acutely reminded of Leon at those times when he would mouth his silent devotions standing with his feet pressed together, the phylactery box on his forehead and the leather straps wrapped around his arm, nothing could be permitted to disturb him. On a flight home from Davos once, descending toward New York over the cemeteries of Queens, Leon, wrapped in plastic tubing to shield him from proximity to the dead forbidden to him as a member of the priestly caste, stood in the aisle with feet pressed together silently praying the Eighteen Benedictions as three stewardesses resorted to brute force to wrestle him back into his seat—but still he would not be budged. Pious Jews in prayer shawls were the original meditation practitioners, Gloria had concluded long ago. Covering their eyes and proclaiming their mantra "Shemah Yisrael," Hear O Israel, they leap ecstatically into the flames and are consumed.

She looked toward the *roshi* for a signal that he had read her thoughts—about meditation, about Jews, about Michael—believing on some mystical level that he might have the power to plumb her soul, wondering if maybe he could relieve her by knowing without her having to explain, because of course she would never explain, it was something she never talked about, it happened a third of a century ago after all, Mel found him cold in the closet, the rope impersonal around his neck, the suitcases packed in the room, he would have set off to college that bright morning like a young prince, everything lay before him. How to absorb such a failure of hope? She glanced toward the roshi seated in his wheelchair against the spectral background of Birkenau for some sign of understanding, but realized instead that she was disturbing the flow and the focus of the meditation, like a foreign intruder who would just never fit in. Let me not look upon the death of the child, she said in her heart as she went on sitting by the now silent train tracks of Birkenau. She closed her eyes. More than anything else she desired at that moment to be restored into the inner circle of the favored and sought after. So she laundered her private loss and donated it to the community. "I just want to say that finding out here in Auschwitz where they tried to wipe us off the face of the planet that I'm going to become a grandmother is like hope reborn, it's like spitting in Hitler's eye," she said, as if moved to speak. "Children are the greatest revenge in the world—and the greatest victory."

"Memory is the greatest revenge in the world, and the greatest victory," Bunny the newly minted Holocaust professional, asserted adamantly. "Really really remembering *all* of the eleven million victims, including the five million others. Roma and Sinti, formerly known as Gypsies. Political prisoners, formerly known as Soviets. And also, of course, our good friends and hosts, the Poles, formerly known as Polacks. And finally, gays, yes, we must never never forget gays—formerly known as fruits, faggots, and fairies, homos and dykes, queens and queers." She gave her mother a laden glance, and looked away.

Maurice was about to remark to Monty that now that Gloria had found Leon's long-lost daughter, maybe she would shell out another ten million to the museum to make Marano codirector with Bunny—what a dynamite duo that would be, Abbot mit Costello, Mutt mit Jeff!—but luckily for him, before he would have had the good sense to stop his mouth from spilling over, he was deflected by Fisher-roshi, who was again strumming his guitar contemplatively, weaving his words mournfully into the waves of the meditating circle. "We'll never know, my beautiful friends, we'll just never know what our final destination may be, even if we achieve the highest level of *samadhi* by meditating in a mountain cave for nine years like Bodhidharma himself in wall-gazing *zazen*. Listen, friends, this is so so deep. You know how when your plane lands, your flight attendant says, Have a nice day in Minsk, or Pinsk, or wherever your final destination may be? Can you think of anything deeper, friends—wherever your final destination may be? This may be the ultimate koan. My sweetest friends, you may imagine that Auschwitz was the final destination—the end of the line, literally and figuratively—for so many souls, and not only for the dead but now also for us, the living, on the journey to knowing. Yet I feel the energy of the dead souls moving restlessly in our midst. It is a healing energy, my beautiful friends. They are giving us permission to heal in their space, and we, in turn, must make space for them in our living circle and allow them to sit with us. We must liberate them and ourselves from torment and passion, we must open the gates to righteousness and enlightenment, He who makes peace in His heavens must also grant to them peace, and to all of us too—peace, shalom—and let us say, Amen."

Fat tears from the roshi's eyes were plopping audibly onto his guitar like raindrops into a metal pot set under a leak, he had lubricated himself so thoroughly with his own words. He let the strumming of his fingers trail off plaintively into a sustained pianissimo that merged with the shades of the silence, giving them shape and substance—the silence of the ongoing meditation practice and the silence of the otherworldly twilight descending in a translucent pale violet haze over the chimneys and train tracks of Birkenau.

Even Monty, the old Holocaust hand, was caught under that heartwarming spell that the roshi had cast—that self-affirming spell attesting to your place on the side of the good that comes at minimal personal cost through virtual victim immersion in such lowest-common-denominator consensus evil and horror as the Holocaust—that it took him just a few seconds longer than usual to realize that the shrill buzz streaking through the circle like an electric current was coming from the inside pocket of his own iridescent fly-blue suit jacket. Retrieving his cell phone, he automatically summoned up that universal voice oblivious to all bystanders, enunciating in an inflection and at a decibel level in a no-man's-land between conversation and proclamation. "Sibyl, sweetie? Yes, I'm sitting—at the unloading ramp in Birkenau at an unscheduled activity with my campers and Uncle Maurice." What followed then for the general listening audience were echolike, bulletlike queries, punctuated by brief pauses. "Mommy?" "The garage?" "Gas?" "Police?" "Hospital?"

"Tomorrow," Monty said finally in those winding-down tones recognizable to one and all as the approaching end of a phone call. "Don't worry, sweetheart, Daddy will be home tomorrow, everything will be all right."

Clicking off, he whispered behind his hand into Maurice's ear. That was Sibyl, Monty said—your little onion, which was what Maurice affectionately called the girl, translating from the Yiddish, he was like a grandpa to her, he had known her all her life. It seems that Honey had attempted to commit suicide in the garage, Monty went on to report matter-of-factly—the bitch!—maybe even with the Zyklon B. There was still a can or two of the contraband left over, stored on the shelf in his suburban garage in Arlington, Virginia, alongside the bicycle oil and the fertilizer and the cremated ashes in a pickle jar of the father of the previous owner, and all the other junk, from the ones he had smuggled into the country in his swashbuckling museum pioneer period to elude the environment Nazis. What a pain! Sibyl had found her unconscious when she came home from school and had called 911—the shit, to traumatize their daughter like that, not to mention the consequences for himself and the museum and the entire Holocaust itself, no way she would ever get custody now, she could kiss it good-bye.

Completing his briefing to Maurice, Monty then turned with an expression of large-type pain on his face, and raised his voice like the part-time rabbi he also was, performing the pastoral duty of clarifying the rumors and gently delivering the bad news to his flock. "Word has just reached me from the United States of America that my wife, the well-known multimedia artist Honey Blank-Pincus, depressed over man's continuing inhumanity to man as exemplified by the Holocaust and other more recent genocides such as Cambodia and Rwanda and Bosnia, has attempted to take her own life, joining the great sorrowful pantheon of such eminent and distinguished figures as Walter Benjamin, Paul Celan, and Primo Levi. Fortunately, Honey's life was saved in the nick of time by fast thinking on the part of our daughter, Sibyl, but the lesson for all of us is that the Holocaust will not go away, its aftereffects remain with us, Holocaust post-traumatic stress disorder is of epidemic proportions. The barbarians have befouled the earth, strewing in their wake desolation and despair and black holes such as this planet called Auschwitz, as the survivor Ka-Tzetnik 135633 described it, in which we struggle to find meaning and a sign of God's face even today—and we are forever condemned to clean up the mess they have left behind."

Maurice nodded his approval. It was a masterful beginning, Monty was a genius, as per usual. For the sake of the museum, for the sake of the six million plus the five million others, it was not one minute too soon to begin spinning this looming scandal in the most sacred and inviolate of Holocaust threads.

The next moment, two blasts from the shofar were sounded, which Monty interpreted as the highest personal compliment, a most rewarding expression of how powerfully Koan Gilguli and the entire audience had been affected by his family tragedy and his stirring existential oratory. Instantly, everyone stood up, fluffed their *zafus*, and bowed toward the cinnabar bowl on the train tracks in the center of their circle with the ring of memorial candles surrounding it, filled with the names of the dead like a poisoned soup. With tiny steps, they began walking silently in a circle behind the roshi as he was pushed nearly soundlessly in his wheelchair by Marano, guided by Koan Gilguli. Slowly they moved around the tracks and the unloading ramp and the ring of flickering candles with the carved red bowl like a votive in the center. Their hands were clasped on their chests, their gazes focused a short distance ahead to the back of the breakable neck of the seeker in front of them, spines erect and chins drawn in, in a posture like the *zazen* from which they had just arisen. To Monty they appeared hypnotized, drugged, like sleepwalkers, but the redhead, who was beginning to bore him profoundly, told him in a whisper that this was *kinhin*—the shofar was being used here in Auschwitz instead of the traditional two strikes of the bell in the zendo to herald its commencement—he should just try to empty himself of all of his habitual egoism and follow her lead in the performance of this walking meditation. Behind him walked Maurice, humming a subversive "Hava Nagila" medley under his breath while slowly and dutifully he circle-danced as at an alien bar mitzvah. Gloria was taking mincing steps in stocking feet, hunched uncharacteristically, pressing on Marano's heels, an unguarded expression of utter grief on her face. Bunny was behind her, straining not to offend. Some distance away, Krystyna made no effort to rein in the swing of her hips in her tight leather miniskirt as she tottered in the mud on her stiletto heels, balancing herself with the weights of Gloria's two shopping bags, which she would not under any circumstances leave on the ground, only a naive American could believe they wouldn't be stolen. Not far behind her came Norman, marching morosely in the circle, his hands clasped over the helmet, like a malignancy on his heart.

Reb Tikkun from the Shtetls made his way to the cinnabar bowl on its rosewood base in the center of the circle and took out a page of names. He began to read: Aronowicz, Nina, age twelve—Auschwitz. Bulka, Albert, age four—Auschwitz. Friedler, Lucienne, age five—Auschwitz. Goldberg, Henri-Chaim, age thirteen—Auschwitz. Halpern, Georges, age eight—Auschwitz. Krochmal, Renate, age eight—Auschwitz. Mermelstein, Marcel, age seven—Auschwitz. Spiegel, Martha, age ten—Auschwitz. Wertheimer, Otto, age twelve—Auschwitz.

When he completed his recitation, there was again the liquid silence of the quest for inner collectedness accented by the soft brushing of feet as they continued to circle in walking meditation. In the middle of this silken silence Gloria was moved to speak. "This is for all the children of Auschwitz," she said. She began to sing off-key in the thin creaking voice of an old woman. "Hush little baby don't you say a word"—it was the only lullaby she could remember—"Mama's gonna buy you a something-something."

And after that, it was all la, la, la.

PART THREE

Lessons of the Holocaust

1

THE TAKEOVER OF THE UNITED STATES Holocaust Memorial Museum in Washington, D.C., began a short time after noon on a Tuesday in late August, the hottest recorded day of the debut decade of the new millennium. A large crowd consisting primarily of advance-ticketed visitors to the museum, mostly tour groups of captive black and Latino kids in shorts and tank tops from summer schools, camps, and other assorted enrichment and holding programs, but also conscientious local citizens driven to come out specifically for this event even in the humidity of the capital's sublimated swampland, was standing in the Hall of Witness at the foot of the grand staircase for a public rally to "express outrage and reject silence" concerning the Tibetan Holocaust. Maurice Messer had pulled every possible string to engineer an appearance at this program by the Dalai Lama himself—"a close personal friend from mine," he confided. "When I first heard his name I thought he was maybe some kind of camel or something," he added off the record when it became clear that his holiness would not materialize. Years earlier, Maurice had escorted this simple Buddhist monk, as he called himself—"a public relations genius and fund raiser par excellence," Maurice had pronounced him—on a VIP tour through the three floors of the museum's permanent exhibition amid a bracing sauna of media bulbs. Afterward, blinking in unison as they emerged on the Raoul Wallenberg Place side of the building, on the Eisenhower Plaza near the abstract

Loss and Regeneration sculpture, the chairman and the spiritual leader—in his "trademark one-sleeved toga number," as Blanche had put it at breakfast the next morning, gazing down through her half-moon glasses perched on the tip of her nose at the front-page photo above the fold from which her Maurice had been cropped—had issued a joint statement declaring that the Holocaust is redeemed through the lessons it teaches.

This time, though, a functionary from the Tibetan government-in-exile had advised the museum's external affairs and special events and press and public relations offices that, regrettably, his holiness would be cloistered at a Buddhist retreat on Martha's Vineyard throughout the summer, at the beachfront estate, as it happened, of the museum's backup choice as guest of honor for this rally, who would unfortunately obviously also not be available, "that movie actor, what's-his-name, you know, that *alter cocker* Buddhist, the one mit the gray hair and the little squinty eyes mit the wrinkles or the crinkles you might call them on a good day who always gets all the young chiclets, God alone knows what they see in him. Tell me something," Maurice simply could not hold back this outpouring of his frustration and disgust, "is it strictly kosher for an ort'odox Buddhist to be shtupping all the time mit the opposite gender?"

All Maurice got personally for knocking himself out like this for the Tibetans was a memo from the White House assuring him that the president looked forward to supporting his reappointment as museum chairman in the coming year attached to a letter from the embassy of the People's Republic of China at Kalorama Circle protesting the Tibetan Holocaust program and the slurs it cast on China, upon receipt of which Maurice had his secretary immediately fax to the Oval Office, with a copy to the Chinese embassy, a first draft hastily put together by Monty's team of an announcement of a Chinese Holocaust program scheduled for the thirteenth of the coming December, the anniversary of the day in 1937 when the Rape of Nanking by the Japanese began, which, as Maurice very well knew, would provoke an outcry from the Japanese embassy on Massachusetts Avenue demanding a program for the Japanese Holocaust on the anniversary of the bombing of Hiroshima. Well, there was no way in hell Maurice was going there, no way he was going to fire up U.S. veterans and patriots by getting his museum mixed up in some atomic bombshell Japan-versus-America moral equivalency controversy like what happened when his friends and neighbors on the Mall, the Air and Space Museum of the Smithsonian Institution, put up its *Enola Gay* exhibit with a script giving equal time to the Japanese on the bombing of Hiroshima by that U.S. B-29, and the American right wing went ballistic. No, Maurice had his principles, that's where he drew the line. Hitler's Axis partner would get a program in his museum only over his own dead body. To hell with the Japanese. Still, what did he get from the Tibetans for knocking himself out like this? Did these little climbing monks have any conception at all of what is required in terms of organizational infrastructure and financial outlays to raise a voice of conscience in this way? The sad truth was that all they got by way of appreciation from the Tibetans was an anorexic Jewish girl with little round glasses from Scarsdale, the casualty of a lifetime of enrichment overscheduling from tap dance to French horn to lacrosse, who, probably in fulfillment of her so-called volunteer community service requirement for high school graduation, to the indiscriminate applause of the audience, had just read a letter in the name of the Tibetan government-in-exile in Dharamsala acknowledging the lessons to be

learned from Jewish survival strategies in the face of persecution and Diaspora, and thanking the Holocaust.

As far as Maurice knew, to his utter disgust, when he had
opened the rally in the Hall of Witness with a short but powerful speech welcoming the "Members from Congress and the
Diplomatic Corpse, Fellow Partisan Fighters and Survivors,
Mine Fellow Americans," the highest-ranking official present
was Abu Shahid, minister of jihad of the extremist Palestinian
organization From the River to the Sea (FRS), now tugging
his luxuriant black mustache frosted with silver or working
his string of carnelian worry beads and perfecting the drape
of his red-checked kaffiyeh over his Armani suit jacket as he
sat through the ceremony in the place of honor accorded him
beside Maurice, on special chairs set up on the landing of the
grand staircase that served as the stage. Nor had it escaped
Maurice's notice that all through his speech this oiled Omar
Sharif clone had rudely and inconsiderately conferred with an
aide whom he had introduced as his chief of staff, a distract-
ingly stunning woman, as it happened, not quite young any
longer but still devastatingly gorgeous, dressed in full military
fatigues, leather boots, and a bandolier of cartridges like a
beauty queen sash crossing her size thirty-six C bust—Maurice
had eyeballed her as a professional from his years in the foundation business. In a patronizing British accent, she had informed
the security guards as she sailed past the metal detectors into
the museum alongside her boss that her outfit was an ethnic
diversity guerrilla-theater folk costume, and were they to discriminate against it by barring her entry, they would be doing
so at the risk of massive civil-liberties and human-rights violation litigation; in any case, couldn't they see, the idiots, that she
had no weapon, she added, raising her empty hands to highlight

the curves of her body and pirouetting, dizzying them all with her otherworldly lusciousness, like a promised reward only in paradise. Persuaded, Maurice nodded permission and waved her in. And this was how they thanked him, with complete lack of attention during his important remarks, leaning over and consulting each other with mouths so intimately close that their breaths mingled in public, talking throughout Maurice's entire presentation and stopping only when he finished, just the way Monty always did? It was one of Monty's least attractive habits, by the way, by no means something to emulate, Maurice could certainly do without it, thank you very much, it drove him crazy. Yet also, despite himself, a part of him interpreted this style of regal disdain and contempt as a sign of superiority, perhaps because it so particularly identified Monty, for whom he still maintained such a passion and such regard, leading him to privately parse such behavior as the mark of a chosen and blessed breed who are above listening, who are excused from the common courtesies due to their special election, the higher sphere they inhabited.

It was Monty, in fact, who had written this speech, as he wrote all the others—or, more precisely, the speech was a product of Monty's shop, from a boilerplate drawn up years ago, probably by Honey, tailored for each specific occasion such as this Tibetan Holocaust program by one of his cute little interns the age of his daughter, Sibyl, since, following his filthy divorce, Monty no longer had Honey to do the ghostwriting for him. Providing speeches was one of Monty's responsibilities as Maurice's chief of staff, the job he had been given as a consolation prize after that whole mess, when he had found out through a press release that Bunny Bacon had been named director of the museum. Rattling drunk, he had showed up after midnight, banging on the door of Maurice's suite at the Four Seasons hotel, threatening to destroy him together with the entire museum and the whole goddamn Holocaust by leaking everything to the media, every sordid scrap, which he not only had filed away in his head but about which he also had in his possession real documentation in black and white and on tape, both video and audio, the least being the data on the unsavory acts they had been required to perform re that geriatric Zelda Knecht, White House liaison to the Jewish community, to get Maurice named chairman.

"Chief of staff?" Monty had wailed when Maurice had made this compensatory offer. "Are you out of your fucking mind? You know what you can do with your fucking chief of staff?" In vain had Maurice struggled to convince him that while he, Monty, had a life and above all the blessing of a family, of children, Bunny was alone, she had nothing—nothing! She needed the job far more than he did to give her something resembling a purpose on this earth. "What for you need this headache?" Maurice had tried to rationalize with him. In the end, though, Monty had been placated with the promise of complete independence as Maurice's chief of staff, minimal duties along with a bloated staff to carry them out, the unlimited pro bono services of a museum lawyer in his divorce case, and then the deal clincher, a salary in the stratospheric six figures, which Maurice had to squeeze out annually from private donations rather than federal appropriations to avoid a major whopper of a scandal, justifying the expenditure in a top-secret confidential behind-closed-doors executive session of the council's Politics and Perks Committee with the cry, "I need him, I need him for mine work, the six million need him, Jewish survival needs him!" That was also the cry he would raise each time some constipated federal GS–7 stickler bureaucrat caught Monty falsifying his expense account records, claiming reimbursement, for example, for a four-star business lunch at Galileo's or Gerard's Place with a representative of the Anti-Defamation League or the Pentagon or a similar gourmet type, when actually he had dined there for three hours of applied personal orientation with the newest female Holocaust hire not hopelessly hideous under age twenty-five, who then staggered back to the office to buckshot the details to all of her friends and family via e-mail. "I'm telling you, I need him," Maurice would cry on those occasions of looming exposure as well. "Don't worry! I'll take care from him. I'll take the boy behind the woodshed and give him a few good *potches*."

But for all his tragic heroic flaws, this time, too, Monty had created a brilliant product customized for the Tibetan Holocaust program. When Maurice returned to his seat after delivering the speech, Abu Shahid leaned over cordially and the two men shook their equally fastidiously manicured hands as the jihad minister, in a gonadic voice deepened even more by a lifetime of smoking, like the late lamented King Hussein's of Jordan, muttered, "Excellent, first-rate—truly inspiring!" And it *was* inspiring, Maurice could not but agree, even if he had to say so himself, even if this cold sensualist had not listened to a single word—about the lessons of the Holocaust, "learning from the past for the sake of the future," that brilliant motto coined by Monty one ordinary Sunday morning while casually shopping for brunch items at the Georgetown Safeway with Joy something-or-other who covered museums for the Style section of the *Washington Post* at the time, and he had noticed in the gourmet freezer a package of lox produced by some venerable smoked-fish company with the slogan "Emulating the past to preserve the future," to which he gave a creative little Holocaust twist, and—voilà! As Maurice now proclaimed to all the assembled concerning the lessons of the Holocaust, "irregardless of what we suffered and lost from this horror of horrors, in the end made it all wort'while." Those lessons, he elaborated, were many and rich, but the one we must take to heart now, the one that history and memory and conscience demand of us and teach us so compellingly, is that it is ethically and morally unconscionable to remain silent bystanders in the face of the Tibetan genocide. History, memory, conscience, ethical, moral—"peepee words," was how Norman characterized them to Maurice not long after the poor nebbish had been passed over for the directorship, "pieties and platitudes." But for Maurice they were juicy words, words that never failed to thrill, they were all-purpose words that formed a great pool into which you could dip, and however many times you dipped, you always came up looking refreshed and good.

Maurice definitely looked good this sizzling noon in the Hall of Witness, even with the cutting-edge air-conditioning system pumping desperately and increasingly futilely against the massed body heat. And the fact was, if Maurice looked good, the museum looked good, the Holocaust looked good, which was the bottom line, after all, the reason he was still going full blast on borrowed time—he was driven, he was obsessed, pushing on day and night, never resting even now, well past his allotted three score and ten, well beyond the paltry number of years doled out to his luckless and, let's face it, less resourceful companions in the shtetl of his boyhood. Too bad Monty wasn't here to witness his performance today, Maurice reflected, he would have been very proud of his handiwork, he would have been very gratified indeed, though probably the boy was just doing his job outside in the pendulous humidity; despite his wise-guy image, deep down there was nobody more loyal and dedicated than Monty. Most likely he had gone across the street, to the National Park Service grassy knoll on the other side of Raoul Wallenberg Place where that useless gang of protesters was penned behind barriers, to try to keep them from buttonholing the media and agitating the crowd streaming in, in solidarity with the Tibetans.

Maurice didn't even have to bother to glance out of the window of the red brick administration building that morning to know who was already yelling out there bright and early with the roosters and the cock-a-doodles—the usual suspects, naturally, that *yutz*, Herzl Lieb, Leon's crazy rabble-rousing son, a rabbi no less, recklessly attacking in front of all the goyim this sacred temple of his own people in the Diaspora, a fringe character if ever there was one, along with two of his sidekicks, those *alter cockers* who might, you never know, finally *cholesh* from the heat once and for all, it was time already, Maurice's enemies from the hair wars during the formative years of the museum, those so called survivors, Lipman Krakowski and Henny Soskis. You could count on these three stooges to show up like clockwork, screaming their heads off and waving their signs and shoving their flyers into the face of every passerby whenever Maurice invited another Arab such as this Shahid fellow to the museum as his personal guest as an element of his Teach a Terrorist program, or whenever he presumed to give the persecution of another people, such as these pathetic Tibetans, equal time as part of his You-Too-Can-Prevent-a-Holocaust initiative. This was a lucky day for Herzl and his cronies, they had scored a double whammy, the Tibetans and the Arabs in a single shot, two birds with one stone, yelling bloody murder

for all they were worth like the world was coming to an end.
How dare you invite Jew killers and Holocaust deniers into
the shrine to Hitler's victims! How dare you undermine the
uniqueness of the Shoah by implied comparisons! We are out-
raged! We are shocked! Shame, shame!

Maurice was not moved. What did these naive troublemak-
ing nothings know of the kinds of pressures that are exerted
on someone in his position, especially the pressure to maintain
such a fine balance between the museum's mission to memori-
alize the Jewish dead and the priceless federal mandate, with all
the advantages it conferred in terms of status, prestige, power,
funding, visibility, location, location, location, and on and on,
not to mention the annual Days of Remembrance ceremony in
the Capitol rotunda itself, with that tasteful display of pomp
and pageantry—the presentation of the flags and the colors as
the U.S. Army Band (Pershing's Own) played the processional,
and then that singing sergeant first-class in her military suit
skimming her shapely figure, who gave every donor and survivor a richly deserved hard-on when she belted out not only the
national anthem but especially "Es Brent," that heartrending
lament on the burning shtetls, in the original Yiddish no less. It
was phenomenal, unbelievable! Who would ever have thought
that the Jewish people would have been kept alive and sustained
to reach such a moment? As far as Maurice was concerned,
instead of screaming and hollering, we should open our prayer
books to page sixteen and bow our heads in gratitude, every
male member should stand up as the cantor leads the congregation in a recitation of the blessing of a "Shehechiyanu." Which
other ethnic group in America could claim such an affirmation
of its tragedy, in the Capitol rotunda no less? Why the Jews?
Why not your so-called Native Americans, or your so-called

African-Americans? Because unlike those poor suckers, we weren't screwed by America—at least not yet. The truth is, the Holocaust Museum on the Mall was a testament to Jewish success and clout in America, a "Jewish power testicle," as Maurice phrased it in strictest confidence, it made the Nazi hunting office in the Justice Department, which everyone used to think was such a big hoo-hah, look like peanuts in comparison. This was not a talking point to be shared with our enemies, Maurice would have cautioned, but as he expressed it to his Blanche in the privacy of their boudoir, the museum was like a Jewish fist in the world's eye, like, you should pardon me, a proud circumcised Jewish cock erect in the body politic of the country. Every prince and prime minister and president who came to Washington on a state visit was required to pass through the museum, to light a candle in the Hall of Remembrance, place a wreath at the base of the marble altar containing soil samples and God alone knows what else from the concentration camps, and bow his head solemnly, be cleansed and purified as in a *mikvah,* a ritual bath, for God's sake.

So if the price of such unprecedented power was to cloak it in the somewhat debasing but nevertheless unassailable armor of historical Jewish victimization—was that too much to pay? And if once in a while the White House or the State Department or another branch or big shot requests a favor for diplomatic or other high-level purposes touching on international or national affairs, to escort a visiting foreign dictator, let's say, or a documented mass murderer or a local racist or your constituency's favorite anti-Semite through the exhibition and give him the VIP treatment—what was the big deal? Didn't the government have a right to expect some return on its investment? Who is hurt if some fascist gets a peek at the Ringelblum milk can in which the archives of the Warsaw Ghetto were hidden, or a brief tutorial about the scale model of Jews being processed through the gas chambers and crematoria? The payoff in terms of publicity and recognition for the institution, for the Holocaust itself, was incalculable. Furthermore—who could say?—maybe, just maybe, your average war criminal would have a conversion episode on the spot as he was led through one of the tower rooms, for example, and his attention was pedagogically drawn to the display of the shoes of the victims of the Majdanek death camp, or to the prewar photographs of the Jews of the Lithuanian town of Eiszyszki, celebrating birthdays and mugging for the camera like normal human beings who believed they had their lives under control, that everything was all right, almost all thirty-five hundred of them slaughtered in two days by mobile killing squads. Even a despot has a heart and a mother or maybe a dog or at least a goldfish that he loves, even for someone who committed crimes against humanity such wrenching sights can be life-altering, even a universally despised creature is capable of learning the lessons of the Holocaust and becoming a better person if only somebody out there cares enough to provide him with a little personal attention and quality time. Maurice regarded this as one of his sacred missions, his personal Sponsor a Sociopath campaign, and he subscribed to it not because he was afraid he would not be reappointed chairman if he refused a high-level government request, God forbid, and not because he enjoyed rubbing shoulders with big shots, even if they were bloodstained, but rather because he sincerely believed in the possibility for change through education and enlightenment. The honor that would reflect on the museum dead from an atonement moment by an instantly reformed tyrant would be incalculable. Instead of being desecrated, as the protesters mindlessly chanted like a broken record, the six million would be sanctified, they would be blessed, their suffering and torment would acquire purpose, the Holocaust would have meaning.

Education—that's what it was all about, "to capture the hearts and minds of the people," as Maurice liked to say. And it was not just a matter of educating those willing pupils who sign up on their own for the grueling three-hour text-intensive narrative tour of the museum, from Nazi Assault to Final Solution to Last Chapter, from harbingers to horror to healing, savoring the well-deserved reward of a cathartic, side-of-the-good cry at the end as they watch the heartwarming survivor testimony films with endless boxes of Kleenex thoughtfully provided by the management, and then proceed to the hexagonal Hall of Remembrance, like a triumphant Star of David, for a moment of reflection, to light a memorial candle, and to hum "God Bless America" as they gaze out the tall, narrow window at that mighty American phallus known as the Washington Monument, their appreciation of the bounty of liberty and democracy newly strengthened and revitalized—which is why, by the way, of all the museums on the Mall, this one was the most American, believe it or not, its funding most justified, Congress should just shut up already and give it the money. No, above all, the museum's task, in Maurice's view, was to educate the difficult cases, the students with the bad attitudes, the students who do not work and play well with others, the students who get a zero in conduct, cunning perfumed Arabs like this minister of jihad, Abu Shahid, for example, who out of ignorance or perhaps an understandable interest in advancing their own cause claim that the entire Holocaust is a lie, an exaggerated Jewish yarn, sly propaganda fabricated by malodorous

Jews and Zionists to gain the sympathy of world opinion, to blackmail the powerful nations in support of Israel. *These* were the visitors that Maurice was targeting in his Teach a Terrorist program—specimens labeled by the unimaginative as beyond redemption, for example, Osama, or Saddam, or the late Yasser ("a sweetie pie, a pussycat," as Blanche pronounced him after shaking his hand as he stepped out of the men's room during a White House reception), and others like them, and yes, also this lesser-known figure, this Abu Shahid of the FRS, From the River to the Sea, which Maurice very well knew stood for the Jordan River to the Mediterranean Sea—stood for a Palestinian state with borders that would mean the end of an Israel that was the only sure refuge for Jews in the event of another Holocaust.

But Maurice was not afraid. He was never afraid, as he always proclaimed; it would have been the motto on his coat of arms, had he had one. For the sake of peace it was necessary to take risks; peace would be the crowning achievement of his career. Yes, despite the protests and the threats and the abuse, he would invite Osama and Saddam, "mit joy in mine heart," he would invite them—and Mr. Kim Jong Il, too, send him over, Maurice was not afraid—give them the VIP tour of the museum just as soon as the State Department for whatever reasons begins the inevitable rehabilitation process and lets them into the country, and certainly the repackaged Yasser after he got his makeover job would have been welcome to the museum any time as Maurice's personal guest, he would have had a standing open invitation. Maurice would have walked Yasser through the railway car on the third floor of the museum, just like the one in which as many as one hundred Jews at a time would be packed like sardines and shipped to the death camps. He would have brought him out face-to-face with the photo mural of the dazed men, women, and children just unloaded from the train, lined up for processing and selection, funneled to be murdered in the gas chambers or to be imprisoned and enslaved—arbitrarily to have their lives protracted temporarily or by a whim to die at once. He would have pointed to these lethal pictures, this undeniable evidence, and in a mighty voice trembling with emotion he would have cried, "This, *this* is why we need Israel!" Yasser's eyes would have opened wide with instant understanding and recognition, in a life-altering epiphany. The lessons of the Holocaust would have sunk in at last. In front of all the assembled—diplomats, distinguished guests, and media—he would have wept copiously, declaring that he now believes in the Holocaust, and vowing to change his ways. He and Maurice would have embraced with overwhelming feeling. The photo of the two of them bonding through clasped hands would have been splashed across the front page of every newspaper on the planet. And the Middle East problem would have been solved once and for all.

The fact that this Shahid fellow strode through the railcar that morning as if it were nothing more than some kind of shortcut to get to the other side on the traffic-controlled tour route through the storyline exhibition was inconsequential. He was not a major player in any case, merely a two-bit commander of a small squad of marginal suicide bombers. He was impeccably polite throughout the tour, of course, it was hard to believe he moonlighted as a killer, nodding courteously whenever Maurice or Bunny or Monty or another senior staff member who made up the escorting entourage took a moment to point something out, but he did not seem to be particularly engaged until they came to the narrow passage-

way where the monitors were located displaying atrocities
behind "privacy walls" to shield children from the violent
images. Pushing imperiously through a large clump of kids
yelling "Ooh, Neat! Cool! Awesome!" as they squeezed up
against each other and stretched on their toes over the pro-
tective barrier to get a peek, as in an X-rated video booth,
of naked Jews being tortured or raped or murdered, he stationed himself in front of one of the monitors and watched
for a long time. It was a silent film taken by an Einsatzgruppen
Nazi, showing Jews being positioned by mobile killing unit
officers for execution at the edge of a ditch—and then a dog
would begin to run around frantically. Clearly, the jihad minister had figured out that a shot had been fired, because each
time the dog was set off, Abu Shahid gave a start, as if he'd
heard a bang. When he had had his fill of watching the dog go
berserk and the victims fall over and die, and die yet again, he
turned to his hosts with glazed eyes and commented, "Fascinating, yes fascinating!" After that, they had to rush through
the rest of the exhibition, because of the scheduled Tibetan
Holocaust program at noon, but Maurice nevertheless took
a moment, as he did with every visiting dignitary, to stop in
front of the resistance segment on the second floor to recount
his experiences as a "leader from the partisans who fought
against the Nazis in the woods," stroking the side of his leg
as he described his precious tommy gun, which he had kept
pressed against his body throughout the war as he slept in
the forest at night. "So you were a guerrilla fighter too," Abu
Shahid said, "just like me." "No, no," Maurice replied, taken
aback for a moment, a rare event for him. "Ah, but you're just
being modest," the minister of jihad said, displaying his long
tobacco-stained teeth in a smile like a camel's. "Of course you

can't deny you were a guerrilla fighter, just as you can't deny there was a Holocaust."

And this playboy was the fellow who was provoking that uproar outside? Please! Save your fire, Maurice the veteran operator would have counseled Herzl and his perspiring senior citizens across the street, save it for the really big fish. What amateurs like Herzl Lieb and his merry pranksters failed to understand, no matter how many times you tried to drill it through their thick skulls, was that this was not a Jewish museum. It was a federal institution—or, at the very least, it was in everyone's interest to maintain that perception, and especially in the interest of the American Jewish community. Yet even so, if there was one thing that Maurice had learned in his years as chairman—may they go on in good health to one hundred and twenty!—it was that no matter what the damage to the well-being and survival of the institution, there was nothing like a perceived slur or threat to Israel to flush the Jewish hotheads out of their holes—that, and even the implied blasphemy that the Jewish Holocaust was in any way not unique, that it was not the mother of all Holocausts, that some other atrocity or genocide or horror or injustice could in any way be compared to it. The first transgression went under the euphemism of politicization, the second was called universalization. Well, this was a subject that Maurice knew a thing or two about. If you were too precious for politics, you should get the hell out of this town. And if you were a uniquist, a Holocaust purist, too proud and possessive to share the wealth and selectively universalize your Holocaust a little bit when necessary—to stamp an atrocity such as Kosovo, for example, with the moral seal of the Holocaust, or conversely, as in the case of Rwanda, to withhold that seal, depending on what was at stake and the interests involved—then you might as well pack up and close shop for good. Without universalization there would be no lessons, no payoff. There would be no point to the museum. The Holocaust would have been a total waste.

*

Bunny was definitely a universalist, Maurice reflected, as he observed her now standing behind the opulent wooden lectern emblazoned with the museum seal, reading her remarks for the Tibetan Holocaust program, benumbed with beta-blockers and Valium prescribed by her shrink for stage fright, while he, Maurice, had never in his life experienced even a tremor of fear engendered by public speaking. Indeed, as Bunny took the liberty of commenting affectionately even within his earshot, Maurice had never met a microphone he did not want to make love to. In general terms, this was true, Maurice admitted it proudly. However, he wanted to make it absolutely clear that he did not enjoy public speaking for his own glory or honor, God forbid, but rather one hundred percent for the sake of the six million. In Maurice's opinion, the obligation of the world to listen to him now, an old survivor with a chopped-liver accent and gefilte-fish grammar, like private family smells not meant to be aired in public—for the world to be condemned to listen to him going on at length even in the rotunda of the United States Capitol itself during the Days of Remembrance ceremony broadcast throughout the entire world on C-Span—was nothing less than just reparations to be exacted from those who had stood by and turned a deaf ear as the Jews of Europe cried out to be heard. You didn't listen to us then, you rotten no-goodniks, you didn't pay attention while it was happening—now you will pay attention with interest, you will damned well listen now, now we will grate your ears raw with the Holocaust until you fall to your knees and beg for mercy, we will never shut up. Mostly Bunny let him go on to his heart's content, she humored him that way, but when it was an occasion that "really really mattered," such as the annual event in the Capitol, for instance, she would tear through the drafts of his speeches ruthlessly, slashing away promiscuously at Monty's prose. "Not dignified, not dignified," she would mutter. "Too Jewish, too Jewish!" There was no denying it, the lady was a card-carrying member of the universalist party.

Maurice only half listened now as Bunny pounded away at her usual universalist theme—the "others," the non-Jews targeted by the Nazis, launching into her well-rubbed laundry list, starting with the "Roma," pedantically emphasizing *Roma* as the only acceptable usage, "formerly known as 'Gypsies,' " she added by way of necessary clarification though she recoiled from uttering that taboo word, then on down to political prisoners, Freemasons, Jehovah's Witnesses, Soviet prisoners of war, political dissenters, homosexuals, the handicapped and disabled—"Useless eaters, as far as the Nazis were concerned, useless eaters all," she declared. She glanced furtively at Mickey Fisher-roshi in his wheelchair, already planted on the stage like an overgrown potted bush; the Zen monk was the guest speaker they had had to settle for in the end for this Tibetan Holocaust program. Between the two of them, Maurice noted, between those two big-eating *fressers,* Bunny and the guru, they must have put on the weight of about a medium-sized goat since they had first met at Auschwitz. It had been quite a spectacle, before the program began, to watch four black linebacker security guards, together weighing in at over half a ton, huffing and puffing, polished to mahogany by the sweat that was pouring down their faces, as they carried Fisher in a kind of improvised palanquin up the flight of stairs to the landing that served as the stage, with his chief of staff, Koan Gilguli, shuffling along behind lugging the wheelchair, and bringing up the rear, Leon's problem daughter in her Buddhist nun's getup and shaven head and little round glasses, Rama, as she now called herself, along with her twins, Rumi and Rumi, already at least four years old, nobody knew if they were male or female or both, it was rumored that even the mother had requested not to be told.

As for Bunny, it registered on Maurice that she was now even more "broad from the beam" than she had been during her Holocaust deflowering on the Auschwitz junket, which was why, as Blanche explained to him, letting him in on a harmless little feminine subterfuge, she wore those long suit jackets, "to camouflage the chassis," in food colors like eggplant, raisin, chocolate, or wine, her personal interpretation of the professional woman's executive uniform. Bunny was dressed in one of those outfits today, in a *cholent* color, Maurice would have described it, since it reminded him of the heavy meat and bean and potato stew that used to sit simmering on the stove for twenty-four hours that his mother would ladle out for Sabbath lunch. Pinned to her lapel, as always, was that diamond and ruby brooch in the shape of a royal crown, like her badge of office, the daytime version of the tiara she wore in her lank dark hair at black-tie evening functions, to symbolize her ascension to the role of a self-styled latter-day Queen Esther, a Jewess with enough balls to speak up on behalf of her people against the anti-Semites, especially against Holocaust deniers, which Bunny had made her specialty, her pet project, even going so far as to advocate that laws be put on the books making Holocaust denial illegal, thereby, in Monty's opinion, not only threatening free speech and civil liberties, so critical to Jewish survival in the Diaspora, but also shunting these crackpot and kook deniers from the lunatic fringe to center stage.

"Queen Esther?" Monty had sneered. "More like Cleopatra, Queen of De-Ni'al—minus the sex appeal, of course." For as Rabbi Monty reminded Maurice with respect to the Esther story, the real queen was also a dish, marinated six months in fragrant oils and six months in spices, the pièce de résistance of the Persian harem. That, however, was the racy part of the story with which Bunny did not identify, the sexist part that she rejected on principle. She explained all this one night to Krystyna by the light of a sandalwood-scented candle on the terrace overlooking the Potomac River of the Watergate apartment that they shared, which her mother had bought for her around the time she ascended to the directorship of the Holocaust, and which she justified on the grounds that, as she put it, "I do genocide all day, at night I deserve to be nice to myself." With respect to the Esther story, however, as she told Krystyna, it was the speaking-up part that spoke to her. Her inner Queen Esther could not in conscience remain silent, especially on the subject of deniers. It was precisely for a crisis of this sort—the epidemic of historical revisionism, the plague of Holocaust denial—that she had reached the perilous throne. "And if I perish," she added selflessly, "I perish." Of course, in the case of Abu Shahid and others like him targeted by Maurice's Teach a Terrorist program, she told Krystyna, there was a competing human rights imperative that obliged her to hold back and refrain from speaking out against them, because when you considered the persecution and humiliation that the Palestinian people had endured at the hands of the Zionists, the motivation behind their Holocaust denial—to undermine the right of Israel to exist—was not only understandable, it was, in the end, forgivable. And even the Palestinians who conceded that there might have been a Holocaust really really had a point when they insisted that *they* after all were not the ones who were responsible; they didn't do it, the Germans did it, for God's sake—so why should their land be stolen, why should they suffer? Oh, Israel was such a pain in the neck; it really really got in the way of orderly Holocaust programming. And to top it all off, it was such an unsafe place, Bunny wished it would just go away, at the slightest hint of a crisis she automatically banned travel to that live volcano by all staff members. But when it came to the matter of the Palestinians, she insisted, all that was required was a little education. With a little education, the Palestinians would not only learn about the Holocaust and its lessons, but even more important for their cause, they would come to appreciate how they might creatively channel and shape and control the narrative for their own advancement.

From the landing where he was sitting next to Abu Shahid, Maurice had a direct view of the top of Krystyna's head as she leaned against the railing halfway down the flight of stairs between the improvised stage and the long expanse of the Hall of Witness where the crowd stood listening to Bunny. He could follow the straight part in her flaxen hair like a row in a Polish wheat field, her hairstyle vastly subdued since Bunny had taken her in hand, sponsoring her as a protégée and making her her chief of staff. Everyone and his uncle has a chief of staff these days, Maurice reflected—Bunny, this Abu Shahid guy, and even he himself, the Honorable Maurice Messer, for his sins. Without a chief of staff, you were a nothing. Over Krystyna's shoulder, Maurice could see, was slung that famous tote bag containing Bunny's essential supplies, most notoriously the DustBuster—

in case, while making her daily directorial inspection rounds through the museum, Bunny noticed a telltale pile of dirt or litter in a corner that required a quick vacuuming job. She was "seriously anal," as Norman had painstakingly explained to his father, a disgusting modern concept when you visualized it that unfortunately seemed to fit, "an obsessive-compulsive control freak," Norman said—Dust Bunny, the staff called her, not to her face, of course. Rummaging among the equipment in that tote bag for a stick of gum that she needed to chew full-time now that Bunny had forced her to give up smoking, Krystyna abruptly looked up with concern during what seemed to be far too long a pause in the speech—the gap was not lost on Maurice either—as if Bunny had suddenly grown confused and lost her place just as she was coming to the end of her account of the Nazi euthanasia program and the fate of those "other" victims—the disabled, the paralyzed, the syphilitic, the retarded, the mentally ill, the demented, the senile—eliminated, Bunny intoned in a rhetorical refrain, as "life unworthy of life, useless eaters, useless eaters all."

These were the very words she had used at dinner the previous evening, Krystyna recalled—useless eaters, life unworthy of life—when she had disclosed that she had authorized the staff at the Parklawn nursing home in which her stepfather, Leon Lieb, was still a silent partner even after the scandals, to stop all feeding of her mother. Setting down her glass of chardonnay, she added pointedly, "It's not like a Holocaust thing, you know. It's not like I'm some kind of Nazi and my mom's a useless eater or life unworthy of life or something like that. I definitely know the lessons of the Holocaust, but this is different, this is a quality-of-life issue—you see what I'm saying? Basically, what it all boils down to is that my mom just needs

a bit of help from all of us who care about her in order to give
herself permission to move on." She expected that her mother
would expire sometime the next day, she told Krystyna. That
was the timetable she had been given by the professionals now
that the feeding had been stopped totally. She had been advised
by the head nurse that Gloria was phasing in and out of coma.
She intended to catch the shuttle to New York right after the
Tibetan Holocaust program tomorrow, she said, in order to be
at her mother's side for as long as her schedule permitted. Of
course, as Krystyna was aware, she needed to be back at the
museum by ten o'clock Wednesday morning for the monthly
meeting of the Politics and Perks Committee, so if Gloria
took her sweet time and did not pass before say, seven a.m. on
Wednesday morning at the very latest, well, Bunny would just
have to say her good-byes and leave. In any case, knowing her
mom as well as she did, Bunny was certain that Gloria would
prefer to be alone for her final moment, her preference would
definitely be to have her own space in which to die. Gloria was
such a private person, after all, and dying was really really such
a private and personal act, like going to the bathroom or looking in a mirror. You didn't want anyone else watching while
you did it. It was something you did when you were alone.
Only the condemned died in public.

   Yes, it had probably been that summoning up of those Nazi
classifications—useless eaters, life unworthy of life—specifically in reference to the demented and the senile, that had
shaken Bunny so, Krystyna was convinced, evoking a disturbing image of her mother dying of starvation in the nursing
home bed even as she, Bunny, was speaking before this Tibetan
Holocaust audience. It was this vision that must have floated
before Bunny's eyes as she spoke those words, causing her to

fumble for a moment. But she was back on track again, thank goodness, moving right along toward the finale of her speech, about how we must all learn from the Holocaust the lesson that silence is intolerable, that complacency is not permissible as the Tibetan people face extinction along with their heavenly bird, the black-necked crane. As moral and ethical human beings, we owe it to history, to memory, to conscience, and to the eleven million victims—the six million Jews and the five million others—to raise our voices and cry out against the Tibetan Holocaust and the Holocaust of the Black-Necked Crane.

Krystyna was sincerely relieved that Bunny had recovered her bearings and made it to the end of her remarks. The whole business with her mother had been an awful drain. It had dragged her down, especially after Gloria's husband Leon had thrown up his hands and declared, "I'm sorry, I can't deal with another sick wife," and dumped the whole problem in Bunny's lap—and he was supposed to be a rabbi and a Holocaust survivor, of all things. Though his own daughter Rama, as she now insisted upon being called, who had been reconciled with her father after the Auschwitz camp reunion by Gloria no less, had sought to chasten him with her pronouncement that sick wives were his karma, he had probably been a gynecologist or an abortionist or a female genital mutilator in one of his previous incarnations, he had just better accept his place on the wheel of life, Leon had bailed out, literally moved from the Fifth Avenue duplex back to his old apartment on Riverside Drive in which he had lived with his first wife, Rose, handing the entire mess over to Bunny.

And it was a mess, Krystyna reflected, shaking her head. Gloria's decline beginning soon after her return from Auschwitz was shocking. It seemed, at first, almost selfishly purposeful and intentional, almost like a case of gross self-indulgence. Bunny had been furious. Until she finally found a doctor who would sign off on a diagnosis of Alzheimer's or, at the very least, dementia, Bunny could not forgive her mother for what she interpreted as cold abandonment and neglect, just like what had happened to poor little Binjamin Wilkormirski in his memoir, which she had no doubt, though she knew very well that some spiteful people now regarded it as a pathological fantasy and a fraud, was truer than true; she and Krystyna still maintained the ritual of reading a passage out loud from its pages each and every night, faithfully, at bedtime. With no consideration whatsoever for Bunny's needs or feelings, shortly after she came home from Auschwitz, Gloria totally and almost maliciously gave up taking care of herself. She began to eat desperately, as if she had herself been a victim of starvation in the camps and had just been liberated, anything she could lay her hands on she ate, from morning to night, never pausing through all of her waking hours. She was never without food in her mouth, as if there were no tomorrow and yesterday had all been deprivation. Bunny was obliged to dispatch Krystyna to secondhand thrift shops to purchase extra-large T-shirts for Gloria and polyester skirts with elastic waistbands. It was astonishing to witness this once supremely elegant and impeccably groomed woman wearing a purple shirt from a rock concert stamped with the logo of a forgotten band called Brain Dead, strands of gray hair wilting around her bloated face. The only personal item she held on to, struggling ferociously to assert her claim to it even while being bathed by her caretakers or manipulated by licensed health care providers or when the Chinese herbalist and acupuncturist brought over by Marano attempted to apply three fingers to her pulse for diagnostic purposes, to pinpoint exactly where the flow of vital energy from the bodily organs had become unbalanced or been interrupted, was a heavy charm bracelet that Marano had fashioned for her, weighted down with single earrings that had languished forlorn in her drawer when their mates were lost—To transform your losses into healing, Marano said therapeutically; to keep before me at all times a reminder of what I have lost, Gloria thought.

A little more than a year after the Auschwitz trip, following a private meeting with Maurice, the last non-family member she saw not including medical and household personnel, on the day that Bunny was installed as director of the museum in a solemn ceremony in the Hall of Remembrance by the eternal flame atop the altar filled with museum-quality soil collected from the concentration camps, Gloria stopped walking. "I'm not playing anymore," she said. Then she stopped opening her eyes. "You haven't shown me anything about the boy," she said. Finally she stopped talking, except for rare occasions, such as during one of Bunny's visits, when Gloria suddenly turned to her Filipino caretaker and inquired, "Who is that old lady, Loretta?" She must have opened her eyes for a flash to have a peek at the visitor, and unfortunately they had missed it. She also stopped feeding herself, though her devotion to eating remained as single-minded as ever. "Your mama have very good appetite," Loretta told Bunny—pints of vanilla ice cream, slabs of chocolate cake, bowls of melon and oranges, potatoes and pickles and pasta, chicken and lamb chops and loaves of crusty bread. Her teeth were phenomenal, a rich woman's teeth, the best that money could buy in dentistry; she ate voraciously. "All right already," Gloria would say, "give me another cookie." Bunny had heard this herself when she visited the Fifth Avenue duplex to observe one of the marathon feeding sessions,

Loretta cooing encouragingly, like a mother feeding her baby, opening her own mouth sympathetically as she pushed into Gloria's perpetually open mouth like a ragged fledgling's poking upward from the nest spoonful after spoonful, each feeding session lasting a minimum of an hour and a half. But when, after more than three years of faithful service, never missing a day, Loretta informed Bunny that she planned to begin training a substitute to cover for her over a period of a few weeks while she returned to Manila to visit her own mother, who was also ailing, and then traveled on to Puttaparthi in India for a short retreat at the ashram of her guru, Sai Baba—she really really needed a break, she needed to clear her head and refresh her soul—Bunny announced that this would be the perfect time to put Gloria in the nursing facility, it was something she had long intended to do, keeping her at home in this ridiculous patched-together substandard setup was just so unprofessional. "But who will feed your mama?" Loretta had cried. "Nursing home will put feeding tube in her." "Never, no way," Bunny said. "Absolutely no feeding tube, it's against our principles. No drastic measures, Mother would never have wanted that." "Your mama not need feeding tube anyway," Loretta said glumly. "She need somebody to feed her." Then she added in desperation, "Your mama love to eat, but she cannot feed self. If nobody sit and feed your mama how long it takes, I afraid she die." Bunny closed her eyes to express her thinly concealed impatience with Loretta's incapacity to get it. The nursing home had professional feeders to deal with clients who for whatever reasons refused to feed themselves, she coldly informed the subordinate. Mother will just have to get used to it.

"I'm not used to it yet," Gloria had said as Loretta leaned over the railing of her hospital bed on her second day at the nursing home. This, at least, was what Loretta reported in a telephone call to the museum, which Krystyna had been obliged to take in her chief of staff's office since Bunny refused to talk to her former employee. It was in that phone call, too, at Bunny's behest, that Krystyna ordered Loretta to cease and desist at once from visiting Gloria; in any event, Director Bacon had given firm instructions to the nursing home administration to eject Loretta should she make any further attempts to invade the premises. And by the way, Director Bacon did not for one minute believe that Gloria ever said anything coherent at all such as that she wasn't used to it yet; these were just quotes that Loretta invented to convince Director Bacon that Gloria was not a goner, that she still had a claim on life, so that she, Loretta, could keep her job. If Gloria really could speak, why on earth would she talk to a stranger, to an alien from a Third World country, instead of to her own daughter, to a benighted follower of this Baba boy guru, no less, a well-known pedophile and pederast and sexual harasser, as it happened, his name was on a list to be considered for condemnation by the museum's Conscience Committee, speaking out against abusers and cults was definitely one of the important lessons of the Holocaust. Finally, in her capacity as Director Bacon's official spokesperson, Krystyna advised Loretta that if Gloria persisted in refusing to make productive and efficient use of her turn with the nursing home's professional feeder, who of course in all fairness had to divide the meal hour equitably among all the other geriatric clients on the floor who also required her assistance, which was only right and appropriate, she was in danger of losing her eating skills, of forgetting how to chew and swallow and so on, the staff would be afraid to risk the liability of feeding her lest she choke or aspirate or something.

The bottom line was, Krystyna told Loretta, if Gloria wanted to survive, she had just better descend from her high horse and get used to it.

That was about two weeks ago when Gloria had been delivered to the nursing home. Krystyna could hardly believe it, it seemed so much longer, she and Bunny had gone through so much. And now Gloria was dying. Just as Bunny had predicted, the professionals had thrown up their hands, they had determined that Gloria was as good as dead, she was just too spoiled and stubborn for her own good, they had drawn up the stop-all-feeding papers for Bunny's approval and signature. It was a truism that at any given moment on this earth, someone is being born and someone is dying, but it really made a difference, Krystyna reflected resentfully, it was in its way an uncomfortable intrusion and imposition and irritation, to know who it was while it was happening. Especially in the matter of dying, it was unseemly, prurient, disturbing information to have forced upon you, well beyond what you cared to know.

Krystyna's eyes fell upon the twins, Rumi and Rumi, at the bottom of the staircase. The dying woman had doted upon them for a while after their birth, but had progressively lost interest as she continued deliberately to shut down into nothing more than an eating machine, divesting from the twins just as she had divested from her own daughter. They were striking children, like exotic display pieces, dressed in white embroidered kurtas over their loincloths, in bare feet, with shaved skulls punctuated by their silky ponytails, and dark eyes rimmed in kohl. As Gloria went on relentlessly with her business of dying at the Parklawn nursing home in New York, one of the Rumis at the Holocaust Museum in Washington, D.C., was being bounced to the chanting of the Monotone Monks, now entertaining the crowd, on the lap of that coddled teenage princess who earlier in the program had read the greeting from the Tibetan government-in-exile. Krystyna had heard that she was related to Rama in some fashion, which explained how one so young and unimpressive had landed such a singular honor—another personalized extracurricular to be added to the résumé on her college application. The other Rumi was perched a step or two higher, dancing with beguiling innocence and abandon to the delight of the audience, as the Buddhist singers with their shaved heads, in their mango-colored robes and yellow rubber flip-flops, sat cross-legged on the makeshift stage and intoned their mantras to the rhythms of their cymbals and bells, their drums and gongs.

The Monotone Monks had been creatively recruited by Monty only the day before to be the entertainment portion of the Tibetan Holocaust program. After their lucky break of a gig at the Tibetan pavilion during the Smithsonian Folk Life Festival on the Mall in the early days of the summer, they had just casually ignored their visas and neglected to use the other half of their plane tickets to return home to their place of exile in a remote village in Bhutan with no electricity or running water or McDonald's. Monty, walking leisurely back to the museum the day before the Tibetan program at around three-thirty in the afternoon from lunch at Gerard's Place with the newest intern in the survivors' affairs department, showing her the sights, had spotted them busking in Lafayette Park in front of the White House, coins and wrinkled bills tossed by passersby piling up in an empty bottle of the moonshine they had learned to appreciate from their Folk Life costars in the Mississippi Delta pavilion. The crowd at the museum was going wild over them. From the honorable chairman, to the minister of jihad, to the lowliest overweight Holocaust voyeur in backward baseball cap with a Coors Beer patch and exposed rear cleavage, this entire collection of mortality in the Hall of Witness that broiling afternoon had lost all awareness of its own transience on earth, united in moist sentiment as the Monks led the singing of the Tibetan national anthem, after which the whole house exploded with cries of "Free Tibet! Free Tibet!"—swaying and clapping, rocking and rolling along with the Monotones until their hearts nearly burst in palpable ecstasy from the swelling of their own goodness and virtue.

It was a rousing warm-up for the featured speaker, and as the Monotone Monks took their triumphant bows with the rhythmic clapping segueing to crashing applause, Rama and Koan Gilguli, waving bouquets of burning incense sticks, pushed Roshi Mickey Fisher forward in his wheelchair, right to the brink of the landing at the top of the flight of stairs, extracting an audible gasp from some of the spectators standing in the front rows of the pit who would have received the full brunt of the impact had he cascaded over. Fisher-roshi good-naturedly jiggled his generous girth in his seat, rocking the wheelchair playfully to demonstrate that it was securely braked. He smiled with mystical wisdom, his grizzled beard splaying across the neckline of his magenta robe lit up with gold threads. It pleased him to alarm his audience in this way. There was an important teaching to be gleaned from it. Life was illusion. Whether we have an awareness of it or not, we are always on the edge. Behind him to his right, on the black granite wall carved with the words of the prophet Isaiah, "You are my witnesses," the projected image of the bejeweled cover of the Tibetan Book of the Dead was superimposed over the intricate pattern of a mandala fashioned out of ephemeral sand. Fisher-roshi raised both of his heavy arms in an appeal for order. "My holy, holy friends," he said when they quieted down at last, "let us meditate."

Most in that crowd simply bowed their heads, deprived as they were of meditation training and skills, assuming for the occasion the familiar moment-of-silence position that is the price of admission to the ball game, but there were a few adepts who instantly folded into authentic lotuses on the spot and smoothly glided into their measured breathing, showing off with the swagger and display of insiders in a house of worship who know the tune and belt out by heart every word of the prayers in a dead language. Fisher-roshi, aided by Rama and Koan Gilguli seated on the floor on either side of his wheelchair, then began the mantra—*ohm mani padme hum*—until, very soon, as if captured in the expanding web of a trance, the entire audience was chanting along with them—*ohm mani padme hum*, peace and love, compassion and enlightenment, *ohm, ohm*, behold, behold, the jewel in the lotus, behold the Jew. Koan Gilguli held up a large prayer wheel, spinning out the mantra printed in Tibetan script on diaphanous paper as the congregation went on chanting, while Rama nestled the glossy-eyed Rumi and Rumi in the cradle of her folded legs, each child nursing at a breast.

"Hey!" the roshi suddenly bellowed, startling them out of their enchantment, setting their hearts pounding in a panic as if they had been hurled from the clutch of a paralyzing dream. "Hey, you dead souls in this mausoleum to memory! Hey, you who were once called Chazkel and Chatsche in Warsaw, Tenzing and Tenzin in Lhasa, Norodom in Cambodia, Kagame in Rwanda, Omar in Bosnia, Vartan in Armenia, listen with full attention, do not be distracted. Your oppressors are defeated—

the Germans, the Chinese, the Khmer Rouge, the Hutus, the Serbs, the Turks—all are maya and illusion. Do not be terrified, do not tremble, do not cling to your suffering as you wander in the spiritual transition, in the narrow *bardo* of the cycle of samsara. Do not be overcome, do not be embittered, do not fear. Attain liberation. Seek release from your physical body. Seek rebirth."

The roshi gripped both arms of his wheelchair with his two thick-fingered hands, hoisting himself to his feet with a rushing noise like fluttering seraph wings. At the same time, Koan Gilguli quickly stepped forward to pull the wheelchair back from where his master was rising.

"What is happening to me?" Fisher-roshi cried.

Under the stupefied gaze of the audience he began to move in his place, then to dance rapturously. "I have transcended my body," he exulted. "I am liberated. I am released. I am transformed. I am reborn. I am dazzled by light—wisdom, perfection, clarity. My holy, holy friends"—and here Fisher-roshi opened his arms in an all-encompassing universal embrace—"praised be the Lord Buddha, hallelujah!"

*

Whether it was from the shock of the roshi's resurrection or from the ponderous heat, which was becoming more and more liquefied and oppressive, no one could say, but as Mickey Fisher thrust forward a crimson velvet slipper from under his goldthreaded magenta robe to begin his descent of the stairs into the bosom of his flock, like Moses from the Mount, someone in the crowd fainted—the news was broadcast in alarm by the voice of an unidentified woman. At first, the quarantine-like circle that had already formed around the fainter who now lay in a dark heap on the floor—a creature in a torn woolen cloak that enshrouded its entire body and hooded its face, male or female, nobody could make a definitive diagnosis—grew wider rather than contracted. Bystanders leapt even farther back, listening in stunned horror as the cowbell around its neck engraved with the warning "leper"—or was it its former owner's name, "Pepper"?—tinkled steadily as the body spiraled dreamily downward, as in a slow-motion replay, collapsing finally against the battered baby carriage filled with brown paper grocery bags that it had wheeled into this lessons-of-the-Holocaust program in the Hall of Witness.

Within a moment, however, a young Hasid rushed forward in his shoulder-padded, boxy black suit and wide brimmed black felt Borsalino hat that hid his face except for the tuft of sparse beard pointing like an arrow in the direction of the overcome creature, his long sidelocks and the fringes of his ritual garment flying as he pushed ahead. "Hatzolah, I'm from Hatzolah!" he cried. "Volunteer lifesaver coming through! Move back! Out of my way!" Behind him came a nun with lowered head carrying a half-empty plastic bottle of water, murmuring, "The paralytic, the leprous, I will go and heal them, Jesus said." From the height of the landing where he sat in his place of honor, Abu Shahid had an excellent view of the action. Flashing a gold ring set with a glittering diamond as he stroked his mustache with his trigger finger, he turned to his host, Maurice Messer, who was fuming at Rama for exposing her "maternity brassiere filling mit out the brassiere," as he phrased it from his first career in the foundation business, "like this state-of-the-art museum is some kind of bazaar in Calcutta mit overage suckling babies mit flies walking on their eyes," and at Fisher-roshi for his preposterous grandstanding—"I'm gonna eat that swami-salami faker alive," he growled into Bunny's ear. "What does he think this is, some kind of revival preacher show in a *fershtunkene* circus tent maybe?"

The minister of jihad indicated the Hasid, who was now crouching down, pulling equipment out of his luminous orange bag, and attending to the fallen body on the floor of the Hall of Witness, and confided in a familiar way to Maurice, "That's my son the doctor."

"He's a doctor?" Maurice asked incredulously. Almost nothing could surprise him anymore.

"Ah well, you'll excuse a poor father's forgivable embellishments," Abu Shahid conceded, working his worry beads. "Actually, he's merely an emergency medical technician. But, alas, he *is* my son, Shahid, a crazy boy unfortunately. They should call me Abu Majnun, not Abu Shahid! I sent him to the Harvard of terrorist training camps in Afghanistan, he was on track to become the world's greatest jihad martyr for Allah, a hero of Islam. But then the rabbis got hold of him when he was on holiday in Ukraine looking for a preview of paradise—the rabbis of Chabad. He mixed them up with the mullahs of Hamas, my poor Shahid. Chabad, Hamas—what's the difference? A bunch of beards on the prowl for lost souls, promising deliverance, salvation, the Messiah—the boy was never too discriminating. And this is my reward—a Jewish doctor without even a shingle."

"I see, I see," Maurice replied, nodding his head sympathetically. "Well, if that's your son the doctor, then maybe that holy *schwester* nun over there talking to herself holding that urine analysis *pish* bottle is mine daughter the nurse. It looks like a *shidduch* made in heaven. Maybe we should introduce them."

That was the last time anyone connected to the museum saw or spoke to Abu Shahid, though his chief of staff, Leyla

Salmani, having at some point changed out of her military gear
into a civilian public relations suit with an elegant leather brief-
case, the rich black tresses of her hair pinned neatly back in a
stern chignon that revealed the coiled wire descending from
the plug in her ear, took up her post in front of the Fourteenth
Street entrance as the official spokesperson for United Holocausts throughout the ensuing takeover of the museum. Afterward it was determined that the minister of jihad had probably
vanished during the wild confusion of the opening salvos of
the action, when the strobe lights on the ceilings throughout
the museum began to flash, the fire alarm started blaring, and
the public address system came on with calm authority. "Ladies
and gentlemen, this is a Holocaust simulation role-playing
exercise. It is only a test, but all visitors are required by law to
just follow orders as if it were the real event. Remain calm and
do not panic. Collect all your belongings and valuables, and
proceed to the designated *Umschlagplatz* assembly points for
resettlement. Uniformed guards with batons will conduct you
down the stairs, which for the purposes of this exercise will
serve as virtual cattle cars to be unloaded at the Department of
Agriculture as you exit the building on the Fourteenth Street
side, or, if you are sent to the right, Raoul Wallenberg Place
and the official entrance to the popular Bureau of Engraving
and Printing on the Fifteenth Street side. Once again, please
remain calm and refrain from talking—and have a nice day." It
had been Monty's brainstorm to frame the fire-drill announcement in this way, in line with the overall concept of immersing
visitors in a virtual Holocaust experience from the perspective
of the victims, as reflected also in the raw crematorium-like
brick and steel design of the building with such atmospheric
details as its narrowing central staircase and its watchtower-

like structures on one side, and the ID cards distributed to visitors upon entering the exhibition personally linking them to a random victim in the creepy journey through the haunted house of the Holocaust in the lottery of ultimate extermination or survivorship—all carried out within psychologically tested parameters set by the comfort-level consultant, of course, visitors safely aware throughout that it was all not real, that it was all just for fun, that after undergoing this self-improvement tour, and after inscribing their selected deep thoughts in the comment book at the end, "I enjoyed it very much, thank you for making the Holocaust possible," they will walk out *Homo erectus* as they had walked in, resuming once again the hunt for something to eat.

Now as the visitors, prodded and hustled by the guards, streamed down the stairs and out of the vaulting gallery of the Hall of Witness to the two exits on either side of the building, mostly calmly but also on occasion with sporadic flurries of muted cries and mounting panic that were swiftly and decisively brought under control by the uniformed personnel, Bunny turned in a fury to Maurice. "Is this really really for real?" she demanded. "Who authorized this, if I may ask?" Maurice simply flipped out his palms and elevated his shoulders with a look of utter confusion on his face; it was one of the rare occasions in his life when he truly had nothing to say and did not say it anyway. The next moment, though, he and Bunny, along with Krystyna, as well as Fisher-roshi and his complete entourage, including Koan Gilguli, and the twins Rumi and Rumi, one carried by Rama, the other in the arms of her niece, the teenager who had read the message from the Tibetan government-in-exile, were borne down the steps like pieces of a shipwreck along with the massive tide of fleeing visitors and museum personnel. Incense and prayer wheels and copies of speeches and other props for the Tibetan Holocaust program were trampled underfoot. The chairs for honored guests and the costly speaker's podium that had been placed on the landing were also swept or levitated down the stairs at some point in the midst of the stampede, miraculously injuring no one. As for the now-empty wheelchair, only toward the end, when the building had been almost totally evacuated, a visitor with a handicapped-parking-space gripe, who unfortunately had not had time to absorb the lessons of the Holocaust before the alarm went off, gave it a definitive push. As if in a dream, they all watched from the floor of the Hall of Witness as it went bumping down, steered, it seemed, by some invisible divine hand, until it came to a halt upright and undamaged at the foot of the stairs. Maurice immediately sat down in it. He did this unthinkingly, for in every other known public circumstance without exception he took great pains and pride in separating himself from the signs and symbols of infirmity and old age that afflicted lesser mortals. He was simply not himself at that moment. That moment, it could reliably be said—and, indeed, Maurice did say so himself to his Blanche afterward, when it was all over—was the worst moment he had ever experienced in his entire life, not excluding the actual Holocaust itself, which, however terrible it was, with the humiliation and torture and murder of his mother and father, his brothers and sisters, and so on and so forth, not to mention all that he had personally suffered and gone through, at least had a reason. What was that reason? "What kind stupid question is that? To make lessons, of course, to make memorials mit morals," Maurice stated categorically.

Seated in the wheelchair, Maurice now regarded this beloved

estate of his in which he would have vowed that the mortar between every brick was mixed with his own life's blood, you could probably prove this with a DNA test. He saw that the place was already almost entirely empty. It gave off the hollow ghostly residue and vibrations of a space that was forlorn and solitary after having once been tumultuous with life. It seemed now to have finally truly been turned over to the dead. Looking around, Maurice observed someone he did not immediately recognize taking great pains to adjust a large notice of some sort behind the glass on the Fourteenth Street entrance of the building and locking securely the doors from within; he assumed that another thug was carrying out a similar criminal act on the other side. Apart from himself and Bunny and Krystyna, representing the museum, and apart from Fisher's Buddhist delegation with the twins Rumi and Rumi, supervised by their cousin, now chasing each other with wild squeals and skidding delightedly on their rumps along these vast, polished, evacuated spaces, the only other people he could see in the shadows of the lofty Hall of Witness were the nun, the Hasid, and the cloaked creature now evidently recovered, the three of them unloading the grocery bags from the baby carriage in front of the entrance to the Remember the Children exhibition. Maurice's eye turned to the information desk in the center of the atrium. Information, he thought, that's what I need. With remarkable speed and dexterity, he rolled the wheelchair across the floor to this visitors' service facility. Though it was now completely abandoned, he was determined nevertheless to exercise his right as a taxpayer to get his money's worth. "*Gottenyu,*" Maurice cried, "what's going on here?"

As if in answer to his question, a deep voice came down from the monumental heights of the Hall of Witness with its great

angled skylights letting in the fragmented light of the brooding heavens. "Brothers and sisters, rejoice! The United States
Holocaust Memorial Museum is liberated. The Holocaust has
been returned to the people. All Holocausts are created equal.
United Holocausts, the umbrella group for all Holocausts,
known and unknown, past, present, and future, has occupied
this infrastructure. The occupation will continue until equal
representation is given to all Holocausts, public and private,
personal and global, animal, vegetable, and mineral. The Jewish Holocaust will be apportioned an equal place among all
other Holocausts, no better and no worse, no more and no less
in the universe of Holocausts. Stand by for the posting of the
details of our nonnegotiable demands on our Web site and in
the media. Museum personnel still on the premises are free to
leave unharmed. We take no human hostages. We take hostage
only the infrastructure and everything it contains, pledging our
lives, our fortunes, and our sacred honor not to leave until
the Holocaust is returned to We the People, to all Holocausts
united. Remember, when it comes to Holocausts, a laboratory
rat is a force-fed chicken is an endangered-species whale is your
grandma. Brothers and sisters, take back your Holocaust!"

"I'm out of here," Krystyna declared, and, dropping the tote
bag at Bunny's feet so that the DustBuster came spilling out,
she loped on her high heels across the vacated expanse of the
Hall of Witness toward the exit on the Fourteenth Street side,
where she was quickly let out by a tall menacing figure in a
three-piece suit with the leg of a pantyhose in a mocha latte
hue squashing the features of his face beyond recognition.

Bunny turned sharply to Mickey Fisher. "How could you do
this to me after I gave you this gig today in the Tibetan Holocaust?" she demanded with barely suppressed hysteria. Then,

glaring in a rage at Rama, she hissed, "And I thought we were sisters!"

"You're free to leave too, you know," Rama said serenely. "You heard the man."

"Are you out of your mind? I should leave this place for trash like you to vandalize and muck up like nobody's business? Never! You'll have to carry me out in a box first!" Bunny bent down furiously to retrieve her DustBuster. Then, noticing some dirt a short distance away, she could not stop herself. She flicked on the switch and began to vacuum. As she spotted more and more places that required attention, she started to crawl on her hands and knees, vacuuming as she went along. Fisher-roshi, Rama, and Koan Gilguli intuited that it was a tremendous relief to Bunny to be engaged in this useful chore, it was overwhelmingly healing and therapeutic under the circumstances, it helped her enormously in dealing with this extremely stressful situation. They watched with enlightened and tolerant interest as Bunny continued to do her thing, crawling away from them on all fours, behind the staircase in the direction of the Donor's Lounge, vacuuming all the way. Only when she came suddenly to a stop, depositing herself with a thud directly on the floor with her head sunk in the palms of her two hands and her shoulders heaving, did they judge it to be the correct time to approach.

Bunny lifted her flushed face with her red-framed glasses all askew, resembling a portrait by Picasso. "I need a Valium," she said.

"We don't do Valium," Rama responded. "I can roll you a joint though."

"Just do me one favor please?" Bunny said. "No marijuana in the museum—out of respect for the dead? It's the least you could do for me when I've really really always been on your side, after all. Who has worked harder for Holocaust equality and diversity than I have?—only I've been doing it the whole time by peaceful means, bit by bit, and now you've come in like gangbusters and blown it all to hell. Thanks a lot! Why are you doing this to me of all people—especially at a time like this? My mother is dying in your deadbeat dad's crappy nursing home," she spat out, glaring at Rama. "I was supposed to catch the shuttle right after today's program to visit her on her deathbed—and now I can't go. By tomorrow she'll be gone. Because of you, I'm never going to see my mommy again. And afterward I won't even have a chance to do the appropriate grief work. I'm going to have to sign up for a three-week session at bereavement camp when this is all over if I ever want to get closure—and where am I going to find time for that with my schedule? It's all your fault." She began to grope desperately around on the floor for her DustBuster, her fingers itching again for the relief of at least one more small dose of vacuuming.

Rama looked down at her unmoved. "The way I see it," she said, "you have two options. You can split like the man said and catch your old lady before she heads out to the *bardo,* or you can call off your final-solution orders and hire a private nurse to give her something to eat—you dig what I'm saying? You can afford a private nurse, right? That way, if she's not too far gone already, since you're so uptight about doing the right thing when it comes to looking good in this bourgeois town, maybe you'd have a little more lebensraum to get to her in time for the deathbed trip."

"Starving your own mommy to death?" Koan Gilguli put in, gliding his two forefingers over each other. "Shame, shame, not very nice, especially for the director of the formerly Jewish

Holocaust Museum. What about the lessons of the Holocaust? I truly hope and pray that reports of this don't get out—so unseemly, such a tacky Third Reich thing, life unworthy of life and all that yucky stuff. And scheduling the mercy killing at such an inconvenient time, too, when it's so hard to slot a deathbed visit into your calendar—who would have ever thought? We heard all about it through the grapevine, by the way, that you've given the order to hasten the end so to speak, from Rama-sensei's sister, Naomi-zenchin's mom," and he indicated the teenager now positioning herself for meditation on the floor, not far from the information desk where Maurice remained parked in his wheelchair, absorbed in watching three figures drawing closer, grimacing as they struggled to peel the pantyhose off their heads.

Bunny stood up, suddenly feeling herself to be at an extreme disadvantage on the floor, looked down upon and reduced like a child by these emboldened inquisitors. "Excuse me," she said, "but just who do you think you are? What happens between my mom and me is none of your business—is that clear? I, and I alone, am privy to her living will, and I alone have the legal authority to make decisions in her best interest. Furthermore, for your information, there is no reason in hell why I should feel obliged to justify myself to a gang of terrorists and pot-heads who don't understand the first thing about it." Her voice was rising shrilly. "Now if you don't mind, I need a time out, I need some space to make a call." She extracted her cell phone from the pocket of her extra-long suit jacket and pressed the top number on her speed-dialing list, instantly reaching her psychiatrist's answering machine. Even after all her years in therapy with him, going on half a century, he still had never disclosed to her his August number at his vacation house, paid for in large measure, she had no doubt, by the steady flow of her hefty checks, somewhere on Cape Cod or in the Hamptons, she thought, even that detail he had not revealed to her, it had become a bitter theme in their sessions when other topics ran dry.

"Ah, that beautiful soul, the holy holy Jiriki, is poised at the threshold of the fourth *bardo*, the *bardo* of the moment of death," Fisher-roshi now somberly intoned. "How I wish I could be at her side at this moment to guide her toward the liberation of the after-death plane. But I must remain here to claim this memorial in the name of the oneness of all Holocausts, in the name of all the dead of all Holocausts who call out to me now to guide them to rebirth in this holy holy place." Closing his eyes and raising his arms, he cried out in a voice pitched to pierce the high brick and masonry walls of the Hall of Witness and travel hundreds of miles to penetrate the ears of the hollow-cheeked and dry-lipped Gloria as she lay curled up on her side, clutching a pillow to her breast in a strange institutional bed. "Oh noble one, you who were called Gloria-Jiriki in this life, what is known as death has now come upon you. You are departing from this world. Do not cling to this life out of weakness or fondness or fear. You have no power to remain. Open yourself to the shock of the transition and seek your liberation."

*

Maurice shook his head as this madness engulfed him. What had he done to deserve it? He had heard that Gloria was dying. He had even heard the rumor that Bunny had helped her along with a grateful daughterly kick out the door. She was going to become a very wealthy lady, this money Bunny. If he ever managed to get out of this present mess, he should not forget to consult with the council lawyer about the public perception and the appearance of impropriety, never mind the ethics, of accepting mega-donations from the in-house sitting director. He could count on his lawyer to deliver the desired opinion, his lawyer was his own personal lapdog, maybe he wasn't so bright upstairs as lawyers go, but he was his slave, there was nothing he wouldn't do to hold on to his place of honor at the head of the table at the twice-yearly festive meetings of the full board. Bunny would be forced to resign in order to really really contribute, Maurice fantasized. That would be a blessing from heaven, he would seize the opportunity when this mess was over as he had snatched opportunity from other dark moments in his life, beginning with the Holocaust. Oh, where was Monty now when Maurice truly needed him? Monty would have had the brains and guts to stand beside him in this perilous hour, with the survival of the museum and the entire Holocaust and the memory of the six million at the very top of the severely endangered species list. They would have been an unbeatable team, he and Monty, the two of them together would have instantly vaporized the three goons now stationed in front of him, two of whom, to his dismay but not to his shock, he of course recognized instantly—Jews, what then? Why was it the case that Jews are always the ones who are so liberally ready to sacrifice everything that they've struggled so hard to earn, including this powerful monument to their unrivaled, spectacular pain and suffering, for the sake of some soft, deluded, utopian ideal? The third terrorist in front of him, the black guy in the three-piece suit wired for radio communication, the one who looked like the affirmative-action ringleader, standing a head taller between the other two like the African in the Olympics who always wins the gold medal—well, Maurice reflected, that one also looked familiar, Maurice definitely knew him from somewhere too. What, Maurice repeated to himself, oh what had he ever done to deserve this? Bunny, his sole ally on the ground in this crisis, had already fallen to pieces beyond repair, hanging on to her vacuum cleaner like it was a ventilator, life support. She could now be seen shambling around in circles pressing her cell phone to her ear with her right hand, plugging a finger of her left hand into her other ear, engaging in a therapy session with her shrink's answering machine, speed-dialing over and over again whenever the machine timed out. This was Maurice's reward for his selflessness in accepting Gloria's lousy ten million for the sake of the museum. Had he been thinking about his own interests and preferences, of course Monty would be his director today, never mind the potentially explosive scandals such as the refugee calamity due to reckless reporting, or the cans of Zyklon B in the garage, or the police rap for wife and prostitute beating—he and Monty together would have found creative ways to spin all of that, and, for that matter, anything else that might have come popping up out of the sewers. Had Maurice been thinking of himself instead of the museum, he would have turned down Gloria's money no matter how much she offered, even if she had written out a check on the spot for one hundred million dollars—and Monty would be standing at his side at this very moment, Maurice would not have been so desperately alone.

He looked at the two Jews in front of him. He could hardly believe it—Honey Pincus, Monty's ex—and after all he had done for her, arranging for a private *din Torah* grievance hearing in his own suite at the Four Seasons hotel after she was released from the hospital due to injuries from so-called spouse abuse, a hearing over which he had presided himself as the impartial arbitrator in order to avoid, for the sake of the children, a public airing of all that domestic *schmutz*. He could still picture her bruised face and both of her swollen eyes and her arm in a sling as she had sat in a wheelchair then, just as he was sitting now. "Honey," Maurice now said with unconcealed disappointment, "is this the thank-you what I get?" She turned toward her black boss as if requesting permission to speak. Divorce seemed to suit her, Maurice could not but notice. She looked fit, trim, dressed in black jeans and a sleeveless black shirt, her gray hair barbered in a crew cut, small silver hoops studding the lobes of her ears—no discernible scars, so far as Maurice could tell, from her suicide exhibitionism with the gas a couple of years ago. "I'm not your Honey," was all she said finally.

"Not mine Honey?" Maurice responded. "And maybe also your partner in crime over there"—and he pointed to the other Jew, the one with the flamboyant feather pluming from his hippie headband—"is not mine Schmaltz, Eliot Schmaltz, the son from mine dear friend and fellow partisan fighter, the distinguished proctologist and medical mogul, Dr. Adolf Schmaltz, M.D.?"

"I'm not Eliot Schmaltz," the answer came, in this case without a prior request for permission from the leader.

"Not Eliot Schmaltz? So what kind of Schmaltz are you?"

The feathered friend regarded Maurice with a mixture of pity and contempt. "In the tradition of my people, the Hopi peaceful nation," he explained with a sigh, "I take the name of the greatest natural wonder wherever I happen to find myself. Thus, while I am in Washington, D.C., as a warrior for United Holocausts, I answer only to the name Foggy Bottom."

"And your big chief kick-in-the-pants over there," Maurice

inquired, "the one, you should excuse me, mit his flyer open—
does he also have a special Washington title, may I ask?"

The leader answered for himself. "Wherever I go, I am
known as Pushkin Jones," he said. "We've had the pleasure at
Auschwitz." And he cordially extended the hand he had just
used to zip up. Of course, Maurice refused to take it. Maurice
did not shake hands with terrorists.

Unfazed, Pushkin Jones exposed his glistening teeth in
a grin. "Brother Maurice," he declared, "we of the United
Holocausts rainbow coalition of all Holocausts, personal and
global, have come here today to offer ourselves as your allies
in your noble battle, and, I might add, the noble battle of your
esteemed director, Sister Bunny"—he indicated the place
where Bunny was still wrapped up in her therapy session, with
the phone now clamped between shoulder and jaw in order to
free both hands to search in a panic through her tote bag for
the DustBuster's portable recharger—"against the travesty
and disgrace of Holocaust denial. I am referring now to the
denial of all Holocausts other than the Jewish Holocaust. We
shall combat this kind of Holocaust denial unto death. I am
speaking of the denial of the African-American Holocaust,
for example, which I have the distinct honor and privilege of
representing today, claiming our forty-acres-and-a mule just
reparations for the depredations of slavery. I am speaking, to
cite yet other examples, of the denial of the Holocausts of
my two chiefs of staff—Sister Honey's Women's Holocaust
reflecting the confluence of fascism and misogyny, both dead-
ending in violence, and the Native American Holocaust of
Brother Foggy Bottom here, and, by extension, the Holocausts of all aboriginal and indigenous peoples everywhere

brutally uprooted by conquerors and colonialists and impe-
rialists from their native soils since time immemorial, with
special recognition due the Palestinian Holocaust, a direct
side effect of the monopoly by the marketers of memory of
your Jewish Holocaust."

Oho, Maurice was thinking, *two* chiefs of staff—this must
be a very important guy, and obviously with an intelligence
quotient, you had to hand it to him, he talked very good,
Maurice acknowledged to himself, a very cool rapper, a very
sophisticated cucumber but a genuine anti-Semite through and
through, the real McGoy. Maurice would need to conserve
every neuron for this crisis, he would have to gather every
remaining ounce of his strength to survive this one. This was a
command performance, and he was the resistance star.

"This of course does not mean we exclude other Holocausts," Jones elaborated. "The Children's Holocaust, the Gay
and Lesbian Holocaust, the Christian Holocaust, the Muslim
Holocaust, the Tibetan Holocaust, and so on and so forth, all
are gathered up equally under our great Holocaust tent." His
eyes swept across the Hall of Witness, from the weird threesome with the baby carriage in front of the Save the Children
exhibition to Fisher's Buddhists, now seated on the floor by the
staircase engaged in joint meditation practice. This was when it
dawned on Maurice for the first time, with a kind of staggering
internal jolt, that they had been in cahoots all along, they were
all in this together. "Nor should we neglect to make mention
of the other Holocausts not in our line of vision at the moment
who have rallied to our support both inside and outside of this
building," Jones added. "The Holocausts, past, present, and
future, of nations too numerous to list, from Cambodia to
Chechnya, from Russia to Rwanda, from Kosovo to Kurdistan,

from Armenia to East Timor, *plus* Ecological and Environmental Holocausts, the impending Nuclear Holocaust, the Herbal Holocaust targeting marijuana and other fruits and vegetables, the Endangered Species Holocausts of plants and animals from bluegrass to baby seals, from bladderpods to lesser long-nosed bats, *plus* the personal and private Holocausts of our brothers and sisters everywhere on this earth, from Brother Kwame in the Oppenheimer diamond mines of South Africa to Sister Katya in the brothels of Tel Aviv, from Brother Unborn Fetus tossed in a Dumpster in Los Angeles County to Sister Granny set adrift on an iceberg to starve to death in the Eskimo sea, and on and on in an ancient and endless cycle of sorrow and woe. We are all survivors—cancer survivors, AIDS survivors, sexual abuse survivors, alcoholism survivors, mental illness survivors, circumcision survivors, menstruation survivors, propaganda survivors, et cetera et cetera. Move over, Brother Maurice, the neighborhood is changing, you are not alone, and you are not unique. No longer can you sit there on the ground like a tribe of Jeremiahs girded in sackcloth, covered in ashes, crying out in lamentation, Behold and see, if there be any pain like unto my pain! Your monopoly has been busted, Brother Maurice, your Holy-cause is history. We reject the hierarchy and caste system of Holocausts. All Holocausts are equal in the eye of God. No one Holocaust is superior to another, no one Holocaust is deserving of special treatment or recognition. All Holocausts are unique."

Maurice's brain had grown numb. He had tuned out before the full litany of Holocausts and the rhetoric had been exhausted, at the point at which Jones had implied that other terrorists, not visible at the moment to the naked eye, were present in the museum, not only outside the building but also, most ominously, within it. They could be anywhere, Maurice reflected with a shudder, on any of the three floors of the permanent exhibition, lurking in the Gypsy wagon or in the Auschwitz barrack or in the Danish rescue boat, they could be hiding in one of the theaters on the concourse level or in the archives on the top floor. They had scoped out the territory thoroughly, they slinked around like phantoms, as slick and ungraspable as the jellied calf-bone *ptscha* that his mother used to boil, as cold and heartless as ice, they knew the location of every urinal and piece of art and did not discriminate between them, they set off the fire alarm flawlessly, flushing and voiding the entire building of everyone but themselves within five minutes flat. Maurice was now fully alert to how formidable his enemies were. Sitting in that wheelchair facing Jones and his henchmen, who were lined up like a firing squad in front of him, he prayed in his heart that his dogged will to survive and to prevail, which had carried him through so brilliantly over the years, would not desert him now.

"Brother Pusher," Maurice began, attempting to inject a diplomatic polish into his voice, "I hear you, I feel your pain, I know where you're coming from, believe me. I myself started a very successful business from mine own, Holocaust Connections, Inc., mit a similar idea—sharing the moral capital from the Holocaust. But between you and me, you're barking up the wrong fire hydrant this time. The Jewish Holocaust is bigger from both of us. It's the super Holocaust, the state-sponsored systematic extermination from the Jewish people for the 'crime' of existing by the most advanced and civilized nation on earth—that's the scientific definition. There was nothing like it before or after and there never will be. Nothing can compete. You should quit while you're still ahead, you got a lost cause. Believe me, I understand how you feel. Everybody likes to think their Holocaust is the best, everybody likes to think their Holocaust is unique, but face it, the Jewish Holocaust is the most unique. So let me give you a little piece of advice from an old man who has seen a thing or two in his time, okay? Give up this crazy, childish *narishkeit* what you're doing, and come express yourself constructively by joining me in mine business. I'll make you a senior vice president mit complete control from the African-American Holocaust portfolio. What do you say, Pushka? Is it a deal?"

"That's a very fine offer, Brother Messer, I'm truly honored, but I'm afraid it's an offer I shall have to refuse. I have a dream, Brother. My dream is that all Holocausts are one and united from sea to shining sea in brotherhood and sisterhood, from the red hills of Georgia to the desert states of Mongolia, and I can never give up my dream. But you can rest assured that we at United Holocausts shall always be mindful of our debt to the pioneering work of the Jewish people in the creative and conceptual uses of victimhood and survivorship and Holocausts, a stellar achievement, truly—memorials and museums across the globe as a reward for your persecution, reparations and restitution, and finally, the greatest prize of all, a country of your own. You are the model that all of our equally special and equally unique and equally equal Holocausts aspire to and strive to emulate. And we *shall* overcome, Brother, trust me. Today we begin with the museum. Tomorrow we redraw the map of the world. Our eye is on the prize."

The man was deranged, a megalomaniac, Maurice now realized. How much longer was he obliged to go on eating this dreck? There would be no payoff, Maurice recognized, from continuing to swallow this crap, twisting himself into contortions to avoid giving offense. This was where he drew the line. The time had come to quit making nice. "Listen to me, Pushy," Maurice said. "I have just one word for you. That word is *never*! We will *never* give in to your terrorist demands. When it comes to genocides, we are the genocide mit the capital G, and you are nothing but a lightweight genocide, a Holocaust *pisher*, Pushy. And you will *never* get away mit this. This is the major leagues you're playing in now, mine friend. You are now dealing mit the greatest Shoah on earth mixed up mit the greatest power on earth, the government from the United States of America and the Joint Chiefs of Staff. Before you can say the name from your greatest hero in the area in which your people happen to excel, the department from at'letics—I'm talking Jackie Robinson here—the marines will come marching into this occupied territory and carry you out mit your whole gang of hooligans in body bags. Trust *me*! They will be showing up any minute—and boy are you going to be sorry!"

But even as he pronounced these brave words with such ardor and conviction, Maurice seemed to shrivel in his wheelchair in front of the eyes of Pushkin Jones and his two enforcers, Honey Pincus and Eliot Foggy Bottom Schmaltz, as the realization overwhelmed him that it had been a long while now since the masses had poured out of the museum in a panic. It had been a lifetime, or so it seemed, since these outlaws had seized control and unleashed their terror, and yet no one had come to his aid and to the aid of the six million. In spite of the terrible lessons of the Holocaust, Maurice had heard no voice of conscience being raised, no one had spoken out, no one had lifted a finger to save him.

"Yo, Sister Honey," Pushkin Jones now barked, barely glancing at Monty's liberated ex as he addressed her, "get the old man a drink of water. You know where our fountains are."

Yes, Maurice thought in despair, they knew where their fountains were, they knew where everything was, the air, the fire, the water, the source of all life. Jones directed his gaze back to the chairman slumping in his wheelchair. "You are wondering whence cometh your help, eh Brother Messer? Well, as soon as your director, Sister Bunny, gets off the horn with her mental health provider, if there's any jazz left in it, perhaps you may borrow it to communicate with your spokespersons on the outside, your son Brother Norman and your chief of staff Brother Monty. I'll tell you something, Brother Messer. There's not very much that your two guys can see eye to eye on. According to the briefings I'm receiving"—and here he tapped the radio plug in his ear—"the two brothers are squabbling with each other like Jeroboam and Rehoboam over the kingship, now that you have been incapacitated and are out of the picture. But there is one thing, Brother Messer, that the two of them have very wisely and prudently agreed upon—namely, that it would be most unseemly, it would look very bad indeed, if your federal storm troopers come breaking into the United States Holocaust Memorial Museum of all places, this noble monument to your six million or however many Jews slaughtered by the Hitlerites, and turn this place into another Waco Holocaust. Because, Brother Messer, you should know that if every single one of our demands is not met, *all* of our people inside this museum, not excepting the children"—he pointed by way of illustration to Rumi and Rumi, now entwined in sleep with their thumbs in each other's mouth as once they might have slept in the womb they had shared—"literally, every child and woman and man of us, every last sister and brother, is prepared to make the ultimate sacrifice. Trust *me*."

Incapacitated? Out of the picture? Was that how they were spinning him right out of the playing field? Maurice shook his head. Well, we shall just see about that. Clearly, they had forgotten whom they were dealing with—the Honorable Maurice Messer, Maurice the Knife. He could scarcely believe it—such betrayal, such ingratitude. His own son Norman and his cherished protégé Monty already battling each other over the succession—and the body not yet cold. Maybe, Maurice speculated, maybe someone had caught a glimpse of the body in the wheelchair. Good, he decided, he would remain in the wheelchair, let them think he was weak, "incapacitated, out of the picture," in the words of this psychopath and suicide artist Jones—an invalid, invalidated. Then, at the right moment, he would stun them by rising up like a mythical superhero from the comic books that his Norman used to keep in a wet pile next to the toilet bowl, and pow!—he would destroy them all. Swelling with indignation, Maurice flung out his hand and slapped away the plastic cup being held out to him by that sick-in-the-head Honey, sending it flying across the Hall of Witness, the water splashing into the face of this former punching bag of that traitor Monty. "Never!" Maurice cried. "I will never give in to your demands! I will never negotiate mit terrorists! I will never sell out the six million! You will have to carry me out feet first, mit mine nose pointing straight up to God Almighty in His heavens above!"

With one decisive motion, Maurice swiveled his wheelchair and rolled off in the direction of his favorite spot in the museum—the alcove containing his beloved Founders' Wall. He wanted in this his hour of need to commune with the spirits of his major donors. Bringing his wheelchair to a stop in this sacred space, Maurice felt immediately restored, renewed. This wall was his supreme creation. It was the monument to his greatest achievements, inscribed like a Rosetta stone with the chronicle of his triumphs, which only he could truly decipher. For a long time he gazed at the names on the wall, the roster of his precious donors of one million dollars or more, and was suffused with emotion as he recalled the details of each and every individual deal—how to reach this one on his private island he had retched nonstop over the side of a boat in the Bermuda Triangle, how at the second meeting in the San Francisco penthouse to extract the gift of a lifetime in the estate planning of that one, the prospect had appeared wearing a surgical mask because, as his *feygele* assistant nonchalantly explained, Maurice had a habit of standing too close and spitting too wildly from excitement in the climactic moments of a fund-raising pitch, and so on and so forth down the roll of his princely benefactors. Those happy days were gone, alas, they had been his finest hour, he was like a retired general returning to the shrine to his historic victories.

With quivering reverence, Maurice stretched out his hand to stroke the familiar names carved into the stone. He felt himself to be in a sanctuary, a holy place, like the Western Wall of the ancient Temple Mount. It occurred to him that maybe he should compose a little note, a *kvittel,* to God—"Master of the Universe," he would write, "Save Your Holocaust!"—but there was no place on the wall to put it, no stones and no crannies as there were in Jerusalem in which to insert it, no way to dispatch his petition express to the celestial spheres. He considered affixing it with a drop of his own earwax or mucus or other bodily fluid, but he knew that it would inevitably slip down;

Bunny would spot it on the floor instantly, as she had spotted his gold-embossed chairman's card on the floor, which he had presented to Jones in good faith, in an opening attempt to deal with this gangster as if he were a civilized human being—like a bird of prey Bunny would swoop now as she had swooped then, and suck it up with her DustBuster. Instead, he drew up his wheelchair, butting it against the wall and cramming himself as close as was humanly possible. He took out the yarmulke that his Blanche now presciently stowed in the pocket of each pair of trousers for ready availability in the religious situations that a man in his position regularly encountered, and placed it upon his head. Elevating his upper body within the confinement of the chair, he leaned his head forward and pressed his brow to the cool stone by the letter S, imprinting like a quality meat stamp upon his own flesh the name of his brave partisan comrade, the Honorable Dr. Adolf Schmaltz, M.D., the hospital tycoon and unfortunate father to the terrorist Foggy Bottom Schmaltz. He closed his eyes. And trembling with passion and need at the wall in the presence of the names, Maurice Messer prayed.

2

D UE TO A COMBINATION of unfortunate circumstances, following the takeover of the museum, Rabbi Herzl Lieb missed the opening salvos at the epicenter of the action outside the building, which coalesced on the Fourteenth Street side across from the Department of Agriculture, demarcated by barriers swiftly erected and patrolled by the police of the District of Columbia. Regrettably, however, during those critical first moments, Herzl was on the patch of Park Department turf on the Fifteenth Street side to which he and his demonstration had been consigned that morning, renamed for that stretch Raoul Wallenberg Place, where he had chained himself by the waist to a tree, and sweating extravagantly on this sweltering day under the blanket of his capacious cream wool fringed prayer shawl with its licorice-black stripes and neckpiece trimming of embroidered silver and gold threads, was blowing his heart out through a shofar. Planted in the ground beside him was a cluster of signs and posters on sticks. One depicted Abu Shahid in full face and profile, with the caption "Wanted: Terrorist, Murderer, Holocaust Denier," and then in bloodred capital letters, the question, "Should This Man Be Welcomed into the United States Holocaust Memorial Museum?" Another showed a photograph of heaps of charred and emaciated Jewish cadavers discovered in the camps after the war juxtaposed against a picture of a smiling Dalai Lama in tinted aviator glasses licking an ice cream cone, with the Hebrew word *Lehavdil* scrawled

boldly across, and in English, "How Can You Compare?"
And yet another declared in banner block letters, "Maurice
Messer, You've Made a Mess of Morality and Memory and the
Museum—Move Aside!" Peering through binoculars from the
tall window of the director's office in the red brick administration building across Raoul Wallenberg Place that morning,
Maurice had clutched his breast in bitterness as if physically
struck by this crude ad hominem shot and was muttering, "I'll
move aside your little *schmeckie*, that's what I'll move aside, you
momzer," just as Abu Shahid was being ushered into the room
by Bunny, followed by a uniformed steward rolling in a table
covered with a crisp white linen cloth, heaped with fruits and
pastries on china plates, fragrant, steaming coffee and tea in
silver pitchers, and a sprig of white orchid tinged with mauve
in a crystal vase in the center.

While Herzl remained attached to his tree, Henny Soskis
was taking a break from protesting, sitting atop the coffin
meant to represent the six million, which was one of Herzl's
signature props and visual aids in Holocaust-related demonstrations, generously provided free of charge by one of his legion
of admirers, Alvin Tepel of Tepel and Tepel Funeral Arrangements. Al always came through like a trouper with exemplary
good humor every single time the Jewish people were in danger.
"Your coffin's on the way, Rabbi, top of the line, you don't have
to hold your breath." Al never failed him. Sitting herself down
on this sturdy, deluxe coffin, Henny Soskis let out a profound
sigh and, staking her well-earned claim, announced, "I'm sure
the six million won't mind this close personal contact with an
old survivor's fat *tuches*."

Really, it was much too hot for a protest, Henny reflected as
she fanned herself vigorously with a bunch of the flyers she had

been passing out. Her dress, which she had bought on sale in
the back room of Loehmann's in Rockville for $49.95 with the
designer label torn out after seeing the same exact number at
Saks for five times as much, was soaked through and through,
sticking to her skin like a brisket; her pastel-colored hair, which
she had just had done the day before at Marie's beauty parlor on
the basement level of her senior citizen's retirement complex in
Silver Spring, had collapsed like cotton candy—but what could
she do? Herzl was so intense and persistent, so devoted to the
Jewish people, she could never say no to him. If only they had
had someone like Rabbi Herzl Lieb during the war, she always
commented to the ladies in her synagogue sisterhood, it would
have been a whole different story entirely, believe me.

But of course, all the other survivors had no trouble whatsoever refusing Herzl. And it wasn't just the temperature, as in
this particular instance. It was the heat all of the time, it was the
pressure and the fear. Herzl was too noisy, too radical, too in-
your-face and over-the-top. Establishment Jews cringed at his
shenanigans, and gentiles got this nauseated look on their faces,
not to mention the fact that he regularly infuriated the great
survivor-in-chief Maurice Messer, so that if it became known
that they were associated with this public enemy number one,
all of those nice invitations to museum functions might come
screeching to a halt, especially to those fancy receptions in the
children's tile wall area on the concourse level with those tasty
little noshes and the white wine, strictly kosher, a meal in itself
actually, and for dessert, a political smorgasbord, a veritable
Viennese table of big shots strolling around with name tags like
a list of their ingredients, you could stuff yourself on them as
much as you wanted until you were ready to bust.

But she, Henny, she was not afraid of Maurice Messer, not

one iota, there was no way in the world he would dare to black-ball her if he knew what was good for him; on the contrary, he was afraid of *her*. She had beaten him once soundly, *schmeissed* him good, when he was prepared to desecrate the dead by put-ting bales of their shorn hair on display in the museum exhibi-tion for their sensationalistic value, and, if necessary, she was ready to go after him again if he tried any of his monkey busi-ness with her—she would not hesitate for one minute, and he knew it, she knew his secrets and his lies, she knew him inside out. All it had taken to deflate him during that ugly hair feud was a little word to the president of the United States himself from the brilliant mouth of her granddaughter the intern just like a doctor M.D., her beautiful and exceptional Samantha Brittney, and Maurice had retreated in a flash, coward that he was.

Oh yes, Maurice was a famous coward, everyone knew that, it was far from a secret. That was why, as her son Arnold the psychologist also almost exactly like a doctor M.D., Samantha Brittney's daddy in fact, had once explained to her, Maurice always made such a federal case about how he was never afraid, it was a well-known mental health symptom called overcopu-lating or something like that. Even during the war he was a coward—shaking, *tzittering, pishing* in his pants, getting up the nerve once in a blue moon to venture out at night to steal a sick chicken, trembling at every sound, a liability; they had let him join their hiding place in the woods only after he had promised on everything that's holy to marry the sister with the limp of one of the leaders, a promise he had promptly broken after the war the minute he met his hoity-toity Blanche Bialystok from Bialystok in her little maroon velvet cloche with the veil and the feather. Among the survivors, it was simply the big-

gest inside joke in the world that he now passed himself off
as a resistance fighter commander during the Holocaust. The
only reason the ones who remembered him from those days
who weren't themselves in danger of reciprocal exposure due
to their own concocted stories about their exploits during the
war refrained from coming forward to denounce Maurice was
because they were afraid the disclosure of the lies of such a
prominent Holocaust operator would be grist for the mill of
the deniers and revisionists and skinheads. If the story of the
chairman of the United States Holocaust Memorial Museum
was made up, who could say what else might also be made
up, perhaps even the gas chambers themselves—and without
the gas chambers, ladies and gentlemen, where would we
be? Just another ordinary genocide, that's where, our status
as *the* Holocaust lost like innocence. But if not for this very
real worry and concern, Henny knew that there was nothing
the other survivors would have enjoyed more than to witness
this pompous old liar, this self-promoter at the expense of the
dead, this Holocaust hustler, this Shoah shyster, brought down
low, exposed and disgraced, twisting slowly in the fire like a
broiler on the spit.

Still, Henny could not help wondering—what was she
doing here on such a hot day, she, a seventy-six-year-old widow,
sweating and *schvitzing* on top of a coffin not too different, she
figured, from one she would probably in the not too distant
future be stretched out inside, as if she were in training? It was
a good question. The answer very simply was that she was not
thinking about her own comfort, but about the survival of her
people now facing the hidden Holocausts of intermarriage and
assimilation, against which the only defense was strengthening
Jewish identity through personal awareness of past and poten-

tial victimization. And Henny was not afraid. What did she have to be afraid of after all she had gone through in the first and still number-one Holocaust—ghettos, cattle cars, selections, death camps, forced marches, and so on and so forth through all the stations of the iron cross. Never mind her arthritis and her bunions and her headaches brought on by aggravation. She had come out even in this terrible temperature to stand beside Rabbi Herzl Lieb, to raise a voice of conscience against inviting terrorists and Tibetans into this temple to the six million. Meanwhile, her fellow survivors, lazy bums one and all, stayed home safe from heatstroke and dehydration, watching their soap operas and polishing their dentures.

Of course, Lipman Krakowski had also come out in this heat and humidity to stand with her and the rabbi, though at the moment he was out of commission, he had gone off to use the facilities in the museum's air-conditioned administration building. He had taken along the *New York Times* and the *Washington Post*, which he pored over meticulously front to back, including the sports and classified sections and the obituaries, one of his favorites, as well as every morsel of wisdom in the editorials, sometimes even dashing off a letter to the editor while still perched on the pot, depending on the level of inspiration that seized him, he carried a pencil and pad wherever he went for just such emergencies. The newspapers, as Lipman explained, were extremely relaxing, at one and the same time expanding mind and body. So Henny knew for a fact that she would not be seeing him for a while. She also knew that even though they were engaged in protesting against the museum, there was no question that Lipman would be allowed into the building to use the men's room; staff bureaucrats would never risk refusing him access, impressed with a deep awareness of the horrifying ruckus he was capable of stirring up if provoked. The scandal would be plastered across all the newspapers the next day: "Holocaust Museum Toilet Denied to Survivor in Distress." Scandal was the one thing this museum dreaded above all, and Lipman knew it. Given the nature of its self-righteous subject matter with its attendant vulnerability to ethical scrutiny, and given the sucking up and selling out it was required to do simply to exist much less survive, as Lipman was very well aware, it set an enormously high premium on the appearance of impeccable virtue—like a professional virgin, Lipman thought appreciatively, condemned forever to protest her virginity.

"I'll give you a full report," Lipman said cheerily to Henny as he set off with the newspapers under his arm. He did not mean a report about what he would encounter as he tried to get into the building; there was no doubt at all in the mind of either one of them that he would be admitted without a murmur. Rather, as Henny understood very well, he meant a full report about the outcome and success of his session in the stall, a sacred, inviolable hour during which no disturbance would be tolerated or forgiven, but about which, afterward, he loved to hold forth at length and in detail. As Lipman always said, "At my age, a jumbo movement in the morning is the high point of the day." And, on this particular occasion, he also meant that he would be coming back to her with a full report about the spectacular effects of the Metamucil apple crisp wafer he had ingested, the subject of a vehement argument they had been having over the past hour or so as they distributed their protest flyers, an argument made all the more irritating because Lipman was hard of hearing and Rabbi Herzl Lieb by the tree would not let up for one minute with his shofar blasting. For regularity, Lipman insisted, there was nothing to compare with Metamucil in all of its tasty varieties, solid and liquid—and also gas, ha ha ha; why, the oldest astronaut in the world, Senator John Glenn himself, refused to leave earth without it—because it made all systems go, ha ha. Henny, for her part, with equal ardor and adamancy, shouted into his ear until her voice was as rough as grit a testimonial to the superior efficacy of her own old-fashioned remedy, passed down from generation to generation, from mother to daughter—prune juice with a little hot water and a squeeze of lemon. Sitting there now on the coffin, she fished around in her overstuffed Frugal Fannie's shopping bag to find her thermos bottle filled with this elixir, for the very practical reason that after Lipman returned from doing his business, then it would be her turn.

The truth was, Henny was thinking as she sipped her concoction, she had always had her doubts about the sincerity and genuineness of Lipman's devotion to the well-being of the Jewish people. To give just one example, even when he narrated his oral testimony on Holocaust Remembrance Day in front of high school assemblies of bored kids jiggling around desperately inside their pants, for some unfathomably shameless reason he would always provocatively profess himself to be an atheist. "After all what I seen," he would announce to the fascinated teenagers, "either this so-called God doesn't exist, or if he does, I don't want nothing to do with him." Of course, Henny had to admit, these and other similarly outrageous stunts, such as identifying each Jewish girl in the audience to publicly appraise her face and figure in the interest of determining who might successfully evade the Nazis by blending in with the Aryans and who would not have a chance of passing, or singling out the prettiest blond cheerleader as an illustration of the type that for obvious uses and purposes would have been spared by the SS in the selection process, made him a great favorite on the juvenile Holocaust testimony circuit, utterly immune by virtue of age and a certified track record of suffering from corruption-of-youth charges and sexual harassment accusations. It was as if Lipman simply could not bear having grown old, Henny reflected, he was deliberately rebellious and contrary like an adolescent himself, which, in her opinion, was the true reason he had joined forces with her during the hair war and also why he was out here on this miserable day in this foul heat—not because of his concern for Jewish destiny but from sheer orneriness, the perverse thrill of standing out, of exhibiting himself, to demonstrate that there was still some juice left in him, to put the world on notice that he was not dead yet, to strut and to preen so that maybe the girls would turn their heads and flip him a salute one more time.

Henny sitting there on the coffin was so immersed in this analysis of Lipman Krakowski's borderline character, drinking her prune-juice cocktail and enjoying the exercise of applying some of the mental health concepts such as infested development and cystic personality elucidated to her by her son Arnie the psychologist, that she was completely oblivious at first to the crowds pouring out of the museum. Nor had she noticed that Rabbi Herzl Lieb had quit blowing his shofar and, still tethered to his tree, was calling out to her in mounting frustration and anxiety to run and find out what was happening.

Run? She—Henny Soskis? The last time Henny had run was in 1945, with the SS panting behind her on the forced march from the extermination camp, and she weighed eighty pounds from starvation; now she tipped the scale at over two hundred and twenty. No, Henny did not do running, except maybe for vice president in charge of snacks of her synagogue's ladies' auxiliary club, if you counted that. Taking her time as befitted a woman of her age and size and history, Henny sealed up her thermos flask, stuffed it back into her shopping bag, and, creaking like a rusty old apparatus that had seen better days, hoisted herself up from the coffin onto her swollen legs in their high heels. As she made her way across the street to the museum, the great advancing shelf of her bosom leading the rest of her through the heavy air, she stopped a few of the more alert-looking goyim streaming out and discovered that the crisis was nothing more than a routine fire drill. But when she noticed the barriers going up on the Eisenhower Plaza and the line of uniformed guards closing ranks, she decided she had better investigate further. Barreling through the phalanx of officers with the cry, "Hitler tried to stop me—you also wanna try?" she made her way to the locked entrance. Adjusting on her nose the spectacles that dangled from a string of fake pearls around her neck, Henny read through the glass the sign that had been posted from the inside.

"It's finally happened," she reported to Herzl when she returned to the tree. "The takeover by the universalists that we were all expecting one day. A *cholera* on them all! What did I always tell you, Rabbi? We can just kiss our one-and-only Holocaust good-bye."

Moreover, she informed Herzl, the "bystanders," as she called them, namely the riffraff and slime that always appeared instantaneously the minute there was word of a disaster, spontaneously generated like maggots on rotting meat—the press, the politicians, the big shots and the big-shot wannabes, every single one of them with an opinion, the hucksters and hustlers and hangers-on, the vultures and buzzards, parasites and scavengers of every shape and size, indecent onlookers and weirdos and freaks of every race, religion, and creed—were collecting on the *other* side of the building, on the Fourteenth Street side. This is what she had been told by one of the guards, a very nice-looking young man, an American giant with a nose of such cavernous breadth that Henny could see directly inside by tilting her head back and looking up from below. The Fourteenth Street side of the museum was where all the action was, she advised Herzl in a let's-face-facts tone. It was where they—she, Herzl, and Lipman—ought to go at once without wasting another minute, where they of all people had the right to be, where they above all belonged in this critical hour for Jewish history and memory. The only problem was, as both she and the rabbi understood without acknowledging it out loud, the two of them delicately averting their eyes from the chain that encircled Herzl's waist and bound him in a grotesque union with the tree, Lipman was hopelessly unreachable at the moment—and it was Lipman who had the key.

*

To Lipman's credit, however, when he finally did show up to liberate the rabbi, and the two men bearing the coffin with Henny bringing up the rear then raced within the limits of their individual speed plateaus to the Fourteenth Street side of the building, it was mainly thanks to his cultivated brazenness, Henny had to admit, that they were able to cut through the massing crowd and slide the coffin under the police barrier into the section directly in front of the museum reserved for the "privileged characters," as Henny referred to them until she too gained entry into their midst. Taking the lead from Lipman, Henny turned up her bare arm below the elbow to display the blue concentration camp numbers, with Lipman crying out as they pushed boldly across the line, "Holocaust survivors com-

ing through—wanna see our tattoos? What—you think maybe
this is my telephone number in case I forget? Don't try no funny
business!" With this fanfare, they hauled the rabbi between them
by his armpits with his shoes levitating off the ground into the
restricted zone. It was a passkey into an exclusive society with
an elite membership, the blue numbers burned into their flesh
and seared between their eyes into the memories of their dying
bodies. They were the crème de la crème of survivors, more
authentically survivors than those who had also been in the
camps but had not been branded, those who had been in work
camps but not death camps, those who had been in the greatest
number of camps for the most years, those who had been in
ghettos but not camps, those who had survived by hiding, by
blending in with the local populace, by fleeing to Russia, by
being rescued by a Schindler or a Sugihara or a Sousa Mendes,
those who had been evacuated on a Kindertransport, those
who had been hidden as children in monasteries and convents
and stables, those who could claim passage aboard the doomed
ship *Saint Louis,* those who left Europe before the war but could
boast the greatest number of family members killed, and so on
and so forth down the survivor food chain. The blue numbers
etched into their flesh were an indelible code that admitted
them into the inner circle of the exclusive Holocaust club now,
by popular demand, being opened to the general public.

Immediately, of course, all the other survivors similarly set
apart who had gathered from the greater Washington metro-
politan area and beyond also turned up their arms to flaunt
their own numbers, the whole lot of them, Henny observed
with disgust, the lesser and the superior survivors, too slothful
and passive until now to take action against the assorted Holocaust poachers and deniers and minimizers and trivializers,

finally condescending to make an appearance even in the face of the emergency heat warning directed emphatically toward the elderly, as word got out that their Holocaust was under siege from the competition. The numbered elite flapped their forearms in the stagnant air like ragged flags. "What about me? I'm not a survivor too? Who made them the boss?" But it was as if their voices could not project beyond the O of their mouths, like in a paralyzing dream, as if no sound could be emitted no matter how hard they tried to expel their protests. No one regarded them, no one recognized them for who they were. After Lipman and Henny with the rabbi dangling between them got through, the gate crashed down with a thud of finality and they were condemned to stand on the other side of the tracks with all those alien American nonentities whose history was transparent and whose suffering had borders.

"Thank you, dear friends, for lifting me up—in every respect," the rabbi said when they finally set him down again in the VIP section.

Beyond the blockades, the mob of gawkers and gloaters was multiplying by the minute, Henny could see, flowing north to Independence Avenue and streaming onto the lawns of the Mall itself, packed not only with the malcontented survivors who huddled together for spiritual warmth and security like immigrants from a single country settling in the same neighborhood, but also with the full palette of America partaking of the communal entertainment of the latest news from the Jews. Represented in their numbers, among other onlookers and bystanders, was the stodgy majority citizenry of the District of Columbia in a spectrum from pale bisque to the darkest chocolate, their young manipulating stereophonic equipment where their voluminous pants crotched at the knees; spectral

government beetles with ties askew and hair wrung out by
the humidity scuttling out of the monumental white marble
tombs; fry-fed families yoked to their cameras and ready to
strangle each other, thankfully released from the dogged misery of touring to which they had condemned themselves by
this lucky stroke of crisis and spectacle coinciding with their
visits to the nation's capital. Foreigners, too, and immigrants
in all their vaunted diversity were everywhere Henny cast her
eye, their outstretched arms with a five-dollar bill fluttering
from their fists reaching out toward the peddler in the shim-
mering lavender shirt open to the belly button and the rows of
glittering gold chains who had managed somehow to finagle
his way into the VIP section with his cart hauled by a white
donkey and trailing red, white, and blue streamers in honor
of the United States of America. At five dollars apiece, the
peddler was hawking little plastic capsules filled with blessed
dirt collected from the base of the Holocaust Museum, as if
any minute the entire edifice would crumble to the ground
in a pulverized ruin and disappear. Africans, Asians, and South
Americans from such backward cultures they had no concept
really as to why Jews were so vital to human existence were
clamoring for these sacred souvenirs. Germans, whom Henny
could always smell a mile away, waved soiled bills clutched in
the raw hands they employed to carry out their unsavory private habits. Even Arabs, usually so immemorially slow about
parting with all payment except revenge, took time off from
secretly plotting whatever it was that they plotted, acts Henny
did not even want to begin to imagine, to claim a piece of this
unfolding history. Only the Israelis, annoyingly present in that
crowd as everywhere else on earth in numbers vastly out of
proportion to the size of their tiny, expendable state, were not

buying. "They want the fucking Holocaust? *Bevakasha*, let them have it! Good-bye and good riddance!"—screaming like barbarians over the heads of the delegates from the more civilized nations, jolting Lipman Krakowski with their harsh Hebrew out of the hum of his leveling deafness.

Lipman's Hebrew derived from his decade in Israel after the war, smuggled by night from a D.P. camp in Germany through the snowy mountain passes of Italy to descend into the dark holds of the ghostly ship *Galila* at Brindisi, disembarking in the port of Haifa to circle madly in an underworld hora with kindred lost souls. He could make himself understood in thirteen languages, in fact, or so he claimed, a "linguist from necessity due to persecution and exile," as he romanticized himself when hitting on the immigrant Latin American or Haitian or Chinese girls in their native tongues. "I love the ladies—so what can I do?—I love them even when they don't smell so good," he always said. He used this line now too, in Hebrew this time, addressing a gorgeous executive type, like an actress playing the part in a movie, who was inside the winner's circle along with himself and the other luminaries, and not only that, she had a hearing aid too just like his; despite her richly deserved vanity she could not fully hide the wire descending from her ear. Their eyes had met in mutual recognition at the offending stimulus of the shrill shouted Hebrew, and he had sealed their connection by personally employing the holy tongue. There was no question that she got his message. "Pardon me, missus," Lipman inquired, switching now to English, "you from the embassy—from Israel?"

"Palestine," was Leyla Salmani's clipped retort.

"Did you say Philistine? Ha, ha! That's okay, lady, that's okay, don't worry your pretty little head about it. When I first came to Israel it was also called Palestine. Israel, Palestine, it's all the same thing, back and forth, all the same, I'm a big believer in intercourse between the human animal." Then, stung by the sight of her turning disinterestedly away from his insignificance, he called out in desperation, "Tell me something, lady—you know what a Jew is? I bet you think a Jew is a scrawny pathetic little pimple on the backside of the planet. Lady, look at me for a minute, I wanna show you something, I'm telling you, one little look, you won't be sorry."

With italicized indifference, Leyla turned her head to bestow on the lowly supplicant the begged-for look. In captive amazement she went on looking as Lipman smoothly stripped off his shirt and trousers to expose a remarkably well preserved and fit physique in a snug red Speedo swimsuit packaging a proud tight bulge, a flawless body if you forgave the subtle betrayal of a nearly negligible graveward sag in the pectoral zone and a practically indiscernible looseness and mottling of the skin. He spanned his well-defined muscular arms, raised his fists over his weightlifter's shoulders, and swiveled, displaying himself like a champion in the ring. "Does this look to you like the body of your average stereotype? Tell the truth, lady. Feel free to look—it don't cost you nothing. Go on, missus, you can also touch, don't be afraid, it don't bite, no obligation, money-back guarantee if you're not one hundred percent satisfied."

Lipman's nakedness flashed by the corner of Henny's eye like a bizarre streak of light in the wrong climate. Was he out of his mind, she wondered, undressing like this in public, and in such a holy place too, and at such a time, with all the media cameras pointed like a firing squad at an execution? Did he want to get himself arrested? she fretted anxiously, waddling over as fast as her heavy legs in the wrong shoes could transport her to rescue this old troublemaker's skin from the two swarthy guards who had broken from their squad and were also drawing closer. "Officers, officers sir," Henny cried out, "this gentleman is a Holocaust survivor. Lipman—show them your numbers! You see, officers, like cattle they branded us! Let me explain to you, officers. Mr. Krakowski here took off his clothing as a sign of mourning to protest about what's happening inside our holy memorial museum here this very minute. You know what I mean—the takeover, they're stealing our Holocaust in broad daylight right in front of our eyes. It's highway robbery. Can you believe such a thing should happen after all what we went through? Mr. Krakowski needed to show the whole world the defenseless human body that Hitler, he should rot in hell, tried to exterminate, so the world should know and never forget. I can vouch for him, officers. Mr. Krakowski is a museum volunteer, a respectable citizen, eighty years old—an old man—harmless. It won't look so good for your police blotter if you lay a hand on a senior citizen Holocaust survivor right in front of the Holocaust Museum of all places, believe me, I'm telling you this for your own good."

"Seventy-nine," Lipman observed glumly to Henny in Polish. "I heard what you said. I'm seventy-nine, not eighty. You're the one who's eighty minimum no matter what you tell to yourself and to everybody else is your true age. You can't fool me, Henn'sche, the two of us go very far back, all the way back to the dark ages. Please, I'm asking you, don't do me no favors—okay? Don't try to help me out, I don't need your help. And don't call me harmless, it's the same thing like castrated, with the you-know-what cut off, it's not a compliment to a red-blooded American male, for your information. And also, if you don't mind, can you hold back maybe from calling me an old man in public—a senior citizen?You thought I didn't heard? Well, Henn'sche'le, I heard very good! Who asked you to go ahead and broadcast my age right here like a loudspeaker in front of this beautiful *kura*? Maybe now you also want to go ahead and announce how I fought in the Israeli army in the War of Independence in 1948—and spoil one hundred percent whatever crumbs are left over from my chances with this hoo-hah Arabische chicken?" Almost imperceptibly, Lipman indicated Leyla Salmani, who was still observing the scene in fascination. He referred to all desirable women as chickens, as Henny knew very well because of her name. It was a tired joke between them based on the implicit understanding that she was like a piece of wood to his arousal organs, irredeemably unattractive, she might be a hen but she was no spring chicken. And Lipman was genuinely stirred by chickens. He had been an egg candler by profession until his retirement to full-time bodybuilding and newspaper monitoring. He had a long and distinguished career behind him of lovingly cupping in his hands the products of chickens and holding them up to the light to reveal their bloody secrets.

"Mr. Krakowski is also a very famous author, officers, I'll have you know," Henny went on, deliberately ignoring Lipman's infantile petulance in this emergency. "Extremely prophylactic, if you know my meaning—the author of so many articles you couldn't even count them." She turned to Lipman, yelling urgently in Yiddish, "How many letters to the editor did you write so far, Lippa?" She had seen them yellowing with her own eyes, pinned up over every space of the cork-covered walls of his garden apartment in Wheaton, Maryland, and glued into piles of scrapbooks cramming the metal bookshelves.

"Three thousand four hundred and sixty-seven," Lipman

answered her sullenly in Russian this time. "But I don't need to impress these peasants, these imbecile kulaks." He gave the two officers a charmingly insincere smile and patted his little red swim trunks. "So maybe I mixed up the Holocaust Museum with a beach in Puerto Rico," he said to them in Spanish. "So sue me. It's hot out, amigos, very hot. Maybe you noticed. And then this *pollo* comes along," again he indicated Leyla, discreetly, as he chose to believe, "and if it was hot already, boy, did my bubble boil. You get my meaning, compadres?"

With a proprietary look, Lipman reinforced his claim on Leyla, earned, in his mind, by this close brush with the indigenous authorities that she had witnessed, an immigrant bonding experience between them as far as he was concerned. Addressing her in Hebrew, he said, "Lady, on a hot day like this there are only two things to do—make love, and eat ice cream." He puffed out his bare chest, which revealed only the slightest of droops under a faint cumulus of white hairs, and, glancing from Leyla across the restricted area to the vendor, who went on frenetically unloading the capsules of holy Holocaust Museum dust to the clamoring customers, he added slyly, "You think maybe that distinguished entrepreneur over there has some ice cream he can sell to us?"

Henny shook her head tragically. How had it all come to this? she asked herself. Her eyes moved from Lipman, pathetic in his nakedness, to the cops wandering off bludgeoned by their own incomprehension, to Leyla, who had detached herself from Lipman's death stink as from contagion and was now chatting familiarly over the back of the white ass with the vendor still cashing in on the devastation, the vast alien mob spreading from his wares as far as Henny could see. Lipman, too, was gazing at the dark pair on either side of the white beast. "Go ahead," Henny heard him spew out with a shrug, "make him a *matzah brei*—what do I care?"

On the prime real estate spots nearest to the entrance of the building clustered the heaving mass of politicians and journalists, with Congressman Jedediah Jaspers sounding off into a bank of microphones as he loosened his tie and opened the top button of his shirt to the steamy seductions of the cameras. Museum and community leaders were conferring in important clots, officials and experts of all pretensions rubbing against each other like killer ants on the last sweet bit of crust, Henny observed. Circulating among them was that weird couple they had all noticed but whom no one could claim, the veiled nun and the Hasid in the shade of his black hat pushing their carriage with a "Remember the Children" banner fluttering from it, their dark oversize porcine baby within, legs draped over the sides, sucking on a bottle of liquid supplement that poked out from under the raised hood. Like a parody of new parenthood they strolled unmolested into and out of the museum the way the lunatic birds used to fly freely over and through the electrified fences—even as she remembered this in the sanctuary of America, Henny felt a twinge of envy—into and out of the death camp.

Her eyes followed the pair as they steered their baby carriage among her fellow survivors, stopping alongside Dr. Adolf Schmaltz the proctologist, a real doctor M.D., yes, but not a specialty you would wish for your child. From her privileged vantage point, Henny watched as Schmaltz bent his head to read the letter they handed him, then scribbled something probably illegible on what looked like a prescription pad, tore off the sheet of paper, and gave it to them. She was exceptionally gratified to note that this millionaire *macher* and big-shot doctor was consigned at least for now to the lowly general-public side of the barrier. Such a major donor like him, she couldn't figure out why he hadn't made a big stink yet, demanding his rightful place in the precincts of power and prominence. Ever since Schmaltz had collaborated with Maurice Messer in distorting history and endangering Holocaust credibility by claiming to have been the aide-de-camp to that great resistance liar, following which he was immediately appointed to the museum council and named chairman of the Ethics Committee, Henny had despised him. Then he dumped his poor Yetta like used goods for Vonda with the legs, from the casinos. Only when Henny learned that Schmaltz's son had dropped out of school to become a Hopi Indian on a reservation in Arizona, and had stubbornly dug in there sucking mushrooms all day long even in the face of the deprogramming interventions lavishly funded by the old man, most notably the mission in a private luxury jet of Rabbi Dr. Monty Pincus to demonstrate to the boy the superiority of the Holocaust high over all other forms of highs—only then, perhaps for the first time in all the long years since she had been marched off to the cattle cars with the Nazis behind her sealing up the house in which her mother and baby sisters were hiding, did Henny feel once again that maybe there was a God in heaven after all and some measure of justice on this earth.

She watched now as the heat of the day congealed and became concentrated, the sky began to darken and blister, and the police helicopters that had been hovering overhead all afternoon started to give chase to a small commuter plane that suddenly appeared, circling wildly. As if to shelter their baby from the coming storm, the Hasid papa and the nun mama picked up their pace with their beat-up buggy, moving rapidly from Schmaltz's humble place among the masses into the restricted VIP area. Pausing one more time before dashing back into the museum, the nun slipped a crumpled sheet of paper to Rabbi Herzl Lieb's sister, who lowered her head and read swiftly. Passing the note to her brother, the sister then swirled down to the top of the coffin in a kind of faint, surrendering all self-consciousness with respect to how she looked to the rows of judging eyes such as Henny's that were fixed upon her, and sat there hunched over in a tragic pose, her elbows planted on her thighs, her palms pressed into her cheeks, her fingertips raking her temples.

This was not the rabbi's hippie sister, Henny realized as she continued staring, the lost Mara, not the prodigal dropout daughter who had caused so much embarrassment and anguish to her father, that indicted nursing-home-fraud criminal and Warsaw Ghetto partisan impersonator Leon Lieb—further heartwarming proof, in Henny's opinion, of the existence of divine justice unto the tenth generation. This was the good sister, the proper, *balabatish* one, the one who had married the psychiatrist, not strictly a real M.D. no matter what they said—more like an unfrocked rabbi, in Henny's opinion. This was the daughter whom Leon Lieb had set up at the head of his charitable foundation that funded such worthy and noble causes as obesity clinics in memory of his late wife Rose, as well as centers for the study and recognition of Jewish courage and resistance during the Holocaust in his own honor. This sister had latched herself on to the rabbi the minute that he and Lipman with Henny puffing behind had arrived with their coffin, her long ashen face exactly like her brother's only without the punctuation of a beard. Never releasing the rabbi from her sight for a minute, trailing closely behind him, she clutched the edge of his prayer shawl like a life jacket as he carried on with his pastoral duties, leaning over the barricades to kiss and embrace and stroke the aged cheeks of his congregation of compromised survivors, greeting them as My rebbes, my holy teachers, my spiritual guides, while they in return bent toward his dimming light as to their last hope.

He was a fearless, dedicated leader, Rabbi Herzl Lieb, Henny could not deny it, faithful and steadfast at their side from the very beginning. But in those innocent days long ago, when they had first started out with their original and startling Never Agains and their Remembers, their Kaddishes and their candles, their testimonies and lessons, their memorials and museums, who would ever have imagined that this would be the consequence, who could have predicted that their small band of idealistic survivor saints would metastasize into a fatal plague of persecutees, an epidemic of victims, a pestilence of freelance and copycat Holocausts? In those early days it had been Rabbi Herzl Lieb, young and brash, who had valiantly risen before them to lead them into battle with his rallying cry against the Six Silences—how well Henny remembered being struck by the epiphany of his formulations at that time before they had deteriorated into pieties and manipulations and clichés: the silence of the perpetrators, who trusted the world to collude in covering up their crimes; the silence of the collaborators, who muted and muffled their participation in the unspoken understanding that they were victims too; the silence of the bystanders, witnesses who did not raise a voice of conscience to help; the silence of the American Jewish leadership, too frightened to speak truth to power; the silence of the survivors, too traumatized to come forward with their testimony; and the silence of the six million victims, who could not speak for themselves. "I am hoarse from all these silences," the rabbi had mystically declared. But then, in reaction to these toxic silences, such tumult and cacophony had been generated, Henny thought mournfully, unconsciously elevating her hands as if to stop up her ears, such screaming and yelling culminating with everyone tearing at the remains of the Holocaust to claim their own personally monogrammed piece, memorials and museums sprouting up everywhere, even El Paso, Texas, had to have its own Holocaust museum for the cowboys, even Whitwell, Tennessee, had to have its own cattle car to contain its plague of paper clips, that now a little silence would definitely be appreciated—yes, a little peace and quiet, if you don't mind, the dignity and refinement of a time when there were still no words, when the words had not yet been mass-produced and packaged and made universally available for instant consumption.

In those heady days, when the rabbi was still young and the Holocaust was still unique, Henny recalled, he had led his demonstrations decked out in a striped concentration-camp-prisoner uniform, blasting his ram's horn and lamenting with thunderous sincerity that he himself had not been privileged to be among the martyrs of the gas chambers and the furnaces. She and her good-hearted Milton the CPA newly retired from the Internal Revenue Service, may he rest in peace, who had first taken her captive as his future tax deduction when he had penetrated the Buchenwald concentration camp at the end of the war with his American GI battalion, had debuted with their acclaimed long-running hit routine as husband-and-wife liberator-and-survivor duo, including triumphant personal appearances and prizewinning documentary films, on the Holocaust testimony circuit. And they were the real goods, the two of them, one hundred percent certified—she an authentic survivor, branded with the official tattoo seal of approval, he a genuine liberator, not one of those blacks or Afro-Americans or whatever they called them nowadays mythologized in the flush of affirmative action by this very museum supposedly dedicated to historical truth as the first to charge into Buchenwald and free the slaves. But when she and her innocent Milton first took their show on the road, those were the undisputed glory days, the golden age when Holocaust survivors reigned unopposed as victim royalty, the rewards of their universally acknowledged unparalleled and preeminent suffering laid lavishly at their feet, climaxing in the jewel in the crown, this monumental museum, rising audaciously on United States government soil, dead Jews bearing witness to the goodness of America in an unambiguously just war, and also in peace. It was an astounding feat, which Henny fully appreciated—the transformation of our Jewish Holocaust into an American memory, almost too stupendous to absorb.

Her eyes moved from the imposing museum, now overrun and crawling with the hordes of demonic baby Holocausts that they had spawned, to her growing tribe of eternally aging and dying and soon-to-be-no-longer-with-us fellow survivors. We have used this institution and the Holocaust it packages for our own glory and pride, she admitted to herself, and we have been used by it in turn for legitimization and sanctimoniousness. We have been greedy for the spoils of our suffering in the form of restitution and reparations, and have allowed our names, our plundered assets, and our dormant claims to be exploited for the greed of others. We have let ourselves be seduced by power and profit in no way different from those who had not been purified in the fires so that our entire enterprise has become fatally tainted and our time has truly run out.

"We have been guilty, we have betrayed, we have robbed, we have spoken slander," Rabbi Herzl Lieb was intoning to his congregation of defeated survivors who had come out searching for the salvation of meaning in that punishing August heat but were now either fleeing the approaching storm or standing there wretchedly, the thin hair and translucent skin defining their mortal skulls shielded with newspapers or crackling plastic bags as the drops began to fall. The rabbi was invoking the litany of transgressions from the breast-pounding confession of the Day of Atonement descending unrelentingly upon them as summer declined to fall. "We have extorted, we have been perverse, we have been loathsome, we have committed abominations, we have strayed. *Gevalt*, my friends, it is what I have told you from the very beginning. This museum and everything associated with it is a corrupter and a seducer, mired in politics and deals and compromise from its conception in 1978 as a sop to Jews who were making feeble little noises against the sale of F-15 fighter planes to Saudi Arabia, and it continues to be steeped in special interest agendas to this very day, dragging the six million and the entire Holocaust down to universal cynicism and revulsion along with it. As I said to Jimmy Carter when it was my turn to shake his hand at a White House reception for rabbis, 'Mr. President,' I said, 'don't give us the Holocaust in exchange for the State of Israel.' Needless to add," Herzl Lieb added, looking with wonder at his own right hand, which had been complicit in insulting the most powerful man on earth, "I have never been invited to the White House again."

The rabbi now extended that hand to his sister and helped her to rise from the coffin. "My friends, I want you to meet my sister, Rashi," he told his audience. "Rashi, say hello to these nice people."

She shook her head, uncharacteristically oblivious to the rain soaking and flattening her hairdo. Tightening her lips to a rippled chalkiness and closing her eyes, she metronomed a finger in the negative in front of her face, too overcome to speak.

"This is what it has all come to, my dear faithful companions," the rabbi shouted over the fat drops of rain slapping against the sidewalk, the thunder in the distance, the helicopters and light commuter plane looping overhead, the squawking of birds diving headlong to the ground like dark mythic omens. "It's the end of the line for us," the rabbi bellowed. "We have given away our past, our history and our Holocaust. Now they are claiming our future too. The terrorists have stated that nobody inside this building will come out alive unless all their demands are met. My sister's daughter, Naomi, is inside that building."

Those who had remained from among the survivors and could hear above the rain exhaled a collective gasp. Herzl did not go on to elaborate that not only his niece, Rashi's daughter, but also their other sister, the strayed Mara, and her two children were in there too; that would have been more detail than these old folks could process in this weather, much too complicated and strange, and far less effective in wringing out their quivering hearts. The sight of a stricken mother standing before them over whose child's head doom was throbbing was as much stimulation as they could bear. Every living Jewish child was a survivor, a firebrand snatched from the burning, yet still the lessons had not been learned.

"Naomi has written a letter to her mother," the rabbi revealed. "We believe that the girl has been brainwashed. With Rashi's permission, I will read you the letter."

Rashi was unable to respond. She was not so sure it was such a good idea. The rabbi raised his voice over the storm and read: "Dear Mommy, peace and love. I'm writing this letter to you to say good-bye. The old man in the wheelchair says they'll never give in so I guess we won't be coming out alive. Maybe Grandpa Leon can like dialogue with him? I think they fought together during the Holocaust or whatever. This whole museum is so bogus. Don't be sad, Mommy, it's okay. It's part of the cycle, it's samsara. I'm here with my cousins, Rumi and Rumi. They are so cute you can just die. Their mom, Auntie Mara aka Marano aka Rama-sensei the Buddhist nun, is also here for sure. She's like the coolest person in the whole world, totally awesome. She says I'm just like her when she was my age. It's like the biggest compliment. She says I'm channeling the Mara she's sloughed off, so I've changed my name to Mara. So Mommy, if like by some miracle or whatever I make it out of here, please don't call me Naomi anymore."

*

The delivery of this letter was the last stop on the route of the nun and the Hasid steering their black baby carriage before vanishing behind the screen of the rain back into the hollows of the museum. Leyla Salmani's eyes had followed their circuit, observing them fade away in the darkening downpour after their visitation among the survivors as she had kept track of them from the moment they had first materialized, floating unobstructed in the white haze of the heat among the inflated power brokers pressing closest to the entrance of the besieged museum. She and Tommy Messiah's donkey were standing side by side, regarding them together.

Leyla had come over to inquire if Tommy Messiah had any ice cream. He gestured with thumb and index finger rounded

into a circlet for her to have a little patience please and wait
a second while he completed giving instructions to the two
urchins of color he had recruited on the correct way to fill
the little plastic tubes with dirt from the base of the Holocaust Museum, now doubled in price due to increased overhead costs and continued heavy demand for these relics by the
public. Having adjusted the production of his assembly line to
his satisfaction and while still executing a fever of transactions
without pause, Tommy Messiah then managed to snatch the
opportunity to slip his hand into the donkey's carpet saddlebag,
extract a few pink and white pills, and with an almost imper-
ceptible movement deposit them inside the breast pocket of
Leyla's man-tailored suit jacket, taking as he did so in the form
of his rightful payment a sly pinch, as a reminder, of the living
nipple underneath. "Strawberry and vanilla," Tommy Messiah
said, "flavors of the day."

Leyla stood frozen in her place beside the donkey, her beautiful chocolate eyes fixed on the Hasid and the nun wading into
the knot of personages of consequence, wielding their baby
carriage before them as a kind of implement to clear their path
and hack their way into the jungle. They were doing their job.
What was she waiting for? She too ought to proceed into the
heart of the heart of the action, Leyla knew, to pound away
on behalf of United Holocausts. The media were all in place,
parched for adjectives, all the usual suspects set out like putty
for her to mold, from the hard-liner former reporter, now
exalted to pundit and talking head, Crusher Casey, to her
old movie director and screenwriter, R. C. Hammer, filming
importantly, and every specimen in between. Pushkin Jones
and all the holy martyrs were fulfilling their part, sacrificing
themselves inside the museum, relying on her on the outside to

articulate in the cool persuasive polish of her Oxford English
the message of United Holocausts. Her own people too were
counting on her for special recognition, among the hosts of
all the other Holocausts, of their Palestinian Holocaust perpetrated to rectify that holiest-of-holies Holocaust of the Jews to
which the entire world was required to pay daily deference and
render hourly homage. Really, she ought to seize the opening of
the wake created behind the progress of the pram, Leyla knew,
in order to reenter the precincts of influence and power, but
for the moment she was unable, she felt for the moment dull
and emptied, as if all her energy were leaking into a shameful
little puddle forming on the sidewalk around her like the dung
dropping under the donkey. To lift a foot and take a single step
forward was beyond what she could imagine.

Not removing her eyes from the shadowy couple as they
smoothly penetrated the innermost circles with their weird
offspring, with a subtle sweep of her hand, as if she were wiping her mouth, Leyla positioned one of Tommy Messiah's pills
in the well of her tongue, worked up a quantity of saliva, and
swallowed it down. Then she took another, just in case. She
recognized the Hasid of course from his past life as a *shabab,* for
which, it seemed, he was now making demented atonement,
and the nun too was known to her, but the deformed creature
in the buggy was a special effect wrought by these two creative types of their own peculiar devising—she wondered what
could possibly have possessed such a pro as Pushkin Jones to
sign off on such grotesquerie. The alarming thought struck her
that the contents of that carriage might even be the monstrous
offspring of her old companion, the fanatic settlement leader
Yehudi HaGoel, behind whom in an hour of wild recklessness
she had ridden on the bare backs of white stallions over the

brown hills of Judea, admitting him into the secret chambers
of her citadel, where he had planted his bomb and blown off
her father's legs. This strange fruit of one of his wives, named
in a dead language for the onset of the redemption, as a child
almost transparent in her slightness, had been lowered by a
rope through the most minuscule of orifices in the floor of
Al-Haram Al-Ibrahimi, the Tomb of the Patriarchs in Hebron,
Leyla had heard, to seek out the haunted beds of the forefathers
and mothers in the subterranean caves below. After that, the
girl was never again the same, or so the story goes, like the
docile boy Isaac after he was bound atop the altar on Moriah.
Abraham had descended from the mountain without him,
alone. Or more to the point, without Ishmael. It had been over
the throat of his other son, Ishmael, her own untamed ancestor
falling upon all of his brothers, Leyla was convinced, that the
father had brandished his knife on the mountaintop.

Ishmael and Isaac, two traumatized sons of one God-obsessed
father. No record exists that they ever had contact again with
their faith-crazed old man until together they buried him in
the Cave of the Machpelah. Arab and Jew, partners in the business of death, bleeding into each other, like Shahid metamor-
phosed into a Hasid, Leyla reflected, the boy who was once his
father's plumage, groomed for splendor and legend, swindled
by the rabbis into trading in the material rewards of Islam in
paradise for the material rewards of the Jews in the Garden
of Eden, seventy-two perfumed houris with translucent skin
and eternally renewable virginities forfeited in exchange for
an old wife converted into a footstool reeking of overcooked
wild ox and leviathan, a lousy deal in anyone's book. Leyla's
eyes followed Shahid, freely infiltrating the innermost circles
nearest to the museum with the buggy and the veiled sister

at his side. Had he still resembled the lithe Arab boy with the checked kaffiyeh drawn across his face and the taut slingshot taking aim in the alleys of Ramallah that he once was in an earlier chapter, it would have been inconceivable for him to be admitted into those rarefied zones. Here was the best of all incognitos, Leyla saw, if only he could still be enticed and conscripted. Who would suspect a pious Jew? Under his fringed garment they would strap enough explosives to blow up the entire Israeli Knesset and all of its Jewish clowns one sunny day as the Arab delegation sucks in the fragrant smoke of their narghiles in their bright new cabanas on the beaches of Tel Aviv; in the creamy satin band inside his black Borsalino hat a dagger would be slipped with which to overcome the pilot in the cockpit and slam the jet with all of its passengers swaying in prayer into the sands of the Negev, straight into the nuclear reactor of Dimona, which doesn't exist.

"Too Jew for you?" Tommy Messiah whispered into her ear, cohabiting her thoughts, his eye, like hers, on the Hasid while not for even one second divesting from pushing his dirt. "Checked out Shimshon lately? This is his ass." He gave the donkey's bridle an emphatic tug.

This was the jolt Leyla needed to propel herself forward. She began to make her way toward the ring of the movers and shakers nearest to the hijacked museum. Yes, she knew she had recognized this ass from somewhere, she realized as she approached the epicenter. She had seen Shimshon straddling its bare back, riding among the olive trees along the terraced hills of Samaria. This was only a short while after he had been released from Tel Mond prison, where he had been sent on drug-dealing charges, and where, until his spectacular penance and return to the original faith under the influence of fellow

inmates serving time for conspiring to replace the golden
Dome of the Rock with the Third Temple, he had sat in his
cell all day composing his pathetic letters to her, expecting a
reply merely because for once in his life this Zionist boor had
done the gallant thing and taken the rap on himself rather than
passing the buck, as usual, to the woman who made him do
it, the woman who had beguiled him. Leyla had been behind
the wheel of her silver Mercedes with the top down when she
had spotted him on the ass. Her hair was bound up in her silk
Hermes scarf, her eyes were protected from betraying her by
her celebrity shades, and Abu Shahid was beside her in the
passenger seat, smoking a foul-smelling Noblesse to which he
had remained true from his bohemian days in Sheikh Jarrah
and Abu Tor, flicking the ashes onto the road, when they were
inconvenienced by being obliged to come to a complete halt to
allow the procession of jokers to pass: Shimshon with full black
Nazirite beard riding atop the ass in his Israelite turban and
white biblical tunic with its blue fringes, strumming a Davidic
harp; behind him a bride, arrayed in a golden crown delineat-
ing the walls of the old city of Jerusalem, being transported
to her domed wedding canopy in a royal Solomonic litter carried on poles by four bearers, among whom Leyla immediately
recognized the hallucinating twins Eldad and Medad, from the
class trip to the Auschwitz death camp so many years before,
adorned in wreaths of rosemary and myrrh. "I know that guy,"
Leyla had said to Abu Shahid. "An ex-con. A dealer in Ecstasy."

What sort of comfort might now be derived from the
recognition that, as Tommy Messiah had correctly insinuated,
however extreme Shahid might appear in his Jewish emana-
tion—and he was definitely a cultic case, Leyla kept her eye
fastened upon him as she drew closer to where the Hasid and

his nun with their carriage were navigating the labyrinth of eminences—next to a freak like Shimshon he looked more or less like one of the boys? But the real question was, Who in a million years would ever have imagined that she would run into Shimshon's white ass again of all asses, right here on Fourteenth Street in Washington, D.C., in front of the United States Holocaust Memorial Museum, of all places, in the middle of a takeover crisis no less? And how could she be sure that this really was Shimshon's ass, as Tommy Messiah maintained? Was she supposed to be able to tell one ass from another merely because she was from the Middle East? Wasn't it possible, after all, that the livestock had simply strayed across the street from the Department of Agriculture? Above all, why in the world would Tommy Messiah have gone to all the trouble and expense of importing an ass for special effects all the way from the Holy Land when no doubt there were more than enough available right here in the land of plenty, in Christian America, where snow-white redemption asses were probably already being mass-produced just as red heifers were being bred, perfect and without a blemish, for purification rituals in the restored Temple? The answer was obvious, Leyla finally understood. Tommy Messiah was putting her on; he had invented this preposterous story of Shimshon's ass either to test her or to make a fool of her—to test if she got the joke, to make an ass of her by pushing in her face the corrosive fact that *she* was the joke.

Stiffening to shake off her own female absurdity and fraudulence, Leyla now sought to position herself among the main players in the inner circle, where, she noted, not a single other woman was present. She took pains to keep as far away as possible from the representatives of alternative Holocausts who had materialized to stake their claim as word of the universalist occupation of the museum spread. It was not only critical to establish her position as the chief intermediary and public relations spokesman for United Holocausts, a coalition of serious prime-time Holocausts in every way at least as worthy as the Jewish Holocaust, but for Leyla personally, it was no less important to ensure that the Palestinian Holocaust, her own people's *naqba*, be accorded its rightful place in the first tier of the pantheon of Holocausts. True, the credo of United Holocausts was to respect all Holocausts equally in all their multifarious diversity of suffering and victimization, but Leyla was exquisitely mindful to keep her distance publicly from the chicken holocaust lady, for example, who, even in that heat, was present to bear witness in her heavy feathered costume strung with heartbreaking photos of abused poultry rescued from the processing industry, pounding on her drum and chanting, "All broilers are my brothers, all fowl are my 'family.'" The ferret holocaust, the mad cow holocaust, the experimental and research animals holocaust, the right-to-bear-arms holocaust, the Confederate flag holocaust, the Falun Gong holocaust, the witches and Wiccans holocaust, the aliens and extraterrestrials holocaust, and so on and so forth across a topography populated by seeming crackpots and cranks—each and every one of these lowercase holocausts without exception had to be shunned in the short run for the sake of the ultimate legitimization and triumph of their cause.

For this strategic reason, Leyla also pretended not to notice her old friend from the interfaith and feminist and human rights scene in Greater Israel or Greater Palestine, depending on which side of the line you squatted at, Ivriya Himmelhoch—because Ivriya's deserted wives holocaust, and more specifically her Jewish deserted wives holocaust, her *agunot*'s holocaust of

wives chained by the harshness of rabbinical decree to husbands who had vanished without a trace or a death certificate,
was, while worthy, by no means a major-league Holocaust.
Technically, it was a sub-subspecialty of the larger Women's
Holocaust—in some respects, though far less understandable
and forgivable in cultural and human terms, like the murders
by blood relatives of Muslim women accused of dishonoring
their families, another subcategory of the Women's Holocaust
that happened to be close to Leyla's heart but that also regrettably had to be put for the moment on the back burner in the
overriding interest of the greater joint effort.

Leyla had heard through the New Age and interfaith and
vegan grapevine that Ivriya was in the States to advocate on
behalf of the deserted wives of the World Trade Center in New
York, which had been reduced to the dust from which it had
risen. This was an added reason to try to avoid her, since of
course there was the delicate issue that it had been Leyla's
own people, provoked beyond endurance by a justified hatred
of that shitty little country Israel, the cause of all the trouble,
and its best friend America, who had ignited the conflagration
resulting in these deserted wives whom the legalistic rabbis
now refused to release into widowhood, rejecting as proof of
death in the absence of a body the fact that the missing husbands
never returned after setting out to their regular jobs in the
towers that morning in September and sending home e-mails
of farewell from their offices in the fiery clouds. Perhaps that
was the morning of all mornings that they had been inspired
to wander off to the land where deserting husbands go, and
as for e-mails, they can be beamed from anywhere in the universe, as even the most rigid and reactionary of the rabbis in
their black satin caftans knew very well as they conducted their

question-and-answer responsa exchanges regarding law and practice via high-tech Internet hookups—Is a golem (provided it's not a female golem) acceptable as one of the ten worshippers required for a *minyan*? May a man lie in a woman's bosom in the sunlight if she needs to check him for head lice? If your PalmPilot in which you have programmed holy texts containing God's name falls to the ground, should you kiss it when you pick it up?

Still, it was not a simple matter for Leyla to pretend that she had not noticed Ivriya Himmelhoch. In the solidity of her wheelchair, to which she had been confined years earlier when she was still a young woman after a fall from a horse, the price exacted from her for riding carefree and bare-breasted, the Lady Godiva of the Galilee, Ivriya was a focal point and axis in whichever setting she happened to be. If she was there, you noticed her, like a centerpiece on the table. You had to communicate over or around her. She was a manifest obstruction requiring the acknowledgment of a detour, and she recognized her power. Now, as Leyla followed the Hasid and the nun with their baby carriage to the heart of the action at the very front of the museum, Ivriya followed from behind. Leyla was wedged in by wheels, and Ivriya was calling her name.

In this way they made their passage through the tangle of men who mattered, piled up against each other in a killer sport huddle, the knots of their ties loosened, great craters of perspiration at their armpits, their jackets slung campaign-style over one shoulder, sweat pouring down from their temples, arriving at the frontline just as those two museum titans, Chief of Staff Rabbi Dr. Monty Pincus and Council Member the Honorable Norman Messer Esquire son of the chairman, addressing a team of top officers in full battle gear from the highest ranks of the FBI's Bureau of Alcohol, Tobacco and Firearms special commando force, uttered in unison their immortal words, "I'm in charge here!"

With a seamless movement, Leyla Salmani and Ivriya Himmelhoch turned to each other. "Jinx," they absurdly burst out in unison. Then, caught up together high on the wave of the ridiculous, taking care not to break the spell by uttering another word, they instantly linked pinkies to make a wish, inspired by the remembered stimulus from their childhood games—the astonishing and potentially incredibly auspicious coincidence of two people saying the exact same thing at the exact same time, even though technically, according to the rules for optimal wish-granting success, it was the two men, and not they, who had first spoken at once. Still, the women registered their wishes mutely, with fingers hooked. Then, still precisely together, they exploded, erupting into great honks and snorts of helpless laughter. It was impossible to hold back, even as all the important men turned to glare at them for their failure of seriousness and Norman, surreptitiously checking his fly, inquired, "Excuse me, ladies, is something funny?" and Monty took the liberty in this emergency of whispering into Leyla's unplugged ear an offer to bring her a drink of water— or maybe, from that Balaam prophet-for-hire over there with his donkey, an ice cream cone to lick? They were doubled over, Leyla and Ivriya, choking, retching up convulsive shreds of laughter, charged with surging currents of laughter, their thoughts entwined as their fingers had been, the corroboration of words unnecessary between them—trembling as one lest the terrible laughter merge into terrible weeping and tears come streaming from their eyes and mortifying wetness from who knows where else as they shared their acute consciousness of the ridiculousness of these puny mortal men puffed up with their affairs and strutting about like cocks under the indifferent eye of the sun.

A moment or two later, however, again almost exactly in concert, the two women recovered, startling themselves back to propriety and business. They turned from each other without a word, as from a mutual embarrassment, which, in order to be expunged, demanded mutual denial and rejection. To Ivriya it was evident that she would not acquire Holocaust certification for her deserted wives through Leyla. Adroitly maneuvering her wheelchair through the power clot, she made her way to the fringes where the celebrity columnist Crusher Casey was dictating into a phone his seven-hundred-and-fifty-word featured commentary for his appearance on the prime-time news that evening, to be recycled as the print version in the next morning's newspapers. Ivriya was well aware that Casey, in his bow tie and spats and three-piece pinstripe suit, even in that heat, was a conservative ideologue and therefore not prone to be correctly solicitous of a woman in a wheelchair paralyzed from the waist down whose cause, moreover, challenged traditional male establishment religious authority. Even so, she was sufficiently politically savvy to appreciate that Casey had an unmatched forum and following, Casey's columns were published and broadcast worldwide, he was disproportionately powerful and influential; if by a stroke of good luck—a breakthrough for her cause was what she had secretly wished for, after all—he inclined himself favorably toward her and her flock of *agunot* twisting their tissues in desolate unresolved abandonment, the benefits in terms of public awareness and raised consciousness could be stupendous. In the face of this potential outcome, what did her own personal dignity or self-respect matter? Ivriya was prepared to demean herself, she would assume the posture of a supplicant, hover at the edge of the great man's overrefined orbit while he went on dictating, wheezing through his rhetorical flourishes in consequence of a full frontal assault by the allergens to which he was so exquisitely sensitive in that hot pendulous air, loath nevertheless to sully the finely spun twin-peaked silk handkerchief poking up from his breast pocket, wheezing and dictating relentlessly while rigidly ignoring Ivriya at his periphery except for the instances when he automatically lowered his hand in her direction without actually glancing her way to receive another Kleenex after the taken-for-granted appearance of the first, claiming one after another, which she dutifully placed in his palm from the traveling box she kept among her essential supplies in an easily accessible case in her wheelchair, tucked against the arm.

Cocking her chin perkily upward, fixing her eyes upon the media star with the adoration she calculated might soften him, passing the tissues up as needed to the powdery hand dangling blindly above her from time to time to receive them, Ivriya dedicated herself to earning her petitioner's chits as Casey held forth and expatiated—opening with a witty account of the naked grab for power in the museum leadership vacuum created by the takeover, the leap into the breach of those two pushy little poo-bahs, Pincus the wife beater, whom Casey had once sensationally profiled when he still wore his reporter's hat (and by the way, in all due modesty, Casey parenthesized, he was firmly convinced that thanks to that rigorous bit of investigative work, he deserved full credit for keeping this cowboy out of the director's saddle of this sui generis museum), and Messer junior, that pompous little weasel and jerk; these two pitiful climbers, Casey intoned, had certainly come off way too

Al open quote "I'm-In-Charge-Here" close quote Haig—the memorable words uttered by the clueless general slash secretary of state following the assassination attempt on President Ronald Reagan, a gaffe he would drag along behind him as his main piece of baggage directly into his *New York Times* obituary. From there Casey moved on to an arch and entertaining laundry list of the sundry assortment of Holocaust pretenders who had precipitated this crisis, including—would you believe?—an ambassador from the so-called Fur Holocaust, insisting on a moral equivalency with the Jewish Holocaust, the entire vile usurpation spearheaded by an African-American for whom even the benefits personally accrued from affirmative action were not regarded as reparation enough; as far as Casey was concerned, and here, before ending this section with a quotation from Machiavelli concerning the fundamental beastlike nature of humankind, he repeated his policy proposal, which he had articulated several times before, namely, that every Negro male and female in America who is a proven descendant of slaves should be handed a onetime lump-sum payment of restitution on condition they sign an agreement to shut up once and for all about lowered self-esteem and being dissed and any and all other useless gripes and grievances—enough is enough, final payment, case closed. The concluding and most crucial section of Casey's commentary commenced with a forceful reiteration of his unyielding guiding principle—No Negotiating With Terrorists, Period. This principle, he asserted, overrides all hostage considerations, all moral and ethical scruples and niceties, and, it goes without saying, all potential consequences to the museum infrastructure and collections, which essentially contained very few unique artifacts in any case or objects of value; an international fund-raising campaign of the sort the museum's contributors and creators were legendary at mounting would do the trick of replacing every item and then some in no time at all. Whatever it takes to get the job done, that's what we have to do, Casey asserted, segueing directly from there to the laying out of his battle plan: A lightning strike, that was the crux of it, blitz the buggers to kingdom come, all kinds of sexy stuff, swoop and poop—for God's sake, what's needed here is a little adult supervision! The M.O. would be a limited friendly-fire air war to storm the complex—first, by the insertion of an entry device into the roof through which deluge hoses would be trained on the targets to scare the living you-know-what out of them; then, an infusion of tear gas to smoke them out of their holes; last, if resistance persists, the delivery of a small compact bomb, neatly pinpointed and targeted for minimum collateral damage and maximum percussive and explosive effect. "Nice is nice," Crusher Casey hurtled triumphantly to the finish with his familiar epigrammatic sign-off as Ivriya Himmelhoch cleared her throat huskily and gesticulated desperately for his attention, "but Right is right!" Satisfied that he had the handle on the situation, that there was nothing new here that he had not already seen and heard and known before, as usual, and mindful of the need to ration his public appearances as a major media figure to maintain their market value, Casey clicked off his phone, slipped it into its designated compartment inside his jacket pocket, and strode off briskly, executing, in passing, a satisfying dunk shot with his wadded-up ball of used tissues into the receptacle conveniently presented by the lap that was Ivriya.

*

The incident of the attempted Holocaust power grab by the rivals Monty Pincus and Norman Messer was also being communicated by Leyla Salmani, reporting through a miniature microphone attached to her wristwatch into the ear of Pushkin Jones at his command post at ground zero inside the Hall of Witness of the museum. Guarding her position close to the source, Leyla riveted her gaze on the movements of the nun and Hasid wriggling their carriage to the very front of the enemy lines, as she went on providing Jones with a blow-by-blow account of the Monty and Norman show, the squalid temporary marriage of convenience hastily consummated between these two senior museum officials who patently despised each other, conjoined in a befouled bed at this critical juncture to prevent the military types from doing what military types were evolutionarily programmed to do—launching a full-scale air and ground assault on their sacred institution to fumigate it of the invaders. "Perish the thought," Norman the clown declared. "For shame!" Monty the straight man echoed. "The violation of violence within the holy precincts of the six million violated by violence, gas on the sacred ground of the gassed—a sacrilege, an outrage!" "It would be the Mother of all Holocausts," Norman eked out laboriously, momentously, "the Holocaust Holocaust. We would have to erect a new museum to commemorate it."

That was a truly scary prospect. For the moment, Leyla confirmed to Jones, all parties agreed to put the attack scenario on hold. But overhead helicopters were suspended, on the ground troops in full gear were poised. It was a combustible situation, a tinderbox that required only a spark to ignite and consume everything around it, the living and the dead in one great pyre. Now, Leyla reported, continuing with her complete eyewitness coverage as she observed the nun attempt to pass one of her letters to Norman Messer, the august leaders were battling over procedures for the implementation of Plan B—namely, how to secure the good offices of the universally exalted Holocaust High Priest, the only living personage who might embody the moral authority and cultivated prestige to intervene and negotiate with the renegades and bring them to their senses before it was too late.

"I know the High Priest personally, the High Priest's a close personal friend of mine," Norman blurted out, sounding to his own ears alarmingly like his father. Even so, he could not contain his excitement, sputtering out blooming corsages of saliva to keep from using the common pronoun to designate so hallowed a figure as the High Priest while at the same time swatting away the nun's proffered letter as he waved his arms wildly in the air. But, Norman added, in the attitude of privileged insider, calming down now as befitted his public role, stretching the pleasure of forcing them to hang on his every word, the High Priest is a very difficult number to book, scheduled years in advance, a rare catch. However, if by some miracle the High Priest's services as arbitrator and peacemaker and savior can be secured in this emergency, Norman most definitely must be the one to personally escort the High Priest into the combat zone. Naturally, Norman in his position could not be expected to take upon himself the responsibility of soliciting the High Priest due to the impossibility of personally guaranteeing the High Priest's safety in this perilous situation. Nevertheless, like a brain surgeon making his entrance into the operating theater to perform the delicate life-and-death procedure only after the patient has been fully laid out on the table and the gross incision has already been made, Norman was committed to undertaking the risky and dangerous role of aide-de-camp whatever the consequences to himself personally, yes, provided support staff and other subordinate team members paved the way before-hand as appropriate, handling the preliminaries, working out arrangements.

"No problem," Tommy Messiah said, stepping forward as if summoned.

The deal was swiftly concluded: fifty thousand dollars for the immediate services of the High Priest, plus a limousine to transport him back and forth from his suite in the Washington hotel where he happened by a stroke of good fortune to be ensconced at the moment in a meeting with the first lady in connection with her project on children and dogs, plus a twenty-five-thousand-dollar commission for Tommy Messiah as the fixer, the agent, and go-between—all payments in advance, naturally, no strings attached, irrespective of outcome or success, and, needless to say, in cash.

"No problem," Tommy Messiah said again when they raised the predictable obstacles. They could go to the Bureau of Engraving and Printing next door to obtain the bills, it was all part of the same federal outfit anyway, he had no objections whatsoever to government greens, bring them to him hot off the presses, in a white cardboard box tied up with string, fragrant and moist, like freshly baked rolls straight from the oven. Frankly, he didn't give a damn how they got the bread. But the bottom line was—no payment, no priest. "Bottom line, friends," Tommy Messiah stressed.

Norman decorously stepped back as the transaction was carried out, preferring in this instance the discretion of silence to the unforeseeable consequences to himself of exposing this operator for the crook he knew him to be. He consoled himself for his noninterference bystander's policy with the thought that this would by no means be the first time the museum threw away the taxpayers' money. And who could say? Maybe the High Priest would be delivered after all. He glanced at Tommy Messiah counting the loot, adeptly flipping through the bound wads of lettuce like a seasoned Gypsy accordionist. The snake had obviously not recognized Norman at all. On the one hand, this invisibility felt safely reassuring. On the other hand, considering the humiliation Norman had endured due to having been ripped off by this charlatan with respect to the phony Holocaust artifacts at Auschwitz, not to mention the major personal trauma of the museum check that this swindler had forced him to sign, such dismissive nonrecognition was profoundly insulting. His father, thank God, the honorable chairman, had managed in the end to justify the check in the ledgers as a contribution to Polish-Jewish dialogue, but for the panic and anxiety that Norman had gone through, the pain and suffering, no recompense was possible.

Satisfied that all was in order with the payment, Tommy Messiah detached the donkey's nearly empty feedbag, deftly stuffed the bills inside, then strung it at the creature's other end positioned just so, under its tail, inspiring by these manipulations a fresh deposit of steaming cover-up for the cash. The task completed, Tommy Messiah stepped up to Norman and handed him a card. "This is where the H.P. is headquartered," he said. "He'll be expecting you. Don't forget the limo. He won't leave home without it." He leaned over intimately so that Norman could distinctly smell essence of ass, and whispered into his ear. "Last time we did business you paid me to get you into the fucking convent, you *paskundyak*. You didn't pay me to see your daughter. That would have been a much more expensive proposition."

Norman started visibly, as if accosted on the road by a man

or an angel holding aloft a flaming drawn sword that could
pierce his heart. Reminding himself, however, that divine mes-
sengers do not after all appear in this day and age, he rushed off
toward the fulfillment of his earthly mission, shouting in parting orders to museum underlings concerning the requisitioning
of the limousine, "Lincoln Continental, uniformed chauffeur,
latest model, fully loaded, make sure it's red, I happen to know
that the High Priest prefers red," and concerning the nun who
was attempting yet again to hand him her letter, "Jesus Christ!
Put her in touch with interfaith or external affairs, for God's
sake. Why am I expected to micromanage everything? We need
to delegate, guys! We're losing our Holocaust. It's slipping away
right in front of our eyes. This is a life and death situation."

"Our best and brightest," Monty Pincus whispered much
too close to Leyla Salmani, his eyes pointedly following Norman's exit. She took a step backward, to obtain a better view
of the receding black figures of the Hasid and nun with their
freak offspring swelling over the rim of the perambulator as
they departed the camp of the power elite. "I know who you
are, Leyla Salmani," the chief of staff was miming through the
din of her own inner buzz, insinuating himself again into the
space she had just vacated. "You're just another idealistic chick
who wants to change the world—classic type who uses tits
and ass to get through the door, and once inside, expects to be
respected for her mind. *Entre nous*, babe, you and your cronies
inside the museum don't know what the fuck you're doing. No
offense, sweetheart, but you're all just a bunch of stupid pissers
and pikers. You're headed straight down the yellow brick road
toward one colossal goat fuck."

The sensible thing to do, Leyla recognized, would be to
get away from this creep, block him from using her physical

existence to turn himself on through his own verbiage. But
again her energy had forsaken her. What had Tommy Messiah sold her? Sugar pills, placebos. Discreetly she placed two
more on her tongue and swallowed them down in a single
gulp, attending inwardly for a burst of optimism, a faint pop
of rapture. Everything seemed pointless, without meaning. In
any case, beyond her internal borders it appeared as if all activity had ceased in the sphere of the eminent persons closest to
the museum, an extended intermission was apparently unde
way as they awaited the redemptive arrival of the High Priest.
Utterly bereft of spirit, failing disgracefully in her mission, as
she very well knew, she nevertheless could not bring herself to
perform. Her gaze followed the carriage of the nun and Hasid
in its funereal march toward the survivors' camp. The heat was
boiling down and thickening, the sky beginning to darken. To
move forward in this air was impossible, like wading through a
gray aspic in which all animation was suspended. Passively she
remained in place without will, submitting to the verbal violation perpetrated by this secretion of male protoplasm closing
in upon her, made even more repulsive because he believed
himself to be charming, droning through her thoughts with his
insider's expertise about how deluded she and her comrades
were, destined for failure, for ridicule and oblivion. What had
they expected to accomplish anyway with their anachronistic
sixties-tactics victims'-power takeover of the museum premises?
The whole joint from kitsch to cattle-car clone would have
been handed over to genocides-dot-com soon enough anyway
without a struggle, and in the not too distant future. If only
they'd had the patience to wait another few years at most, this
precious little Jewish Holocaust boutique museum would have
been forced to diversify to general human rights products to

have any chance at all of surviving even marginally. Because the Holocaust is finished, passé; it's no longer relevant. The perspective has shifted. But in its heyday, in the days when it still mattered, it's important to note for whatever it's worth, no one could have matched the Jewish Holocaust with its mass industrial gassings—come on, who could top that? But the fact of the matter is, finally, at long last, even the Jewish Holocaust with its gas chambers and ovens, its mobile killing squads and extermination camps and all of its endlessly fascinating fetishist exotica, is being removed from the active file for interment in the vaults of history alongside all the other forgotten centuries-old slaughters and atrocities and sufferings. Holocaust chic is out, baby—yours, mine, ours. The age of memorialization is over. The past is a story with an ending—simple, orderly, false. The future is what it's all about now—unknown, uncertain, unsafe, like sex and death, the raw wild forces ramming out of the sky, gashing the buildings, incinerating the earth, the dark savage forces out of control.

Was he really daring to say these things to her, taking these liberties, speaking to her in this way? She was tuning in and out as if in a trance, catching the bullets, extracting the gist. Lighten up, Leyla baby—was that what he was saying?—the world is coming to an end, you might as well let yourself go. Her gaze listlessly kept track of the nun and Hasid wheeling their carriage into the camp of the well-fed survivors toward Foggy Bottom's father the ass man, while, repellently intimate, like a fleshy-tailed demon inside her brain, his words were lashing. Too bad you guys don't have Jewish heads, he was saying, or something like that—could it have been, too bad you don't have Jewish deads? Instead of wasting your time on the museum, required reading today but an abandoned tome tomorrow, you should have gone for the gold, cashed in your pain for lucre. Jesus Christ, a little creativity's in order here, a little imagination, please! Your Palestinian Holocaust, for instance, your pathetic little *naqba*—rather than crying piteously to the whole world to pay deference to your catastrophe, you should have demanded that they just pay. You should have shaken down the Germans for reparations, the Swiss for the heirless dormant accounts, the Austrians for unclaimed looted art, the Italians for insurance policies collecting dust, and the Jews for a cut and a percentage of their entire take. The Jewish Holocaust is your Holocaust too. Hitler screwed the Jews, and in return they and everyone else screwed you. Because of Hitler you were exiled from your gardens trellised with bougainvillea in Jerusalem, from your Ottoman terraces overlooking the sea in Jaffa, from your arbors of purple grapes on the Carmel. They owe you, baby. Where are your brains? You're such a dumb bitch.

She did not resist but absorbed it all, partially closing her eyes and letting him take his pleasure orally even as she could hear the rain pounding down in heavy sheets beyond the canopied entry area where she was standing, and the door slamming as the limousine roared to a halt on the sidewalk as near to the overhead projection of the building as possible, and Norman Messer panting, doubled over and creaking as he unrolled a red carpet under the fine leather shoes of the High Priest the entire distance until his hindquarters smacked against the locked door of the museum. Only when she heard the shriek of the chicken holocaust lady, "The Jews are killing my pullets!" did Leyla Salmani commit to the immense exertion of fully opening her eyes again.

Chickens were being hurled out of the dark sky, fluttering grotesquely, letting out bloodcurdling squawks, scattering their droppings and feathers, striking the pavement with the bluntness of doom. Holding an umbrella with one hand over Monty Pincus's head and waving a cigarette with her other hand, Krystyna Jesudowicz opened her mouth wide to receive the last of the ice cream he was stuffing inside in order to avoid mixing milk with meat as he bent down to pick up one of the bird carcasses. He examined the tag attached to a string around its pitiful twist-off neck and read aloud: "This is your replacement. This is your substitute and exchange. This is your penance. This rooster takes on your sins and goes to its death for you. And you? Where do you think you're going?"

Rabbi Dr. Monty Pincus lifted up his eyes unto the heavens. "Somebody up there is *shlugging kaporos* for us," he interpreted for his congregation. "It's the atonement ritual. Yom Kippur is coming. Look up in the sky. It's an end-of-days prophet calling on us to repent."

Up in the sky a small airplane was accelerating brazenly, whirling ecstatically in circles with a tail of helicopters in grinding pursuit. On the ground, now that all the customers had fled, Tommy Messiah was leading his donkey and cart away. Leyla caught his eye for confirmation. Tommy Messiah nodded his head. Yes, it was what she had thought. Shimshon, of course, the penitent, the zealot, the avenger, the harbinger—who else could it be? The original kamikaze, crashing them with him into the abyss—Shimshon. He was the pilot. Tommy Messiah nodded again. And Eldad and Medad, the minor prophets, casting down the birds.

PART FOUR

The Third Generation

W HEN THE POWER WAS CUT inside the museum, and darkness and heat engulfed them, and they were besieged by
the pounding rain, Rumi and Rumi threw back their heads to
open the black holes of their throats and howl at the injustice of
the universe. They howled without respite, and nothing would
quiet them—not their mother's attempts to nurse them while
crooning their favorite personalized lullaby, "Oh Rumi Concentration Oh Rumi Contemplation Oh Rama Meditation," to
the tune of Bessie Smith's "Oh Daddy Blues," not the wild ride
in the baby carriage pushed by their cousin Naomi-zenchin in
dizzying rings around the granite floor of the deserted Hall of
Witness, especially not the carob lollipops on recycled paper
sticks from the grocery-bag supplies held out by the nightmare cloaked figure whimpering in solidarity, bell trembling
in empathy, who had ceded to the twins its nest in the black
buggy, not even the offer from Foggy Bottom Schmaltz to tell
them once again the story of the imminent return of the comet
Hale-Bopp crashing to earth and the end of days in accordance
with the lore of the Hopi peaceful little people, topped by the
ultimate temptation—permission to touch, albeit very carefully touch, the live grenades strapped to his body, with which
he intended to blow himself and all of them up if their demands
were not met.

All of these treats they spurned, wailed and would not
be comforted. For Maurice Messer in the wheelchair at the

Founders' Wall, praying now with even greater fervor after having absorbed the bitter medicine of the note scribbled on the prescription stationery of his so-called comrade in arms and resistance collaborator, Adolf Schmaltz, the relentless piercing crying of these strange-smelling creatures was simply the limit. How much more could a man take? They're gonna wake up the dead, all six million of them, he wanted to shriek, including the one and one half million innocent children, I'm gonna strangle those little *cockers*. But instead, for propriety's sake, over the personal assault of their screeching, he attempted to put forth the more civilized point of theological etiquette—a little respect please if you don't mind, there are people here who are trying to pray, this is a house of worship, curb your children, for God's sakes. Schmaltz's message had been dropped into Maurice's lap by the nun and Hasid along with the letter they had sought to deliver to Norman. Maurice had just had a few seconds to absorb this treacherous blow from his good friend Schmaltz, the man of the rear, right where it hurt the most, when the lights went out. Then that intolerable bawling of those alien beings commenced and would not let up. Maurice felt himself at last to be utterly unmanned. They were all against him. What was the use of going on?

Only a few moments before, before the plagues of darkness and the wailing of the firstborns had descended upon him, he had begun to feel again the stirrings of hope, he could not say exactly why, perhaps it was naive foolishness, a natural human instinct toward healing and recovery, his innate survivor's optimism, but still, whatever the reason, even his appetite had begun to revive in some measure. Of course he would never have considered partaking of anything from the brown paper grocery bags of that deranged trio over there, macro this, organic that, spread out in front of the Remember the Children exhibition on a filthy cloth like a picnic in the underworld by the black river, with Bunny posted as sentinel at the bridge alongside her new pal, Honey Pincus, brandishing her rejuiced DustBuster in readiness for the banquet's inevitable fallout and debris. To Maurice this offering of seeds and dried fruit droppings looked like what went into a bird at one end and what came out at the other, he definitely did not recommend it to himself for his own health. Still, before the lights went out and the brats began to howl, Maurice could almost summon up in his memory the warm fragrance that would waft out of the tall bags deposited each morning at the entrance to the museum cafeteria, the words "Holocaust Bagels" scrawled in bold letters with black marker. He was already mentally skimming the cafeteria menu, indulging an impossible fantasy of ordering out. He would even have been willing to settle for one of those cat-food tuna sandwiches if that was all that was left, even on one of those air buns sprinkled with little sesame seeds like lice nits, a very insensitive reminder for survivors of the camps.

Maurice did not even like tuna fish, as it happened, he had wanted to ban it from the menu entirely along with the lice-nit buns, that's how keenly his appetite had been rekindled just a few minutes earlier, but now all thoughts of preferences, all thoughts of physical comfort and nourishment, went out with the lights, drowned out by the nonstop screaming of the Rumis, dashed by Schmaltz's note curling like a special delivery of poison in Maurice's lap. The whole Holocaust had gone to hell. This is what Maurice Messer now acknowledged to himself as he watched from his sacred Founders' Wall the underworld procession descending the grand staircase, bearing flickering memorial candles from the Hall of Remembrance and setting

them down in a demonic circle on the floor to illuminate the
Hall of Witness, in accordance with instructions from Bunny
Bacon and her latest discovery, Honey Pincus, to whom Bunny
had promised the directorship of the academic branch of the
museum, Monty's old job, as soon as this nasty crisis could be
put behind them and they could get on with their lives. The
two women were already planning a special exhibition on the
Gynecological and Menstrual Holocaust, which, as Honey
correctly pointed out, has already claimed many many more
millions and billions of victims, gay and straight, than the
conventional bourgeois Holocaust, and is, as a matter of fact,
still ongoing. "Don't worry," Honey reassured Bunny, "you can
handle it. You already know much more about this Holocaust
from personal victimization than you ever knew or will know
about the other one. It's going to be an absolutely sensational
show—really really transgressive," Honey added delightedly. It
would include, they both agreed, in addition to such testimonies of gynecological atrocities as a video of a doctor with one
hand inside a patient and the other holding a cell phone, "Hi,
what's up? It's me, I'm in the examining room, doing a pel-
vic," a large artifact as its centerpiece, a major installation—a
menstrual hut, an exact replica of the structure into which,
in some African cultures, women were banished during their
lunar periods of pollution, so offensive and inimical to spiritual
devotions within the house. Museum customers could sit in
the menstrual hut just as they are invited to pass through and
even linger in the railcar upstairs on the third floor, in order
to personally experience the suffering and humiliation from
the point of view of the victim. "A room of one's own," Honey
said.

The brainstorm of co-opting the lights of the memorial

candles came from Jake Koan Gilguli, who was sitting on the red granite floor of the Hall of Remembrance at the foot of the altar with the tongue of the eternal flame lapping above him, plunging into a past-life therapy session with Rama-sensei, when the power was cut off and darkness fell. Nodding beneficently and smiling with heartening serenity and acceptance, Rama was seeking to help Koan Gilguli delve even further back, to access an incarnation prior to Yankel Galitzianer of Przemysl, Poland, murdered in Crematorium III at Birkenau. An awesomely learned and revered rabbi in Israel had declared that the six million who were exterminated in the Holocaust were actually resurrected sinners, atoning for their evil deeds in a previous life. That explained everything. No longer could the question of why with respect to the Holocaust ever again be asked. Koan Gilguli therefore set himself the task of discovering this *gilgul*, this former incarnation of himself who had sinned so grievously as to merit in the next life the fate of Yankel Galitzianer in the gas chamber. As he sat on the floor of the Hall of Remembrance opposite Rama-sensei, the two of them intimately passing from mouth to mouth something green she had rolled and sealed with her spittle and ignited with the flame of a memorial candle in its jar doubling now as an ashtray, he permitted his eyes to stream idly, as if for inspiration, over the names affixed in a burnished metal dirgelike procession upon the hexagonal walls—Auschwitz-Birkenau, Treblinka, Chelmno, Sobibor, Dachau, Buchenwald, Ponary, Jasenovac, Transnistria, Ninth Fort, Babi Yar, and so on through the familiar stations of torture and murder slipping from the sharp edge of memory into mindless refrain and litany, doggerel and kitsch. Then, in a flash, just a moment before the lights were extinguished and the children began to wail, the phrase "Death Marches" snagged his vision, like the mystical odd bead on a frayed old string. It was then that Koan Gilguli recovered it all: the death march on the night of August 1915; the Knights of Mary Phagan just a few months before their transformation into the new knights of the Ku Klux Klan; the Jew Leo Frank, abducted from a cell in the Georgia State Prison in Milledgeville, hanged from a tree limb in Frey's Grove.

"Jim Gilchrist, member of the lynch mob—that's who I was," Koan Gilguli announced to Rama-sensei. "Reborn for my sins as Yankel Galitzianer to feel Frank's pain."

Rama nodded sagely, displaying her small milky teeth in a beatific smile. Then, like a goddess rising from the bestowal of blessed knowledge, she rose to attend to the crying of her children. The flames of the rows of memorial candles set out on the ledge along the wall of the Hall of Remembrance cast their reflections in the pools of her steel-rimmed glasses.

Koan Gilguli carried two of these burning candles, one in each hand, to light the path for his master, Roshi Mickey Fisher, as he made his way toward Maurice Messer at the Founders' Wall. He's coming to take back the wheelchair, Maurice fathomed. His old brain was still ticking, thank God, he had instantly figured it all out. No way I'm gonna let him have it, the lousy putz, he resolved, and shimmying backward on his rump, Maurice wedged himself more securely into the seat, staking his claim, his feet dangling childlike in space above the footrests. Just let him try to kick me out, I'll scream bloody murder, even louder than those rotten kids I'll scream. The roshi, though a minimum thirty years younger, Maurice was pleased to note, was puffing like an obsolete boiler beside him, a fat *zhlub* with gefilte pipes. Koan Gilguli was holding aloft the memorial lights to illuminate the wall, for his master's edification. Without even condescending to glance at the faker, Maurice demanded that he do something about those kids. "Can't you make them shut up? You're the poppa—right? You get the credit—correct me if I'm wrong. So nu—maybe it's time already for a little discipline from the daddy department, you know what I mean? I'm going crazy here. What you think this is? A rumpus room? This is a holy place, for God's sakes!"

"Holy, holy, holy," Fisher-roshi chanted along in tune with the wailing of the children, impervious to Maurice's gross self-display. "The crying of babies—holy music, celestial music. We have fallen into the place where everything is music, the Persian poet sang. If it fades, we fade. Apocalypso—the latest musical sensation! Attend closely to the teaching in the crying of the children, I say to you. Planes crashing into buildings, towers crumbling to the ground, men leaping headfirst from the clouds—this is not a silent movie. It is screaming and yelling, howling and sobbing, crying, crying, crying, all the way down. Did you imagine it was silent in the gas chambers? Consider this screaming as you gaze at your halls and walls and contemplate the imminent destruction of all the creations of your pride. The crying of the babes, the bleating of the lambs, holy, holy, holy, Adonai Tzevaoth, all the earth is filled with His glory. It is the music of enlightenment, the music of the divine—purer than Bach, sweeter even than Coltrane." His eyes squeezed shut, as if in a trance, the roshi was swaying and dancing, boogying to the rhythm of the children's shrill lamentations rocking the stone and steel of this mausoleum in which they had buried the Holocaust.

Maurice was in hell, and the howling of the children was a wind bladder, a rattling tumor he was condemned to drag through eternity. His eardrums were stretched to the bursting point; they were ringing, vibrating, frizzing like seltzer; the only comfort in all this for him was that now he would have a license to tune in and tune out selectively in accordance with what he chose to hear, yet Fisher's voice cut through the din with his blasphemy. "So this is your Death Wall, like they have in all the synagogues—you know, the *yahrzeit* wall, with the memorial tablets for dead members, bigger tablets for bigger members?"

"You some kind of *apikores* or something?" Maurice cried. "What you talking, you *fershtunkene* heretic? This is mine holy donors' wall, for your information. Mine donors are alive and well, thank you very much—and still donating. Till one hundred and twenty—years, I'm talking, not millions. What kind of grubber you think I am?"

"Ah," the roshi intoned, starting in again with his unbearable chanting, "I see only death on this wall. The physical bodies behind these names may believe they're alive, they may flatter themselves that they're buying and selling, getting and spending, strutting and preening, fucking and farting, moving and shaking, attending functions, posing for pictures, but it is all maya and illusion. Out of one stinking hole they have been excreted, and into another stinking hole crawling with maggots and worms they're fated to be shoved. They can be likened to broken pottery, to withered grass, a passing shadow, a blowing wind, a fleeting dream, they're nothing but scattering dust, though they believe they're alive. Let them like the ancient monks dig up the cadavers of young women at night to watch them decay. Then they will grasp the true meaning of their desires and appetites. On this earth they are as transient and impermanent and forgotten as the suffering and torment of the millions of souls you've exploited in the erection of this vainglorious self-aggrandizing monument. On this wall they are already counted among the dead. What I see here on this wall are only the names of the dead."

The roshi took a memorial candle from Koan Gilguli's hand to hold up against the wall as if to scrutinize it more closely. "This spot here—where it says 'Reserved'? You see it? It's Jiriki's spot—yes? It belongs to Jiriki, to the holy holy soul you call Gloria who at this very moment is struggling to cross over to the *bardo*. But she clings to this life, her mind is agitated, she cannot achieve tranquillity even as I, her transition coach, urge her with all my power to step out boldly. Nevertheless, she holds on desperately despite the inconvenience and annoyance and burden to family and friends. She does not let go though they have denied her all nourishment to body and spirit. She declines the release from worldly illusions and passions due to some unfinished business here on this earth—some unfinished business touching on this wall."

Reserved? What was this bubba-baba yammering? What a low-class, tacky idea—reserving space like in some kind of bargain-basement blowout sale! Show me, go on, show me the word *Reserved,* you miserable fraud, Maurice wanted to yell. Nowhere on this wall could *Reserved* be found. Who would know this better than Maurice? He could recite by heart every word, every name on the wall, Honorables all the way down, from the Honorable Bugsy Ackerman to the Honorable Dutch Zwillman, a ladder of H's reaching up to the heavens, stacked like a poem, Maurice was the troubadour of this epic hymn. Yet Fisher had seen the word *Reserved,* as in a vision, and Maurice was so shaken by this madman's insight that he lurched halfway out of his seat in the wheelchair, sending the two sheets of paper in his lap swirling to the floor, and over the mounting earsplitting ululations of the Rumis, like a harbinger of chaos, it flashed through his mind for a split second that maybe he ought to fall upon his knees at the feet of the roshi and cry, Master, forgive me, you have looked into my soul and exposed my sin, but though the buck stops here, it wasn't I who took advantage of a helpless old woman. Her daughter, my director, made me do it. The inscription the old lady wanted was so inappropriate and undignified—My son Michael, my son, my son Michael, if only I had died instead of you, Michael, my son, my son—sons coming out of your ears, a person can get a headache from all those sons, a Jewish mother tearjerker dripping with schmaltz straight from the Second Avenue Yiddish theater, we could never put something so melodramatic, so unprofessional, up on my wall in our world-class state-of-the-art federal Holocaust headquarters, though the old lady paid for it in advance and in full, it's true, I admit it, and even got a receipt to prove it, but we figured with her mind gone to Poughkeepsie she'd never know the difference, she'd never find out.

Fortunately, though, instead of surrendering to this mad temptation to purge himself through such a radical and demeaning and ultimately self-destructive act of contrition, Maurice came to his senses, thank God, reclaiming his stately position in the wheelchair. And despite the shock to his system from Fisher's revelation that he had endured, he even mustered up enough presence of mind to casually lean over as he regally resettled himself in order to retrieve Schmaltz's prescription from the floor. He crumpled it soundlessly in his fist and shredded it with his pearlized manicured fingernails. He moistened it discreetly in his mouth and dispatched it with a shot of saliva down his gullet through all the tubes and coils of his system straight to the sphincter at the lower depths, the good doctor's department as it happened, returned to sender in new and improved form.

Fisher-roshi turned his backside disrespectfully to Maurice's wall, pressed his palms prayerfully together in front of his heart, and dipped his head in a gentle bow. "*Namaste*, Jiriki," he pronounced softly, yet like a shark fin slicing through the unceasing roiling waves of the children's screams, his words headed straight for Maurice. "You may rest in peace now, Jiriki. If this little specialty-shop museum survives the coming doomsday, old man Messer will put up your son's plaque on his precious wall exactly as you ordered it. Trust me. As for what Schmaltz is prepared to do to preserve *his* son—Messer has just eaten the evidence. If he's truly that hungry, we can probably spare a few of the copies of Schmaltz's letter that we xeroxed on the equipment upstairs in the learning center of this user-friendly Holocaust."

Then the roshi lifted his head and raised his voice, not only projecting it over the continuing wailing of the two Rumis but launching it like a missile targeted for the warehouse in which Gloria lay in desolation moaning mama, mama on her mean bed three hundred miles away. "Listen, oh Jiriki," Fisher-roshi shouted. "The time has come for you to detach yourself from all this noise and set out on your journey to the noble silence within. Liberate yourself now from the impermanence of all things, my holy holy Jiriki. Break your attachment to all worldly passions and illusions. Cross over to the silence of luminous oneness. Fly out to the grace of this silence. Transcend the cycle of life and death and achieve enlightenment. Loosen your grip from the metal bars of your bed. Ease your body out of the iron cage of your personality. Float out on your good energy to the place where you are no longer old or young, no longer woman or man, no longer desired or cast off, no longer Gloria or Jiriki—to where you simply and purely are."The roshi held the memorial light against his grizzled beard, casting the nether part of his face in diabolical shadow. "I'm blowing out the flame now, my holy holy Jiriki," he whispered, tears darkening his beard. "I honor the place where our spirits are one. *Namaste,* seeker. It's okay to stop fighting."

Was it at that moment, when Fisher's voice glided legato-like to a whisper and he blew out the light, that Maurice suddenly realized that the children had stopped torturing him with their screaming, or was it a moment later, when Bunny let out that horror-stricken shriek? For Maurice, that was just about the last straw, a shriek that nearly put the finishing touches to what was left of his hearing. Bunny was positioned, when she erupted, with a direct line to his ear, straightening out beside his wheelchair from bending over with her DustBuster after having vacuumed up the letter originally meant for Norman, which had been affronting her across the floor, glaring white detritus spotlighted by Koan Gilguli's memorial candle, refusing to let her rest. Maurice could actually discern through his canals the paper being sucked in by her appliance and crunched into quarks, thank God, which was a gratifying sign in the aural prognosis department, but then came the trauma of Bunny's blistering scream, an animal cry, the kind of savage, otherworldly sound she probably never knew she had it within her to emit, she most likely didn't even recognize her own voice, and once more Maurice could not vouch for the integrity of what he was hearing. My heart, over and over again, My heart, My heart, Bunny cried, They've taken my heart, My conceptual heart, My God, My heart. She was bereft, in anguish from the knowledge that had just dropped like a meteorite out of the sky and crushed her. She was motherless. Her mother had been taken from her. Her mother was gone. But when his eardrums stopped quivering after the initial puncture of her scream, Maurice thought he could make it out more clearly as she raved on and on—My art, she cried again and again, My art, My art, They've taken my art, My conceptual art, My God, My art.

Within the circle of memorial candles on the floor of the Hall of Witness, the twins Rumi and Rumi were contentedly playing with plastic Lego blocks—building toy concentration camp barracks and toy crematoria, setting out a complete *Konzentrationlager* model in accordance with the illustrated instructions in the set as read to them by Naomi-zenchin, little toy white skeleton prisoner figures and little toy black helmeted guard figures administering beatings, electrocutions, burnings, hangings on miniature toy gallows, shoving bodies into toy gas chambers and toy ovens, little white toy corpses heaped up in pyres. While the lights were still burning, the nun, wandering through the floors of the museum, had paused before the Lager Lego installation on exhibit in a glass display case outside the Hall of Remembrance. It was conceptual art that the museum had to own, one of the more recent additions to the permanent collection, it asked you to consider how history and truth and evil are plastic; the artist was Polish, the legend informed, and therefore, he explained, poisoned. With the inconsolable cries of the children pressing in all around her, the nun revisited this exhibit. By the light of a memorial candle, she removed from the nearby wall a brass and burl-wood plaque, as heavy as a millstone, which mediated and gave context to the art. The inscription on the plaque hailed Maurice Messer for his courage and selflessness as a partisan and resistance fighter during the Holocaust. Wielding this testimonial plaque with two hands like a club, she smashed the glass of the display case. The power had been cut; there was no danger of the alarm going off. When she brought the Auschwitz concept as an offering to the children, they were pacified at last.

*

He imagines they've stopped crying, but I still hear them, the ones who are present in this place and those far away, the living and the dead, the cherished and the discarded, the dark babies with swollen bellies and overexposed eyes, the benumbed babies set down alone on a rag in the marketplace with a beggar's tin can at their feet, the ashen babies ripped from their mothers and tossed alive into the burning pits. It is my calling to keep their cries acute in my ears, not so loud that I am benumbed, not so even that I grow complacent to the disturbance, not so soft that I become corrupted by the illusion of distance in time, in place, in fortune, but always piercing, jagged, present, like stigmata eternally renewing themselves between my eyes, perpetual pain, with no escape into oblivion, and no relief. Beyond vocation, it is also my passion—to keep all the suffering that ever was and ever will be everlastingly fresh in my mind, a seal set on my heart, undistanced and uncorrupted by memory, to take the never-ending anguish into account every minute, to be forever in a state of shock, of not believing my eyes, of being unable to breathe, of not being able to comprehend. Again and again, minute after minute, my hand must spring to my mouth in horror. Don't let me get used to it, Lord; that's all I ask. Let it always hurt just as much, it is the desire of my body and my blood. Keep me forever suspended in thin air, in complete consciousness and pure terror, in the space between the leap from the burning tower and the final crash onto the cold ground.

I float through this ruin of a museum to illuminate the images and icons by the light of a memorial candle. The young girl struggling to cover her breasts will always be transfixed in the moment after rape. The old man with the half-butchered beard will always be in the grip of his tormenters. The dark-eyed boy with the cap on his head and his hands in the air will always be frozen at the point of the gun. The respectable matrons bizarrely naked out of doors in an open field under the shivering sky will always be mortified by our lurid gaze as they stand in line, awaiting their turn to be murdered. And always in full awareness they will be awaiting their turn.

You will always be nailed to your cross.

I am nailed to you.

I immerse my hands up to the wrists in the ashes of the Jewish dead from the base of the remembrance altar, and move through the darkness of these chambers bearing my candle. I am your watchdog faithfully making rounds, guardian of the awake and the sleeping, protector of all damaged children, the grown and not yet grown, suffering them all to come to you, bestowing your tenderness on all survivors, the consolation of your pity upon my dying companions. I touch Naomi lightly on the brow. A blue vein pulses on her temple as she sleeps. I touch Shahid between eyes that race frantically back and forth under diaphanous lids. The defenseless puffs of his breath warm the pale hairs of my arm.

In the center of the hall, Foggy Bottom is at his post, glaring fixedly into the void. He sits upright on the floor, legs folded, back straight, chest bare, the harness of grenades exposed at his midriff. The old man brakes in front of him in the wheelchair. Your papa's lost his noodle, Big Chief Hassenfeffer, the old man says. If Schmaltz the proctologist thinks for one minute that by threatening to go public with the so-called truth about what we did in the war he can blackmail the Honorable Maurice Messer, chairman of the Holocaust, to give in to the demands of terrorists, then his brain must have migrated south to the area of his specialty. He thinks I'm afraid, your papa? He should know better by now that I'm never afraid. Let him say whatever he wants. Who's going to believe him? That's the beauty of our Holocaust, that's what makes it so popular. It's unbelievable. It was always unbelievable, even while it was happening. It has made anything possible.

Foggy Bottom's fingers constrict around his detonator switch. I calm him with my touch, and pass on.

The High Priest is stopped at the checkpoint on the other side of the glass doors, seeking entry into the promised land. His forehead and the palms of his hands are pressed against the glass as he squints into the darkness. He starts when I touch the glass partition at each of his three points of contact—father, son, holy spirit—but he does not notice me; I am not a player, insignificant, invisible to him. He has been equipped with a cutting-edge-model headset telephone through which he communicates with Pushkin Jones. Pushkin Jones will not let him in until he makes a solemn promise and pledge signed and sealed before witnesses to join the Million Martyrs March coming soon to the local Mall. I can hear only Pushkin Jones's side of the negotiations that have been stretching through the night. The High Priest is holding back for reasons of appearances. Brother, why you keep asking me who else is going to be on the speakers' platform? Pushkin Jones says into his phone. Why you keep fretting how it's going to look?

Pushkin Jones is lounging at his ease across the cushions borrowed from the post–Holocaust tour contemplation benches in

the Hall of Remembrance. The cushions are now piled up luxu-
riantly in the typical Gypsy wagon. Over the vest of his three-
piece suit Pushkin Jones has slipped into the typical Gypsy dress,
suitable for wild dancing with its full lacy skirt and polka-dotted
bodice, on which he has pinned the pink triangle for homosexuals. Now and then he punctuates his remarks to the High Priest
with incidental music by passing the bow over the strings of the
typical Gypsy fiddle, or by quoting supporting passages from the
brittle pages of the Jehovah's Witness Bible open in his lap, lit
by a memorial candle. These and other items are on loan from
the Other Victims exhibition on the fourth floor, Pushkin Jones
has stated, and while they amount to little more than pathetic
inclusivist tokenism, these non-Jewish artifacts may ultimately
be likened to the irritant around which a pearl of magnificent
lustrous proportions will form following the universal triumph
of United Holocausts, Pushkin Jones says.

As I draw near, Pushkin Jones calls out, Touch me, bitch, go
on, touch me. Swiftly I touch him on the brow, and I make my
mark on the old man too. He has pulled up in the wheelchair
to observe Pushkin Jones's negotiations with the High Priest.
The old man parks and will not budge. He gives an appreciative
connoisseur's nod toward Pushkin Jones. One of the world's
great preachers and rap artists par excellence, the old man says,
well worth the price of admission. The old man is speaking to
a general audience, not to me; he cannot see me, this station
is too close, I am too low. You're a man after my own heart,
brother, the old man says to Pushkin Jones—a fellow survivor,
a *megillah* guerrilla, the old man says.

I crouch down at my place at the hitch of the wagon, awaiting the lash to pull. Blot me out, Lord, I pray You, from the
book You have written.

"Ich bin ein Berliner," Pushkin Jones addresses the High
Priest. I am a Middle Passager. I am Roma. I am Lesbian. All of
them I am, Pushkin Jones sings, spiraling down into the profun-
dities of the testosterone basso of his persecuted brother Paul. I
am Christian, Muslim, Jew—Pashtun Jones, descendant of the
tribe of Benjamin through Pithon and Afghana in the lineage of
King Saul son of Kish hiding among the vessels, exiled with the
Ten Lost Tribes of Israel across the churning river Sambatyon
hurling up her boulders six days of the week and on the Sabbath
she rests, in the exile of the kingdom of Samaria by the Assyr-
ian Shalmaneser. I am mounted upon my mighty white steed,
galloping across the deserts beyond Kandahar and the mountains of Tora Bora, the jihad of Pathan burned into my flesh.
I am the boy prophet Samuel, child of Hannah and Elkanah
of the tribe of Levi from Ramatayim-Tzofim in the mountain
of Ephraim, Pushkin Jones says. And you—you are the High
Priest at Shiloh, blind and forsaken, confined to your holding
cell outside the door of the tent of meeting. Your descendants
have corrupted and befouled the sanctuary. They have grown
fat and depraved on the gifts and the offerings, despoiling the
holy place, devouring the sacrifices, deluding and violating the
faithful for profit and power and pleasure, glory and renown.
You have not taught them well, you too have battened on the
dead, you have not been a good example. You have outlived
your time, your line has been cut off, you are no longer relevant. The schools of prophecy have been passed to me and
to mine, affirmative action—torn from our mothers' breasts,
sold into lifelong servitude, alone and bewildered, sacrificed
on our beds, terrified by voices in the dark of night. "*Hineini*,"
I once cried, running to you, Here I am. But you were a false
god, and now the idol is smashed.

You were a transition figure, Pushkin Jones says to the High Priest. And yours was a transition Holocaust. Your Holocaust is history—buried in the archives and the tombs. It had a longer-than-average run for a human tragedy and atrocity, but finally and at long last, the Shoah's over, the curtain has fallen, the thumbs of the people have turned down. It's our turn now. A new universal Holocaust is coming, the horror of which has never been seen before and will never be seen again, Pushkin Jones says. Your Holocaust has been superseded, eclipsed. The blazing signs have been seared across the skies.

Blood. And fire. And columns of smoke.

Total cremation. Everywhere ash.

From the ashes, the old man staggers to his feet, a dazed and battered phoenix. He rises from the wheelchair at dawn amid the congratulatory bouquets of microphones, struggling to resurrect himself in the incubator of the media lights held aloft on this patch of globe spinning in the vast universe to radiate on the passage of him alone. On his forehead a cross of ashes is illuminated, incandescent. The generations of children have vanished, leaving behind only the constant waves of their cries from the abyss for those with ears to hear. The High Priest has turned to vapor outside the gates and only his fractured shadow remains for those with eyes to see. Bent over, an old dog, I haul the wagon into the dead-end caves of the interior where the monsters are bred.

Like a ghost I pass. The old man is telling the world he has seen the light. He is a survivor, and his Holocaust will survive in the coming day. We may have been bought out by the international global Holocaust cartel, the old man says, but we're still in business, thank the Lord. The whole world may be burning, the old man says, but we're still here, *mir zeinen do*, as I used to sing with my comrades when I was a partisan and fought against the Nazis in the woods.

The old man announces the new name of the museum in accordance with the terms of the agreement hammered out: United States Holocausts Memorial Museum.

One little *s*, the old man says. It's no big deal, ladies and gentlemen. But two *s*'s? SS? Never! That's where we draw the line.